JOURNEY TO THE FRINGE

STONE MAGE
WARS

JOURNEY TO
THE FRINGE

KELLI SWOFFORD NIELSEN

SHADOW
MOUNTAIN

Visit us at ShadowMountain.com

Library of Congress Cataloging-in-Publication Data
Nielsen, Kelli Swofford, author.
    Journey to The Fringe / Kelli Swofford Nielsen.
        pages cm. — (Stone mage wars ; book one)
    Summary: When someone kidnaps beloved Princess Ivy, a fool, a witch, a thief, and a sea captain embark on a dangerous journey with the hope of saving Ivy and the kingdom.
    ISBN 978-1-60908-833-0 (hardbound : alk. paper)
    1. Fantasy. [1. Magic—Fiction.   2. Voyages and travels—Fiction.   3. Princesses—Fiction.   4. Fantasy.]   I. Title.   II. Series: Nielsen, Kelli Swofford. Stone mage wars ; book one.
    PZ7.N5673Jou 2012
    [Fic]—dc23   2011041111

Printed in the United States of America
Malloy Lithographing Incorporated, Ann Arbor, MI

10   9   8   7   6   5   4   3   2

For Jack, my brave adventurer

ACKNOWLEDGMENTS

There are so many people who put me on the road to this first novel.

Here are my many thanks to:

Katie, Clark, and Jessica, longtime fellows in all things imaginative.

Mrs. Judd, wherever she is, who announced in the second grade that I had a future as a writer.

Carson, Tawna, and Julie, for friendly support and crucial input.

Mom and Dad, for telling me I could do anything I decided to, and believing it.

Jeff, for making me believe I *should* do it . . . today.

My sons, for taking lots of good naps.

Finally and especially, all the family and friends who read and responded and offered the advice that made the book what it is.

This is your book, too.

PROLOGUE

Great dark figures closed in on Princess Ivy, towering over her, obstructing the light and blocking any chance for escape. She was acutely aware of sharp teeth and hideously grinning faces before she was overtaken by the sheer mass of them, their strong arms trapping her, and the cold feel of steel mace chains slowly encircling her throat. She closed her eyes against their sight, unable to shut out the scent of perspiration and raw meat that caught in her nostrils and turned her stomach. The pressure on her neck increased, the chains pinching and strangling her. Ivy gasped for life.

Abruptly, she sat up. She was alone, bedclothes twisted about her, her hands frantically clasping her grandfather's diamond medallion, her pounding heart the only noise in the fireless chamber where she slept inside a castle that was not really home. Her breathing refused to be slowed, and the room closed in on her as ominously as the Southern warriors from her sleep.

She stood, hastily clothed herself in coarse leggings and a thick cloak, and emerged from her chamber, fumbling down the endless winding staircase and out into the gray mist and sharp contours of the mountain. She staggered on the rocky ground, the browning moss crunching beneath her feet as she descended the hillside.

When she reached the thick wall at the bottom of the castle hill, she stopped, pressing her hands into the cold stones and focusing on the mess of shops and cottages sprawled on the gray hills below. Involuntarily, her eyes traced the narrow road, which began a few feet from her position and ran through the village to where it passed through the two dark cliffs on the horizon—the gateway to the South. Her heart lurched.

There was a blemish in the white space between the dark cliffs. A figure. She pushed back her unruly hair and squinted to see more clearly. The figure was becoming larger on the horizon. She swallowed hard, her hands forming fists as she let go of the wall and moved through the gates and down the road to the open hills outside the castle to get a closer look. The image persisted and then sharpened. The smudge on the canvas of the cold morning grew, racing straight toward her—a rider.

Part of Ivy's consciousness screamed warning. It commanded her to get back within the walls, to run into the castle and up the stairs to her cold dark room, to hide in the thick blankets, hoping for better dreams.

But another, stronger, unbelieving part of Ivy kept her rooted to the spot, eyes wide. *Merely a villager out for a morning ride,* it whispered as she watched the rider move through the village with inhuman speed, neither turning toward the small mountain harbor nor pausing at an inn or tavern.

She considered him as he disappeared and reappeared behind hill and house. But it was not until the rider passed the last cottage on the outskirts and headed up toward the castle that Princess Ivy began to step slowly backward, taking in the tall cloaked figure with powerful movements and a Southern mace at his side.

She turned and ran up the hills for the gate. Only a few seconds passed before she heard hoofbeats close behind her. She pushed harder and then stumbled hastily over the rocky ground.

A throaty laugh grew in her ears, and the stench of raw meat entered her nose. The air pierced her lungs and stung her sides. He was upon her.

It was with terror and resignation that she screamed when a strong, rough limb hoisted her onto the barreling steed. Her last conscious thought was that she had not left the nightmare in her bedroom but had walked outside, right into it.

CHAPTER 1

Simon Adler was a fool. At least that was his profession, a profession at which, lately, he had found very little success.

He now sat at the bar of Wentley Tavern shaking his head at the motley group of villagers for whom he had just performed. He had turned out his usual routine, but the audience had seemed less than impressed with his array of sword tricks, jokes, and balancing acts.

"Worked up a thirst, then, boy?" Karl asked from behind the bar.

"Yes," Simon replied, "for water." He looked once again at the drunken men surrounding him. He felt saddened by the state of his fellow villagers, brought down by their fears of Southern invasion, their displacement from their lands, and their daily struggle to coax crops from the unforgiving rocky soil. "They don't seem to be taking to me much these days, do they?"

Karl handed him a tall mug of water. "True," he said, "but then, you aren't exactly givin' them what they want, are you?"

Simon shrugged. "My routine hasn't changed much—same old tricks."

"The problem is you make the tricks look good. You are a

brilliant acrobat, and a witty comedian. You are skillful. People want a fool to be foolish—trip on banana peels and grin and spout nonsense. These men want fools to make them feel better about themselves, not to remind them of what they lack."

Simon sighed. The tricks of his trade had always come strangely easy to him. He wanted to make good use of his talent; but on a deeper level, a fool's humor was based in truth, and today's truths were not well-received. "They didn't used to be like this."

"No, they didn't," Karl replied as he moved down the bar to help another customer. "But that has very little to do with you, or even them, as you well know."

Simon nodded. He did know. He mentally turned back time four years to when his people had been forced to abandon their farmlands and homes to move into the hills. With the increasingly eminent threat of Southern invasion, King Than had opted to forfeit Lyria and move the people back to the relative safety of the mountains and the ancient castle that still stood at the mountainside. This choice made some sense, considering the Lyrians had almost no army, and the nobles who might have possessed any bargaining power had mostly sold off their lands and property and bought ship passage to safer territory.

Those remaining either moved to the mountain valley for safety or stayed behind to face the Southern warriors. Simon's brother and father had been among the latter. Simon, at the age of fourteen, had been trusted to bring his mother and younger siblings to safety in the mountains. The men who stayed behind were inevitably defeated. His father, Marcus, was wounded and his elder brother, Roger, killed. The early winter was likely the only thing that kept the Southerners from advancing through the mountain pass to face the weakened Lyrians. The Southern warriors, unaccustomed to the severe cold of Lyrian winters, had fled south once more. The only mystery was why they hadn't returned after the frost ended.

Simon looked around the tavern once more. He knew many of these men had experienced losses similar to his. He felt sympathy for them, able farmers, barely subsisting in their new mountain homes. Some had been sailors and merchants whose fine vessels were either abandoned to the South or transformed into smelly fishing boats.

Furthermore, three years later, there was still the feeling of unease that came from knowing the Southerners might return any day. The unrest and fear had only intensified since the disappearance of the younger princess. People seemed more suspicious and likely to whisper and look over their shoulders. Simon found that his own dreams had become nightmarish and fraught with worry. Recently, he had even taken to dreaming about the princess repeatedly. In these dreams was always the overwhelming taste of her despair and the unmistakable urge to aid her.

Simon had never met the Princess Ivy, but he felt the unrest of her absence, as he was sure many Lyrians did. Three months had passed since her disappearance, with no word as to her whereabouts. The king had become more withdrawn than ever, and no one ever saw the elder princess, Mara, anymore. After the death of Queen Achlys, a beautiful but somewhat weak and distant woman, King Than had chosen for his wife a commoner, Cora. She was not the dark beauty Achlys was, but she was wise, strong, and lighthearted. Her subjects knew her and loved her. When she died, the people placed their hope and faith in her daughter, Ivy—who was now gone, or even dead.

He fingered the dark bronze tradestone that hung about his neck, the fool's tradestone. He smiled as he considered the irony of his task—to entertain, to make laugh those whose fears and disappointed hopes made them the toughest crowd imaginable. He thought of his Uncle Miles, who had passed his stone to Simon when it became clear he would have no sons of his own. Simon knew tradestones were more ornamental than anything, and only some still chose to wear the inherited pieces, but he had been flattered to accept this stone from his uncle.

"You have to know your audience, Simon," he had said. "You can't make fun of nobles when you perform in the palace, and a crowd in the town square is not going to have an appreciation for court humor." Simon had listened carefully to the advice, nodding his fair head with pretended understanding. "Learn to read the faces in the crowd. Take their mood and use it to your advantage. Decide whether or not they are interested in a spectacle, or just someone to make them think. If you must feed them truth, first coat it with whatever sugar will make it sweetest to them. Give them what they want to see."

Simon considered this advice in light of his current crowd. He was overwhelmed by the impossibility of giving them what they were looking for by a mere act. He wished his uncle were here now to advise him. But Miles had been like many fools, wandering and without family of his own. He had gone away from Lyria to try his craft in an outlying kingdom before the displacement and had never returned. Now Simon could only imagine what he might say if he were present.

The cold air of an open door moved him from his reverie, and he turned to discover the cause of the draft. A weary looking man in the king's uniform entered. He took a seat at the bar just down from where Simon was sitting and brushed snow from his shoulders and hair.

Karl passed him a mug and leaned on the bar near him. "What news, friend?"

"No news," he gulped his drink. "There lies the problem."

"Ah," Karl responded. "You seek the princess."

The man nodded his assent. "A useless task. We are asked to search high and low, in all the places *except* those where we know she has some chance of being."

"Yes, the South . . ."

"That's what we assumed, but we have found witnesses who swear she was taken away to the harbor, not back through the pass."

Karl raised an eyebrow, "Why the harbor? Where would they take her?"

The man looked around the room, catching Simon's eye before Simon pretended newfound interest in his water. The soldier lowered his voice. "We think they have taken her to the Fringe."

Karl was not convinced. "Impossible. No point in doin' that. They can't use her as a bargaining piece if she's dead. Even if they did decide to kill her, why go to the trouble of takin' her out there to do it?"

"Don't think they took her to bargain. Besides," he lowered his voice more, making it necessary for Simon to lean forward in order to hear him, "her mother died at sea, and you know the old stories of that place. People were dropped there, banished, with nothing but the dinghy under them, the oar in their hand, and their hopes against all the bad luck of the place and the ones who had been left there before. The Southerners aren't negotiators, they're monsters. They meant her abduction as a slap in the face, a call to come out and fight, before they come in. They're just playing with us."

"She could have survived, even the Fringe. Why doesn't the king send soldiers after her, then? Why the useless searching?"

"The chances are slim. People have gotten close enough to the shoal to see it, but none who tried to approach the island has ever returned. Besides, the king must know that he'd just be sacrificing his men to send them—that might have been another of the South's motives in taking her there. I know I wouldn't go. The place is nothing more than a dead end, a death trap. I think he just keeps us looking to maintain the appearance of hope, so that even if he feels the slap on the face and the inevitable threat the South poses, he doesn't want his people to feel it. If the kingdom knows Princess Ivy is dead, they will have lost not only their hope but what they see as their tie to the crown and their willingness to fight. As Lyrians, we connect with Ivy, like we did with her mother. The Southerners knew what they were doing when they took her."

Across the room a brawl broke out between some of the men. Karl rushed away to calm them. Simon sat where he was, heart pounding against the stone at his chest. The feeling of his dreams was once again in his mind, the taste of despair in his mouth. Mostly, he felt again the unexplainable but undeniable urge to find Princess Ivy and bring her back. It was all he could see. He wondered why the rest of the kingdom did not seem to feel as he did.

Simon could understand King Than's wish to maintain morale in the kingdom and safeguard his soldiers, but he felt that to do nothing to save the princess was wrong. He knew how his father felt about King Than's passive leadership. He considered the price his father and Roger had paid to do something about it. He thought about his good mother and younger siblings at home, and what would happen to them if the South invaded. He thought of his own skill, the ease with which he could wield a sword. Finally, he looked around him once more at the brawling, drinking, depressed men of his village and wished that he could give this crowd just what they needed.

CHAPTER 2

An old man held up a jeweled mirror but did not see his own white-bearded face staring back at him. He was not surprised. He wasn't looking for himself in the mirror, as most people do, but for an answer to his question. A picture appeared in the glass, a scene:

A king was standing by a cold fireplace. He was visible only from behind. He might not have been particularly old, but his hair was uniformly gray, and his broad shoulders drooped a bit as he gazed up at a portrait that hung above the mantle. The portrait showed two young women—princesses, as indicated by the crowns they wore. They seemed to share the same straight nose and regal countenance as the king.

But all similarity ended there. The princess on the left was small, with long dark hair, dark eyes, and soft features. Her smile was subtle, and she looked to be the leader in both age and beauty. The princess on the right was taller and had wild, curly, honey-colored hair; clear, unguarded eyes; sharper features; and a calm, open smile. The king's head seemed to be inclined in her direction. He clenched his fist and stormed away from the fireplace, leaving the room.

The mirror fogged, and another image appeared. A young woman sat at a pianoforte. Her head was down, but the old man recognized her as the beautiful dark princess in the portrait. Her appearance was neat and her manner calm. There was no music in front of her, and the melody she played was anything but serene. The old man thought he had never heard something so haunting, so seemingly empty, as it filled the dark halls of the stone palace room.

The scene again shifted to reveal a man, perhaps in his mid-thirties looking over the railings of a ship in the small mountain port. The ship was well worn, and so was the man—his skin tanned and his face unshaven. The chipped lettering on the side of the ship spelled out the word *Sapphire.* The clouds above his head were dark. The man stared straight ahead and appeared to be looking without seeing—deep in thought.

The final image was more remote, merely the troubled face of a young man with a strong, worried brow and reddish hair. It was a face the old man had seen in his mirrors before.

The mirror went dark. The old man scratched his chin. He thought about the images for a while before putting the mirror down on the table in front of him. His question was answered.

CHAPTER 3

Gilda Reed marched resolutely out of the council room, slamming the door behind her. She was normally much too sensible a woman to give way to fits of temper, but she could not conceal her disgust for that ridiculous group of people who took it upon themselves to regulate the affairs of witches—or define them. It was preposterous of Andrews, council leader, to think he had the right to revoke her witch's tradestone simply because she could not actually perform magic. She was an excellent witch, in spite of the fact that she didn't fiddle with silly love potions or wart removers.

No one had paid her unusual witchery (or lack thereof) any mind until she had started urging the council to focus on the abduction of the princess. Gilda could not explain her own feeling of urgency about Princess Ivy except that her dreams gave her the feeling that something must be done about it—and by her. She had always trusted her own dreams, feelings, and intuitions, and they had never led her astray. But now she couldn't help but feel that if she hadn't shared them she would still be in good favor as a witch in spite of her absent magical ability.

"Gilda!" Gilda heard the voice behind her and stopped but did not turn.

"Go back in there, Meg," she said. "It's useless."

"I'm sorry, Gilda," Meg placed her short person in front of Gilda with a look of real concern, which diffused Gilda's anger a bit. "The council," she continued, trying to catch her breath, "they are becoming more and more set in their ways. I tried to explain . . ."

"Explain what, Meg? There is no convincing them I am of any use without spells and magical potions to prove it."

"I know the good you have done in your sector. They will not be able to replace you."

"Well, they'll have to. But they'll do it without a stone. My mother gave this to me, and I'll be hanged before I let Andrews take it." She fingered the dark emerald hanging down the front of her simple black dress.

"Yes. I question his leadership; he and the others have become even more grasping since our removal to the mountains. Perhaps they feel it is the only sphere in which they have some control."

"Perhaps," Gilda replied.

"What will you do?" Meg's eyes betrayed doubt. "Where will you go?"

"I don't know." Gilda considered her lack of options. "But you'd better believe it will be something meaningful." Her face was hard, and Meg couldn't help but be a bit intimidated by this tall, broad, determined woman. "Don't worry, Meg. Just do what you can here. Good-bye."

Meg watched her move away. "Good-bye, Gilda."

Once out in the stark, winter cold and on the road to her little home, Gilda's resoluteness wavered. Meg was right to ask what her plans would be. What could she possibly do?

By the time she reached her cottage, Gilda had worked herself into a lather. She stormed in, pulled the old trunk out from behind the bed and set it open in the middle of the room. She then proceeded to create a ruckus of banging cauldrons, scattered papers, books, various spices and seasonings. When the trunk was full of what she deemed to be her necessaries, Gilda slammed it closed and stood back, hands on her hips.

She sighed. She was packed but still had no idea where she would go. She started a pot of tea on her little stove and sat at the table, eating bits of the leftover pudding she had made yesterday, which, she had to admit, was quite good. She sipped tea and looked out her darkening window, watching the light snowfall coat her rosebushes and pondering her situation.

It wasn't that she loved this house so much—she could barely stand up straight under its low ceilings. Of course, this rocky hillside was much inferior to the tidy garden grove where she had resided most of her life, but she had begun to feel that she was doing some good for the discouraged people in her area. Someone, especially lately, always needed a listening ear, and she had been that for her fellow villagers. People were stopping by to see her at all hours.

She recalled a visitor she had had a month or so ago, one of the king's soldiers. He had been told she was the resident witch and had ridden up to her cottage to ask if she could look into her cauldron and tell him if Princess Ivy was still living and, if so, was she living at the Fringe. She had kindly informed the man that she could not actually perform magic and that he would need to inquire at Tillie Maybury's a few miles down the road; although she doubted even a magic witch would be able to see the princess's whereabouts.

Gilda set aside her tea and began to finger the leaves of the potted plant that sat on her table. The leaves seemed to mold to her fingers, and the vines turned toward her slightly. Her mother had always said she had a way with plants.

She felt dreadfully idle—all packed up and nowhere to go. She sighed, got up from the table, and pushed her trunk aside. It would have to wait. She put on a warm shawl and decided she'd better head down to the inn. This was something she almost never did. She found the place rowdy, and the food was never as good as hers. But it wasn't food she needed tonight. It was news.

CHAPTER 4

It had always been crowded at the Adler home; but when Simon entered tonight, the home seemed overfull and somehow confining. Their mountain home was a good deal smaller than the farm cottage on the Lyrian plain had been. And the family was now grown up enough to fill it to bursting, with nowhere to go.

Simon knew that if the removal to the mountains had not taken place, many of his siblings would have left home by now. His brother Roger had taken a position in the navy before he had died. The others would have followed suit, finding apprenticeships and making their way. But now, as it was, they were all limited to the unvaried and menial jobs they could scrounge up locally. There was some industry in working their little plot of land; but the growing season was shorter and less fruitful in the mountains, and there was hardly enough work to keep a portion of them busy for a time.

Simon emptied his pockets of his meager earnings into the family cache on the mantle before being assailed by younger brothers in a wrestling match. After being bested by their rambunctious energy and sustaining a number of warning glares from his mother when their struggles came too close to the table which was now being set, he escaped to seek out his father.

Marcus was resting in his chair by the fire. Simon greeted him and sat in a nearby chair. He then proceeded to become so lost in his own thoughts that his father had to ask him how his day had been three times before it even occurred to Simon he was being spoken to.

"I'm sorry . . . what?" he stammered. His father smiled, but his eyes still spoke sadness.

"Your silence is thick and heavy, son," he said. "What is on your mind?"

Simon sighed and ran his fingers through his sandy hair, trying to form words from his scattered thoughts. "I don't know, Dad," he mumbled. "Being a fool has never seemed more foolish than it does lately. I feel useless and idle."

His father frowned. "I have told you before, Simon, you are an invaluable asset in our family. You have helped me lead and protect your mother and siblings. You have often been a strength at home that I have not." He glanced down at his lifted leg, an unconscious habit of his that always made the background of his thoughts clear to Simon. "Your 'fooling' puts bread on our table as well—"

Simon cut him off. "I'm glad to have helped our family, Dad, but what good am I merely subsisting while our kingdom falls apart? Lyrians need more than a laugh or a show. They need hope, and it is quickly diminishing." He told his father what he had heard from the soldier about the princess and about his own persistent dreams of her.

His father watched with a peculiar expression on his face while Simon shared his news. He was silent for a while afterward. But then he spoke:

"I heard similar news myself today," he said. "I will tell you

more, but first let me ask you what you are thinking. Are you wanting to stage some kind of rescue?"

Simon shook his head. "Yes. No. I don't know. I just know I
want to be brave like you. Like Roger . . ." Simon saw the pain immediately darken his father's features at the mention of Roger and
regretted bringing him into it. "I spend my time spinning out truth
to unwilling crowds but never acting on it. I'm like a starving wretch
who lies on his floor professing his empty stomach while his brother
goes out to hunt food." Simon smiled slightly, then shook his head.
"I feel like I'm meant to do more with what I have been given, that's
all."

Marcus looked directly into Simon's eyes. "You have been given
a good deal, Simon," he said. "I know of no one more intelligent
than you or agile, hard working, or better with a sword. But there
has always been something more with you; some power under your
boyishness begging to be realized. It makes me proud to see that you
intend to use it well. As such, let me tell you what I heard today."
Simon sat up in his chair.

"Like you, I have heard rumors that Princess Ivy was taken to
the Fringe. If she was banished to a boat there, alone, it is not likely
that she survived; but as you say, this is all a matter of hope. There is
a ship in port now, a fishing vessel under the command of a Captain
Merrick. He is either brave or careless with his life; but it is well
known that he often brings back his catch from places as far west as
the Fringe. If you are serious about finding the princess, I suggest
you find out about this ship and get on it."

Simon was silent, shocked at this speech. "You think I should
go?" he asked, not able to hide his incredulity. "Even if I were able
to get on that ship and somehow make it to the Fringe and find our
princess, what about you? What about my duty here at home?"

"Oh, Simon, I may not be whole, but I am here. Your younger

siblings are not the small children they were when we first came through the pass; in fact, Benjamin is older than you were when you led our family through. It will be okay for you to relinquish that duty for the time being to shoulder a new one. I know as well as you do that a quest for a princess now might seem foolishly lofty to some in light of more practical and pressing needs. But the loftiest aims are the ones worth pursuing. So, use what you have, Simon. Give us all hope."

After this speech, Marcus Adler smiled at his son. This time it was echoed in his eyes.

CHAPTER 5

Well, Gilda Reed," said Nell with surprise when Gilda peeked into the kitchen of the inn. "We have not seen you here in a long time."

Gilda raised an eyebrow behind her tiny spectacles. "I'll not mince words, Nell," she said. "I've come for news." After all, news had to be Nell's specialty. It certainly wasn't her cooking. Nell beckoned her in, and Gilda stood over the stew that was boiling in a big pot. She sniffed.

"It needs more salt," she said. "And something else . . ." She sniffed again. "Perhaps some basil."

Nell brushed the advice aside. "You'll have to taste my cooking before you criticize it," she said. "Anyhow, let me tell you what bits of gossip I've picked up today."

Nell started in on some current drama about a fisherman's son who had recently disappeared with a young nobleman's daughter on one of the last outbound boats. "He's shamefully below her, of course, but that's mattered less since Queen Cora took the throne. I'm sure her parents will dress him up as something grand when they reach their destination, and no one will ever know about his humble origins until he opens his mouth." She giggled, then sighed. "So much for the upper class as 'protectors,'" she scoffed. "Most of them have fled by now and we're stuck here with the Southern army at our throats." She seemed ready to dwell on this for quite some time.

Gilda urged her onward. "What else have you heard?"

"Oh the usual," she said, not easily dissuaded from her soapbox. "You know, now that the princess is gone, who have we got on the throne who understands us anyway? The soldiers have been sayin' they've taken her to the Fringe, but there's no word about a rescue. I guess no one dares go there . . . although now that I think about it, an Adler boy *was* in here earlier trying to find that Captain Merrick who sails out west. He seemed all bent on gettin' to the Fringe. Maybe he plans to rescue the princess himself." She laughed at this like it was some great joke. Gilda did not join in.

"Who is this boy?" she asked.

"You know," she said. "You remember Marcus Adler? He was one of the men who stayed to fight after the removal. I think the oldest son died, and this one . . . Samuel or Simon or something, he was the next oldest—a long-legged boy with all those freckles. He comes in occasionally to entertain the customers. He's merely a local fool."

Gilda frowned. "Did he locate Merrick?"

Nell shrugged. "He was talking to some of those sailors in the far corner." Gilda leaned out of the kitchen, locating the group Nell was referring to. "I think they told him where to look." Gilda thanked Nell and left the kitchen, shaking her head. Nell was agreeable enough but somewhat close-minded, Gilda thought. If this Adler boy was planning to go after the princess, that was nothing to laugh about. It was easy to dismiss people who had no obvious great abilities or worth . . . *but if one only looked deeper*, Gilda thought.

She had been similarly dismissed herself, and only today, but she was not without value. There was much she could do. She was sensible and a good problem solver. She was not a wispy willow, but a strong, hearty woman, not afraid of weather or danger. And somehow, she had always had a sense that she was meant for something greater.

She was going to find out about this boy, and his motivation. Who knew? Maybe they could help each other.

CHAPTER 6

Simon stood on the dirty docks of the harbor, staring up at the white-chipped wording on the boat in front of him. It said *Sapphire*. Simon scrunched up his nose, finished the last bit of his mother's cornbread, and tried to convince himself he had not made a huge mistake in coming here. The *Sapphire* seemed to be more a dilapidated scrap heap than a seaworthy vessel.

He was still deliberating when a distinguished-looking older sailor came walking down the gangplank toward him.

"How do yeh do?" he asked, congenially, nodding to Simon, who smiled in return. "Bit o' nice weather, eh?" He indicated the gray and gathering clouds. "Too bad we're ta set sail first thing in the morning, but it can't be helped."

Simon did not look at the clouds. He cleared his throat and stood up tall. "You must be Captain Merrick."

The man laughed. "Not a bit close, lad, but no matter. I'm 'is first mate, Abner Murray." He extended his hand and Simon shook it.

"Simon Adler."

"Well, Mr. Adler, if it's Merrick you want, he's just there." Mr. Murray pointed to the silhouette of a man who stood on the opposite side of the ship, facing out to sea. "I'd proceed with caution if I were you, though. Foul weather makes for a foul mood where he's concerned." Mr. Murray winked at Simon and disappeared down the dock.

Simon took a deep breath and commenced in climbing up the gangplank. He crossed the deck to where the captain was standing, stopped a few feet from him, and tried to collect his thoughts into words. He cleared his throat.

"Get off my boat!" the captain spoke, back still turned, before Simon could say a thing.

Simon choked, "Excuse me, sir, but . . ."

"I don't have any money to pay you if you've come to collect, so you're wasting your time. Get off." Merrick clenched his fist, and Simon suddenly noticed what an intimidating figure he presented, even from behind. He was a few inches taller than Simon—who was already tall—and he was broad and well-muscled.

Simon backed up a few steps and said, "I'm not here for money, sir."

Captain Merrick turned around abruptly. He was probably only ten or fifteen years older than Simon, but his face looked like it had seen more than enough use and weather. His features were strong, and he had a light beard on his chin. A dark blue tradestone hung about his neck. He studied Simon suspiciously. "Then what do you want?"

Simon bowed, extending his hand with fool's flare. "I'm here to offer you my services."

Captain Merrick laughed roughly. "I don't know what it is you are after, boy, but my ship is fully staffed. I won't be needing your 'services.'"

He moved to turn around again, but Simon proceeded. "Excuse me, sir, but I have been told you sail only with a mate and three other men. Hardly a full staff for a vessel this size."

"This 'vessel,' young man, is nothing more than a broken-down fishing boat that brings in barely enough for the five of us, let alone a pampered youth who has probably never done a bit of sailing in his life—"

"I'm not interested in a share of the catch," Simon cut in.

A trace of curiosity surfaced in the captain's eye. "What do you want, then?"

Simon continued, heartened by even slight interest. "Passage. It is well known, sir, that you are the only person who is sailing as far west as I am interested in going."

"How far west is that?"

"The Fringe."

Captain Merrick laughed out loud but stopped himself when he saw the earnestness of Simon's countenance. "Are you crazy, kid? Haven't you learned a thing? I might sail into more dangerous waters than most, but even I know that it is impossible for any ship to make berth there. I'd be thrashed to pieces."

"I don't want you to make berth, just get me close enough to sail in on a dinghy."

"You would never make it."

Simon smiled at his feet. "Are you a sailor or a prophet?" he mumbled. The captain opened his mouth as if to speak, but Simon beat him to it. "Whether or not I make it is hardly your concern. I can give you this for the dinghy." Simon held out his bag of coins. He knew it wasn't much, but it might offer some incentive.

Captain Merrick held the bag in his hand but just continued to stare quizzically at Simon. "You don't seem suicidal, kid. Why do you want to do a thing like that?"

Simon read the doubt in the captain's face. *Might as well get this over with,* he thought, and then said, "I'm hoping to find the princess."

The corners of Merrick's mouth turned up slightly, and Simon thought he looked vaguely amused.

Simon pressed on: "I know I might not look like much, Captain, but I am hardworking, strong, agile, and willing to learn. I'll help you with the sailing and any fishing you might do between here and my destination."

Captain Merrick watched him for a minute and then shrugged. "What's your name, kid?"

"Simon Adler."

"Adler, huh." Merrick turned his back to Simon once more.

"All right, kid," he said, "we leave at dawn. I'll expect you to work as hard as the rest, so you'd better get a good night's sleep."

"Thank you, Captain." Simon smiled at his success, or undoing, as he walked down the gangplank and off in search of a place to rest.

◆   ◆   ◆

Captain John Merrick always slept on the *Sapphire;* he was more at home on water. However, he was weary of ship rations, and it was with the express desire to eat something warm and semi-edible that he made his way to the nearest inn the night before he was to set sail.

As he walked, coat pulled up around his chin for warmth, he mulled over the conversation he had just had with Simon Adler. He had known another Adler, Roger, some years back and had even fought near him the day he died. If the kid were at all like his brother, he would be a hard worker.

The idea of the princess being taken to the Fringe was not a new one to him. The rumor had been circulating for a good while.

He found it mildly interesting, however, that Simon Adler was so convinced of its truth he was aching to sail out and find her. There was, after all, little evidence of her whereabouts or chance of success.

Merrick could hear the noise of the Arrow from some distance and was not surprised to see it rather full when he entered. He found himself a seat near the back and didn't wait long for Nell, the inn-keeper's wife, to come find him and bring him some warm bread and a hearty but somewhat flavorless stew. He had almost finished eating when Nell came back and placed a sort of cream pie in front of him.

"On the house," she said, and left.

He was about to take a bite when he felt someone standing behind him. He turned around and stared up at a tall, broad-shouldered and somewhat graying woman wearing an emerald tradestone and wire glasses too small for her face.

"Hello, Mr. Merrick," she said. "I've been waiting for you to come in. May I have a seat?"

Merrick only stared up blankly at her; but she, not really seeming to need an invitation, walked around and sat down directly across from him.

"I am Gilda Reed, and I'll be sailing out with you tomorrow," she said, matter-of-factly. "What time do we leave?"

John Merrick, a bit taken aback, said nothing. No one ever paid him any heed, and now in one night the whole kingdom seemed to want a ride on his ship.

Gilda Reed continued, undeterred, "I'll need an approximate time in the morning, you see. There are things to be done and supplies to be gotten. A deadline would be nice."

Merrick wasn't quite sure how to deal with this woman. He took a bite of the cream pie in front of him.

"I can't take you. Sorry," he said, "my ship is no place for a lady."

"Oh, don't be ridiculous! I'm no fragile creature. I need to be on your ship tomorrow, and you will not be a bit the worse for having me, I dare say. Besides, I have good reason to go."

"You seek Princess Ivy."

"Well . . . yes." She seemed a bit surprised at his response but continued, "I am a witch, Mr. Merrick. I intend to use my skills on her behalf."

"Oh?" he said, taking another bite of pie. "You have some spell that is going to help you past death at sea to arrive safely at the Fringe, find the young woman, and transport her back safely—all by yourself? What exactly is your plan?"

"You know as well as I do, I will not be the only person on your ship interested in her rescue," said Gilda.

"Yes," Merrick laughed mildly. "You and barely-a-man off to save royalty. He is probably as likely as you to succeed. Have you met him?"

"I have, actually. We met not long after he talked with you." Gilda did not seem a bit disturbed by his doubts. "He is young, to be sure, but not unwise, and definitely brave. I'm sure we'll manage."

"How?" said Merrick, his mouth full of pie, and growing impatience readable on his face. "Tell me, what are you going to do?"

"The right thing, Mr. Merrick," said Gilda Reed, sounding equally impatient. "We will do the right thing or die trying. You, on the other hand, will catch fish, sail around on your miserable boat, and wait for the Southerners to march in and destroy us all."

John Merrick felt his face turning red. This woman knew nothing. He had tried fighting fate, battling the Southerners. It had gotten him nothing but lost friends and foul memories. He took a deep breath and allowed his usual color to return. He went to take another bite of the cream pie and realized, disappointed, that he had eaten it all.

Gilda went on, "If you are so sure it is impossible to save the princess, Mr. Merrick, why is it you are so eager to sail in those dangerous western waters, and why did you agree to take the young man?"

Merrick frowned at her questions. He had been telling himself for a long time that the catch was better farther out, but he could not discount that there was also some other barely conscious draw to the area that had become more pronounced lately; the place was even in his dreams. He decided to ignore the first question but addressed the second.

"Simon Adler may have rot for brains, Ms. Reed," he said in a condescending tone. "But he will at least be capable of pulling his weight on my ship. He has offered to work, and pay."

"As will I," she said, producing a small handful of coins. "Here is some money, not much, but I will certainly work."

"I don't wish to offend, Ms. Reed, but what good are you going to be at sailing a ship or hauling in fish?"

"None whatsoever, Mr. Merrick."

John Merrick nodded in affirmation.

"I mean," said Gilda Reed, "to earn my passage as your cook."

"You cook?"

"Yes, very well, Mr. Merrick." Gilda Reed smiled. "In fact, I made that pie you have just devoured before me."

Captain John Merrick raised an eyebrow. "Hmmm."

◆   ◆   ◆

On a busy night at an inn like the Arrow, the noise level was such that a person could really only hear the man sitting just next to him, if he talked loud, and nothing else. Perhaps it was for this reason that John Merrick and Gilda Reed did not hear a small figure sliding under their table as they conversed. Or it might have been that the said figure, a boy, had become skilled at making himself undetectable, much like a hungry rat. He was accustomed to hiding, sneaking about, and taking what he needed to survive.

Tonight, for instance, he had slipped into the Arrow's kitchen to rummage for some food and had come across a mostly uneaten pie. He had only just grabbed a handful of crust and cream when he heard Nell coming back through the door. He hid in a nearly empty grain barrel, licking his fingers, as she exclaimed at the missing portion and stormed about cursing his name and telling him to come out and take punishment for his naughty deeds.

"Burr, you sneaky little tyrant! Where are you hiding? I'll go get my Ross to teach you a lesson you'll never forget if you don't leave!"

Burr sat calmly in his barrel, well aware that Nell had no time tonight to comb the kitchen in search of him or pull Ross away from his many customers to do it for her. He waited, hoping she would depart soon and leave him what remained of that delectable pie.

"All right, Burr," Nell continued, her first threat affording no response. "Stay hiding all you want, but the pie is now locked in the ice closet—you won't be having any. You might as well go filch from someone else, you little monster!" She stormed from the kitchen, door swinging behind her.

Burr pushed out of the barrel and scanned the room, cursing his rotten luck a bit and Nell a lot. The pie was gone. He went to the kitchen door and peeked through the crack out into the dining area. Nell was carrying a piece of his pie to a table in the corner. Burr raised his eyebrows. It was no easy task to steal food from the person eating it but he had done it before, and this pie seemed worth the challenge. In a matter of moments, he was across the room and under the target table.

Burr knew if he was going to steal the pie he would have to be quick, but before he could set to work, a word of the ensuing conversation above caught his attention. *Fringe.* He sat very still, listening, until the pie was gone, and so was the woman who had made it. His head buzzed with what he had heard.

When the man, the captain, finally finished his meal and broke out into the dark cold to walk down the docks, a little shadow followed him all the way back to his ship.

CHAPTER 7

Princess Ivy felt the light on her eyes long before she opened them. Her mind told her that she was at home in bed. Her body, however, insisted that these blankets were thinner and more wooly than hers; that the smell was not of stone and candle wax but of fire smoke and mint; and that the very texture of the air here was different.

She heard the old man come into the room and set something by her bedside. Its smell was vaguely pleasant, but she decided she did not want to be awake today and therefore lay very still, concentrating on the backs of her eyelids and wishing they wouldn't tremble so much with her concentration.

"I know you're awake," said the old man, matter-of-factly. "No need to pretend." Ivy did not move. "You've confined yourself to sleep—real or imagined—for over a week now since we talked. You were barely conscious for almost three weeks before that." There was gentleness in his voice that gave her a small pang of guilt, but she did not open her eyes. She heard him sit in the chair at the end of her bed.

He continued. "I'm sure you wish you could really sleep, really forget, indefinitely. However, that body of yours has got to start living again"—he paused—"today, Ivy."

Something in the way he spoke the last two words made Ivy open her eyes.

She looked at the man at the end of her bed. His hair was white, and he had a snowy beard with a bit of red occasionally interspersed, lingering from younger days. His cheeks were rosy, and she had seen them fire up with emotion once or twice in the few conversations they had had. He was simply dressed in brown, practical attire and watched her with wrinkled, almost transparent blue eyes.

"Good," he said. He stood and left the room.

With her eyes now open, and the light streaming in, Ivy allowed herself to really observe the room. It was moderate in size, containing the red-curtained bed she was lying in, a sort of sitting couch on the opposite wall, and, of course, the wooden chair placed at the end of her bed. *So he could watch over me,* she thought. There was a fireplace on the wall across from the bed, and the floors were covered in rugs and carpets of warm hues.

When she leaned out to see beyond the curtains and look above her, she realized what an extraordinary room it was. The walls were tall with no windows, but the whole ceiling was clear glass through which she could see the wispy-clouded morning sky. She had never seen anything like it, and wondered if it was magic. The old man, Medwin, would have to be magic in order to know the things he had told her of a week ago. Suddenly she remembered the conversation again and had a strong desire to close her eyes once more and escape into sleep when Medwin returned.

"I brought you some clothes," he said, setting a simple green dress and some slippers on the small couch. "Yours, I'm afraid, were quite ruined after your ordeal. The waves and rocks tore them to shreds. Luckily, a former guest of mine left these." Ivy sat up a bit to look, wondering how there could have been other guests here, but did not get out of bed. "Although," he continued, winking, "you may wear that ratty old nightgown forever if you so desire."

Ivy looked down at herself and became suddenly aware of her disheveled state. She automatically reached for her grandfather's pendant and was relieved to find it still fast about her neck. She had only a few memories of her mother's father; but his clear stone had been a special gift from her mother when she turned twelve. Her mother wore one identical to it. Its source and familiarity made her feel more grounded. She exhaled.

"There is also a bath drawn for you in the adjoining room, which will be hot for only a short while yet, so I'll leave you to it." He turned to go.

"Wait." Ivy stopped him.

"Hmm?"

"How did you know . . . about my father and everything?"

Medwin looked suddenly tired. "You might say I *see* things, Princess. Beyond that I will explain to you in more detail later. For now, have some of that drink I left you and take a bath. You will feel better. Then, follow this hall, here, to the end on the left where there is a dining area. I will endeavor to make us something edible for dinner." He smiled and left the room, closing the door behind him.

CHAPTER 8

Simon could not believe that a farmer's son and acrobat could be so brought down by the physical task of sailing. He was young and fit, but as he crawled into the swinging hammock for his second night aboard the *Sapphire,* Simon felt muscles complain that had previously gone unnoticed. He had been fascinated by his first day's observation, had avoided seasickness, learned terms and principles quickly, and had looked forward to the chance to prove his knowledge. He had not bargained on how much more difficult it would be to actually perform the tasks. In the course of this second day, Simon had scrubbed the deck, untangled endless amounts of drift nets, and scaled the riggings to topmast and back until Niles was satisfied he was fast enough.

Niles was a sturdy man of very little conversation, whose weathered appearance made him of indeterminate age. He was a patient and accurate teacher but seemed determined that Simon perfect a task before he move on to the next.

Thomas was a thick middle-aged sailor. He was a steady man and always seemed to be humming or singing some sailing tune. He mostly avoided Simon—unlike Hastings. Hastings had red hair and a disposition to match. He was continually asking nautical questions that he knew very well Simon could not understand let alone answer. He strode purposefully across the newly scrubbed deck with his large, filthy shoes, and stood laughing at Simon's early attempts to climb the rigging until Mr. Murray came by and told him to get back to work.

Simon kicked off his boots and relaxed back into his hammock, closing his eyes. He was almost asleep when he was startled awake by a sudden outburst.

"What the—Oh my! Out! Out!"

Simon sat bolt upright. The shrieking, which was obviously being caused by the ship's only female crewmate, was coming from the galley. Simon took a deep breath and slipped out of the hammock. Ms. Reed had probably encountered a rat or something, but he thought he might as well offer some help. As he neared the galley he could hear sounds of struggle, but he was not prepared for the sight that met him there.

Under Ms. Reed's strong arm was the tawny head of a kicking, flour-coated creature whose struggle filled the air with white dust and who was shouting muffled curses as he bit into the side of her dress.

"Ah, Simon," she managed to choke out. "If you wouldn't mind . . ."

Simon lunged for and captured the thrashing feet with older-brother deftness and in a few moments had the flour monster pinned to the floor. Ms. Reed stood, brushed off her black dress, and straightened her tilted spectacles.

"Thank you, very much," she said.

The creature sputtered and began cursing and shouting. "Let go of me you dammmph," he screamed before he was cut off by the bit of nearby dishcloth Simon gagged him with.

"What's going on?" Hastings burst into the galley, followed in a few moments by Mr. Murray.

Simon caught his breath and brushed some flour from the creature's face to reveal a slim-cheeked, very angry-looking young boy.

"Ah," said Murray, kneeling down next to Simon, "it appears we have a stowaway."

"So bravely caught by a fellow three times his size," sneered Hastings.

Simon ignored the taunt as Murray laid a firm hand on the struggling youth. "If we take off the gag, will you leave off cursin', boy?"

The stowaway, a bit more still, moved his head in assent. Murray nodded at Simon, who untied the gag.

"Let go of me, you freckled numbskull!" the boy shouted, and began to kick again. Simon moved to reapply the gag, when the boy shouted, "That wasn't no curse! You said no curses. Leave it off!"

"Then settle down and explain yourself," said Simon, moving the boy to a sitting position. "Who are you?"

The boy scowled but quit kicking. He shook the flour from his hair and wiped his face on his sleeve. "I'm Burr," he said.

"What's yer surname, Burr?" said Murray, kindly.

"Don't have one."

Murray and Simon exchanged looks. "No parents?" Simon asked.

"Nope."

"No one will be missing him, then," said Hastings. "I say we toss him overboard. He'll just eat our food and make a mess."

Simon ignored this comment. "Why did you hide on this boat, Burr?"

The boy pointed at Gilda Reed. "I ate some of her pie and heard her talking to that captain fellow about the Fringe. I was just plain curious, I guess. I followed him back and hid in the fish hold. Only

. . . it smelled so rank, and I was so hungry that I came here to get some food but had to hide in the flour when I heard her coming." He looked at Gilda, who stood watching him with hands on her hips. "I just wanted some good food and a bit of adventure."

"I think a swim in the ocean would be a good adventure," said Hastings. Burr snatched a nearby ladle and threw it at Hastings, missing his head by inches.

Hastings recoiled as though to strike the boy, but Murray detained him. "Back to yer duties, please, Hastings." Hastings stormed from the galley.

Murray continued, "We won't be throwing yeh overboard, Burr, but something must be done. Yer unplanned arrival means more work and less rations fer the rest of us. What do yeh propose?"

Burr just scowled and shrugged his shoulders.

"How old are yeh, then? Seven? Eight?" Murray guessed.

"Ten, you dumb old codger. I'm ten."

"Hmmm. Well, Burr, yeh ought'a know that what yeh've done is illegal, and that Captain Merrick won't have dead weight on his ship. So, yeh've got two choices. Either become our prisoner, and we lock yeh in the fish hold for the rest of our trip and feed yeh nothing but gruel, or, as ten is as good an age as any to learn to sail, yeh work on this ship, respect yer elders, and yeh can sleep in a hammock and have some of Ms. Reed's food here, if she'll let yeh."

"On one condition," interjected the cook. "He reports here first to grind enough of our wheat stores to replace the good quantity of flour he has effectively destroyed."

"Fair enough," said Murray.

"So, what will it be, Burr?" said Simon.

"Not much choice, really," said Burr, flatly. "I'll work. But the food had better be worth it."

"My food always is," replied Gilda, and Simon and Murray nodded their assent.

CHAPTER 9

Bathed and dressed, Princess Ivy had the feeling she was wearing new skin as well as new clothes. The warm water had refreshed her, and with a newly fierce appetite, she left the little bathing room in pursuit of dinner.

Out in the hallway, Ivy froze. She stared down a corridor that was wall on one side and the same kind of seamless glass as on her bedroom ceiling on the other. The exceptional view revealed that the edifice she had been sleeping in for the past month was at the top of a hill, surrounded by dark and jutting icy peaks that gradually emptied into the rocky surf. She watched the cold and angry waves crashing steadily below and felt the hair rise on her arms. A chill ran through her, even though the hallway was rather warm. *She had survived those rocks and waves.*

Ivy still felt confused by her own survival. Memory supplied vivid pictures of being thrown from the little vessel in which she had been placed, her hands bound. She remembered the gasping, terrifying, icy struggle. Her kicking legs had given way, and the waves had overcome her. Ivy recalled her fierce longing for safety and the feel of the cold chain and pendant about her neck. But then, somehow, the next thing she remembered was lying, coughing, with the grit of cold sand at her cheek, salt in her eyes, and air in her lungs.

Ivy began to feel dizzy and turned to follow the hallway to its end when a glimmering at the periphery of her vision caught her attention. Ivy back-stepped to look through an open door on the solid wall at her side.

As she walked through the doorway, she suddenly found herself surrounded by hundreds of images of the same green dress she was wearing. The entire room was full of mirrors. The walls were mirrors; freestanding looking glasses of various shapes and sizes surrounded the room; there was a large table in the middle layered with shimmering hand mirrors. As she moved toward the table, Ivy saw and felt her repeated image moving about the room. She picked up a small, wood-carved hand mirror and looked into it. She was a bit surprised at how thin and pale her face was. She set down the mirror and proceeded to circle, admiring the different cuts and frames, when she heard a voice behind her.

"Seems you've found my mirrors," Medwin said with raised eyebrows.

"Yes . . ." Ivy looked at the floor, feeling it was rather rude of her to be snooping.

"It's no forbidden place. You are welcome to look in any of the rooms you'd like while you're here."

"Which could be forever, I suppose."

"Perhaps." Medwin smiled slightly. There was an uncomfortable silence. "You asked me earlier how I knew the things I told you of last week."

"Yes," Ivy said quickly.

Medwin regarded her quietly for a moment before continuing. "I see things in these mirrors. I don't have much control over what

I see; although at times I may direct my sight by asking to see certain things or get answers to a particular question. Sometimes I get answers, and sometimes I don't. The glimpses don't come with an explanation. I am left on my own to interpret what I see and hear in them."

"Are the mirrors magic?"

"Not necessarily." Medwin pulled at a chain around his neck and drew out from his clothes a tradestone unlike any Ivy had ever seen. It was black, obsidian probably, and highly reflective. "It is my own ability, something I have learned to do."

"And with your ability you saw the things you told me of?"

"More or less. Yes."

Ivy looked down, struggling to restrain pent-up tears.

"But, Ivy, I have seen other things too. I want you to know, as it might give you comfort, that there are people coming for you."

Ivy looked up, her eyes glistening. "People?"

"Yes."

"Coming to the Fringe?"

"Yes."

"But . . ." Ivy thought of the vicious coast she had just viewed in the hallway and remembered the things she had learned about her abduction, "will they make it?"

"That," said Medwin seriously, "remains to be seen."

CHAPTER 10

In the bowels of the *Sapphire*, Burr's feet slipped and skidded on the floor as he pushed a crate of smelly fish with all his might toward the fish hold. His arms were tired, but he liked the idea of them getting stronger so that one day he could give Hastings a nice big black eye. He also liked the feeling in his stomach that came with regular meals, and he wondered when dinner was. The ship lurched, the floor tipped, and Burr lost grip of his crate and fell over, again. He cursed.

"You watch what's coming out of your mouth, young Burr—" Gilda Reed's head appeared at the door to the galley, "or the only thing going in it will be mush."

"Slipped out," said Burr. "The ship is rotten tipsy today."

"It's making me ill," said Gilda, who did look a little green. Just then, Hastings appeared.

"Get those fish to the hold, Burr. That's enough dawdling."

Burr stuck out his tongue but recommenced in pushing the crate to the hold.

"When's dinner?" Hastings addressed Gilda.

"Not any time soon if I keep slipping in this dreadful water. I need more sand for my floor, please, Mr. Hastings."

"I'll see to it," he said, moving down the passage. Just then he bumped into Burr, who was emerging from the fish hold.

"Watch it, shrimp."

"Out of my way, you great lump," Burr retorted.

"All right, just for that, you'll go fetch a bag of sand, and bring it to the galley."

"Like hell, I will."

"More of that, and I'll see you're locked in the hold. Besides, you won't be eating dinner unless Ms. Reed's floor is sufficiently gritty."

"Then you won't neither, I take it!" Burr grinned at him.

"Come here, you little . . ." Hastings lunged, but was caught by the collar and held back. He spun around out of the grip and came face to face with Captain Merrick.

"What's going on here, Hastings?"

"Just teaching our little git of a stowaway a lesson in obedience." Captain Merrick glanced at Burr, who looked particularly red-faced.

"He's under no obligation to take orders from you, Hastings."

"He's a little thief . . ."

"Who has been made a member of the crew. So I suggest you get Ms. Reed her sand and continue about your own business."

"Yes, sir." Hastings's cheeks glared red as he pushed past Burr and disappeared down the corridor.

Burr looked up at the captain with an innocent expression.

"You've already made an enemy here, Burr. I can't afford to have a crew at odds with each other in these wild winter seas, do you understand?"

Burr nodded his head and looked at his feet.

"I understand Hastings is rather hotheaded, but you would be wise to avoid encouraging him."

"Yes, sir."

"Good, now make sure you get some good rest until your watch this evening. It's going to be a rough night."

♦   ♦   ♦

Simon emptied his stomach, once again, over the railings, but had no time to stop and wipe his mouth. He simply buttoned his top coat button, unsheathed his knife, and, as ordered, climbed aloft to loosen a sail. The boat reeled wide, and the noise of the storm raged in his ears. Snow collected in his hair and stung his eyes. His hands and feet slipped on the ropes more often than they held true, but he climbed, with determined strength, up to his destination.

Cutting the sail free was a nearly impossible task in the storm, as its bending folds obscured his vision and he had only one hand free with which to accomplish his task. However, his knife cut true. The sail was loosed then rolled back, and he descended, relieved, jumping the last few feet to the deck.

"That's the last of 'em," yelled Murray, who was standing close by. "Thomas and Niles are on watch now, let's get below."

Simon climbed the ladder down and, now free from wind but not from rocking, staggered to find his hammock. Murray climbed to occupy the one next to his.

"Are yeh alright, Adler?"

"Of course. I rather feel like each of my individual muscles have been stretched and strummed like fiddle strings. Oh, and the room is upside down. Perfect." Simon closed his eyes, wishing the nausea would subside.

Murray chuckled. "The closer we get to the Fringe, yeh know, the worse it gets."

"Yes, I've noticed." Simon paused then wondered aloud, "Why

does Merrick test fate by sailing out here at all, do you think, our current mission excluded?"

Murray was quiet for a moment. "I've often wondered that myself," he said, finally. "There is something about Merrick that is different than any other captain I've sailed with. He's fearless on the water. Not reckless, yeh know, but when he's at sea he always seems more in control of any situation than the storms and swells. It's like the water moves for him."

"Moves for him?" Simon echoed. His tone was doubtful, and yet he could not deny that in his brief time on the *Sapphire* he had noticed that Captain Merrick seemed to move the ship through the water with unusual ease and skill.

"Sounds crazy, I suppose," Murray said. "But he gets us through rough waters, and our hauls out here are always the greatest; although, we've never been quite this far before. Has it occurred to yeh, that yeh're not likely to make it to land?"

"Yes, several times, actually."

"And even if yeh do make it, yeh won't be able to get back off."

"I've considered it, yes."

"But yeh're determined to go."

"Yes."

"Why?"

"It's mostly a feeling I have, like I must be doing something. I feel it all the time, even when I sleep. I can no longer be still while Lyria falls apart and all of her people submit to death and destruction. I realize the princess is small compared to fleets of angry Southern warriors, but she must have been important if they went to such an effort to remove her, even if her only role is to give the people an incentive to wake up and fight. We need her to come home and be for the kingdom what her father is not."

Murray thought quietly for a few moments.

"Well, if yeh're resolute, hadn't yeh better come up with a plan? We're gettin' closer every day." Murray sat up as he said this, looking directly over at Simon. Simon sat up and stared back.

"A plan?"

"Listen, Simon. It's a mate's duty to know every detail of the destined coast, and I know every mapped inch of this side of the Fringe. I'm telling yeh that although there is really no good place ta enter her shoals, there are some better than others. I'm telling yeh that I'm willing ta go with yeh, as yer guide."

Simon couldn't help but smile, nausea notwithstanding, "You'll come?"

"No. He will not."

Simon and Murray turned toward the voice, and faced the captain's dark silhouette on the last step of the ladder.

"But, Captain . . ."

"No, Murray. This ship needs her mate. Not to mention, you are not as young as you used to be. As captain of the *Sapphire* it is my *personal* duty to ensure the safety of her crew."

Murray exhaled and shook his head.

"I will go in your place." John Merrick turned, ascended the ladder, and disappeared above.

From where he had been listening in his hammock in a dark corner of the room, Hastings quietly turned and closed his eyes.

CHAPTER 11

Medwin stood in the middle of his mirror room, eyes closed in concentration. When he opened them, he turned to face a full-length wood-framed mirror to his left. He approached the mirror and looked into it.

The image blurred and then sharpened to reveal a formal room in what appeared to be the stone castle. The king was sitting in a high-backed golden chair looking out a window at his side, his chin resting on his balled fist. His brows were knitted in concern, or was it consternation?

"Excuse me, your majesty." A tall, bearded man dressed in royal uniform entered the room and bowed deeply.

The king did not move. "What is it, Talbot?" he asked, little expression on his tired face.

"There is news concerning your daughter, sir."

The king sat up and turned, abruptly. "Well?" he prompted.

"A small party has set off in search of her, sir."

The king studied his steward carefully. "They have actually set sail?"

"Yes, sir."

"They were heading toward the Fringe?"

"Yes."

"A few brave souls . . ." the king mumbled, while Talbot watched, eyebrows furrowed.

Just then, a movement to the king's side caught his eye, and he turned confrontationally to the shadowy northern corner of the room. His dark-haired daughter, head bowed, moved from the shadows.

King Than composed his features and smiled. "Mara," he said, walking toward her, "you startled me. Come hear the good news."

Princess Mara did not speak, but took his arm when he offered it, and followed both men from the room.

The surface of Medwin's mirror then changed to show the *Sapphire* treading through icy waters. The sky above was unusually clear. The nets were down in the water, and the entire crew was involved in the task of fishing.

Suddenly, the young boy jumped up animatedly, pointing at the particular net he was standing by. Medwin could not hear what was being said over the sounds of the surf, but it was obvious that the child was excited about the catch. The fair-haired youth rushed to his side, pulled up his sleeves, and began to reel in the net. The first mate moved to help. They appeared to be struggling, and the boy left his jumping to take up another portion of the net.

Soon the redhead joined in. The other crew members left their nets and moved to watch the struggle with amused anticipation.

Medwin watched the boy's face become suddenly serious as the contents of the net were raised to a visible level. The redhead looked up and stumbled backward. A large snapper with a long snout and sharp teeth lashed about in the folds of the net. The boy screamed. Cursing, the haulers let go of the net and it plummeted back into the water. The boy broke into laughter, and the surrounding crew members followed suit. The captain appeared on the scene and, concealing a faint smile, shouted orders. The crew returned to their nets, and the scene faded.

Medwin stared at the dark mirror. The amused smile slowly left his face as he considered this group of mismatched travelers. He knew, as they did, that this pleasant reprieve would be brief.

CHAPTER 12

Simon knocked firmly on the door to the captain's chamber with his free hand.

"Enter."

He pushed through into the dimly lit room and set the tray of food on the round table at which the captain and the mate sat, their companionable conversation curtailed by his entrance. He felt their eyes on him.

"Ms. Reed follows with the rest of the meal, sir," he said.

"Thanks, Adler." Abner Murray smiled at him and indicated a chair. Captain Merrick remained silent.

Simon sat at the table quietly, observing the captain's quarters for the first time. Other than the table and four chairs—now all occupied but one—the room contained a hammock and a small writing desk, scattered with papers and charcoal. The walls were dressed in maps, and the floor in books and atlases. The room was devoid of identifying personal items or pictures.

Gilda Reed entered, without knocking, and placed another large tray on the table then stood behind the remaining chair.

"At last," murmured the captain.

Ms. Reed amiably ignored his remark and began ladling and distributing a tantalizing-smelling fish stew and some hearty bread.

The four were silent for a while as they began eating, but after a time the captain spoke.

"We're nearly at the Fringe," he looked at Gilda and Simon. "You've had a small glimpse of rough seas these past few days, and I assure you they are nothing to what you will be encountering in the Fringe's shoal. You are still resolved?"

The two assented.

"Then," he continued, "it is time we discuss the particulars of this undertaking and get everything in order."

"Sir—" Simon cut in, "you have said you will come, but I feel that . . . I should say that you are not obliged to take us. It is not your task."

"It's as much my task as yours," he said quietly

Simon was not finished. "No," he said, "I'm not sure what your motive is, but this seems some forced nobility, and I don't think anyone who is not committed to our purpose—farfetched as it is—should join us."

Merrick raised an eyebrow at the speech. "I am also Her Majesty's subject, am I not?" Simon said nothing, and the captain continued: "But that matters little. If you die in that shoal, I will be personally responsible. You might not be my favorite people"—he eyed Gilda, who smiled serenely—"but you are my crew. I will permit no further argument on this."

"I will, as you know, be leaving the *Sapphire* in the hands of Mr. Murray. He'll have Niles and the boy to help him, but I plan on bringing Thomas and Hastings along with us."

"No, sir," Simon interjected, "not Hastings."

The captain looked mildly amused, "You dislike him, Adler?"

"I don't trust him," Simon said.

"Not much to trust, or like," Gilda assented.

"Well, I've sailed with him enough, and I trust him. Liking is a different matter." He composed a smile. "Besides, he's volunteered."

Simon couldn't hide the surprise on his face, and the captain grinned. "Hastings will come along. I desire to have some *experienced* sailors for such a task. We won't make it without him."

"I will do my best, then, to see that he doesn't accidentally fall overboard when a large rock is near," Simon pledged in mock solemnity. Gilda chuckled quietly.

Merrick ignored the comment completely. "Settled then," he said solidly, and changing tone altogether he turned to Murray. "So, Abner," he said, "tell us about this coastline."

CHAPTER 13

A fat gray rat scurried down the corridor in the depths of the heaving *Sapphire.* It was hugging the crevice of the wall and hurrying toward a tantalizing piece of cheese. The rat's nose moved quickly, its whiskers twitching, as it approached its prize. It had just carefully reached a little paw toward its bit of Swiss when, with a slam, the door of a little wooden cage closed shut behind it, trapping it.

"Got 'im!" shouted Burr, who secured the little door and picked up the cage. "Gilda, Gilda," he cried, running down the corridor and bursting into the galley. "Got your rat, for you! I got 'im!" He held up his prize, proudly.

Gilda made a face at the caged creature in Burr's outstretched hands. She turned away. "Why, thank you, Burr," she said. "Now toss him overboard as soon as you get a chance."

But instead of leaving the galley, Burr put the cage on the floor and sat himself atop a barrel, swinging his feet while he watched Gilda rush about the galley. She was piling simple breads, cheeses, and dried meats into a cloth parcel.

"You takin' that food to the Fringe?" he asked.

"Yes," Gilda didn't look up, "and I have to hurry; we'll be dropping anchor any minute."

The ship suddenly tilted, and several little hard rolls fell to the floor. Burr hopped down from his perch to help Gilda collect them.

"What'll we eat when you're gone?" he asked.

"There are plenty of fish and other food stores here. Niles cooked before I came, I believe, so he'll take care of it."

"Not likely," said Burr, returning to his barrel.

Just then the ship's bell rang out above.

"Oh fiddlesticks," Gilda began to pack more furiously. "Hurry up on deck, Burr, and tell them I'm coming," she said.

Burr quickly grabbed his caged rat and rushed from the galley. Gilda packed the last of the supplies and looked around the galley once more, making sure she wasn't forgetting anything before she hustled into the corridor and up the ladder to emerge onto the ship's deck.

The food dropped from her arms, and she stood paralyzed, staring over the ship's starboard rail, blinking through her little glass frames. Before the ship stretched a garden of jutting rocks over which angry waves crashed. The dark and choppy sea wound around the crags and crashed on a beach-less shore. The rocks of the sea emerged and rose to form a cruel coastline and a high, icy island, the top of which was shrouded in a murky fog.

"Welcome to Fringe paradise," sneered Hastings, close in her ear as he brushed past her, carrying a crate toward the fragile dinghy swaying back and forth madly above the deck. Simon was there, struggling with strong arms to hold it steady. She thought he looked serious but stolid, and the sight got her moving again. She retrieved her dropped items and approached the men.

"This is the last one," said Hastings, lifting his crate onto the little vessel. He then turned and took Gilda's parcel from her, offering a toothy grin that did little to conceal his nervousness.

Captain Merrick and Abner Murray joined them. "Remember, Abner," the captain ordered over the noise of the surf, "wait only as long as conditions allow. After Hastings, Thomas, and I have deposited them, we will try to make our way back, but don't sink the old girl holding your breath for us."

Murray nodded, his eyes troubled.

The captain turned to Simon. "You have three days to search for the girl and get back to the shore. We'll circle back to get you then, if at all possible, but if you are not there waiting for us, you're left."

Simon nodded.

"Ms. Reed," the captain turned to her, "now would be a good time to put into force whatever skills you have as a witch." Without waiting for a response he turned to shout orders to Niles.

Gilda Reed stood quietly, her black shoes up to the ankle in a puddle of water on the deck, her stomach sinking. She pulled the emerald tradestone out from the front of her black buttoned shirt, held it tightly in her hand, thought of her mother, and for the first time in a long time, truly questioned herself.

◆　　◆　　◆

"Row!" shouted John Merrick, hoarsely. The little vessel seemed to be moving backwards in spite of the fierce efforts of its inhabitants. Thomas and Simon rowed front, and Simon couldn't help but notice that the other sailor had no songs or tunes today. Hastings and Merrick rowed in back, and Gilda sat down in the middle. Dark waves rose on either side of them, threatening to consume them and slowly filling the boat with water. The spray inhibited sight, and the oars more often caught air than water as the boat swayed.

Captain Merrick threw a bucket at Simon. "Bail!" he yelled.

Simon passed his oar to Gilda and struggled to throw out the water faster than it was showering in. Merrick threw off his drenched coat, and the rowers breathed heavily with the exertion.

There was a high-pitched scream at the back of the vessel. Simon turned around to the puzzled faces behind him. Hastings threw off the tarp covering the cargo in the back. A wild-eyed Burr sat up, screeching and sputtering out water. Merrick gaped, and Simon started.

"Oh, Burr!" Gilda looked at him with sad eyes.

Hastings looked livid. "Why you little—"

"No time for that!" yelled Merrick, throwing his gaze at Burr. "Bail!" he commanded. Burr continued to cough but began frantically moving out the pooling water with his cupped hands.

"Rock! Port side!" yelled Gilda, too late. The little dinghy collided with a dark mound of stone and wave and threatened to overturn. Gilda lifted her oar to find the end mostly missing and torn. The men moved about and rowed hard to compensate for the shift of weight. Hastings pushed off the rock with his oar, and the dinghy again moved forward. The men rowed furiously as Merrick shouted directions.

Gilda dropped her useless oar and began to bail water with her hands, alongside Simon and Burr. Her blistered palms grew red with the icy water, and her gray hair whipped about her face. Her small spectacles were obscured with water. She reached down deep to shovel out water and pulled back her hands quickly, as if bitten. There was a splinter in her bleeding palm and a look of horror on her face.

"There's a hole," she mumbled, and then yelled, "A hole! The bottom of the boat is torn open!"

"Try to stop it," yelled Merrick. "Use whatever you can find!" He threw her his waterlogged coat. Gilda applied it to the hole, but water continued to seep through. Simon handed her his coat as well. Water still oozed in and was now halfway up Gilda's calf.

"Burr!" she howled, "toss me the food parcel!" Burr complied, but as he stepped back to resume his bailing, Simon yelled a jumbled warning, the boat tipped, and Burr fell backwards into the waves and spray.

Gilda Reed shouted out Burr's name in horror. All five remaining passengers moved instinctually to the side of the boat, which tipped dangerously with their weight and threatened to capsize. Merrick moved back to the other side and pulled Thomas with him by the shirt. Simon knelt at the side of the boat and searched the tossing blackness for any fluctuation. A head bobbed above the waves for a moment, and Simon quickly extended his oar.

"Grab on, Burr," he yelled, just as the head disappeared once again. Gilda Reed clenched her teeth, and Merrick stood stone still. Hastings stared, dazed, over Simon's shoulder. Burr's coughing head appeared once again. He caught sight of the oar and reached to grab it just as another wave rocked the little dinghy away. He was now out of reach.

In an instant, Simon threw off his heavy boots and dived over the side of the boat.

"What are you doing!?" Hastings bellowed to the water where Simon had disappeared. "He'll drown himself!" He began to remove his shoes, but Captain Merrick caught his arm.

"Row to them, Hastings," he said. "Thomas." Hastings and Thomas picked up their oars and put all their strength into the rowing as the captain scanned the water and shouted directions. Simon had surfaced and was swimming toward Burr, who was surfacing less often and coughing with exhaustion and panic.

Gilda moved herself from her stupor. She grabbed some rope

from the bottom of the boat, tied it to the bucket handle, and yelled for Simon to catch it as she threw.

Simon gasped, shook the water from his eyes, and caught the bucket as it came his way. Then, holding it under one arm, he pushed through the stony water toward the last place he had seen Burr. No part of the boy's body was visible. Simon looked around frantically, calling Burr's name.

A pale little palm rose up out of the water to Simon's left, and he caught it fast, pulling an unconscious Burr close to him. The boat was still at least ten feet distant, but the men began reeling in the rope until Simon and Burr were next to it. Simon handed up the boy and then, with Hastings's help, pulled himself in.

The boat was unsteady beneath them and was more than two-thirds full of water. The remaining supplies floated around, damaged and useless. Waves began to crash on them incessantly. Simon handed Burr's limp body to Gilda, and the four men began to bail, madly. Slowly the boat sunk.

"It's no good," cried Merrick. "We've got to jump out and overturn the dinghy to hold on to or we'll surely drown." He moved quickly to Gilda. "Give the boy to me," he said.

Gilda, looking wild, handed him over fearfully.

"Everybody overboard! Now!" Merrick yelled. The others obeyed. Bodies disappeared and surfaced over the side of the sinking dinghy. Simon and Hastings pushed at the sides, and Thomas and Gilda pulled to turn the boat. Merrick held to the little bucket and the waterlogged boy.

After much pushing and screaming, the boat overturned and the companions grasped its edges tightly.

"Hold on!" shouted Captain John Merrick. "Hold on!"

A wave rolled at and over the little boat and its passengers.

Somewhere, high above them, Medwin's mirror went black. He

unclenched his white fists and let a metal hand mirror clash to the floor.

"Hold on," he whispered. Behind him on the floor, her head in her hands, Princess Ivy echoed him.

"Hold on."

CHAPTER 14

Simon sat at a long table in a crowded, low-ceilinged room. His father, Marcus, sat at the head of the table, and many sandy-haired and freckled Adler children occupied all the remaining seats but one.

"Listen up," Marcus said, calling the rowdy room to order. When quiet prevailed, he continued: "Roger has some news for us."

Simon and the rest of the Adlers turned their eyes to Roger, who sat next to Simon, a subtle smile present on his handsome face.

"Tell 'em, Roger."

Roger studied his family.

"Out with it," said Simon, nudging him in the ribs.

"Yes, all right," said Roger. "As many of you know, I have a fondness for the sea . . ."

"I thought you had a fondness for Jane Evans," interrupted a younger sister, and everyone laughed. Roger shot her a threatening look.

"Quiet!" demanded Marcus, urging Roger to continue.

"Well, I've been made an official member of the King's Navy. I'm going to sail."

The announcement brought mottled cheers and congratulations.

"And as such," Marcus bellowed above his offspring, "a bit of celebration!" He indicated the door to the kitchen through which Simon's mother came carrying a large cake.

She placed it in front of Roger, and Simon heard her whisper in his ear, "we couldn't be more proud, son," before returning to the kitchen for plates and forks.

Simon turned to look at Roger, his normally dispassionate face aglow with excitement. "Congratulations, brother," he said, patting him on the back. Roger turned to him.

"Thank you, Simon," he said, and patted Simon's heart.

Simon's chest seared with pain. He clenched his teeth and shut his eyes tighter against the hurt. When he opened them he was staring into a concerned-looking young female face, framed in a wild mane of hair.

"Calm down," she said, and was gone.

Before Simon could wonder who she was or where he was, the young woman returned with a tumbler of sweet steaming liquid.

"Drink," she ordered.

Simon found that his throat was coarse, restricting his speech, so he simply obeyed. He could feel the warming liquid drain down into his chest, easing his pain. He started to breathe more easily. His mind cleared, and he suddenly knew who the young woman was.

"You're alive," he murmured, and tried to sit up. His heart thudded and his vision blurred. He slumped back against the pillow.

"So are you, but you won't be for long if you don't lie back down and rest," she said, helping him down onto the bed. "Just lie still and drink some more of this." She stood up and moved to leave.

"Wait—where are you going, Princess?"

Ivy raised an eyebrow at him. "I'm going to tell Medwin you're awake, and to see to the others."

"Are they alive? Did anyone . . ." Simon blinked as vivid scenes of the watery struggle returned. At the forefront was the sight of Thomas and the look of shock on his stolid face as he was wrenched from the overturned boat into the unforgiving waves. He remembered seeing blood in the spray. He had not seen Thomas again. He moved abruptly to sit, but the princess moved toward the bed quickly, practically shoving him back down.

"Calm down, Simon," she said, and he became still at the mention of his name. "Your captain and Miss Reed are a bit scraped up but doing well. The boy and the redhead, who has received head and leg injuries from unforgiving rocks, are alive but unconscious." She paused, then continued, quietly, "The other man did not make it."

Simon felt a clenching in his chest. "How long have we been here?"

"You made it to shore, barely, about four days ago."

Simon nodded and looked around his nicely furnished room. "What is this place?"

Ivy smiled slightly. "Medwin's glass house."

Simon looked puzzled.

"The Fringe," she said, turning to leave before speaking again, her back still turned. "You are at the Fringe, and according to the captain, the ship, the *Sapphire,* should be gone by now. We are . . ."

"Stranded."

"Stranded."

"I'm sorry," whispered Simon, but Princess Ivy had already left the room.

◆　◆　◆

Gilda wandered from room to room in the glass house, without destination. She stood in the long hallway, blinking through her lenses as she stared out of the large window framing the terrible sea below. The sun was shining on the icy slopes and crashing waves, but Gilda still shivered as she studied the coast, other recollections of the vicious water lingering in her memory.

She had looked in on Burr a little while ago. Medwin seemed to think he was improving, but Gilda felt troubled at the thought of his expressionless face tossing on a foreign pillow. Hastings was even worse. How could she have been so naïve as to endanger the lives of others in the pursuit of a fruitless mission—believing so blindly in its success?

She heard a door close behind her and turned to see Captain Merrick approaching. Her stomach sunk. Here was a man she had knowingly deceived. She decided to confess.

"Captain Merrick." He looked up and acknowledged her.

"Ms. Reed."

"I have to tell you . . . I'm not a witch."

"What?"

"I lied. Just before I came to you I had officially lost the title, as I am technically unable to perform magic."

John Merrick just stared at her, straight-faced.

"I deceived you so that you would bring me here. I take full responsibility for the outcome . . . and ask your forgiveness."

"Ms. Reed, there is no need to ask my forgiveness. I assure you I place very little faith in any witch's magical ability. I knew full well what I was leading you all into and, as captain, it was my responsibility to put a stop to it. I should not have sanctioned a plan that was sure of failure, let alone participated in it. It is my fault entirely."

"Not so." Gilda and Merrick turned to see the third party in the hallway. It was Simon. He addressed them as he approached.

"This idea was mine originally. I cooked it up. I was determined to see it through without thought to anyone's life or warning. I am to blame. No one can convince me otherwise."

"I can." Simon turned around to the doorway at his left and

came face-to-face with Princess Ivy. She was as tall as he, and he could see that her face was set, her eyes discouraging argument. She moved into the hall and addressed her would-be rescuers.

"Don't believe for a second that you cooked this idea up, any of you. It was carefully planned and prepared before you were even aware I was missing."

"By whom?" asked John Merrick with unmasked doubt in his voice.

"By my father," she responded, looking down, "by King Than."

"What do you mean, dear?" Gilda Reed came forward.

Ivy sighed. "I mean that my capture was . . . allowed and agreed upon by my father in collaboration with the South. He has been long joined with them and saw me, for some reason, as a threat. In removing me to the Fringe, he not only ensured my end, but the end of any of those loyal to me. You."

"No," Simon objected. "No one made us come. The idea was my own."

"Oh?" Ivy faced him, "You didn't hear about my disappearance from a man wearing my father's uniform?"

"But—" Simon realized the truth of her words.

Gilda spoke up. "But we are not the only people in Lyria loyal to you."

"Perhaps," said Ivy quietly. "But you were the only ones willing to risk your lives, to face dangerous odds in my behalf. They can subdue the rest."

The hallway was quiet as Ivy's words sank in. The sun streaming through the window wall seemed to mock and laugh at them.

"Well," a voice behind them roused them to turn and face Medwin, who was smiling brightly, "I hate to interrupt such a lovely pity party, but I have tea ready in the library, here. Would you join me?"

CHAPTER 15

Medwin's library was a tall room in the center of the house with another glass ceiling and walls lined with books. It was decorated with an assortment of thick, worn furniture, and a large fireplace stood opposite the door. Princess Ivy sat on a low velvet sofa with Gilda next to her. Simon took a chair by the fire, and Captain Merrick remained standing. Medwin went about calmly distributing tea, seemingly unaware of the uncomfortable silence in the room.

Merrick began to pace. Princess Ivy watched him nervously. Simon watched her.

"If you knew about your father," Simon said, "why didn't you do something? Why didn't you warn someone?"

Ivy turned to face him. "I only found out after I was taken. Medwin told me."

Everyone turned to look at Medwin, who was now at Gilda's side.

"One lump or two, Ms. Reed?" he asked. She indicated one but did not speak. Medwin finished his rounds and sat in a large red armchair.

Merrick faced him. "All right, old man," he said. "I think you'd better explain what you know."

Medwin smiled, "Oh, I think her highness has pretty much cleared it up, don't you?"

Merrick glared at him.

Medwin sat forward in his chair, set his cup on the little table next to him, and then continued. "Well, let's see. King Than has an intense love of power, which has corrupted him slowly over the years. It never happens all at once, you know. Currently his power hunt has led him to make an alliance with the Southern warriors and the forces that lead them. They have offered him a tempting prospect, I'm sure. So he has been trying to weaken the Lyrians little by little. He'd like to hand you all over without a fuss. When he moved his kingdom into the mountains, however, he saw that some were not willing to just submit. Many fought." Medwin nodded toward Merrick.

"At first, he found this uprising against the Southerners to be harmless, but he knew that if they were organized under some authority," Medwin nodded toward Ivy, "they could become a force to reckon with. Hence, he sent her to the Fringe, advertised her absence, and looked forward to getting some of the difficult ones out of the way."

"But we," said Merrick, "are no one. It seems a bit extreme. I mean, what proof did he have that the princess would even do anything about it?"

"He didn't need proof. The mere idea was enough for him, and it was always clear to him that Lyrians' loyalty to the crown was mostly centered on Ivy and her mother. Besides, Princess Ivy and all of you are a more important force than you realize. I must give him credit for understanding that you have the potential to be a real problem for him."

"Had," said Simon.

"I beg your pardon?" Medwin responded.

"We *had* the potential to be a problem."

"Oh, yes, I'm sure he feels very proud of himself for having gotten you out of the way. He must feel sure of his success."

"And rightly so," Gilda mumbled.

"Yes," Simon continued, "even if we were a threat, we are now stuck here, at a dead end, with no way of getting out, fighting back, or warning others."

"Well, that's the interesting part, Simon." Medwin's smile returned. "You see, the word *Fringe* does not signify an end but an edge. Ironically, King Than, with all his knowledge and cunning, sent you to the one place where you could actually do him the most harm, I'd wager."

"What do you mean?" Ivy sat forward.

"I mean, my dear, that the Fringe is not a dead end." Medwin paused, taking in their steady stares. "It is a doorway."

Everyone spoke at once, a cacophony of questions and demands filling the room. Medwin held up one hand to quiet them.

"I will explain." He spoke calmly, and with a hint of parental condescension. The noise abated. "In order for you to understand the nature of this place and how it is a doorway to another, we first need to talk about tradestones."

"Tradestones?" Simon echoed.

"Yes. You see, before tradestones came to merely signify a person's way of earning a living, they had a much more important purpose. What you currently understand of magic is limited to what you have seen local witches enact—mere potions and magic tricks. But generations ago, here and elsewhere, there were performers of great acts of power. It was not 'magic' so much as it was the ability to understand, bend, and utilize the elements and aspects of the earth.

"While no one person has the ability to make all things bend to his will, the mages of which I speak were born with a gift for using a certain element—wind, rain, earth. Pick an element and you'd be certain to find a mage who could harness its full power. Over time, it was discovered that prowess for a particular element was connected to specific minerals and deposits found in various precious gemstones. And so the mages began mining these gems and crafting them for wear as a way to focus their natural abilities and enhance their power. These tradestones were made and passed down, generation to generation, to those in the family who carried the same gifts.

"Of course, there were some mages who desired to use their elemental gifts in a corrupt manner—out of harmony with the earth and all of the elements. But tradestones are interesting little tokens, and they would not work for the corrupt. Instead, those who sought to manipulate the elements for their own gain found other ways of enhancing their powers—dark, evil ways. Those who wore their tradestones honorably came to be known as Stone Mages. They worked to keep the corrupt mages, known as Wrakes, in check; but Wrakes were difficult to find and identify, for they performed their acts in secret and knew how to cleverly mask their powers.

"As the Wrakes increasingly abused their abilities, people without elemental gifts became jealous and suspicious of *anyone* with such power. Those in authority persecuted and shunned all mages. And eventually, even though tradestones continued to be passed down for tradition's sake, knowledge of their true power was lost. Fortunately, a small but worthy number of Stone Mages kept the knowledge and passed it on in secret. The Wrakes, too, continued to practice their art covertly, bending kingdoms to their will and using their powers for evil and destruction.

"When I was a boy in Lyria, many Stone Mages were secretly honing their skills and meeting regularly to keep our art alive. On my twelfth birthday—the age at which children were deemed ready to keep the secret—my parents presented me with my mother's tradestone and brought me into the secret group of Stone Mages. Not many years later, a group of Wrakes practicing secretly in the South began to identify and kill those of our numbers. As the Wrakes' numbers grew, ours dwindled. I became hunted for my gift and was chosen to come here to hide and, more importantly, to protect the literature and knowledge of the Stone Mages until the time when Lyria was again ready for them.

"Today, there are few who actually use the tradestones in the manner for which they were designed. Indeed, many who still wear tradestones have an elemental gift, but very few are aware of them. It is my belief that the reason Abaddon, Southern ruler and the most powerful Wrake of our time, is so interested in the annihilation of a small and seemingly insignificant kingdom, is that he knows there are many Stone Mages in Lyria who, if taught their power, could rise up against him and keep him from enacting whatever dark plan he has devised.

"Each of you, I think, is a Stone Mage with a gift you know nothing about. It is for this reason that I believe you are an important force in opposing the king. I also believe this is the reason you made it to the Fringe alive."

Medwin observed the confused stares on the faces around the room. "Do you not all bear tradestones?" he asked.

Gradually, Simon drew forth his fool's tradestone, Merrick fingered his blue captain's stone, and Gilda took out her witch's stone.

Medwin turned to Gilda. "The emerald, Ms. Reed, or witch's tradestone, originally aided those with the gift of the earth. Witches are now known for their potions in part because the stones were formerly worn by those with a gift for soil, plants, and growing things."

Gilda simply shook her head. "I am not magic. I cannot create great potions," said Gilda. "I have inherited the stone but no gift."

"I believe your cottage has a rose garden?"

"Well, yes," Gilda replied, "but I don't see—"

"The only thriving garden in the rocky hills? Do you not find that to be interesting?"

"Coincidence," said Gilda.

Medwin continued, "Is it also true that you are able to take the earth's bounty and create delicious things to eat?"

"Yes," answered the others in unison.

"Your gift may be undeveloped, Ms. Reed," said Medwin, "but it is present."

He turned to Merrick. "Care to guess what gift the sailor's trade-stone aids?"

Merrick, who didn't generally favor guessing, just stared at him.

"Your sapphire, Captain Merrick, is worn by those with a power over water. Your skill at sea and ability to chart waters no one else dares venture near is evidence enough of that."

He turned to Simon.

"And yours, Simon. Your bronze stone gives you power of time. A very rare gift."

"What do you mean 'power of time'?" Simon asked quizzically.

"Well, you have the power to stretch, shift, maybe even stop or rewind time. I suspect its mages were inclined to the fool's profession because of their excellent timing. A well-told joke is all about timing, yes? And, have you never felt as you were juggling some nasty handful of flames and daggers that you seemed to be able to stretch the moments before they fell from the air?"

Simon nodded, his brows furrowed.

Merrick began to pace again, shaking his head. "I'm afraid this is a bit too much for me to swallow, old man."

Medwin seemed to ignore the comment. "I should also ask you about your dreams," he said.

"Our dreams," Merrick parroted, an eyebrow raised.

"Yes, you see, I suspect that many of you are the unwilling recipients of nightmares or repeating and poignant dreams. It is common for those with elemental gifts to have vivid dreams which might urge them to use their gifts. These dreams are often more persistent in those who have not realized or begun to practice their magic. There have been different theories about why this happens, but my own is that it is your mind's way of telling you to make use of the gifts you have been given. I would not be surprised if your dreams are partially responsible for your being here today."

Medwin studied their faces, gauging their responses, and smiled. "To add further credibility, let me tell you that my tradestone," he pulled the dark, reflective stone from his clothing, "lends me the gift of sight, or the ability to see the happenings in the world surrounding me. It is with the aid of this gift that I knew of the king's treachery, the princess's capture, and of your coming to us. Our quiet princess over there can tell you that she had a detailed description of you and your travels from me before we ever actually laid eyes on you."

Ivy nodded solemnly. "What he says is true."

Merrick sat down.

"What about the others?" asked Gilda. "Hastings and young Burr? Are they Stone Mages as well?"

"Neither wears a stone," Medwin replied. "But I believe Burr has the gift of animals, and Hastings . . . I'm not sure." Medwin seemed momentarily lost in thought, but after an interval he turned back to his audience. "All of you will have to learn to use your stones and gifts before you will be able to accomplish much with them."

"What does all of this have to do with the Fringe being a doorway?" Simon asked.

"Ah," Medwin nodded, "another very unique gift is the one that is enhanced by the clear or diamond stone. Those with this gift are given power over space. They can actually bend space to move and change something's—or someone's—physicality and location. One of these Stone Mages used the gift to create this doorway here, many years ago. It leads to a faraway place on our globe, unknown to you but called Bellaria by its people. The dangerous and rocky shoal has kept the doorway hidden from all but me. I suppose I am its gatekeeper; though it does not open for me."

"Then how would we be able to pass through?" asked Gilda.

"Princess Ivy will have to open it for you."

Ivy stood from her place on the couch. "But Medwin," she stammered, "I don't even have a stone. How could I possibly have the gift of space?"

Medwin walked steadily to where Ivy stood, her hands on her hips. He gently fingered a gold chain that hung about her neck and pulled forth a rough, clear pendant.

"But," Ivy took hold of it, "this is only my grandfather's old diamond necklace."

"Yes," said Medwin, "your mother gave you this. It matches her own tradestone, does it not? She also passed to you her gift—the gift of space."

Ivy's eyes were wide, and she shook her head, bewildered.

"Princess," Medwin prodded, "why don't you tell us how you survived the Fringe's shoal."

Ivy furrowed her brow. "I'm not sure," she said. "I simply remember being thrown from the ship by the Southern warriors. My feet and hands were tied. I went in the water and sunk down, knowing I would drown. I wished desperately for life and shore. I don't remember much more after that."

"You can't explain, then," Medwin said, "how I pulled you up from the shore, alive, with hands and feet still tied."

Ivy blinked. "I must have drifted in."

"Impossible," said Medwin. "In your moment of focused desperation, you moved through space from the edge of the cove to the shore. You used your gift."

Ivy stared at him, doubt still prevailing on her face. "Even if I do have the gift, I have no knowledge of it or how to use it. It would probably take an endless amount of time to gain sufficient skill to open that door."

Medwin's face glowed as he looked at Ivy. "Going anywhere?"

CHAPTER 16

F rom *Forging Stones of Power,* by Wilfred Knowles:

The very first stone matched to a gift was a solid granite stone owned by the early mage Soren Wyline. Wyline possessed powers associated with metals and rocks. It is said that Wyline experienced a regular and persistent dream that drew him to a hidden mountain cavern, where he unconsciously began using only his bare hands to pull unusual and many colored stones from their resting places in the walls and ceiling of the cavern. He said he felt a "stirring in [his] core" when he held a particular granite rock, and so he put it in his pocket. He carried it with him for weeks and found that his powers as a mage had greater focus, and that he was less weary after using his gift.

Wyline then began to surmise what the stones in the cavern really were. He brought his fellow mages to the cavern and soon had identified five different stones to match five known gifts of the mages. They were as follows (the stones are classified according to the resemblance they bear to more commonly known stones):

Powers associated with stones and metals—white granite

Powers associated with earth, soil, and plants—green emerald

Powers associated with water—blue sapphire

Powers associated with fire—red ruby

Powers associated with wind—pale pink stone

He also found at least five other stones that have since been tied to the rarer mage gifts. They are as follows:

Powers associated with sight and reflection—reflective obsidian

Powers associated with time—bronze stone

Powers associated with space—clear diamond

Powers associated with animals—rusty brown stone

Powers associated with people—yellow citrine (Although the yellow stone is common in elemental mines, the corresponding gift remains a matter of debate and hearsay. Some have carried the stone, but there are disagreements as to whether or not people's wills can be bent like animals.)

Some of these gifts, like the gift of time, are rarely seen; while some, like that of animals, have become more frequent.

John Merrick slammed the cover of the dusty book shut and stormed from the glass fortress. Soon, the tips of his fingers and nose began to grow numb as he high-stepped down the snowy hill toward the rocky cove below.

He actually preferred the cold air in his lungs to the stuffy confinement of the fire-lit library. Medwin had offered and encouraged the travelers to read about their gifts from his ancient books in order to improve their knowledge and abilities. But Merrick found that the reading did nothing but give him a headache. He sought some alone time and a chance to exert his "focus" on actual water. He needed to discover what power he had, or didn't have, for himself.

The hill was steep, and he slipped occasionally on his descent. The deep snow, though a nuisance to walk in, served as a cushion for his falls. His long, fur-lined coat was well dusted with snowflakes and ice by the time he reached the water. He turned for a moment to look back up at the glass house and discovered he could no longer see it. He stared back up at pure rock and snow until the sun appeared for a moment from behind the cloud and a glimmer on the hill caught his eye. He then realized that the glass house was not merely glass on the outside, but mirror—reflecting the surrounding peaks and hiding it in their image. He turned back to the water.

The beach-less shoreline was simply a succession of dark rocks jutting up here and there. Merrick stepped and jumped from stone to stone until he found a large rock with a surface horizontal enough to hold him. He knelt down and allowed the spray from the waves to dot his face, making him shiver. He watched the water swirl around his rock. He bent, removing his coat, and immersed his fingers, then hands, and finally his arms to the elbows, moving them around and feeling the power of the water as he resisted the current of the incoming waves then allowed its flow to push his strong forearms back.

He shook his arms dry and laid his palm a few feet above the surface of the undulating water. He focused on it, imagined it, willed it to rise up and meet his hand.

Not one drop moved from its course.

He sighed and looked out ahead of him where the rocks eventually thinned and the vast sea stretched to the clouded horizon. It was certainly the rocks, not the waves, that made this shoal so dangerous. The sea simply pushed on, steadily flowing to its destination, undeterred by obstacles. Who was he to think he could move it? How could he stop it if these rocks could not?

He pulled the sapphire from his shirt and peered into its clear, blue face. It was a deep, crystal blue, like lagoon waters on a sunny day. He thought about his ship, the *Sapphire*. He tried to imagine her sailing. He had been surprised at times by her ability to weather rough seas and survive fierce storms. He thought of how she utilized wind and waves to reach her destination. *Used them, not forced them.*

Merrick let the stone fall back against his chest and could feel it, now cold, pressing at his heart as he closed his eyes. He allowed years of latent energy and unspent ambition to flow from his warm center, over his shoulders, and through his arms. His fingers tingled, and he blindly and gently swayed where he stood. He saw blue on the back of his eyelids, a moving, rushing, roaring blue. His heartbeat quickened and his hands suddenly felt hot. Shocked by the sensation, he opened his eyes abruptly and looked to his hands.

He found that he had unconsciously raised his arms at his sides and that directly beneath them the water swelled and rose to a few inches beneath his palms. It seemed that the water simply flowed larger and higher—as if he held large magnets over a sea of metal, drawing it up to meet him.

He inhaled sharply and sat up straight in surprise. His arms fell, and with them the water. It resumed its swirling course about the rock as if unconcerned by its previous behavior. Merrick stared at the water, his eyes peeled and his mouth hanging open.

"Ha!" he burst out. A smile spread on his usually stoic face and he stood up, hands on his hips.

"Ha!" he repeated, and then, composing himself and realizing how weak he felt, head to toe, he turned to climb back up the hill to the house.

CHAPTER 17

From *Tips for Better Stone Use*, by Bertrand Tibble:

Chapter 5: Know Yourself

Sometimes it is easy to forget that the power you use comes not from the stone itself, but from you. The stone itself is useless (you may have discovered this if you have tried to perform magery of a different kind with a different stone) without your own ability.

For example, a monocle may improve a man's ability to see and add focus to his vision, but it will do nothing for a blind man, and it will not change what a man may do with or think about what he sees. A man who does not want to see what is before him will not have much success in interpreting his surroundings with or without a monocle.

Similarly, in using your stone and your gift, the power will be clearer if you know what you want to do, and you must have sufficient desire and motivation. The gift inside you can come forth only if you give it a good reason to. You have to know what is most important to you and focus on that when learning to use your gift. The stone can aid you in this focusing but it cannot decide for you what is important.

You must also know your limitations. When you use your gift you are putting a bit of yourself out into the world around you. Inevitably you will find that there is an energy cost. Learn to know how much you can do with your gift before fatigue makes magery, or even usual living, impossible. Give yourself time to rest physically and mentally after large magic uses. There are many tales of Stone Mages who performed great magical feats to defeat an enemy only to be easily beaten by a greater enemy afterward.

Gilda removed her small spectacles, clearing away the steam that had condensed on them, and leaned over a large pot in Medwin's kitchen. She fixed them to her nose once more and ladled out a small amount of the brownish liquid she was brewing. She took a careful sip, made a face, and turned into the messy pantry to find the right addition to her concoction.

In her reading about tradestones and elemental gifts, Gilda had learned that effective use of one's power was strongly tied to desire and motivation. She now believed that her previous failure in the realm of potioning had to do with her general distaste of it. She had never been interested in nonsense wart removers or love potions. As such, her potions had not been successful.

It was no matter. She did not regret these failures, as she did not believe in her heart that a quick fix was the best solution to any problem. She had, therefore, been successful in her witching by simply helping people acknowledge and discuss their difficulties. It also didn't hurt to offer them a little spiced cider or a well-baked trifle or pastry.

She was now braving Medwin's terribly disorganized store room full of bottled herbs and juices—some labeled, and some not—in order to create a potion for which she felt great motivation to be successful: a healing draught. Gilda's daily visits to Burr's room made her feel overly anxious about his return to health. She felt a sort of maternal responsibility for the boy. If she really had some sort of gift, she ought to be able to use it for him, and Hastings as well, she supposed.

She had given some of her potion to Burr this very morning, pouring it slowly down his throat and anxiously studying his unresponsive face.

She was now attempting another variation on the draught. She had just lifted a certain flask with a particularly indiscernible label up to her eye level when a loud crash made her drop the flask, the dark liquid spilling down her dress and forming a puddle at her feet.

Mopping her dress with a nearby cloth, Gilda emerged into the hallway. Another crash ensued, and Gilda decided that the noise was coming from the little corridor outside Burr's room. When she reached the narrow hallway she saw shards of glass strewn about the floor. Princess Ivy came running from Burr's little room, followed by a glass tumbler that just missed her and made contact with the wall opposite the door before shattering into more sharp pieces on the floor.

"And stay out, wench!" came the raspy reply from the room. Ivy's mouth dropped in surprised indignation. She turned and saw Gilda. Ivy's face calmed, and she laughed nervously.

"He's awake," she said.

Gilda exhaled and smiled. "It worked, then?" she asked.

"Apparently so," said the princess, swallowing. "I shall leave him to you." She smiled and left to go inform the others.

Gilda wiped the return smile from her face, and, trying to look stern, entered the boy's room.

"What is the meaning of this behavior, Burr?" she reprimanded. She found it difficult to remain stern at the sight of the boy. He was bare to the waist and wearing his old knee-length underwear. He was lounging on the bed, legs crossed, dark hair standing out in all directions above the bandage on his head, a smug grin on his face.

"Well here I am, alive as ever," he announced. And then a bit more apologetically, he said, "I was just havin' a bit of fun. Besides, she was trying to make me put some clothes on, and I feel just fine as I am."

"I don't care what she was trying to do, young man," Gilda bent to pick up the clothes, which had obviously been thrown like the pitcher and tumblers, "that is no way to treat a lady"—she handed the clothes to Burr, who stuck out his tongue but took the clothes —"let alone a princess."

Burr looked at her under furrowed brows. "A princess?"

"Yes, sir," Gilda replied.

"Stinking corpses!" said Burr. "I didn't know she was no princess."

"Don't be vulgar, Burr."

Burr sighed and lowered his head. "Sorry, Ms. Reed," he said.

Gilda nodded a reply and came to sit by him on the bed. "We were worried about you, Burr. You didn't wake up for a long time. I would love to feed you a good meal, and we have so much to tell you about, but first you will have to put on these clothes and, with them, your best behavior. Is that clear?"

Burr looked up. "Yes ma'am," he said.

"Good," said Gilda, ruffling his messy hair. "It's nice to have you back. Now let's go apologize to Princess Ivy and have some food."

CHAPTER 18

From *Being One with the Stone,* by Cecil Fairlight:

> *I often take a walk into the mine, feeling the weight of my stone on my bare chest. I sit on the solid ground and breathe in the air and power of the place. My stone is warm, and so is my heart. I ponder the earth and the universe for many hours that seem like minutes.*
>
> *I am one with the stone. I am one with the earth. I am one with the mine.*
>
> *I venture out into the world. I feel all the leaves on the trees and the tendrils of every little vine. I feel the buds beneath the earth. I know each herb on the ground and can call the flowers.*
>
> *I feel the power flowing through me and from me. I love my little green stone. I am happy. I can move the soil and the plants and the trees but instead I walk, happy in my thoughts and content in my gift.*
>
> *I am one with the earth. I am one with the trees. I am one with the ground. I am one with my stone.*

Simon threw open the heavy door to the glass house, letting it slam loudly behind him as he broke out into the setting sunlight.

He tossed a particularly lengthy and unhelpful volume he had been studying out into the snow. *Be one with the ground, Cecil Fairlight,* he thought, and grinned ruefully.

Weeks had passed at the Fringe, and while most of the travelers were making progress with their gifts, Simon had made none. He began to doubt that he had any power at all.

He thought of the others. Merrick was making water walls as tall as he was down at the shore these days. Gilda had successfully healed Burr and was making progress on Hastings, who was now breathing easier and having short bouts of consciousness, not to mention she had grown a small indoor creeper plant clear up the side of the house in a matter of hours. Burr didn't have a stone, so his magic seemed more chaotic, but he had still managed to command an army of spiders to follow him around the halls, making everyone nervous, especially Gilda, who issued a hearty reprimand.

Everyone slept long and soundly at night, wearied by the use of their gifts; but Simon lay awake, tossing and anxious.

Even Ivy was having more luck than he. Although she was obviously bothered by her lack of success at opening the doorway—making her more withdrawn and irritable—she *was* able to move things from room to room. Sometimes furniture would simply appear in another room, or a desired dish from down the long table would materialize in front of her without her asking for it to be passed.

Medwin had suggested that Simon merely needed to find the proper motivation for his power to surface, but Simon had no idea what that would be. He thought the mere desire to prove himself should be enough, but the gift remained dormant . . . or nonexistent.

Simon distanced himself from the house, climbing the mountain with a vague inclination to explore the higher cliffs. As he followed an upward path and came around the curve of a large rock, he was moved from his thoughts by the sight of Princess Ivy standing a small distance away from him, back turned.

They were at the rim of a small glacial valley, and as Simon looked at the icy mass below, he realized this must be the location of the supposed doorway. Ivy's head was bowed, and it was apparent she was concentrating deeply. Simon quietly advanced a few paces, not wanting to disturb her but hoping for a closer view of the small glacier below. As he came around the rock, he realized that from this location he could look all the way down to the sea. He saw the dark figure of Merrick below returning from his perch on the rocky shore.

He turned back toward the princess. He could see her profile now. Her cheeks were rosy from the cold, and her hair fell freely over the long green cloak she wore. The wind moved the wild curls back and forth about her face, but she did not move from her stance. Her arms were a little outstretched in front of her, and her shoulders moved slightly as she took deep breaths.

She raised her head suddenly, but her eyes stayed closed. She took a small step closer to the edge of the steep slope on the glacier side, and her lips parted slightly. She raised her hands in front of her, and as she did so the surface of the glacier below began to shimmer. It seemed to become slightly transparent, and there was darkness beneath it. Simon felt his heart beating faster and he tried to quiet his quick breathing.

Ivy took another step toward the glacier, but this time her foot hit a patch of ice. She lost her balance and began to topple over the edge of the cliff. Simon lunged forward and thrust his arms out in front of him. He was several paces away from her location, but he started determinedly forward, eyes on the princess. As he did so, his sight became fuzzy. The princess seemed to fall with strange slowness. She was eternally falling, hands sluggishly flying above her head, her hair floating around her. Simon's feet were fast and his speed sure. He ran and then slid toward her until he had her by the waist, pulling her to him. He staggered back from the edge, safe.

The princess was tense in his arms, and Simon felt shaky, so he slowly knelt and allowed her to recline on the snowy ground. His sight was again clear. He pushed Ivy's hair from her face, and she opened her eyes, staring widely up at him.

"Are you all right?" Simon stammered.

Ivy nodded. "Where did you come from?" she said, a bit dazed. "I was alone, something was happening, I think, with my gift . . ."

Simon smiled slightly, his head clearing. "Yes," he said, "a hazy blackness was replacing the solid surface of the glacier. I've never seen anything like it."

Ivy nodded again. "Then I was falling, and suddenly you were there, out of nowhere."

Simon watched her, silently.

"You used your gift," Ivy said finally. It was not a question.

They were both quiet for a moment.

There was a sudden shuffling behind them, and Merrick appeared from around the rock. He rushed to the princess.

"Are you all right?" he asked. Ivy nodded that she was.

"Nice catch. I saw it all from below," he said to Simon. "Can't be leaving her on the cold ground, though. We should get her back to the house." He knelt by Ivy, lifting her effortlessly and supporting her with one strong arm. Ivy looked up at him gratefully as they disappeared behind the rock.

Simon stood and followed them, thinking about how he had just bent time and wondering why he didn't feel more elated.

CHAPTER 19

Medwin entered his mirror room, smiling at the thought of his current guests and their progress. In the back of his mind, however, was a sense of foreboding. He closed the door behind him and stood in front of a tall mirror with a black frame.

An unfamiliar scene materialized before him. He was looking at a large, high-ceilinged chamber with no windows and one large iron door. Its walls, ceilings, and floors were dark stone, and in the center there was a long stone table on which iron candelabras were lit.

The door opened, and a group of Southern warriors entered wearing thick iron armor and helmets that covered their features. Each carried a mace, and they were talking loudly and unintelligibly.

The room became suddenly quiet as two additional men entered. Medwin recognized the first as King Than. The other man was tall also but thinner and more angular than the broad king. He wore a dark crown on his head. He had a handsome, strong face and dark graying hair. Medwin knew he was the ruler of the South, Abaddon.

The warriors took their stations lining the walls of the chamber, and the other two sat at the long table.

"King Than," Abaddon spoke in a relaxed, confident voice. "You are here to tell me that everything is arranged, I presume."

The king nodded his head. "It is. We are prepared for the transition."

Abaddon leaned back in his chair. "You feel the Lyrians are ready for domination, then?"

"I can assure you, it will be an easy victory."

Abaddon nodded slowly. "This is good, Than. We wouldn't want to deny you of your new position as joint ruler of the continent. I'm sure you are looking forward to a great and powerful reign over my people and yours, are you not?"

King Than's hands clenched the spot where they rested on the table. "I am ready to do what is needed to advance my position, and yours."

Abaddon leaned forward again and began to lightly drum his fingers on the stone table. "You have succeeded, then, in the matter of your dangerous daughter? She is out of the way, with a little help from my men, hmm?"

"Dangerous is a strong word for someone completely ignorant of her abilities. But yes, that risk has been dealt with in a way that has also annihilated some of her stronger supporters as well."

"I see." Abaddon drummed his fingers faster. "You remember, King Than of Lyria, that I have a seer in my court?"

The king nodded. "She has been very useful to us."

"Well, this seer of mine managed to have a peculiar vision a few days ago. It featured your daughter . . . alive, healthy, and happy."

King Than pushed his chair away from the table a bit, shaking his head. "Impossible!"

"It seems that she and the 'supporters' you spoke of survived their little trip to the Fringe and are in the care of a seer who we have discovered resides there, a Stone Mage."

"It can't be . . ."

"They are learning to use their gifts, and not only is there a Stone Mage there, King Than of Lyria, there is a doorway."

"A . . . a doorway?" King Than's face was pale. "At the Fringe?"

Abaddon stood from his chair slowly and began to pace the room. King Than watched him nervously. "Where does it lead?" he breathed.

Abaddon circled the table until he was standing behind King Than's chair. He placed his long fingers on it. "That is the question, isn't it?" he said calmly. "I have strong suspicions; but we will, I suppose, have to wait and watch and hope our seer is gifted enough to see to that distance. If she can, the information will be sparse at best."

King Than twisted in his chair, trying to remove himself from his awkward and vulnerable position. "I assure you, Abaddon, I will take action immediately."

Abaddon nodded with mock solemnity. "I'm sure you will, Than. As will I."

"Of course," King Than nodded.

"This problem will be dealt with, or else . . ." Abaddon leaned down until his head was parallel with Than's and turned to whisper something in his ear. Medwin could not hear what was said, but saw King Than's eyes grow wide with fear.

In a quick movement, Abaddon pulled the chair from underneath the speechless king and threw him to the waiting warriors behind him. "Get him out of here," he said. Two large warriors roughly grabbed King Than by the shoulders and ushered him from the room.

Medwin stepped away from the mirror and watched as the image faded and his own face appeared. He looked himself in the eye for a few moments before leaving the room.

CHAPTER 20

From *Magical Departures: Wrakes and the Misuse of Elemental Gifts*, by Magnus Dunne:

> *Never forget that the powers of Wrakes and the powers of Stone Mages are the same at birth. The only difference is whether or not the individual decides to use a gift in harmony with the earth or in opposition to it.*
>
> *Wrakes are defined by their rejection of the stones and their desire to create chaos and destruction on the land rather than use their powers for protection, harmony, and healing.*
>
> *They name themselves by the elements they control. There are Fire Wrakes, Stone Wrakes, Water Wrakes, Creature Wrakes, etc. Two unique categories exist for Wrakes with the power of sight and those with power over space. These are the Seers and the Shifters. Like other Wrakes, they have no use for stones. The Shifters have developed more perverse means of moving themselves through space by focusing on and ill-using the human form. The Seers do not wear a stone but occasionally work with a specific mirror or reflective surface for easier sight. Some will carry it with them at all times.*

Hastings looked out the window at the patterns made by sun and shadow on the cold winter hills and tried to forget his dreams. He sat in a deep chair, his breathing a bit heavy at the mere effort of moving himself a few feet from the bed. It was the first time he had been out of it, and he was glad to leave it behind him for a moment. The mere effort had made his head throb and had sent shots of pain through his injured leg. But the pain was almost a relief, for it distracted him from the dreaming, and the thinking, and the remembering.

Hastings was good at many things, but he was especially adept at forgetting. There was always something to do for distraction, especially for a sailor, but he had been awake for only a day or two and was realizing that his injuries were going to make forgetting difficult merely by keeping him from activity. His isolation was keeping him from people to pester and hate, and that made it difficult to forget to pester and hate himself.

He had seen Ms. Reed a few times when she brought him things to eat and drink, but she seemed awkward around him and never stayed long, leaving him alone to recover—to sleep with dreams and wake with remembering.

He heard a noise and turned to see an old man at the door. His relief at the distraction was almost overwhelming, and he exhaled deeply. The old man raised an eyebrow but did not speak. He merely stood at the door studying Hastings with an odd expression on his face. After what seemed an eternal interval, Hastings cleared his throat.

Thankfully, the old man seemed to remember himself and moved forward, offering his hand. Hastings took it.

"I'm glad to see you're recovering," the old man said, releasing his hand. "I am Medwin, and this is my house." He paused. "I have a lot to tell you; there is a lot you have missed while you were unconscious, but first I think you need to understand that your party leaves here in a few days, and I am doubtful of your ability to be recovered enough to join them."

The old man held out something he had been holding at his side and said, "Take a look."

Hastings looked down to see his own bandaged reflection staring back at him. His reaction was immediate. His hand flew out, knocking the mirror from Medwin's hand and onto the floor where it crashed and broke.

Medwin stood still, studying him; and Hastings knew that his face was red with anger and emotion. "You don't look *that* bad," the old man said quietly.

Hastings shook his head and then quit when he remembered how painful the motion was. "I don't use mirrors," he said. "I don't like them."

"What's not to like?"

Hastings would never normally allow such a personal conversation to continue, but there was some quality about the old man, some strength that demanded an answer.

"I don't like what I see."

"You are unsatisfied with your appearance?"

"Mirrors distort. They show me things about myself, and I'm not interested in seeing myself or anything else I might see by studying myself."

Medwin looked like he wanted to ask more but merely nodded. "Well, then, you will have to take my word that you are not prepared for a journey right now." He turned for the door. "I will go get some things to clean up this glass, and then we will talk some more and get you updated on what has been going on."

After he was gone, Hastings turned again to look out the window. He did not look down to see the mess he had made or the many reflections he knew he would find staring up at him.

CHAPTER 21

From *Clear Stones: Their Purpose and Power,* by Lila Wills:

> The element of space is, of course, not really an element. It is neither tangible nor measurable and is therefore one of the most difficult of the gifts to describe, learn, and master.

> An understanding of space, however, is fundamental. One must understand the makeup of the very matter he or she wishes to move, of the way the particles of air fit, and where the holes lie.

> I classify the different uses of the gift into three categories: moving other objects through space, moving the self and others through visible space, and finally creating passage for moving the self and others through non-visible space. I have listed the uses in order of their complexity. The gift of space is rare, and most who possess it never perform more than the first skill—the transportation of objects through space.

> It is much easier to move things you can see, or have seen, to visible places than to move the complex conglomerate that is the human body to places seen or —especially—places unseen. The space mage's ability depends largely upon their ability of sight.

*They must envision the object/person they wish to move actu-
ally existing in the new space. The clear stone enhances the space
mage's gift of sight enough to make the more difficult skills more
attainable.*

*In fact, the third ability, the creating of passages into un-
seen space, is rarely achieved without the stone. We know of
only a handful of mages experiencing recent success in this area.
These mages have been able to understand the makeup of the
space before them and focus on it enough to rend it. Such Clear
Stone Mages have created doorways perhaps never before seen
on plots previously unexplored on our globe.*

Ivy sat back in her chair and observed her lively bunch of companions. The room was rather loud as they finished off their last bites
of Gilda's sweet pudding and argued over dish duty.

Burr had just suggested Ivy transport them into the kitchen for
washing, when Gilda interrupted.

"I think the princess has done more than her duty today. She
deserves a rest." The group resonated with murmurs of agreement
and respect. Earlier that day each of them had watched Princess Ivy
transform the small glacial valley into a kind of portal. She could see
that their initial amazement had generally transitioned to excitement
at the idea that they might succeed in their mission after all. She felt
relieved as well, and glad of success, but all was still shadowed by the
truth about her father and inconsistencies in her family past. She
was beginning to wish the group would disperse so that she could
ask Medwin some questions.

A dark shadow appeared in the doorway, and the room became
silent as Hastings entered, head bandaged and leaning on a crutch.
He looked around the room awkwardly. Medwin stood and moved
toward him.

"Welcome, Mr. Hastings," he said. "Can we get you some
pudding?"

Hastings shook his head. "No. I've eaten in my room, but I could hear the noise and thought I might venture in and see what all this cheery conversation was about." There was an edge of bitterness in his words, and his face was pale. It was apparent that the journey to the dining room had taken its toll.

"Come have a seat then," said Merrick, who also stood and helped Hastings into his chair.

Ivy looked down at her empty plate, feeling guilty at their free celebration while one of their number was still unwell. Ivy felt hesitant around Hastings. She knew him the least of the people at the Fringe, and she felt, in a way, responsible for his injury. She managed to glance up at Medwin, who had resumed his seat and was characteristically sanguine.

"Now that we're all here together, I think there are a few things it would be wise for us to discuss," he said. "We have concurred that the purpose of this journey will be to seek out any possible assistance that might be had from the people of the kingdom beyond the portal, Bellaria, and to come back and reclaim Lyria from Southern control. As you know, my sight tells me very little about the particulars of this place; the more distant the locale, the hazier my mirror visions are, but I have provided you with the name of a man I saw as trustworthy when I watched previous Stone Mages pass into Bellaria. I believe you are also all aware that the doorway allows passage from the Fringe to Bellaria, but not vice versa. You will have to open your own doorway to the continent when the time comes; there will be no re-entry through this one. This will have to be done with the help of other Stone Mages. Ivy has shown her ability to be great. But to create a doorway is a much more difficult task than to open one. You must find Antoine Beval and his people, understood?" Medwin looked at Ivy, who nodded.

"You should also know," he continued, "that King Than and

Abaddon have many powerful Wrakes at their disposal who have not only informed them of your residence here but who are determined to find you and end your mission. Though they are, to my knowledge, ignorant of where our doorway leads, it is possible that they will be coming after you."

"But how?" Simon asked. "Won't they have to come here to use this doorway?"

"No," said Medwin. "This doorway may only be opened by a Stone Mage. Wrakes who move through space, called Shifters, have other ways of traveling between lands."

"What ways?" asked Ivy.

Medwin's expression darkened. "The most powerful Shifters can create holes in space of their own. But without the focus of the stone, the holes are often unsafe or fade quickly. Generally, Shifters move across our world by transporting themselves, or I should say their essence, into other human bodies. They cannot inhabit any body, only beings called Vessels. These are people who have chosen to live a half-life, allowing themselves to be inhabited by Shifters at will. A Vessel must be created willingly. So, usually in order to gain favors or power, these Vessels undergo a dark transformation that relegates them to mere observer while all control of their body belongs to the Shifter."

"I don't understand," Ivy interrupted. "It seems to me that splitting their soul into another person's body would be more difficult than just moving the whole body. How can these Shifters do something like that without a stone?"

Medwin nodded. "I understand they happened upon the magic accidentally. A certain ambitious but unfocused Wrake long ago was attempting to move himself into unseen space by directing himself toward a fellow Wrake who was miles away. He was careless with his magic and lacked focus; instead of moving his body to his comrade, he split himself into the waiting Wrake's physical form. Both men eventually died from the strange phenomenon, unable to return their souls to normal living in their own physical forms. However, their mistake opened the door to experimentation by their followers."

"Why would anyone choose to be the Vessel?" Hastings asked quietly.

Medwin responded, "You ask a good question, one I'm not sure I have the answer to. Vessels surrender years of their life, and it is a menial existence; but still people choose it. Mages who become Vessels forfeit their power temporarily to the occupant of their bodies and are, therefore, particularly dangerous. A Vessel's only distinguishable feature is a burn mark branded on the upper left arm, making it extremely difficult to recognize who the enemy is. You must be careful and divulge your mission and identity only to those whose names I have given you and those they trust."

Medwin paused for a time as his listeners absorbed his information, then continued, more relaxed. "Mr. Hastings and I have discussed this journey, and we have agreed that it will be best for him to stay with me and recover." Hastings shifted in his chair, and again Ivy found it difficult to look at him. She wondered when he would recover, and if he would ever be able to make it back to the continent. She promised herself that if she was able to help him do so in the future, she would.

Merrick seemed to be thinking the same way. "We will come back for you, Hastings," he said. Ivy looked up at Merrick with relief and admiration.

Hastings shrugged. "I'll be fine here with the old . . . with Medwin."

"I'm sure I'll find plenty of things for him to do here," said Medwin with an odd look. "The rest of you should leave as soon as the princess is sufficiently rested and ready, within the week. You will, of course, only be able to take what you can carry on your backs, so pack carefully."

Minds full, each person at the table slowly stood and left the dining room, Merrick assisting Hastings through the door and into the corridor. Ivy lingered in the room, her underlying questions still begging answers.

Medwin smiled at Ivy. "What can I do for you, your Majesty?"

"I was wondering if you knew . . ."

"Yes?"

"If you knew about my half sister, Mara."

"The other princess."

"Yes, is she . . . does she support my father?"

Medwin's brow furrowed. "I have not been able to determine that. When I see her in the mirrors she is very remote. I cannot tell whether or not she is in your father's confidence."

"I see," said Ivy. "We were quite close when we were young, but in recent years we have become distant. I had hoped . . . Medwin?"

"Yes?"

Ivy spoke softly now, embarrassed at her question. "Do you think my father ever loved me?"

Medwin was quiet for a moment, watching her. "That is more than I can see in my mirrors, Princess, but I can tell you from what I have seen of your father that he wasn't always what he is now. I believe your father once had a multitude of emotions that he has since eradicated with his lust for power.

"I understand, Princess, that recent revelations will have a tendency to make you dwell in the past. So, I have a bit of advice for you."

Ivy nodded, willing.

"Learn from the past," he said. "Remember it, and realize that in a way it is responsible for making you who you are. But also realize that the only you who really matters is who you are right now. That is the you who has the ability to act, to change lives, to do something monumental, and to influence the future you.

"A person you loved has used you and hurt you, but there are more people to love, new paths to pursue, and noble tasks that only you can accomplish—for you and for your entire kingdom. If you must dwell on something, dwell on that."

CHAPTER 22

Simon looked about the small chamber that had been his room for weeks. He had successfully removed every trace of his being there, other than his journey pack leaning against the wall by the door and the stack of books he had studied on the desk. He piled them in his arms and headed for the library to return them to their rightful places.

Princess Ivy was reclining in the chair by the fire when he entered. She started and looked up when she heard his footsteps, then smiled a little.

"Oh, it's just you, Simon."

"Yes," said Simon, moving to the shelves with his armload of books, "it's just me. You're not sitting in here worrying over tomorrow are you?"

Ivy stood from her chair and walked over to where he was. "Not a bit," she said with obvious understatement. The corners of Simon's mouth turned up. "Here," she said, reaching out to take some of the books from his hands, "I can help you with those."

"Thanks." He handed her a couple of volumes. "Don't mind the damaged cover of the Cecil Fairlight. He and I didn't get on so well at first, but we've acclimated."

Ivy smiled knowingly. "You are now 'one with the stone,' then?"

Simon laughed. After a moment he said, "Don't worry too much about tomorrow." He paused. "Although, I might suggest that you try not to fall off a cliff in the process."

Ivy laughed. "I never did thank you for saving me, by the way."

"No, you never did."

"Well, thank you."

"You're welcome." Simon looked at the book in his hand, *Now or Never: A Discussion of the Practice of Time Travel.* "I should thank you, actually. I had begun to think I was thoroughly giftless before that little incident. Although I still have very little consistency in it, I just hope I will be effective when the time comes."

"Yes," Ivy turned to face him. "I know what you mean."

A few of the others began to enter the library. By the time Simon had shelved his books, everyone in the glass house was there.

He looked around the room at them, their faces shadowed by the firelight, their countenances uneasy. His gaze found Hastings who sat in the corner, solemn and withdrawn, much changed from his previous self.

Medwin was calmly reading a book, but everyone else brooded, lost and nervous. Simon, too, felt strange. He did not think it was fear that made his heart pound and his stomach clench, but perhaps foreboding. The idealistic assurance he had felt when he first set out to find and save the princess seemed foreign to him now. The pathway ahead seemed to him as nebulous as the space into which he would be leaping tomorrow morning.

Medwin stood from his chair and left the room briefly. When he returned he was carrying an old instrument. He brought it to where Simon was standing and held it out.

"Here, Simon," he said. "I believe you play. Sing us something, as everyone, I think, could use a little music."

Simon took the instrument, a lute, and held it in his hands for a few moments, searching his mind for the right song for this audience—as Uncle Miles had taught him. A random tune popped into his mind and he hummed it to himself quietly for a moment. It was not a song he had ever performed for a crowd, but a simple tune his brother Roger used to sing quietly with his raspy voice while he was working or thinking. It seemed somehow fitting for this night, so Simon began to play.

Morning sun through the windows crept
of a cottage on a mountain farm.
A young mother rocked her baby, who slept;
his tiny head cradled in her soft arms.

She sang to him,
and her strong heart ached
with a longing to hold him forever.
She bent her head,
and whispered softly,
"I'll never let you go. Never."

Deep in her strong heart
she knew this a lie,
for when the boy into a man grew,
she said good-bye, and with a single tear
she let him go, for she knew
she wanted him to live his brave life.

Some years later, on a stormy afternoon,
the young man in soldier's dress stood,
Making farewell to his wife at the gate of his cottage,
which sat at the edge of a wood.

She embraced him fast
and her strong heart ached
with a longing to hold him forever.
She looked up at him,
and said through the rain,
"I'll never let you go. Never."

Deep in her strong heart
she knew this a lie,
for when the time came to bid him adieu,
she said good-bye, and with a single tear
she let him go, for she knew
he needed to live his brave life.

Then, one moonless night at the edge of the wood
the man, in a lamp lit room lay in his bed.
A lovely young woman, a daughter, was near,
bending close, with her hand on his head.

She kissed his cheek
and her strong heart ached
with a longing to hold him forever.
She looked down at him
as he struggled to breathe and said,
"I'll never let you go. Never."

Deep in her strong heart
she knew this a lie,
for when his eyes closed in slumber true,
she said good-bye, and with a single tear
she let him go, for she knew
he had shown her how to live a brave life.

CHAPTER 23

There was a cold blue light outside the glass house as the travelers ascended the cliff to their departure point. The sun had come up a few hours ago but was hidden behind thick clouds, making it seem earlier than it actually was. Simon pulled his fur-lined cloak more tightly around him and looked in front of him at the line of his companions.

Hastings had come out of his room that morning to wish them luck, and Medwin had offered some brief good-byes and bits of advice before disappearing. Simon suspected that although he appeared calm and unconcerned, he would be watching them carefully from his mirror room.

The climb to the glacial valley seemed more labored than a few days ago with the addition of a pack, but eventually Simon crested the hill and joined the other travelers. Ivy took her stance at the glacier's edge.

"As soon as it's open," she said, "you'll have to jump in, one or two at a time, and don't hesitate too much. It takes a lot of concentration and energy to keep it open."

"I'll go first," said Merrick. "If there is danger waiting on the other side of this doorway, I should be the first to face it. Gilda and the boy next, and Adler, you ought to stay to make sure the princess gets through safely."

Simon felt strangely annoyed by Merrick's take-charge captain attitude but kept back the many snide comments forming in his mind. He stationed himself near Ivy and watched as she closed her eyes, slightly raised her arms, and began to breathe slowly and evenly. Simon turned his attention to the surface of the ice, which was slowly becoming filmy and transparent in appearance. Although he had seen this happen before, he still felt his heartbeat quicken as the surface morphed from cloudy to gray to black, deep, and bottomless. He looked back at Ivy, her brow knit, and saw her gently nod. He turned to the others. "Time to go," he said.

Without hesitation, Merrick grasped the straps of his pack, took a few steps, and jumped over the edge of the little valley, his cloak billowing behind him. The black surface of the doorway rippled like water as he passed through it and disappeared from sight. It was silent on the cliff top. Simon released the breath he had been holding and lightly touched Gilda, who stood paralyzed next to him.

Simon began to worry he would have to push her over the edge until Burr took her other hand. "Come on," he said. Gilda's face relaxed. The two of them stepped toward the edge and, hand-in-hand, jumped. Simon watched them disappear through the liquid-like space, and then turned, knees shaking, toward the Princess.

Her eyes remained closed in deep concentration. Simon touched her shoulder lightly, and she opened her eyes but continued to focus on the doorway in front of her. She held out her hand and Simon took it. He led her gently to the cliff's edge. She squeezed his palm and they both stepped over the edge.

Simon had expected this plunge to feel like dropping into

water, but as he passed through the doorway he felt only a chaffing, tingling emptiness. He did not feel as though he were falling but simply existing in nothingness. He screamed, but only a deafening silence ensued. His head began to ache and throb. He felt dizzy, and the only tangible sensation he had was that of Ivy's hand in his. He tightened his grasp and felt her return it.

The pressure in his head increased. It moved down his spine and extended to his fingers and toes. He slowly began to feel heaviness in his back and on the backs of his legs and arms. The sensation increased, as did his dizziness. He blinked his eyes just to feel their movement, but saw only blackness.

Slowly he realized that the weight in the back of his body was a hard surface, an uneven one, and that he was lying on it. Out of the roaring silence came faint noises, murmurings, and rushing of air. The blackness slowly began to take shape, and he strained his eyes to see what was before him as shadows emerged, moving in and out of view. Slowly, the noises became voices, and Simon realized he was seeing a faint outline of a small head and skinny shoulders hovering over him.

"You dead?" asked Burr.

Simon did not move. He simply allowed his brain to compute the bumpy ground he was lying on, the sound of Burr's voice, the rushing wind in his ears and on his face, a starry sky above, and the feel of Ivy's hand, still holding his. His head continued to ache, but the pressure in his body slowly eased.

"Give him some space, Burr," said Gilda. "He'll just need a moment."

Simon heard Ivy's voice next to him. "Did we make it?" He let go of her hand and slowly sat up to look around.

"We made it," said Merrick, who was offering his hands to help

Ivy sit up. "I couldn't tell you where we made it to, but we're all here."

"You've succeeded, my dear," said Gilda, who was still sitting calmly on the ground, watching them all through her tiny spectacles.

Simon looked around him. It was night, making it difficult to see much of his surroundings, but he observed that they were situated on a roundish open space of hard ground surrounded by thick, low trees. The wind continued to blow around him, but it was a gentle breeze, and the night felt warm and summery.

Simon removed his cloak and stood, a bit surprised at the sureness of his legs. He noticed that Merrick had assisted Ivy over to one of the surrounding trees and was helping her sit to rest at its base. Simon could tell, even in the moonlight, that her face was unusually pale.

"What now?" asked Burr, looking curiously about the clearing.

"Rest," said Simon, thinking of the princess.

Merrick looked at Simon and then at Ivy. "Yes," he said. "I'll look around, make sure we're safe. The rest of you should sleep if you can. I know it seems like we barely woke, but we will need to adjust to the sun here and spend the daytime locating the city and our contact there. I will take a look around and join you again shortly."

"I'll come too," said Burr.

Merrick was looking as though he would never allow it when Gilda spoke. "Of course you may," she said. Her look allowed no argument. So without saying anything, Merrick turned and disappeared through the trees, Burr following closely.

When they were gone, Gilda gathered her belongings and moved over to Ivy's tree, helping her lie down and covering her with a cloak. Ivy's eyes closed, and her face became relaxed. Gilda laid down near her, her head on her pack.

"Might as well," she said to Simon. "It's not as if any of us slept a wink last night."

Simon smiled at her. She was right; he had not gotten any sleep. Simon situated himself at a nearby tree but did not close his eyes; he felt obliged to keep watch over the sleeping women.

◆　　◆　　◆

The sky was shimmering with morning light by the time Merrick and Burr reached the edge of the trees they had been traveling through. Merrick stepped out of the grove and found himself a few feet from what appeared to be a well-traveled road. His eyes followed the road through a bare stretch of rock and sand to where it met the largest city Merrick had ever seen.

Burr swore loudly next to him. Sheer white walls emerged from the desert sand, surrounding even taller buildings and towers. The city was long across the horizon. Merrick noticed that the road led to a large silver gate at its center, which appeared to be heavily guarded. There were no travelers on the road, but Merrick instinctually drew back into the trees, pulling an objecting Burr by the collar after him.

"Come on," he said. "Let's go get the others."

By the time Merrick and Burr had pushed through the trees into the little grove, its occupants were awake and active. Even the princess stood to welcome them and seemed refreshed if not altogether recovered.

Merrick wasted no time. "We're near a city—"

"It's massive!" interjected Burr.

"A large city," Merrick continued. "There is a road just outside this grove that will take us easily there, but I suggest we start now. There is no privacy beyond these trees, and it will be in our best interest to avoid the day's travelers."

"Is it safe?" Gilda asked.

"I have no way of knowing, but we need to locate this Beval person, and I doubt the fellow is in this grove of trees. We have to get to people. Are you fit to travel, Princess?"

Ivy smiled warmly at him. "I think so," she said.

The group made good time getting through the trees, so Merrick allowed them a moment's rest at the grove's edge to admire the distant city. Once on the road, however, their pace slowed. It felt to Merrick that they were going backward, as the road continued to stretch indefinitely before them. The day reached its heat, and Merrick's back was wet where his pack met his shirt.

When the city walls were finally before them, Merrick realized that they had not seen a single traveler. No carriages had passed, no riders on horseback, no farmers' carts. There was an almost eerie isolation on the road. A hot wind blew, but the surroundings were otherwise silent and still. The wall of the city grew larger before them, until inner buildings were obscured by its height. On closer inspection, Merrick could see that the wall was made of stone. But it was smooth, unlike the rough-hewn Lyrian stones he was accustomed to.

Merrick had just begun to examine the line of patrolling soldiers at the gate when Simon approached him, and said quietly, "What do you plan to say to these guards?"

"In case you haven't noticed, Adler, I have no 'plan.' I don't know what I'll say to these men if they refuse to let us pass, so if you have any ideas, please, share them."

Simon arched his eyebrows. "That's what I thought," he said calmly.

The gate was being guarded by at least ten men on foot, but Merrick could see that there were other men stationed at the towers on either side of the huge metal doors. The men were dressed in white uniforms with silver shields, carried long spears, and were all at least as large in stature as he was. The men were not looking directly at the travelers but occasionally stole sideways glances at them under heavy brows. Merrick fingered his tradestone and began to wish for a moat.

As they approached, one of the guards stepped forward, eyeing them curiously but not speaking.

Merrick cleared his throat. "We would like to enter the city," he said. The guard squinted his eyes and continued to stare confusedly at Merrick.

"I don't think he understands," Simon said at Merrick's side.

"Obviously," said Merrick, sighing. He pointed over the guard's head at the large gates. "Go in," he said loudly, gesturing at his group and motioning toward the city.

The guard turned to one of the other men behind him and began speaking quietly and quickly in an unintelligible language. The other guard answered him, and then the first returned to Merrick and held out his hand, palm up.

"Does he want me to pay him?" Merrick asked.

Simon shrugged. "Maybe he just wants to shake your hand."

Merrick held out his right hand warily, and the guard snatched it, turning it palm up and spreading Merrick's fingers as if to examine it. He then dropped it and moved to Simon, holding out his hand and waiting for Simon to offer one in return. The guard proceeded to check the palms of all of the travelers and then, seemingly satisfied, turned back to the other guards, shouted something at them, and moved back to join their ranks.

As he did so, the guards moved aside, still watching the travelers suspiciously. There was a loud creaking sound, and slowly, surely, the large silver gates parted and began to open.

◆　◆　◆

Gilda Reed followed the others through the open gates, squinting at the glaring view that met her eyes. A wide cobblestone road stretched before her, bordered by smooth white buildings of various sizes and heights. A strip of dark soil divided the road in half, and in it grew a perfect line of tall, elegant trees with white bark and shimmering silvery leaves.

People dressed in silky, robe-like garments—all in hues of white, silver, gray, and black—moved about on the street. Tall white horses pulled dark, iron carriages with curtained windows. The sight amazed Gilda, not necessarily for its beauty, but for its smooth perfection.

The street was unusually quiet, and Gilda noticed that people did not wave at one another or stop to converse but moved along their course calmly and coldly. She soon realized that no one had even looked up to acknowledge their entrance or stare at the earthy-toned group that seemed a smudge on the picture of their white, sun-reflecting city.

The travelers moved to the roadside and sauntered on, dazed, for some time before Gilda got up the courage to tap a passerby on the shoulder.

"Excuse me," she said to the cold female figure before her. "I was wondering if—"

The woman, with only a brief suspicious glance over her shoulder, quickly walked away before Gilda could finish. Gilda shook her head. *How utterly rude,* she thought.

The others, having seen Gilda's attempt, began to try for the attention of other passersby, asking for Beval. However, all of them were similarly repulsed. Gilda watched with a degree of amusement as Burr tugged on the black robe of a tall man who attempted to ignore the gesture and walk on, only to find he was tethered by Burr's fast grip. When the tall man turned to scowl at the boy, Burr simply said, "Beval?" The man's face was still and expressionless for a moment. Then he scowled, forcefully removed Burr's hand from his robe, shook his head at him reprovingly, and walked on.

Somewhere in the city, there was a deep chiming, like that of a large clock. Gilda turned in the direction of the sound, hoping to locate the source, but saw nothing much beyond the line of buildings. When she turned her attention to the street again, it was deserted. She watched a solitary black carriage round a corner and caught sight of a flutter of robes disappearing into a nearby building; then all was quiet.

The travelers turned to each other in confused amazement.

"Do you think they were afraid of us?" asked Ivy. "We don't exactly fit in." She gestured to her brown and green clothing.

Merrick shook his head. "They didn't even look at us long enough to have any idea what we were wearing," he said.

"Nor did they stick around long enough for us to point it out," said Simon, indicating the empty street behind him. He glanced at Burr, "What is that you've got there?"

Burr quickly moved his hands behind his back. "Nothin'."

"Produce it," Gilda Reed demanded.

Burr smiled slightly as he pulled a shiny metal pocket watch from behind his back. "I took it from the man's robes," he said with a trace of pride.

"Burr!" Gilda exclaimed. "You know it's wrong to steal."

The boy shrugged. "He deserved it."

A distant but significant noise began to fill the empty streets. It sounded like hoofbeats and, perhaps, carriage wheels. The sound grew louder until, suddenly, a group of soldiers on horseback rounded a corner down the street from the travelers and moved briskly in their direction.

Gilda counted at least a dozen black horses and riders dressed similarly to the men who had inspected them at the city gates. Behind the horses appeared a large, black horse-drawn carriage with unfamiliar silver markings on its side. Behind the carriage half a dozen more riders followed, making an intimidating procession. Gilda dropped the stolen watch into her pocket and pulled Burr toward her, holding his hand so tightly in hers that he grunted and tried to pull it away without success.

When only a few feet from the travelers, the riders stopped and changed formation rapidly until they formed a complete circle around the travelers. Just as rapidly, they lowered long spears and pointed them menacingly at the small group. Gilda saw Simon and Merrick's hands move to their swords, and even she let go of Burr's hand in order to reach for her little dagger.

One of the men shouted something unintelligible at them. Gilda shook her head to indicate she did not understand, but the man shouted once more and pointed toward Merrick's sword hand. Merrick nodded and, dropping his weapon, said quietly, "Lay down your sword, Simon."

Gilda left her dagger hidden, remaining empty handed.

The man yelled something else at the group, holding up his spear-less hand.

"Show them your palms," said Simon, "like at the gate."

Each of the travelers held up their empty palms. The man nodded but did not lower his spear. He shouted something else, this time to the other soldiers, and most of the men dismounted. Before Gilda was aware what was happening, one of the soldiers had grabbed both of her hands, moved them behind her back, and had begun to bind them together with rope. She struggled to free her arms, shouting in frustration, but was unable. "Let go!" she cried. She looked to her friends, who were being similarly bound.

Ivy's captor had just begun to wind rope around her arms, when the rope suddenly flew through the air and landed at the feet of a nearby horse. Burr was biting a grimacing soldier on his strong arm. Merrick had a bleeding cut on his face, but had managed to wrestle the spear from his assailant and was now turning it on him. Simon seemed to be speedily evading two of the soldiers, darting quickly from their grasp. Gilda had just swiftly stomped on the foot of the man behind her when more soldiers, reinforcements, burst in through the circle of horses. She saw two of them coming for her and soon found they had her by the arms and had thrust her to the ground, her face to the dirt. She could hear the others struggling around her, and she could tell by their shouts that her friends did not have the upper hand.

"We didn't do nothin'!" Burr was shouting. "We're just looking for someone, that's all!" His voice was muffled for a moment, and then Gilda heard him burst out with, "We're just looking for Beval! Beval!"

Suddenly there was a man speaking, calmly and steadily. The soldiers were instantly quiet and everyone was still. The two men holding Gilda lifted her from the dirt into a standing position. Her friends were all being held by soldiers, and everyone was looking at the man who had entered the clearing and had just finished speaking to the soldiers.

The first thing Gilda noticed about the man was that he radiated self-importance. He was shorter than her, and considerably plumper, and yet his eyes were lively and full of comprehension. Thick robes of deep purple cascaded over his round frame, made bold by their contrast to the soldiers' white and silver garb. A silver crown sat on his dark curly head. He spoke another order to his watching men, and Gilda soon found herself unbound.

"Welcome to the White City," he said in clear if slightly ac-cented Lyrian. The travelers watched him, their expressions show-ing different degrees of shock. "I hope you will forgive the rude introduction my soldiers gave you, but we do not often receive foreigners here."

"You speak Lyrian?" Burr stammered.

The man's chubby face melted into a smile. "I, unlike my men, am not unfamiliar with foreign places, people, or even tongues." He looked at each of the travelers with an examining eye. "I am Prince Oswald," he declared, "and you are . . ."

"Travelers," Merrick cut in quickly, "from Lyria."

Oswald nodded. "Obviously." He smiled but kept an unfaltering gaze on Merrick. "I heard the boy say you were looking for Beval," he said. "Is that correct?"

Merrick hesitated for a moment but then assented. "Do you know him?"

Oswald's gaze did not waver. "Of course. He is a member of my court; we will find him at the palace." He turned his back on the group and headed toward his large carriage. "Please allow me to take you to him."

CHAPTER 24

The firelight made dancing reflections in King Than's eyes, and he stroked his graying temples. He shivered and moved closer to the fireplace. He could never seem to get warm in these cold mountains. He endeavored to assuage his discomfort with the familiar dream that soon he would be back in his sunny palace on the Lyrian plain in command of the entire continent. This dream, however, had recently grown more remote. Obstacles and doubts filled its place in his thoughts. Even if all the Wrakes from here to the Southlands could find and hinder Ivy and her companions, he wondered if Abaddon would keep the bargain that had cost Than so much already.

The irony of it all was that he had sent Ivy away because of the small chance she might come into her gift and endanger his plans. In doing so he had sent her to a place where she had most likely gained full knowledge and use of her abilities and was an even greater threat. It had always gone thus for him. He had married Cora for the power he believed she wielded; but she had never really trusted him enough to use it for his purposes, or even disclose her knowledge of it to him.

He had the constant feeling of complete powerlessness in his search for power. The effect was wearying.

The chamber door opened, and Talbot strode across the room.

The king barely acknowledged his presence.

Talbot approached his chair and held out a sealed piece of parchment. "A message," he said, "from—"

"Yes, yes," the king interrupted, seizing the message and hastily breaking the seal. It was from Abaddon, of course, and sparse, as usual.

> Perhaps you will be able to move away from your fire, warmed by the thought that the travelers have been located. Bellaria. Walked straight into our hands—The White City. Now we have only to keep them there. Will continue to make use of the Wrakes from your court—those you are aware of, and those you are not.–A

King Than moved away from the fire as a drop of sweat eased down his forehead. He had no doubt that Abaddon's purpose in sending this message was not to pass on good news but to ensure that Than knew he was being watched. But by whom? The king knew Abaddon's seer had better things to do than keep watch over him, as was evidenced by her finding Ivy and the others. Besides, Abaddon had made it perfectly clear that he was employing someone from inside Than's court.

He looked up suspiciously at Talbot. "You may go now."

Talbot nodded. "Any reply, Your Highness?"

"It requires none, Talbot," he said, and watched as the tall man departed. He tried to shake the ever-looming sensation of powerlessness, but he could not help but feel that he was simply a pawn to Abaddon and that once his small part had been played out, and the people of Lyria were subjected or killed, he would simply be swept aside in his uselessness. It was at this point that King Than began to relinquish his dream to rule the continent and began to cling, instead, to his desire to survive.

CHAPTER 25

Princess Ivy of Lyria was uncomfortably wedged between Gilda
Reed's jutting hipbone and Prince Oswald's massive midsection.
The prince's carriage did, indeed, hold six, as he had promised, but
Ivy couldn't help but feel that Oswald was almost the equivalent in
breadth of two regular-sized passengers. Her lack of personal space,
and the annoying fact that the windows were curtained, made her
feel particularly confined.

The prince had been talking congenially and nonstop for the entire ride, asking friendly questions of the travelers and getting sparse
replies in return. Even Burr was more tight-lipped than usual, and
Ivy was glad. Oswald was currently talking to John Merrick, who
was seated directly across from Ivy and next to Burr and Simon.

"So, you are a captain, then." No response. "I would like to tell
you that we have a great fleet of ships here in the White City, but as
you may have seen from your approach the only sea around here is
a sea of sand." He chuckled to himself. "Which gate did you enter
at then?"

Merrick shrugged.

The prince smiled. "It is difficult to get bearings in a city this size, is it not? Well, yes, of course, and all the way from Lyria. What is your business with Beval?"

"It's private," Merrick said, shortly.

"Of course, of course. Didn't mean to pry. He and I are good friends, though. Lucky you ran into me, eh?"

Prince Oswald received no response. He did not seem to mind. He inclined his head toward Gilda. "If you wouldn't mind, ma'am," he said, "could you open that little compartment at your side? I think you will find a drinking flask and some glasses. I'm a bit thirsty." Gilda did manage to slide open the little compartment and pass a large shiny flask and a glass to the prince. "Would anyone else like a drink?" he asked.

Ivy was rather thirsty but felt somehow nervous accepting anything from this unknown prince. She looked across at Merrick, who was staring at Oswald suspiciously. Then she caught Simon's eye, who shrugged.

While the prince waited for a response, he filled the glass he was holding and emptied it rapidly. He smacked his lips, satisfied.

"I'll take some," said Merrick and the others in turn.

The water was refreshing, and Ivy began to relax a little. The rhythm of the moving carriage made her feel sleepy. She rested her head on Gilda's shoulder and tried to keep her eyes open as Oswald droned on about the amazing White City.

CHAPTER 26

Hastings was sitting in the library, his eyes resting on but not reading an open book, when Medwin entered the room and sat directly opposite him. Hastings put the book down and absently rubbed his head where his bandage used to be.

"We have a lot to discuss," said Medwin.

"I suppose so," Hastings replied warily.

Medwin smiled. "I would like to start with your name."

"My . . . name?"

"Yes. We will be spending a considerable amount of time together, and it would be nice if I knew what to call you."

"My name is Hast—"

"Hastings is not your real name, so that will not do."

"I . . ." Hastings had begun a lie, but seeing its futility in Medwin's piercing gaze, reconsidered. "Laith Haverford," he said, and the name felt strange on his tongue.

Medwin nodded slowly. "Laith Haverford, then, only son of Duke and Duchess Haverford. The boy who went missing and was presumed dead."

"Yes."

"You ran away?"

"Yes."

"How old were you?"

"Ten."

"Why did you do it?"

Laith Haverford sighed. "I used to say there were many reasons," he began, eyes downcast, "that I felt confined by my title, or that I was disappointed by my idle life and wanted occupation, or that I craved adventure." He concentrated on the pattern in the rug. "I actually think there was only one reason why I ran away. My parents did not love me. I lived a life that was more than comfortable, with the promise of an important future, and almost my every desire at my asking, but I was lonely and unhappy. "

Medwin nodded. "I see," he said. "Did you find happiness, then, in running away?"

Laith smiled bitterly. "I'm sure you know the answer to that. I changed my name, found work in the shipyards, and waited for my parents to turn the kingdom upside down to find me. I knew they had offered a generous reward for anyone who knew of my whereabouts, but this did not suffice. I understood that they did not seek their lost son but merely the inheritor of the Haverford name and estate. I wanted proof that they had changed, that they loved and missed me.

"Eventually, they forgot the search altogether and were among the first of the nobles to sail away from Lyria when the Southern presence became a threat. After that, I left shipbuilding and became a sailor. I was free from my title, had a real occupation, and even adventure, but no, I did not have happiness. In fact, I was angry with anyone else who seemed to have it." He shook his down-turned head and tightly clenched the arms of the chair he sat in. "I am not proud of the person I have become."

Medwin was still for a while before he spoke. "I know, Laith," he said kindly. "But the life ahead of you is more than the life behind you, and you are not an ordinary man. You are no longer a neglected little boy, and you are not a common sailor. Would you like to begin again?"

Laith relaxed his hands and looked the old man in the eyes. Silently, firmly, he nodded his head.

CHAPTER 27

S imon sat at an empty table in the Adler cottage, carefully polishing an old sword.

"What are you doing, Simon?" asked a soft voice over his shoulder.

Simon did not look up. "You can't fight a war with this tarnished old thing, Roger."

Roger pulled out the chair next to Simon's and sat down. "The sword will do," he said. "You should be packing up your own things. You leave first thing in the morning."

Simon clenched his jaw. "I should be here, fighting with you and father. I feel like a coward retreating to the hills while others stand in my place."

Roger nodded understandingly. "I think I know how you feel, Simon. But would you rather have Mother and the children travel into the hills alone and unprotected?"

"No," Simon sighed. "But I think of you, giving up a good post in the Navy to defy the king and do the fighting he will not. I think of Father, a simple farmer, fighting an enemy that nobles and soldiers run from in cowardice. I hate that I will be among them."

"Among them, Simon, perhaps, but I seem to think that it takes great courage to be a hero among cowards. What you do tomorrow will not be heroic because people are around to applaud you but because it is the right thing to do."

Simon shook his head. "My 'heroism' is only possible because of yours and father's."

Roger placed his hand on Simon's shoulder as he stood to leave the room. "And ours, Simon, is only possible because of yours."

Simon opened his eyes, but saw only darkness. He was lying on a hard, cold surface, and he felt dizzy, and unsettled. He moaned.

"Is that you, Simon?" he heard a whisper to his left. It sounded like Ivy.

Simon sat up slowly. "Where are we?" he asked. The last thing he remembered was riding in the fat man's carriage, that prince, and trying with the others to avoid his pointed questions. He had offered them some water to drink . . .

Simon sighed. "There must have been something in that water."

"Yes," said Ivy. "We were foolish to drink it, I suppose, but I was sure it was safe when he downed that glass."

Simon could hear her shifting about and soon felt her shoulder brush his.

"Are the others here?" he asked, holding out his hands to feel around him and straining his eyes to see through the darkness.

"There's someone next to me," she answered. "Gilda, I think." Simon heard a mumbling and rustling, and then heard Gilda speak.

"Goodness," she said. "What happened?"

As Ivy spoke to Gilda, Simon crawled forward, cautiously, until he came in contact with another, small body. He woke Burr, who accidentally smacked Simon's face with his flailing arm and swore loudly. Soon Simon could hear Merrick's gruff voice somewhere behind him, also swearing.

Simon was relieved that everyone was present, but he had a nagging feeling that something was missing. Impulsively, his hand flew to his neck to feel for a chain that was not there.

"It's gone!" he almost shouted.

"What is, Simon?" Ivy asked.

"My tradestone is gone." A series of gasps and exclamations ensued.

"Mine's gone as well!"

"Missing!"

Within moments, everyone was talking at once, and Simon could not distinguish a single thing being said. Panic filled him. He would have to use his gift. Turn back time again, so that they refuse the water and avoid this dungeon. He reached out for the fabric of time trying to find the past as he had sped to the future, but he felt powerless and unfocused. For a moment time seemed to slow around him, and he thought he could move it back. But momentarily everything returned to normal and he fell to the floor, his head aching and exhaustion pouring over him.

There was pandemonium in the darkness as everyone tried, vainly, to use their gifts without stones. Ivy collided with him, cursing at her weak attempts to move out of this dark space. Gilda and Merrick lacked material to make use of. Even Burr, who was practiced in using his gift without a stone, exclaimed that he "could not find the mind of any living creature in this miserable pit." The worried bits of conversation again filled the small-seeming space.

"Quiet!" yelled Merrick, and the darkness was still again. "We need to find out what kind of space we are in and see if there is a way out."

Everyone moved at once. Simon bumped heads with Burr, who again swore loudly. Simon sat back, dizzy again.

"Stop!" yelled Merrick. "Everyone just stay put. I will move around and see what I can discover about this place." The room was quiet and still again but for the sound of Merrick's shuffling about. After a time he stopped.

"It's square," he said, "or rectangular, and small. The walls are maybe ten feet long, and I can easily touch the ceiling when standing. The walls, floor, and ceiling are all the same smooth stone. I think everyone should take a surface and see if you can find any crack or glitch in it. Move slowly so as not to collide this time."

The others did as they were told, with only a few collisions. Simon found a wall and stood, running his hands over its smooth surface from floor to ceiling. This went on for what seemed like an infinite amount of time. Simon would occasionally cross paths with someone else, and then they would continue on.

Finally he stopped and sat where he was. "There's nothing," he said.

"Keep looking," said Merrick. "We've got to find a way."

"There isn't one," said Gilda. "Simon's right."

"I'm tired and dizzy," Burr complained. "I keep falling over."

"Look," said Merrick, angrily, "we did not come all this way to sit down and give up. I will not tolerate quitters."

Simon scoffed, "Indeed, I'm a quitter and a pessimist, but who is an optimist when they are holding an empty water flask in the middle of a desert."

Merrick laughed roughly. "Yes, give us riddles, fool, that is apparently all you can offer."

"You might recall, Merrick," Simon countered, "that we aren't on your ship anymore. You aren't captain here."

"Then who is?" Merrick yelled. "You? What are you going to do, tell some jokes and hope the room falls apart for laughter?"

Simon squinted at the darkness. "I don't know. I for one thought it was rather funny when you delivered us to a liar who drugged us and stuck us in a stone box."

"Enough!" Ivy interjected.

Simon clenched his fists, feeling suddenly and uncharacteristically unsatisfied with words, and wished he could see well enough for them to make contact with Merrick's overconfident jaw.

"Stop," Ivy spoke again. "Just think for a minute. Obviously, if that prince had wanted to kill us he could have, but he chose to throw us in here instead. Maybe he thinks we can be of some use to him. It is most likely that he'll be back, or someone will, and we will have to work ourselves out and find our stones that way. In the meantime, we should try to maintain some sanity. This darkness is maddening enough without our contributing to it."

"What do you suggest?" asked Merrick roughly. "We sit here in silence?"

"No," Ivy replied, somewhat defensively. "I suggest we talk to each other."

Merrick laughed. "How cozy. What will be our topic of conversation?"

"Now that *is* enough Captain," said Gilda, calmly. "Think about what the princess said. She is the only one in here making any sense."

Ivy sighed. "I just thought since I don't really know any of you very well, maybe you could tell me about yourselves."

"I have nothing to tell," said John Merrick.

"I do!" said Burr.

◆   ◆   ◆

"My parents were the greatest thieves that ever lived in Lyria," came Burr's husky voice through the darkness. "They only stole from the richest folks, and everyone knew they could steal anything they wanted to. No mark was too difficult. Even after I was born, Mum used to strap me to her back, and I would go with them on their nighttime raids.

"Once, when I was still a baby, a man offered my parents a huge batch of money to go steal something real important for them from the house of a very rich lady. This man, though, was a thief himself, and was tired of my parents taking all the good loot. When my parents got to the rich woman's house, soldiers were waiting to arrest them. It was a trap.

"As soon as they saw the men there, Ma and Pa got out the window and tried to run away. The soldiers followed them into a nearby wood. The soldiers were getting closer, so my ma hid me at the bottom of a tree and covered me with leaves. She meant to come back for me when they had escaped the soldiers, but they never did. The soldiers arrested my parents, and they were hung to death.

"Pretty soon, though, a family of bears came along and found me in the woods. The mama bear could see I was all alone, and so she took me in like one of her own cubs."

"Bears, huh?" said Simon.

"Course," Burr said. "I stayed with them and learned how to fish and find berries and all. I was happy with the bears, and I was the bravest one of the whole bunch.

"One day when I was maybe five or six, I was out exploring in the forest with my bear brothers when an evil witch—"

Gilda Reed cleared her throat loudly.

"Um," said Burr, "I mean when an evil old mad lady came into the trees looking for poisonous weeds and saw me with the bears. Before I could attack her or run away, she threw sleeping dust on me, and I fell to the ground. My bear brothers ran to get help, but the evil lady threw me into her sack and dragged me back to her dark ugly cave.

"This cave looked small from the outside where there was an opening in the side of the hill, but it was big inside; and in the back of the cave were large cages where she kept children to test her poisonous potions on. None of the children talked to me until late that night when the wi—mad lady fell asleep. Then one boy whispered to me that if the lady caught any children in the day, or if we woke her up at night, she would cut off our fingers and feed them to her pet snakes. I told him not to worry, that I would find a way out."

Disbelieving laughs began to fill the darkness, but Burr plowed on with his tale, undeterred.

"Every night after that, I began to slowly unwind the threads of the huge sack the old lady gave me to wear until I had made a pretty good rope. Then I waited.

"Eventually the evil lady decided it was my turn to be her testing child for the day. When she went to open the cage, I threw the rope around her neck and wound it until I began to strangle her with it. She thrashed around so much that I eventually had to let go, but the rope was wound pretty tight at her throat.

"While she was rolling on the floor and gagging and such, I stole her keys and freed all of the children. They went running out of the cave to freedom. Then I bent over that mean lady. Her mouth was oozing out foam and spit, and her face was all purple and her eyes were bloodshot, and where the rope was on her neck it was all bloody and—"

"Burr!" Gilda interjected.

"What? I'm just tellin' it how it was," Burr retorted.

"Well, skip that part."

"Fine, fine. So anyway," Burr continued. "I was pretty sure she was going to die when I left her, but I guess I was wrong. Once I got out of the cave, I was living on my own, sleeping here and there, finding my own food, and doing magic tricks for money. But that old mean lady, she was just biding her time until her strength was back, and then she disguised herself and came after me.

"By this time, I had joined up with some traveling performers, and I was the assistant to the lion tamer. He wasn't the nicest chap, but he gave me money and a place to sleep in his wagon at night.

"Well, one dark night, the lion tamer sent me out to catch some rabbits for lion food. I was real quick and could catch 'em with my bare hands. So I went off the streets into a little wood nearby. I was walking around when I started to hear footsteps behind me. I just kept walking, and the person kept on following, until I came to a tree. I jumped behind it to hide and turned around to see if I could catch a glimpse of my follower. All I could see were shadowy trees. I kept walking again, and the footsteps started again. This time, they were closer. I started shakin' real bad and I started to walk faster, but the footsteps got faster. I started to run, and the person started to run. There was nowhere for me to go, so I decided I'd have to face 'em. I was about to turn around when I felt a hand on my shoulder, gripping hard. I stopped, and slowly turned, and—"

Burr was cut short by the deafening sound of stone grinding on stone, and suddenly the blinding light of a lantern revealed the head and shoulders of a person, a woman, peering out at the group of blinking travelers from a perfectly square hole in the floor. She pushed aside the large slab of smooth stone she had displaced and held up the light, squinting.

"Are you the Lyrian idiots who have been parading around the White City asking for Beval?"

The travelers all stared dumbly at the intruder as she pulled herself out of the hole and handed her lantern to John Merrick.

"Could you hold this please?" she said patronizingly. Then she turned back to the hole where a thin-faced man with a beard had just emerged. She offered him her hand and pulled him up into the small, square room. She dusted her hands and put them on her hips as she stared at the dumbstruck group.

"You're lucky the city is filled with our spies, and even luckier Oswald threw you in the dark dungeons instead of the fire pits."

Simon was the first to find his voice. "Can you take us to Beval, then?"

The woman smiled condescendingly. "I *am* Beval," she said.

John Merrick coughed and stepped closer to the woman. "*You* are Antoine Beval?" he asked, incredulously.

The woman turned to him and sized him up briefly before re-claiming her lantern from his outstretched hand. "No," she said, "I am his daughter, Saffi."

"Can you take us to Antoine, then?" Burr asked.

"My father is dead," Saffi replied, eyes still on Merrick. "I'll have to do." She gestured to the other man. "This is my cousin Fergus," she said. "He came to help me get you out of here. No one knows these passageways better than he does, but he does not speak Lyrian, so you needn't pester him with questions."

"How is it *you* speak Lyrian?" asked Merrick.

Saffi turned back to him. "No time for lengthy explanations now Mr.—"

"Merrick. John Merrick."

"And the others?"

Merrick took introductions upon himself. "This is Simon Adler, Gilda Reed, Burr, and—"

"The Princess." Saffi finished for him. She had nodded indiffer-ently to the others but watched Ivy with unmasked interest.

"Ivy," the princess said kindly, extending her hand.

Saffi smiled and took Ivy's hand. "An honor to meet you."

John Merrick watched this interaction with puzzled interest, wondering how this woman who had treated him with such cavalier disinterest could now seem so sincere. Saffi was a little shorter than the princess, with dark regal features and black hair pulled into a modest knot at the back of her head. She was dressed practically in leggings and a sort of form-fitting jacket.

"We'd better get going," she said. "There's not much time."

"But our stones," Gilda said quietly. "We can't leave without our stones."

Saffi turned on Gilda. "You've lost your stones of power?" she asked.

"I didn't," Burr interjected.

"You never had one to lose," said Simon. "We woke without them."

Saffi muttered something under her breath resembling a curse. "Well, there's nothing we can do at the moment. I expect someone will be back to check on you within the hour, and then they'll turn the place upside down trying to find you. We'll come back for your stones when the lookout is over."

"Just leave them?" Ivy asked.

Saffi nodded to her. "Yes, Princess, but don't worry. They can't use them and wouldn't dare try to destroy them. We'll get them back eventually." She turned to the hole in the floor and said something foreign to Fergus, who lowered himself into the hole. She bent to follow.

"Where does this lead?" asked Merrick, behind her.

"Out," Saffi replied. "You had other plans?" She lowered herself into the hole.

"No," said Merrick, who watched her with one eyebrow slightly raised before following her through the floor.

CHAPTER 28

"Concentrate," Medwin urged from his comfortable armchair at the end of the glass-sided hallway. He was addressing the man at the opposite end of the corridor, Laith Haverford, who was standing with one hand on the wall for support and endeavoring to walk. His crutch was lying abandoned on the floor behind him. "You'll have to show me you can do it without hands."

Laith breathed heavily and cursed the old man under his breath. He lifted his hand from the wall and began to take slow, belabored steps down the hallway. His face was red, partly with the strain of walking and partly with anger at being made to do so. He began to feel dizzy but pushed forward.

"Can't you go any faster?" asked Medwin.

Laith silently cursed the old man again but kept walking. After a seeming eternity, Laith was close enough to Medwin that he could have reached out and thumped his white head. Instead, he dropped to his hands and knees and let the fiery anger welling inside him course through his body as his beating heart began to decelerate.

"Congratulations," Medwin said calmly. "You have just walked down a hall."

Laith felt his cheeks burn and he clenched his fists. "Who do you think you are?" he spat out, looking up at the sanguine face of the man in front of him. "I thought you were trying to help me, not kill me."

Medwin smiled. "I'm glad to see there is still some fight in you, Laith."

Laith shook his head bitterly and looked at the floor.

"Besides," Medwin continued, "you are not dead, are you? I am trying to push you, Laith, because until you are strong in body and mind, you will not have the strength to control the power in you. The power I plan to teach you to use."

Laith scoffed. "That means nothing to me, old man." He paused as he placed one hand on the wall next to him and stood up again, looking down at Medwin. "You keep telling me I have a gift, or a power, or something. But what? What can I do that is so great? Do you really have something to teach me, or are you just bored and lonely here and enjoying having someone to torment?"

Medwin looked up from his armchair. His expression was unchanged, but Laith thought he saw a touch of red in the old man's cheek that gave him a surge of joy at having touched a nerve.

When Medwin spoke, however, his response was characteristically composed. "I don't like your anger, Laith, but I like the strength behind it. There is something very real that I have to teach you, but you will need this strength to do it." The old man stood and looked the young man in the eyes. He pulled on the chain around his neck and drew the reflective stone from his shirt. "I am going to show you something. When I hold this up, I want you to focus all that energy inside you into this one object." He held the stone up for Laith to look into.

"I told you, old man," Laith said, "I don't like mirrors."

"You are afraid of them, you mean." Medwin held up his hand to forestall Laith's reply. "It is time for you to quit being afraid of your own reflection," he said. "Now, look."

It took a surprising amount of will, but Laith finally lifted his gaze to the little stone; and when he did, he saw only his blue eye staring back. He felt the anger surge inside him and he looked down. He concentrated on the trapped energy inside of him and looked up at the stone again, releasing a long hot breath as he did so. A single eye stared back. *This is not my eye,* said a voice inside him. It was dark brown and magnified by the liquid brimming in it. The lashes were long and wet. The eye blinked. A tear rolled. Slowly, Laith lifted his hand to his dry eyes and felt them widen. What was he seeing? The image blurred, and again his own blue eye was staring back at him.

The stone fell away, and Laith found that he was staring at the old man once again. "What did you do?" he whispered to Medwin.

"You saw something, then?" There was an excitement in Medwin's eyes that took Laith by surprise. He nodded in reply.

"You share my gift, Laith. You have the gift of sight."

CHAPTER 29

Prince Oswald pulled the flesh from a drumstick with his teeth and threw the bone onto a platter now full with chicken bones. He chewed briefly before swallowing a mouthful of juicy meat and signaled for a nearby servant to clear the platter and bring more. He wiped his greasy mouth with the back of his hand, and decided that he was definitely nervous, or even . . . afraid.

Prince Oswald always downed large portions of food when he was afraid. Of course, he also binged when he was happy, angry, victorious, or depressed. But this nervous eating was unique in that it seemed he needed to get as much food down his throat as fast as he was able. Tasting was irrelevant. He must merely consume.

He had now been eating various meats for the last half hour, ever since he saw with his own eyes the empty room in the dark dungeons. His prisoners had disappeared. He had sent all of his men, except those who waited on him personally, to search the palace and the surrounding city. He had ordered the clock to chime early so that the streets would be clear for the search. Now all that remained for him to do was eat and push aside impending thoughts of the punishment he might receive for his negligence.

The servant reentered the room with a large hambone on a platter. Oswald yelled at the man to hurry. The servant, however, continued to move very slowly across the long room, his eyes downcast. Prince Oswald stood angrily, meaning to severely chastise the lazy man, when the servant suddenly looked up.

The prince took a step backward. This was not the servant he had sent to the kitchens, but another of his employ whom he knew well. He glanced instinctually to the man's left arm. It was covered by the long-sleeved servant's shirt he wore, but Oswald knew what he would see on that arm if it were visible. This man was a Vessel. And judging by the menacing stare which he fixed on the trembling prince, he was currently in use.

The Vessel had now reached the table and was staring across it at the prince. "Good evening," he said in perfect snakelike Bellarian. Prince Oswald nodded stiffly. The vacant-eyed Vessel set the hambone on the table and leaned across it. "I have a message for you."

Prince Oswald nodded and took another step backward.

"My Lord Abaddon is aware that you have had a small mishap, correct?"

The prince nodded again, dumbly. The Vessel reached down and grasped the large, sharp, two-pronged fork on the ham platter and inclined it toward the prince.

"My Lord Abaddon commands me to say that until the Lyrian scum are found you shall not eat another bite." He moved the fork closer to the prince until the sharp prongs were brushing the thick folds of skin at his throat. Prince Oswald swallowed nervously.

The messenger continued. "He also says that if you fail once more, you will never eat again." The man drew the prongs slowly back and forth across the prince's neck. Then, in one quick movement, he flipped the fork around and stabbed it violently into the ham on the table in front of him.

Prince Oswald fell back into the chair behind him, breathing heavily, and watched the Vessel back away from him, stop at the door of the room, arms folded across his chest, and smile wickedly as he stood there at his post, watching his charge. "Where shall we begin?"

The prince coughed, hoping to clear away the obstruction in his throat and speak confidently. "I have two things," he squeaked. "The name of a longtime vexation, Beval; and these." Oswald drew from the inside of his generous robe four chains, on the bottom of which four stones glimmered.

CHAPTER 30

Six shadowy forms obscured the lamplight ahead of Simon as he crawled on hands and knees through the dusty tunnel. The group had been traversing these passages on all fours for a portion of an hour that seemed indefinite. There had been several turns, as the tunnel had many different forks and bends, and Simon was convinced that in spite of his fair sense of direction he would not be able to find his way back to the dark prison room even if he had desired it.

"Are you sure Oswald is ignorant of how to access these tunnels?" he asked the lantern holder.

"Yes," Saffi replied curtly.

"None of his men know how to get in here?"

"None."

Simon glanced behind him then continued crawling. He looked down at his hands as they pushed through the dust. Just then, his head collided with Ivy's back. She had stopped crawling and was sitting on her legs in front of him. Simon's blow knocked her forward slightly.

"Oh, um . . . sorry," he stammered as he helplessly watched Ivy bump Gilda in front of her, and a procession of shuffles and angry grunts issued from the line of people in front of her. "I didn't know you had stopped," he addressed the mumbling group.

"It's alright, Simon," Ivy turned to him, and he thought he heard a smile in her words. She was backlit, her face dark as she faced him.

"Why have we stopped?" he asked her in a whisper.

"Fergus seems to be deliberating over whether to take this left or the next one." She leaned closer to him and lowered her voice further. "Frankly, I've never seen such a maze. I don't know how he can possibly keep it straight."

Simon nodded and sat up, rubbing his sore back. "Yes. I don't know how much more crawling my back will stand for. How are you holding up?"

Ivy shrugged, "I'm fine. These passageways weren't made for tall Lyrians, though, that's for sure."

"Yes," said Simon, "you are rather tall for a Lyrian woman." He felt stupid the moment he'd said it but was helpless to retract it. Why was it that he always had something smooth to say until he was talking to the princess.

He could hear the smile enter Ivy's speech again. "I'm as tall as you, I'd wager."

The group began moving again, straight on to the next left, and Ivy and Simon followed. They had reached the turn and had begun proceeding down the side tunnel when Simon again addressed the group leader.

"Does anyone else besides you know of the passages?"

There was annoyance in Saffi's voice when she answered back to him. "I told you," she said, "only my people know these tunnels, and there isn't anyone who knows them as well as Fergus here."

Simon was silent momentarily, and the group moved on.

"It's just—"

"Give it a rest, Adler," Merrick shouted back at him.

Simon shook his head in the darkness and looked behind him. "I'm not trying to annoy," he said.

"Then what is the point of your incessant questioning?" Merrick retorted.

Simon raised his voice, irritated by Merrick's rudeness. "I keep hearing something behind us," he said. "It's getting louder."

Fergus halted immediately. Saffi set down the lantern and turned her head abruptly. "Everyone be still!" she commanded.

A steady, almost machine-like hum sounded from somewhere in the darkness. The sound was, indeed, getting slowly louder. Ivy grabbed Simon's arm instinctively, and he heard Gilda Reed draw a sharp breath.

◆　　◆　　◆

"Move!" ordered Saffi. "As fast as you can."

As the group frantically began to move forward, Merrick breathed out, "I thought you said there was no one in here."

Saffi replied breathlessly, "There is nothing human in these tunnels."

"Then what is it?" yelled Burr.

Fergus grunted something unintelligible, and Saffi translated. "Ants."

"Ants?" Merrick choked out. "I don't think you have the right word. Do you expect me to believe that the loud grinding is a bunch of little bugs?"

"I mean for you to believe that an army of hungry, angry desert ants is almost upon us. It will consume anything in its sight, Mr. Mark."

"Merrick," the captain corrected, as he and the others began scrambling more frantically. "How much further?"

"Too far," Saffi barked. The impending hum was increasing in volume. She shouted something at Fergus, who answered her back in quick, strained tones.

Merrick's limbs ached with helpless dread. He focused on the lithe form before him and struggled to match her rapid pace. He glanced behind him momentarily. The others seemed to be keeping up, but he cursed himself for not taking up the rear.

Fergus and Saffi were engaged in a noisy argument. The insect hum was morphing into a roar.

They had just crawled past another tunnel on the right, when Fergus stopped. Saffi pointed at the opening and yelled, "Get in there, Simon. Everyone else follow." Ivy had only just entered the tunnel behind him when Merrick heard Simon shout back, "It's a dead end!"

"I know it is." Saffi's voice behind him was firm. "It will be close, but we must all fit in there. You'll have to sit, or kneel, but you can't stay on all fours."

John Merrick felt his chest constrict. There was more than one reason he had chosen a life at sea, and wide-open space was one of them. His stomach sunk at the thought of being trapped between people in that little space. He hesitated at the threshold. He turned to Saffi, expecting her to yell at him, but she simply looked into his eyes, placed her hands on his arms, and pushed him backward into the opening.

Merrick took deep breaths as Saffi backed into the passageway after him. He could see over her shoulder that Fergus followed. The roaring of the insects was nearing. Merrick could see a few straggling ants scatter around the edges of the passageway and scale the walls of their little hole. He began to feel the sting of bites on his ankles.

Then John Merrick witnessed two extraordinary things. The first was that Fergus, his hands at the tunnel's opening, was actually moving the sides of the tunnel in. The empty space began to slowly fill as the mud and stone stretched to close the opening. Then, quietly behind Merrick, Burr started to hum. The sound was low for a boy so young and the tune strange, but as he hummed the straggling ants in the tunnel began to retreat toward the remaining gap at the entrance. Merrick forgot his claustrophobia as he watched, amazed.

Suddenly, Saffi's lantern burned out. John Merrick held his breath. The collective thrum of thousands of moving insect legs and pincers was close in his ears. It was the only thing to hear, just feet away from where he was sitting. He could feel Burr behind him, struggling to be still. He could smell sweetness in Saffi's hair where it brushed against his nose and cheek.

Slowly, the thrum swelled and ebbed. It became a buzz, and then merely a distant humming once more.

John Merrick released his breath.

CHAPTER 31

Lord Abaddon sat in silence, clenching and unclenching his jaw. In all other appearances, he seemed perfectly calm as he glared over the shoulder of a small, gray-haired woman who seemed to be studying the smooth surface of the flat, dark stone she held.

Presently, she set the stone on her lap and shook her head. "Nothing."

Abaddon exhaled slowly through his teeth.

"Their location is hidden," the old woman continued as Abaddon walked around her chair and stood facing her. "I need more information if I am to trace them as far as Bellaria."

Abaddon bowed his head toward her in a slight gesture of respect, his face impassive. He turned and left the chamber, closing the door firmly behind him and striding confidently down a long, dimly lit corridor. His body felt warm with the anger that raged inside of him, and he allowed it to course through him, beginning in his chest and then spreading, oozing into his limbs, fingers, and toes.

He threw open the door to his private rooms and stood in the dark, cold chamber, not bothering to call for the fire to be lit. It had taken extreme self-control for him not to instruct his Shifter to slit Prince Oswald's throat. He knew he needed the corpulent imbecile in order to recapture that which had so quickly slipped through his fat fingers.

Abaddon was certain this ignorant group of travelers was no match for him—he had never had to worry about a *real* adversary. However, these escaped Stone Mages were a thorn in his side, one he could not remove, and the thought was maddening. *Someone will pay for this.* He rang for his man.

By the time the solemn-countenanced Wrake entered, Abaddon was sitting calmly in his large chair hidden in the shadows of the dark room.

The Wrake cleared his throat. "My Lord?"

"I want you to collect some qualified Wrakes, Shifters, and our friend in King Than's court and get to the Fringe."

The man started slightly. "But, sir," he stuttered, "the travelers are gone, and that doorway is useless to us."

Abaddon stood from his shadowy seat and then stepped back slightly. "Get to the Fringe," he said smoothly, "and kill the old man." His eyes glowed in the darkness. "Kill the gatekeeper."

◆　　◆　　◆

"What do you see?" Medwin's calm voice broke Laith's reverie.

He looked up from the wooden hand mirror he held, and shook his head, fingering Medwin's tradestone that hung around his neck.

"Only images. Bits and pieces of things."

"No clear scenes? No concrete moments with meanings?"

"No," Hastings sighed, frustrated. "Why don't you just tell me what I should be looking for? You might help me find what I need to see."

"I can't tell you what to see in that mirror, Laith. No two human beings, with or without sight, ever see the same thing in a mirror. It is reflective. Personal." He paused for a moment, thinking. "Tell me about the images."

"I see green on the hills outside the glass house; spring. I see a great dark ship being prepared for a long voyage. Mostly, I just see a woman, her face."

"You know this woman?"

"I don't recognize her. Her hair is dark, and her eyes are deep and sad. It was the eye I first saw in your stone that day in the hallway."

Medwin nodded. "It is her image that holds the greatest importance. We don't need a mirror to know spring is coming again to the Fringe. The ship may be significant to us in some way; but for now, Laith, just focus on her. Form a question about her in your mind that must be answered, then look."

"What question?"

"You must decide."

Dozens of questions flitted through Laith's mind. Who is she? Where is she? Why is she so sad? He closed his eyes. He thought of where these past few months had taken him. He never would have guessed when he boarded the *Sapphire* for another fishing voyage that he would have ended up here, knowing what and whom he now knew. He opened his eyes and looked in the mirror. *What does she have to do with me?* He wondered.

Again, Laith was looking at the dark-haired woman, but this time he could see her entire person. Her long hair fell over finely clad shoulders, and on her head she wore a silver circlet. *Princess.* He thought. *The other Princess. Mara.* She was looking down at the floor, and she was enveloped in shadow. Suddenly she looked up, and Laith looked straight into her dark, dull, melancholy eyes.

He dropped the mirror. It fell off his knee and crashed to the floor, breaking.

His head jerked toward Medwin, who stared back at him, eyebrows raised.

"What did you ask?" inquired the old man.

"Why she was important to me."

"And what did you see?"

"She is the Princess Mara."

"Oh," said Medwin. "Yes, I see."

The old man met his eyes momentarily, and Laith knew he understood. He shrugged. "Sorry about the mirror."

Medwin waved away the apology. "I've got a few others," he said.

·　　·　　·

King Than rolled out a large scroll on the wide table in front of him and glanced nervously over his shoulder. He scanned the rough paper with his index finger, searching the map before him with careful attention. After a few brief moments of rapt investigation, he angrily pushed the map aside. Its edges folded under, and the scroll rolled to the floor. He opened another map and repeated the same process.

The king's eyes were bloodshot and framed in dark circles of worry. His appearance was unkempt, and his hair disheveled. He pushed the last scroll aside and dropped his head into his hands.

King Than had known he was alone in the chamber and therefore nearly fell backward when he heard a movement behind him. There was a figure in the dark curtained alcove of his window seat. He gasped.

The figure moved slowly toward him, and as the light gradually illuminated its features, he began to recognize the face. His shoulders drooped.

"Mara," he sighed. "You startled me."

She moved from the alcove, and the light shone fully on her person. "Sorry, Father," she said, her eyes down.

"How long have you been there?" the king asked.

"Oh, I must have fallen asleep here earlier, waiting for you to come back. I've only just woken up."

The king nodded, glancing briefly at the scrolls. "I see."

Mara glanced at him momentarily and then looked away. "You seem out of sorts, Father. Are you well?"

"Well enough. A bit tired, I suppose."

She moved toward the decanter of brandy and a few glasses that stood on the table on the opposite wall. "Something to drink, Father?"

King Than slumped into one of two thick armchairs at his side. "Yes," he said, looking toward the dark alcove distractedly. "Thank you."

The princess was soon at his side, assuming the other armchair and handing him the glass. Her long dark hair hid her features from his view.

King Than realized he was rather shaky. He drained the glass. He closed his eyes and felt the liquid descend his throat.

"Better?" Mara's quiet voice asked at his side.

"Mmm."

The king started to feel a bit dizzy. He took deep breaths. His throat began to burn and his head ache. He opened his eyes and turned to his daughter. She was looking directly at him, her face a picture of curious fascination.

His throat began to constrict. His deep breaths became short and fast. Hazily, he noticed that his daughter's dark eyes were not now dark, but a sickly green. His eyes became wide. His hands moved to his throat.

"H-helpp me," he said to his staring child. An eerie smile spread over her usually melancholy features.

He shook his head disbelievingly and gasped for air. "N-not-t y-you?" He watched the triumphant features of the woman swim and swirl as he fell from his chair. He hit his head on the floor, and his body sprawled limp over the discarded maps.

The dark daughter sedately bent over the lifeless body. Her fingers found his neck. Determining there was no pulse in the prostrate king, Mara quietly stood and left the chamber.

CHAPTER 32

The remainder of the journey through the tunnels seemed a blur to Ivy. Her head was filled with stalking hoards of insects and humans who could mold earth and communicate with creatures. She was vaguely aware that the tunnels had become wider and taller as the group moved from hands and knees to feet. She hardly blinked when the group halted, their passageway dead-ending at a solid wall of mud.

She watched as Fergus laid his large hands on the muddy wall, willing it to recede from the top. The earth moved slowly this time, and Ivy suspected that the opening's size was less influential in the pace than Fergus's apparent weariness. She noticed Saffi place a supportive hand on his shoulder.

Ivy could not see beyond the opening as the group proceeded through it, her vision obscured by backs and heads and arms. But presently, the passageway opened out to a wide, flat precipice in front of her that circled an underground chamber of vast proportions. The ceiling was not tall, but their current path surrounded a hole that extended downward in the chamber. Ivy followed the others to the drop-off and looked down at a vast chasm extending into dark oblivion far below.

It was extraordinary. Built into the sides of the massive round pit below were dozens of torch-lit, cave-like dwelling places filled with people. The caves were of various sizes and connected by rough wooden bridges and rope ladders, which were traversed with ease by the inhabitants of the little underground city. There was a busy hum in the chamber, and the torchlight gave the place a glow that Ivy found a pleasant contrast to the dark dungeon and shadowy tunnels from which she had emerged.

The travelers stood in collective silence at the chasm's edge, and Ivy blinked in amazement. She began to notice a few upturned eyes and curious glances from some of the people nearer the top and realized that their entrance here, unlike in the White City, would not be ignored.

She gradually became aware of an animated foreign conversation behind her and turned, as did the others, to see Saffi speaking with a tall older man Ivy had not noticed before. Fergus said a few words to the man and then, with a nod at the travelers and a brief squeeze of Saffi's shoulder, mounted a ladder and disappeared over the edge. Ivy assumed he sought rest and realized how tired she was herself as Saffi approached with the tall man, who looked at them excitedly. She introduced him as Eben, Council Head.

"Welcome to our home," he said in rough but practiced Lyrian. He proceeded to grasp hands with every traveler in turn, inclining his head to each. When he came to Ivy, however, he bowed deeply and pressed his forehead to her outstretched hands. "Welcome," he said again.

This attitude of honor was not new to the Lyrian princess but surprised her in this strange and foreign place, and she wondered at the worshipful greeting. Confused, she nodded her head respectfully to Eben and said, "Thank you."

He rose, beaming, and then, bowing his head once more to the entire group, moved to descend the same ladder Fergus had taken. Saffi smiled at the group tiredly, beckoning them to follow her to the precipice's edge.

"What is this place?" Merrick asked her.

"The Pit," she said, extending her arms over the precipice in mock grandeur. Merrick merely stared at her.

She shrugged. "Sanctuary or Hell," she said, "you decide." Saffi turned to mount the ladder. "This way to food and rest," she called over her shoulder. The travelers followed without protest.

CHAPTER 33

It was raining at the Fringe, a heavy spring rain that darkened the skies and saturated the greening slopes. Medwin, sitting near his chamber window, watched the downpour and felt unusually weary. He endeavored to ignore the worn wooden mirror in his lap. He felt his eyes grow heavy, and he hungered for rest, the sound of the rain lulling him into sleep.

But a familiar tugging at the outskirts of his consciousness compelled him to open his eyes, raise the mirror, and look. He knew there was something that needed seeing.

A great, dark ship was leaving the Lyrian harbor at high speed. It cut smoothly through the stormy waters, undeterred by the howling wind and engorged waves.

On closer inspection, Medwin could see that the ship was well armored and bore the flag of the South. Strong Southern sailors moved with ease about the ship, and the upper deck was filled with a cluster of passengers, notwithstanding the driving rain. They all seemed to be watching the hooded figure at the ship's bow. The person was leaning forward at the prow, and Medwin would have mistaken it for a figurehead had he not seen the dramatic movement of its outstretched arms.

Medwin knew that this unearthly symphony conductor was a Wrake, and that its orchestra was wave and water. He knew that the ship's easy passage through impassible waters was not a result of muscular Southern arms, but of these small, lithe ones.

Somehow he also knew that the group of passengers on the deck was comprised of powerful Wrakes. He knew that only Abaddon could have sent them. He knew that they would be reaching their destination in half the time it would take a normal ship, and all at once he knew what that destination was.

Medwin's hand began shaking, and he put down his mirror. He stood from his comfortable chair, all thoughts of sleep abandoned. He hurried through the glass house, down the stairs, through the windowed corridor and into the library where Laith sat in his favorite chair at the fire.

"We've got trouble," Medwin announced as the fiery head turned at his entrance.

Laith straightened in his chair as Medwin hastily described his vision in the mirror. He watched the young man's brow furrow in confusion as he unfolded the image.

"How can you be sure they are coming here?" asked Laith, unconvinced. "What could they want with you?"

The old man shrugged, his weariness returning with more force. "You will learn, Laith, that while being a seer is a wonderful gift and a rare one—surely we are the only Lyrian Stone Mages who possess it—it makes us a sought-after lot. Why else would I choose to live at the Fringe? We see things, and others often want access to what we can see, or seek revenge for what our sight may have cost them."

"They know you aided the princess?"

"Perhaps. We can be sure, however, that they mean us only ill."

"What can we do?"

Medwin stood from his chair. "Come," he said, turning to leave the library, "your training just became much more imperative, and we have very little time."

CHAPTER 34

John Merrick's dreams faded, and he felt rested and content as he lay in his ship's hammock. He was vaguely aware that the familiar lull of the *Sapphire*'s rocking was absent and wondered if the crew had made port without his command. He sat up abruptly and opened his eyes.

He was in a small earthen chamber barely large enough for the hammock he had slept in. The only other item in the room, an extinguished candle, sat in a carved-out shelf in the wall next to him. Light gleamed around the edges of the thick cloth that acted as door to the little room. Merrick exhaled deeply, remembering his current situation all at once. He stood and pushed aside the cloth.

He stepped into a large circular room lined on one half by other cloth-draped doorways. He gazed across this larger chamber and saw that it was open to the massive main pit of the underground city. In the center of the room was a large stone table surrounded by at least ten stone seats. His group had been led directly here last night, and Merrick recalled a hasty meal of dried meat and hard bread before being directed to his sleeping chamber.

It was impossible to tell the hour without sky or sun, but the lit chamber and general noise issuing from the outer pit indicated that waking hours had arrived.

He made his way to one of the chairs as Simon emerged from the chamber adjacent his. The youth's blond hair stood out in all directions as he mumbled "Morning?" and seated himself next to Merrick.

The young girl of about twelve or thirteen who had served them the night before entered through the passageway, carrying a tray with stone mugs on it. She was followed by an alert-looking Gilda Reed and Princess Ivy, who stifled a laugh when she caught sight of Simon's hair.

The four at the table had begun drinking the warm, sweet liquid when Saffi Beval entered with her usual confidence, followed closely by Eben from the previous night, Fergus, and a very old woman with white hair and an intelligent smile. Saffi introduced the woman as Beathas and indicated that this group made up the council. Saffi and Fergus were seated, and the other two bowed a warm welcome to the guests.

After a short debate about who should have to wake Burr, which Gilda lost, the boy came stumbling and swearing from his sleeping chamber and then sat at the table, hastily devouring the porridge and hard bread placed before him.

The food was tasteless but satisfying, and soon, as the serving girl was clearing away the dishes, Eben spoke. Saffi translated for him.

"Eben wishes to again offer you humble welcome to our community." Merrick smiled as Saffi uttered the kind words, her voice devoid of any trace of humility. Eben continued to speak while she translated. "He, with the rest of us, is wondering what reason you have for coming at this time."

Merrick would normally have answered for the group, but it was obvious that the question was directed to the princess. She, noticing their gaze, glanced briefly at her companions before clearing her throat and offering an answer.

"Your people are obviously aware of Lyria. Miss Beval even speaks our language. I am not sure, however, what you know about us and what you do not."

Saffi translated, but Eben and the others offered no reply, so Ivy continued. She told them of the Southern threat and the removal of her people to the hills. She explained how her father had turned traitor to his people and how it was only a matter of time before they came completely under the dominion of the South and Abaddon. She explained her capture, the rescue that her companions attempted, and of the training and guidance they had received by Medwin. She told of how she had opened the doorway and of the strange welcome they had received in the White City, of their meeting with Prince Oswald, and finally their imprisonment.

The council at the table listened quietly and with interest. They did not interrupt but exchanged meaningful glances at the mention of Abaddon's name and of the doorway at the Fringe.

Ivy glanced toward the others at the finish of her speech. "We have come here to ask for your aid," she said. "It is apparent that the ways of the elements and the power of stones are not new to you. We are hoping that with your help, we can regain our stones, open another doorway, return to Lyria, and with the power of many Stone Mages at our aid, defeat Abaddon and his warriors."

There was silence after this speech, and Merrick noted a defeated look in the eyes of the council members. Saffi shook her head.

"We can't help you," she said. She did not look pleased to deliver such an edict, but something about the automatic rejection in her tone touched a nerve in John Merrick.

"You mean you won't help us," he said, eyes boring into hers as she turned to his rebuttal.

Her eyes flashed, but her voice remained calm. "No," she said, "I mean we can't. We are Stone Mages here, and many of us are powerful, but none of us bears the gift of the clear stone. No one here has power over space. If the princess is the only such Mage you have among you, then you have no way of opening a door and are stuck here."

Merrick blinked, shocked, and Ivy's head fell into her hands.

"Not necessarily." It was the old woman, Beathas, who had spoken. Her voice was soft, but her Lyrian was unmistakable. She said something in Bellarian, and the others looked at her confused. "There may be a way," she said to the travelers.

Beathas turned to the young woman at her side. "Saffi," she said, "tell our guests our history. Then I will be able to explain my idea."

•　　•　　•

"What are we doing in here?" Laith looked around the familiar mirror room, annoyed. "Seeing is not going to keep that ship of killers from our shores. If your plan is in this room, I hope you'll forgive me when I ask where you keep the swords."

"I will explain, Duke Patience," Medwin said, leading Laith to the center of the room. Endless reflections greeted the men, all at different angles and vantages but all basic depictions of a gray old man and a redheaded youth. "What do you see?" the old man asked.

"Us," Laith replied dully.

"Ah, yes, Laith." Medwin began circling Laith as he spoke. "Your mind tells you that you see a wilted old man and a fiery youth in those mirrors. But is that really us, or just a replication? Is what you are seeing in each mirror an accurate representation, or are some skewed, stretched, or disproportioned?

Laith shrugged.

"One ability a seer may develop is that of illusion, or placing before the eyes of others thwarted truths, making things appear different than they really are."

Laith continued to stare quizzically at the man. "I thought our gifts were to use the elements, not change them. What you are describing sounds unnatural."

"Not necessarily," Medwin replied. "Nature has long been deceiving our eyes. Have you never seen a puddle of water on the dusty road ahead of you when the sun is hot and then discovered as you approached that it was merely a mirage? Have you ever picked up what you were sure was a small stick, only to watch with wonder as it crawled off your hand? Even nature thwarts our reflection as we see ourselves in the surface of a still pond. Why does it not follow that we could do the same?"

Laith nodded slowly.

"Let me illustrate," said Medwin. He moved closer to the table in the middle of the room and put his hand over it. Laith watched as the table slowly stretched and grew outward, seeming to fill the room. He blinked. Medwin dropped his hands, and the table was suddenly its normal size again.

"Hmm," Laith replied, eyebrows raised. "So how is this going to help us beat the enemy?"

Medwin smiled. "The shoal at the Fringe is a treacherous one. But Wrakes with water gifts could likely navigate safely through it. We cannot physically put a rock in their path, but we might be able to trick them into thinking one is there with our powers of sight."

"Okay, fair enough," Laith sighed. "But I'll still be brushing up on my swordplay if you don't mind."

"Fair enough," repeated Medwin. "But this training begins

immediately. I can perform illusion but cannot sustain it long on my own. I will need your help."

Laith nodded again.

Medwin reached into the folds of his clothing and pulled forth something that he kept clasped in his hand. "I also have been meaning to give you something," he said. Laith held out his hand, but Medwin's fist remained closed. "It belonged to my wife," he whispered.

Laith withdrew his hand. He had never imagined that Medwin would have had love and a life other than this lonely one at the Fringe. He cocked his head to observe the man he thought he knew so well.

"It should be passed to my child," Medwin said, looking slowly up to meet Laith's gaze. "But since I never reproduced, I suppose you'll do. It's such a strange coincidence that you came to be here to receive it." The old man smiled and opened his fist, holding his hand out toward the young man.

Laith reached out slowly and lifted the gold chain, a reflective stone dangling from its links. He drew in his breath sharply and then exhaled as he draped the stone of power over his neck.

•   •   •

"The use of elemental gifts in Bellaria is ancient," Saffi began. "From the beginning of our recorded history, people knew of their gifts and learned to use them for good. Those with elemental gifts became the royal family—nobility, really—and were placed in a position of power. Their role was not to dominate but to protect the people under their stewardship. It is likely that the earliest knowledge of mines and stones of power also originated in Bellaria. Indeed, here, where you stand, a great deposit of stones of power was extensively mined but kept a secret from all but a few Stone Mages and ruling nobles.

"It was not long after the mine's discovery that those with the power of space began to realize that the stones increased their ability not only to move within Bellaria, but to move outside of it as well. Our nobles began to travel to other places, Lyria among them, helping others to discover their elemental gifts and sharing the knowledge of stones with the worthy leaders they encountered.

"Of course, there were some who abused that knowledge, discarding stones that worked in harmony with the elements, and using their powers in evil, unnatural ways. As evil and distrust grew, travel between lands diminished, and our Bellarian Stone Mages chose to close doorways and discontinue the intercourse they once held with many worlds, where magical knowledge became secret and scarce.

"For many, many years, life for Bellaria went on as normal, with the Bellarian Stone Mages quietly practicing their powers in their own closed-off kingdom. And then around thirty years ago, one of our nobles, a distant cousin without direct access to the throne, became hungry for power. He was one of the rare few with the power of space, and he began to learn of dark magic ways, gathering many followers in secret. His plan was to get the throne by marrying the crown princess, who was the only child of the current king and queen. She, however, saw through this charming front to his dark heart and refused him, choosing instead another noble whom she loved and trusted. He was an upright and honorable Mage who mined the stones of power.

"Angry and defeated, the cousin continued to rally people to his dark cause. One night they carried out an attack on the palace. The cousin moved in first, killing the king and queen in their beds. He then proceeded to the princess and killed her. But in doing so, he woke her husband, Antoine Beval, who fled with their baby daughter to warn the rest of the nobles." Saffi paused here to let the impact of her words sink in.

"Antoine led them to an escape through the secret underground tunnels that led to the mine." Saffi held out her hand to the space behind her, which opened out into the great pit.

"The nobles were safe underground," she continued, "but knew that execution awaited if they resurfaced. The cousin, whom you know as Abaddon, took control of Bellaria. He destroyed the royal city and built up the White City in its place."

Saffi held up her right hand. A perfect circle was imprinted on the flesh of her palm. "It was ancient tradition for Bellarian nobles to wear a mark on their palms—made at birth as a symbol of our commitment to use our gifts to serve the people—and that mark became our identifying brand. Anyone appearing at the gates of the White City with the royal mark was killed, and regular sweeps of the streets were made to catch anyone else loyal to us—even our young children who bear no mark.

"So our people have remained hidden, only surfacing through the tunnels to steal supplies and food. We have become great thieves. There are a few citizens of the White City who are still loyal to us and who act as spies or give us aid; but most are either afraid of being put to death or are charmed by Abaddon and are happy to forget us.

"Not long after our displacement, Abaddon felt satisfied that we were sufficiently defeated and thus placed Oswald, one of his pawns, in control of the city. He then forced an imprisoned Space Mage to open an old doorway for him, and he left with some of his most powerful Wrakes to Lyria, his next planned conquest.

"When I was a young girl, one of our spies in the city spotted a small group of foreigners and passed word of their arrival to my father, who was able to find them and bring them here before they were captured by Oswald and his men. The foreigners were Lyrians. Some of our royals had continued to learn and speak Lyrian in case our contact with your people renewed some day, but we were surprised to see them in our lifetime.

"They were three women, Stone Mages and sisters, who were among the few left in Lyria to hold knowledge of the past. They had journeyed to a Lyrian outpost, searching for a man of wisdom—a seer—said to possess the ability to advise and aid them against the increasing threat posed by Abaddon and his forces. The seer told them that he had seen my father in a mirror vision and knew that he was a good man who might lead his people to help them. These women, all mages with power of space, then opened the doorway here.

"We welcomed them and agreed to assist them. If these women would open another doorway and allow all of us to follow them back to Lyria, we would help them defeat our common enemy and in return they promised us lands and a new life above ground.

"The women found a place far out in the desert, away from the White City, and began the work of forging a new doorway. They worked at night, using the darkness for cover, and were always accompanied by my father and a few other strong Mages for protection. The process took weeks, and while they stayed here we grew to love and respect these women; our community was full of hope for a new future.

"One night, however, on return to the site of the doorway, these women and the men protecting them, including my father, were met by Oswald and an army of men—all Wrakes and warriors. They revealed that Abaddon's seer had apprised them of our activities and Abaddon had ordered them to put an end to our plan. They killed the three women and their protectors. My father was the only survivor; he fled the onslaught to bring us the dreadful news, his wounds so severe that he died only a few months later.

"We have remained here since, in our underground prison, rarely seeing the light of day. One of the Lyrian women, the most important and powerful, had mentioned a daughter to us. This woman had left her deceased father's stone with that daughter, in hopes that her daughter would learn to use it if the need arose. We have hoped through these years that she would return, with others, to complete the task left unfinished and deliver us. Imagine our excitement when that daughter appeared with companions. We are only sorry she did not bring other Space Mages with her." As Saffi spoke the last words, she was focused on the face of the princess, who became very pale.

"You cannot mean me," Ivy whispered. "My mother was captured and killed at sea when I was a young girl."

Saffi smiled sadly at her. "No, Princess," she said. "It would take more than that to kill a woman as great as Queen Cora. Your mother died here, fighting to save us and all of Lyria. You look just like her."

Tears sprang to Princess Ivy's eyes, and she looked down at the table, watching its surface blur, as her eyes became pools of salty liquid. Although Ivy's mother had passed away when she was only five, there remained in her consciousness a few very clear images of that face, framed by soft, light hair. These images swam through Ivy's mind as tears fell freely to the table.

After many moments of warm silence, Ivy heard Beathas speaking. "I believe," she said, "that there may be a way to finish the work your mother began years ago, Princess."

Ivy caught tears with a soft handkerchief that Simon had gently placed in her hand, and looked up at the gray-haired woman.

"It is true," Beathas began, "that the task of creating a doorway has never been accomplished by the power of one Stone Mage alone.

However, we don't know if . . . that is . . . if it may be possible for someone with the power of space to finish a door already begun. Your mother and aunts began a fissure in space years ago that still remains—nothing could undo their work, although it was halted before its completion. We believe that they were close to finishing. It might, perhaps, be possible for you to finish what they began."

Silence again reigned at the table after this speech. Ivy stared back at the stone table thoughtfully, fingering the edges of the handkerchief she held. Saffi mumbled a brief explanation of Beathas's Lyrian to Fergus and Eben, her brow furrowed. Eben looked thoughtful for a moment, then nodded, but Fergus's eyes were dark and doubtful. He spoke roughly as Saffi translated.

"Fergus says that the risk is too great. Oswald and his minions know where that doorway is located and might be more likely to watch it now that he has seen these Lyrians. He says that we have no way of knowing if the task is possible, but we do know that it is dangerous. We cannot afford to lose more people in this attempt. There are few of us left, as it is, and they should not be forced to do this."

John Merrick laid his large hand forcefully on the table. "What alternatives are there?"

He spoke to Fergus as Saffi translated. "Do you have a better idea, or do you mean to continue hiding underground forever?"

Fergus stared back at Merrick before replying.

Saffi spoke, "He says, he merely thinks we should take some time, think things out, and consider other options."

Ivy spoke, her voice quiet but strong. "I understand that you have lost people before, and that your chief concern is for survival," she said, looking at Fergus and the other Bellarians, "but, the time you speak of taking is time we do not have. Our kingdom will be overrun by Abaddon and his warriors any day, perhaps it has begun already, and when that happens, our people will be destroyed, or made slaves, or worse. I will attempt to finish the work my mother began, and it would do us great honor if you would help us. If you do, we can promise you a free life above ground in Lyria. If you choose not to help, we will do the best we can on our own."

Beathas smiled warmly at Ivy. "You *are* your mother's child after all. Of course we'll help you." The old woman repeated her sentiment in Bellarian. Eben nodded in agreement, but Fergus shook his head and spoke again.

Saffi translated, "We might help you, but we cannot open that door, and you cannot do it without a stone."

Saffi inclined her head to Ivy. "He's right," she said, "we're going to have to get your stones back from *reyne morel.*"

"Who?" asked Gilda.

Saffi looked at her. "It means 'prince swine.'" Burr laughed.

Simon looked lost in thought. "I thought you said that this was a mine, here," he said. "Can we not just locate new stones?"

"Yeah," Merrick said, nudging Saffi, "or are you out of Rock Mages as well?"

"This is a mine, Simon," Saffi replied, completely ignoring Merrick. "A few of us have the gift of stones. I am one, but it is a long process to locate, mine, and cut a stone. By the time we replaced what you had lost, your kingdom would be destroyed. We will have to steal them back."

Fergus shook his head again, and spoke with translation, "*You* will have to steal them back. If you can show us you can retrieve your stones, using the raw power of your gifts with all the limitations involved, then the people here will *want* to follow you."

"Okay," said Ivy. "Let's make a plan."

CHAPTER 35

Sweat dripped from Laith Haverford's forehead as he focused his entire attention on the little daisy in a vase on a small table in the library. He memorized its every curve and inflection of color. He took in the smooth surface of the white vase and the gradual undulation of the flower's stem. He closed his eyes, holding the image there as he slowly turned to face the fireplace.

He opened his eyes and endeavored to picture the daisy on the mantle. He forced himself to picture its position, the way the light would fall on it. He strained his eyes. His face was red with heat. His head was pounding. Again, the flower did not appear.

The heat welled up inside Laith's chest. He roared angrily and flailed his strong arm at the flower on the table, sending the vase crashing to the floor. "It's no use," he growled.

Medwin did not stir from his armchair at the side of the room. "You've got to quit breaking my things," he said simply, almost cheerfully.

Laith roared again. "I've been at this for hours, days. I'm just not strong enough. We're going to have to hide you, and I'll face them as best I can with the sword. This just won't work."

"It will. Keep practicing."

Laith turned to face the old man, fists clenched and eyes blazing. "No. My mind just doesn't work that way. The flower is not on the mantle, and it is not in me to make it appear there. I can't create this kind of deception. I'm through."

He made for the door, but Medwin stopped him, moving from his chair with surprising speed and grasping Laith's arm. The old man looked him straight in the eye, and Laith saw a rare fire in the stare. "Don't you dare tell me, Laith, that deception is beyond you. I will not accept that from a boy who has spent half his life convincing hoards of people that the son of a duke was nothing but a common sailor. You imbibed fraud daily, and you did it to run away from your problems. Don't have the gall to give up, to be so easy on yourself. You are a master at creating illusion, and now finally you have the chance to use it for good. Now is the time for you to stop being weak, to face your problems and persevere." Medwin grabbed the front of Laith's tunic and pulled him forward forcefully, their noses almost touching. "Be a man."

Medwin released his hand and moved slowly back to his armchair. Laith's heart was pounding in his chest as he watched the old man retreat. Laith noticed that Medwin's face was every bit as red as his own, and also observed for the first time tiny flecks of red in the man's beard. The youth unclenched his fists.

He reached down at his side and unsheathed the sword he had begun carrying with him at all times. It was not the most ornate sword in Medwin's odd collection, but it was certainly the sturdiest. Laith had cleaned it and sharpened it thoroughly. He held the thick blade in front of him, continuing to stare into the old man's eyes.

Medwin stood, one arm resting on the armchair, and stared back. He raised an eyebrow.

For a moment the two men just stood there, eye to eye, and then Laith turned and placed the sword on the table where the flower had been. He sighed. "All right," he said, his voice even and low, "but no *man* should have a flower on his mantle. Let's try for the sword."

CHAPTER 36

Ivy sat in the dark dining chamber overlooking the pit. She wound a curled strand of hair around her finger, absentmindedly observing the interactions and movements of the people in the caves and on the bridges and ladders of the mine.

In one chamber opposite hers, she could see Simon and Burr. Simon was teaching the boy to juggle balls of string and having little success.

In another chamber, a young mother was grinding some kind of grain on a slightly concave stone, her young daughter kneeling close by. She watched the mother hand the pestle to her daughter and guide the girl's movements. Something about the little scene struck Ivy. The mother's movements were patient and gentle. The daughter was concentrated and eager to please.

Ivy had a mental picture of herself as a young princess—about the age of the girl at the pestle—running down the vast corridor in the Lyrian castle. She held a fistful of new daffodils she had picked for her mother, and she looked over her shoulder periodically, anxious to escape the angry gardener. She pushed her messy curls from her face with her free hand as she ran, her new blue dress now coated in fresh brown mud. When she burst into the library, her mother looked up, that soft hair falling on her shoulders, and laughed. She swatted Ivy playfully and swung her up into an embrace.

Ivy sighed at the memory. Meeting these people who had known and respected her mother opened fresh recollections, and Ivy wondered anew about the woman who had given her life. The details she had received this very morning about the actual final days of her mother's life had answered questions—and posed new ones.

New movement in another, opposite chamber caught Ivy's attention. The chamber was actually more of a long storage passageway, lined with boxes and miscellaneous items. Saffi Beval had just entered, followed closely by John Merrick. The young woman began rifling through one of the boxes, pulling out haggard pieces of clothing. Merrick had taken on a role in the plan to retrieve the stones that required him to become a *Pelasar,* or pit dweller. Saffi stood and began holding up different garments to his frame, obviously searching for the most credible attire. The items in her hand were too slight for his broad shoulders. She tossed them aside and returned to the boxes.

Merrick was talking to Saffi, and both had their backs turned to Ivy, who was lost in thought, wondering what the captain might be saying to her and what, if any, were her replies.

"She'll have quite a task, trying to fit anything to that man," came a voice behind Ivy, who turned to see Gilda Reed standing behind her in the dark.

"How long have you been there?" she stuttered. She could see Gilda smile in the darkness.

"Just a minute or so." The older woman came to stand by the younger and they quietly observed the pair opposite them. Merrick had moved closer to Saffi, hovering over her, so that when she stood again, arms full, she bumped into him. She pushed him back, annoyed. He smiled at her provokingly as he tried to regain his balance.

"He seems to fall all over himself when he's around her," Ivy observed quietly.

Gilda Reed chuckled. "Yes," she said, "she has certainly made an impression."

Merrick's arms were raised as Saffi held up a rough brown jacket to the captain's frame. The two were standing very close.

"He is a wandering sailor," Gilda continued, "and she seems to be something of a true north."

"Yes." Ivy's voice betrayed a small sound of bitterness, and she restrained herself from speaking more. Across the way, Merrick had spoken again to Saffi, who started angrily at his comment, shoved the clothes in to his chest, and left the corridor. He followed her out, and the room was again dark and empty.

Ivy turned to Gilda. "Are you ready for tomorrow?" she asked, conversationally.

"I suppose so. I feel I won't be much help without my stone, but Fergus, who also wears an emerald, you know, has been showing me a few things that I can do without it."

Ivy nodded. "I wish I could come and help. How can I prove myself to these people if I am not with you?"

Gilda placed a hand on her shoulder briefly. "You'll get your chance," she replied, turning to leave the chamber.

When she was at the threshold, she turned back momentarily. "You are also a true north, Princess," she said kindly. She turned again to leave. "Just not his."

Ivy sat in the chamber a while longer, eyes closed, thinking. She could hear laughter, and opened her eyes to glance once more at the pair of jugglers across the way, their faces lit up in shared mirth. Watching them, she smiled.

•   •   •

Saffi walked quickly through the dark tunnel leading up from the mine. She knew this tunnel well, for she often went down to the mine to be alone. Today, however, she had gone down into the lower regions of the pit not for solitude but to retrieve a certain object.

It felt heavy in her hand, and holding it made her stomach sink. She hated this long piece of metal and had long ago wished to dispose of it. She now loathed having to dig it up and put it to use.

The tunnel came to an opening, from which she emerged before climbing a nearby ladder with her free hand and ascending to the chamber where she knew John Merrick was waiting for her.

She pictured his tanned, bearded face, his mouth curled up in that infuriating smile. She was puzzled about this arrogant man—a strange combination of stubborn selfishness and bravery. She could not help but feel admiration for his willingness to undertake this dangerous task but was simultaneously annoyed at his insistence that it be his.

She reached the room and pushed aside the door cloth to enter. She blinked. The John Merrick that stood waiting for her was hardly recognizable as the man she had talked with only this morning. He was wearing the rough clothing she had found for him. His sun-tanned face was clean-shaven, and his dark hair was trimmed quite short. *He looks like a Pelasar,* she thought, *a* handsome *Pelasar.* She wrinkled her nose.

"What do you think?" Merrick asked, holding out his arms.

Saffi nodded at the jacket. "It's a bit short in the arms, but I suppose it will do."

There was a quiet moment between them, and Saffi noticed that Merrick's gaze had turned to the object in her hand. "That it?" he asked, quietly.

"Yes." Saffi bit her lip. "You don't have to do this."

Merrick shrugged casually, but Saffi noticed that his eyes were serious. "I do," he said. "You said yourself that the only time Oswald is guaranteed to leave his palace is for a hanging. He only rarely attends the sweeps of the city. He won't hang a Lyrian; he'd want to keep us like a prize for Abaddon. And a real Pelasar man should not be asked to do our dirty work for us.

"Besides," he continued, in a lighter tone, "I've been practicing all afternoon." He glanced at a pitcher of water and cup on the table behind him. "The fire's hot."

Saffi turned to look into the little fireplace. The flame was getting low, and the coals were glowing red. She swallowed. She inserted the hated metal brand, crest down, into the hot coals.

"Sit down," she commanded. Merrick obeyed, and Saffi drew another chair adjacent his so that she was facing him. She drew the tray of items she had prepared close to her and dipped the cloth into the cleansing liquid in a little bowl. She took his right hand—a large, rough hand—in hers, palm up.

"Sailor's hands," he said unapologetically.

Saffi began washing the hand with the cloth. "Why did you choose sailing?" she asked, wanting to take his mind off the impending task.

"Don't know. I guess I always loved water, obviously, but I also just wanted to be away," Merrick said thoughtfully.

"Was there never a wife or children to await your return?"

"No family at all," Merrick replied matter-of-factly. He shifted in his chair. "My hand is clean," he said. "Let's get on with it."

Saffi released his hand and looked nervously at the fire. Merrick watched her carefully.

"If you're not up to the task," he said, "you might as well go get a man to do it."

Saffi flashed him an indignant look.

"I don't want you fainting on me," he said.

Saffi angrily stood from her chair and removed the brand from the fire, the circular tip now glowing red.

Merrick took a long swig from the bottle sitting on the tray, and then, flashing Saffi that provoking smile and holding out his right hand, said, "Do your worst."

CHAPTER 37

Simon's muscles murmured complaints leftover from his last journey through the tunnels as he ascended the ladder to the uppermost level of the pit. He frowned slightly when he thought of entering the tunnels again but did not hesitate as he pulled himself over the edge of the precipice and stood where he had that night when they first entered the mine.

He looked back down into the pit. The morning lamps were just being lit, and people were coming to the openings at the pit's edge, quietly preparing to watch the departure.

Simon turned again and walked over to join the gathering group. Most of the people were already there. John Merrick stood to one side of the group, looking very much like a Pelasar and donning his unmistakable no-nonsense demeanor. He would be the first to go—alone.

Burr stood nearby with two other Bellarians Simon vaguely recognized. Like Burr, these men also had the gift of animals and had volunteered to help the boy. Simon had been amazed at the number of Pelasars who had volunteered and began to think that Fergus was wise to create a circumstance for the people to choose to follow the Lyrians rather than being forced to. These particular men seemed to be impressed by Burr's youth and the strength of his skill even without a stone. The three of them were dressed in dark robes like those worn by the people in the White City. Burr's hair was standing on end, and his usual morning countenance deterred anyone from making conversation with him.

Simon moved toward Saffi, Fergus, and another Pelasar woman. He would join them on this morning's mission. Gilda Reed had just emerged from the pit and moved to join them as well. She nodded a "good morning" to Simon, which he returned.

Simon saw all of these people, but his attention—and eyes— focused on the princess. He knew Ivy must remain in the pit. But here she was, moving among the people, wishing them well. She had pulled away from the group now and was standing alone. She caught Simon's eye and held it. In that look, Simon recognized a familiar disappointment. He knew exactly what Ivy was feeling, and all the memories of sending Roger and his father off flooded back, the helplessness in which he watched them go, and the frustration at not being able to help.

She began walking toward him, and he watched her, trying to form in his mind something he could say to bring her comfort and reassurance, something eloquent and understanding, but as she drew near, he heard himself blurt out, "You wish you could go."

Ivy's face fell, and she nodded. "I should be helping."

Simon stepped closer to her so that only she could hear him when he spoke. "When the South invaded, my father and older brother were among those who took up arms to fight for their lands. I wanted nothing more than to stand with them but was forced to lead my family though the pass and into the hills. The day they stood to fight, I ran away."

"You had no choice. You were protecting your family."

Simon nodded. "Part of me knows that, but the other part of me wonders if I did have a choice. My brother died in that fight, and my father was injured. I felt guilty for being alive and healthy after that."

Ivy's expression communicated understanding.

Simon continued, "Who knows, princess. Maybe today I will be able to do something important, something no one else could do, to help our kingdom and these people. Because my brother fought and died for me I can live to do this today. Surely because we go for you today, you will be able to do something more for us tomorrow."

Ivy nodded, slowly, and looked away toward the others. "Thank you, Simon," she said.

She turned to look at him again, intensely. "Please come safely back," she said, then blushed for some reason. "All of you, I mean." She looked toward Burr. "I worry for Burr. He's young, and won't even be able to communicate with those two."

Simon nodded, gravely. "Yes," he said solemnly. "Unfortunately, they will be unable to hear his fascinating life story as they travel."

Ivy smiled.

Simon was encouraged. "I suppose the real worry will be that he'll teach them *his* version of Lyrian."

This time Ivy laughed, and Simon reveled that he was the cause of such a magnificent thing.

CHAPTER 38

Someone was shaking Laith Haverford, vigorously. He pushed the man off of him and sat up in bed.

"Get up," Medwin commanded. "It's time."

Laith threw off the covers, sheathed his sword, and shouldered his dark cloak as he ran after Medwin through the hall of the glass house and out into the cool night.

The moon was full, offering a clear view of the approaching vessel out beyond the shoal. Medwin led Laith down the mossy slope, sticking to the shadows of the cliffs for cover. He had repeatedly impressed upon the young man the importance of concealment. Their known presence would compromise the effectiveness of their illusion.

They stationed themselves behind a long, low rock and peered out across the tempestuous cove. Medwin nodded toward a large stone jutting from a nearby wave crest.

"That is our illusion," he whispered. "Study it."

Laith breathed deeply and focused all his powers of observation on that stone, its shape, and the way the waves moved about it.

Just as Laith began to feel he had mastered the details, Medwin gasped. Laith looked to the distant vessel and immediately understood what had caused the old man alarm. There were two long boats being lowered from the ship. They had planned on one boat, one illusion, and one success. There was no way they could sink two.

"Will we both have to create a stone?" Laith whispered.

Medwin shook his head. "Impossible. We will just have to target the boat that poses the greatest threat and hope the sea deals with the other."

The lantern-lit long boats inched closer, one slightly ahead of the other. Laith began to distinguish a form at the head of the first boat, standing with hands extended.

"There," Medwin pointed. "That person is the Water Wrake. He will be doing the navigating. It is that boat we will focus on."

The boats crept forward, and Laith found that he was sweating in spite of the cool breeze ruffling his red hair.

"Now," whispered the old man, "I'll begin."

Laith watched the sea, eyes peeled, and began to see their stone take form in the water, directly in the path of the first boat but far enough from its sight not to draw attention. It was situated as they had planned, between two swells. These swells indicated that other dangers lurked nearby and would likely cause damage to the boat when it turned away from the illusion. The outline began to solidify, and Laith watched as the image became firm. He took another deep breath and extended his arm slightly, adding his focus to the image, reinforcing its presence into the sea.

Laith was soon aware that the first long boat was coming in sight of the rock, and that the other had fallen directly behind the first. The Wrake in the first boat was moving his arms back and forth when the wind swelled and the hood fell from his head, revealing long dark hair. The Water Wrake was a woman. The young man started, and for a moment the illusion shimmered.

"Focus," urged Medwin between clenched teeth, and Laith renewed his focus on the stone.

The boats had entered the roughest waters. Laith could hear the shouting of the rowers, and he became aware of the frantic movements of the boat's passengers. The Water Wrake, however, remained at her post. As they neared the illusion, an outcry came from the first boat. The rowers moved frantically, and the boat began to shift course slightly.

Laith smiled, hoping their plan would work, that they would hit a real rock as they steered away from the illusion. His head was pounding with the strain of maintaining the deception, and his hands began to tingle.

Suddenly, a loud shriek pierced the night air. The Water Wrake had lowered her arms and was screaming a horrid song at the sea. The waters swelled under the long boat, carrying it, last minute, from the path of an underlying crag—a real one. Her motion saved the bottom of the boat but caused it to capsize. Laith held his breath, watching as the inhabitants of the little vessel disappeared beneath the dark water.

The second boat, catching sight of the illusion, turned quickly the other direction, and Laith heard the tearing of wood on stone and the screams issuing from the inhabitants of the now destroyed second vessel. Next to Laith, Medwin dropped to the ground limply. The illusion vanished.

Laith, dizzy and exhausted, moved to aid the old man, but Medwin raised a hand. "Watch the surface," he rasped.

Laith's hand suddenly moved to the hilt of his sword. Obviously he and the others had survived this shoal, couldn't these Wrakes as well? He peered again over their rock to examine the surface of the water and the rising of the waves. He could see the capsized vessel and identify floating bits of the ruined one. No human forms were readily visible. His eyes darted back and forth across the shoal.

He paused abruptly and clenched his sword. There, less than fifty yards distant, were two swimmers. Laith swallowed hard.

"Medwin," he whispered violently, "run! You've got to get back to the house, hide, anything. There are two who might make it to shore."

The old man shook his head and began to get to his feet shakily. He drew a sword Laith was surprised to see at his side.

Laith had intended to argue, when out of the corner of his eye, he saw two figures emerging from the crashing waves, moving closer. The first, a great hulking figure, found his hands and feet and began climbing over the rocks directly toward where they were standing.

Behind him, the other figure appeared, dark hair plastered to her face, a heavy torn cloak skirting the water around her. The Water Wrake crawled from the waves, undeterred by the jagged path before her, and pushed back the straggling strands of her wet hair. The moonlight illuminated her features as she stared up toward Laith, and the young man choked in recognition. It was Mara, Princess of Lyria.

CHAPTER 39

John Merrick took one final look at the roughly drawn map of the tunnels on his scrap of parchment and then at the opening directly above his head. Setting down his lantern, he stood and gently pushed at the smooth stone that perfectly fit the opening. He felt it move upward and quickly extinguished the lamp, then tore the map into tiny bits which fell and scattered on the floor of the passage. Carefully, he pressed the stone up a little farther and peeked out.

The room into which he looked was dark and quiet. He slid the stone away from the opening completely and pulled himself up into the room. He then gradually pressed the stone back into place and brushed dust around the edges to conceal its presence.

Around him, he could see the dim outlines of wine kegs. He ran his hands over them, feeling his way to the narrow stairway on the far wall. He ascended the stairs and pressed his ear to the door at the top, listening carefully for a few minutes before turning the knob and opening it. He found himself in a pub kitchen, strangely tidy, and currently empty.

He stood outside the door for a moment, watching the swinging door that led to what Merrick assumed was the dining room, and waiting for someone to come in and discover him. When no one did, he moved to the door and peeked through a crack in the doorway. The customers of the pub sat at long tables in a dimly lit room. They were robed in their white, gray, and black robes and made very little conversation with each other.

Merrick moved back into the room, snatching a loaf of bread from a shelf full of them and biting off the end. Still, no one came into the kitchen. He was pondering whether or not to take a ladle from the low countertop and swing it across a hanging rack of pans, when a short, gray-robed woman pushed through the swinging door. She halted when she saw Merrick and dropped the tray of cups she was carrying. They fell to the kitchen floor with a crash, and the woman's sharp-featured face contracted as she screeched unintelligibly and at such a pitch that Merrick cringed and dropped his bread loaf.

He feigned a confused flight for an exit. The woman continued screaming and chasing him about the room, finally grasping one of his arms in her bony fingers with surprising strength. He was enacting a struggle when two other large men entered the room.

One man thrust Merrick to the ground, delivering a swift kick to the gut that left him writhing on the floor. The other man wrenched Merrick's right hand away from his body, examining the circular brand on his palm. Merrick hoped the healing herbs that had been applied to it gave it a look of time and authenticity. The man tossed away the hand dismissively.

"Pelasar," he growled. The other man grunted in agreement and spat disgustedly.

The last thing John Merrick saw before the darkness was a big black shoe aimed at his head.

◆　　◆　　◆

Gilda Reed emerged, relieved, from the tunnels and pulled herself upright. In spite of Saffi's assurances that the likelihood of encountering ants again was slight, Gilda felt much more at ease with both feet on the ground and the warm, thick air in her lungs. She stood stretching as Fergus and the other woman, Nabra, moved the earth to close the opening.

The tunnel had opened into a shaded orchard lined with the same silver-leaved trees Gilda had noticed on her first entrance into the White City. She now observed a white, pear-like fruit weighing down the branches. Curious and thirsty, she plucked one from a nearby branch, examining it briefly and feeling that it was good before biting into it lustily. The fruit was soft and sweet, and juice leaked out the corners of her mouth and down her chin. It was a feast of flavor after days of the Pelasars' bland meal and burnt tea.

She looked up from her happy chewing to notice her five companions staring at her.

Gilda briefly stopped chewing and raised her eyebrows at them. Saffi put a finger to her lips and shot a warning glance at Gilda, then turned and proceeded quietly through the orchard, beckoning the others to follow.

Sighing, Gilda dropped what was left of the fruit on the dusty ground and followed. Ahead, through the leaves above, she could make out the massive, rising white walls of the palace. She wondered if the stone was naturally that color, or if it had been bleached by its continued exposure to the relentless sun.

As the group neared the end of the orchard, Saffi directed them to remain in the shelter of the trees while she investigated. Gilda watched as the young woman cautiously moved to the edge of the tree-cover, sticking to the shadows, then paused, listening. The group waited in silence for an indefinite period.

Soon, cutting through the stillness and echoing through the

city, came the deep chiming Gilda had heard once before. This time, however, it was not an even, clocklike pealing. Instead, the low bell thrummed a rapid, uneven rhythm: *da-dong, da-dong, da-dong.*

Gilda knew this meant the hanging. She felt proud of Merrick for his effectiveness but anxious for his safety. A nudge from Simon told her they were moving again, and she followed the group quietly out of the orchard and to the base of a large tower of the white palace.

Saffi glanced up at a small balcony high above them and then stood back with Simon as the Earth Stone Mages knelt at the ground.

Gilda watched Fergus and Nabra gently fingering the climbing vine that reached three or four feet up the wall. The vine had wide leaves of a green so light it was almost transparent. She placed her hands on a nearby tendril and, with concentration, tried to re-enact the expanding and growing feat she had performed on many of Medwin's ivy plants at the Fringe. Her progress here was much slower, and she wished for her mother's stone, her emerald.

Still, she could feel energy flowing through her and the movement of the vine in her palms as it twisted upward and outward, climbing slowly toward its destination. As the vine wrapped itself firmly around the top of the balcony, Gilda let out a little yelp of triumph. The vine was now a perfect climbing rope as thick as her wrist.

She noticed that the other two had finished theirs as well and were already working the final two. She moved to help them, and soon, they were ready for their ascent.

A nagging feeling of foreboding crept over Gilda. She was a fit woman, and active, but she was not as young, strong, or *thin* as these others, and she knew that climbing this wall, her excellent vine notwithstanding, would be no easy task. She felt tired from the mere growing of the vine but took a deep breath and stepped forward.

She grasped on to the thick, green tendril and used the contours and jutting rocks of the wall to hoist herself up. She moved carefully and steadily, as she had practiced in the pit, finding the best footholds and ignoring the exhaustion in her arms. The others were much faster, and she could soon see the Pelasars climbing far ahead. Simon climbed next to her at a similar pace, probably to keep watch over her.

When she had gone about halfway, she longed for a rest but knew that stopping would only prolong the misery and further tire her weary arm muscles, so she pressed on. She was sweating and huffing. She was vaguely aware that the three others had reached the top and were climbing over the stone railing onto the balcony. Her destination was drawing closer, but slowly.

Gilda's eyes were watering, and perspiration dotted the lenses of her little spectacles, blurring her vision. She moved her left foot toward what she thought was a foothold and felt it slip against the rock. Her feet fell from the wall, and her hands began sliding down the vine. She gasped, her hold weakening and hands slipping. She felt a strong hand on hers.

"Don't let go," Simon commanded. "I've got your hands, now see if you can swing in closer and get your feet back on the wall."

Simon's voice was steady, and Gilda forced herself to calm down. She moved her legs and felt the vine swing. As they neared the wall she extended them, floundering for a foothold, and felt them make contact but slip off.

"Again," Simon said, his voice now betraying the strain of holding her weight.

Gilda swung the vine once more. This time her whole body

made contact with the wall, and her feet found holds. She was secure.

She nodded to Simon, unable to speak. He released her hands, and they both resumed climbing.

Gilda's progress was quickened, and she realized, reassured and slightly embarrassed, that the others were reeling in her vine from above. When Fergus pulled her over the railing onto the safety of the balcony she felt her arms turn to mush as she knelt, relieved, on the solid stone floor.

Simon climbed up after her, and she turned to thank him, but was arrested by the look on his face as he gazed over her head toward the big glass doors that led from balcony to palace interior.

She turned to look where he was looking and saw the shiny door handle turn and the doors slowly open. Standing before them were three armed guards pointing sharp swords at the five weary climbers.

CHAPTER 40

Laith and Medwin were still for only a few moments as they watched the two Wrakes shake the water from their hair and clothing, draw swords, and ascend the mossy hill toward their rock.

The younger man turned to the older. "I'll take the brute," he said. Then he hoisted himself onto the rock he had been hiding behind and held his sword in the air. The massive Wrake extended his own sword, howled, and moved straight toward Laith in an angry run.

With adrenaline coursing through him, Laith jumped down from his perch and ran out to meet his opponent. Their blades met in a grinding clash, and the fight began. The Wrake lunged powerfully, and Laith barely evaded his blade, moving to the side and thrusting unsuccessfully with his own. The Wrake thrust again; and this time Laith blocked with his sword, pushing the larger blade aside with a shriek of metal.

As the larger man continued his attacks, Laith found it more difficult to move offensively. In what seemed like mere seconds, he found himself slowly being forced backwards up the hill toward a large cliff face. If he could not move around the blade soon, he would be trapped against the rock and defeated.

The Wrake quickly became aware of the impending cliff as well, and, smiling grimly, increased the forward thrust of his blows. Laith blocked, and blocked, the swords clanking and screeching. The cliff was nearing. The Wrake lunged low and, in spite of Laith's evasive movement, the large blade pierced the side of his calf. Laith gasped. Then suddenly, eyes narrowed, head burning, and fists clenched, he stood and growled. Now, he was angry.

The Wrake's purple, moonlit face morphed into a sickening grin as Laith thrust, heat overtaking him. His opponent blocked, and the two engaged in rapid attacks and counterattacks of equal force. Laith was aware of the stinging pain in his leg, but only vaguely. He moved quickly, and his feet were sure. He ducked, thrust, blocked, jumped aside, and then went in again for the attack. Slowly, Laith began to gain the advantage, pushing his opponent back down the slope toward the water.

The Wrake's movements became more frantic. Holding his sword with both of his hands, he swung forcefully for Laith's neck. The young man ducked, and quickly countered with a jab to his enemy's chest. The Wrake blocked the attack just in time but stumbled backward over a rock, which robbed his balance and allowed Laith to slice him across the shoulder. Shocked, the huge man continued to stumble backwards down the hill. Laith pursued him, but before he could overtake him, the Wrake had stopped, dropped his sword, and grasped a large rock with his strong arm.

Laith was blinking, surprised, when the Wrake made a low grinding sound in his throat, and the rock suddenly flew from his outstretched hand toward Laith. Laith ducked just in time, crouching on the hillside. Below him the Wrake extended his hand, and another rock simply lifted into it. Laith stood slowly, moving backwards tentatively, and swallowing hard. It occurred to him that their sword fight was over; this man was a Wrake, probably with some kind of power for stone or space, and he would use this power on Laith until he finished him. The second rock hurtled forward, and Laith moved aside. This time the rock grazed his arm, and he yelped.

Laith was again backing toward the cliff as the Wrake moved toward him, another boulder in hand. This time, the rock flew at Laith with unbelievable speed and slammed into the young man's gut, knocking him to the ground. Laith groaned, unable to move. He rolled, turning his back to the Wrake and staring at the blurred cliff face ten or fifteen feet away.

Far above him Laith heard the loud grinding of stone on stone. He rolled to his back, looking at the sky, and saw, at the top of the cliff, the shudder and undulation of an immense boulder resting near the edge. He looked down at the Wrake. His eyes were closed, and he was again making a loud, rough noise in his throat. *He's going to crush me,* thought Laith, almost resignedly. *He's going to bring the mountain down upon me.* He turned his gaze up again to the substantial mass of rock above. It was slowly moving toward the cliff's edge, its weight shifting as it came. The boulder teetered, and then fell.

With sudden clarity, and a mad grasp at survival, Laith rolled. He rolled uphill, quickly, until he was flush against the cliff face. The boulder made impact, missing Laith by only a few feet, and began to roll down the slope to the sea. He closed his eyes and listened to the pounding, crushing roll, the deep and dreadful scream of the Wrake, and the final roaring splash as it fell into the sea.

Laith opened his eyes. The boulder was resting calmly in the water, waves washing over its visible curve. Below, his vast opponent was sprawled on the mossy incline, body crushed and jutting at odd angles. Laith looked aside, nauseated, and caught sight of his forgotten comrade, locked in combat with the dark-haired Water Wrake.

Both were moving with strained motions, tired from battle and the use of their powers. Laith stood, alarmed, and moved, belabored with pain, toward the pair. The fighters were nearing the coast. Medwin thrust, and missed. Suddenly, with a low moan, the dark princess raised her sword above her head and motioned toward the sea with her other hand. Behind her, a torrent of water rose up and crashed down upon the old man, who fell to the ground, his sword washing away from him with the surf.

Laith was now close enough to see the weariness on Medwin's face as he looked up at his attacker, defenseless. Laith increased his pace, sword extended.

Princess Mara lowered her sword arm and in a wild frenzy thrust her blade into Medwin's gut.

Laith screamed with anguish as he came upon the wild-eyed girl. She turned to meet him with her bloody sword, but Laith swung first, angrily and blindly, cutting her on the side of her leg. She fell, dropping her sword.

He was standing over her now, his blade extended. She stared up at him weakly. The eyes that had been so bright and wild moments ago were dull, brown, and sad. He moved the point of his sword to her throat.

"No!" Medwin was speaking to him. Laith looked over at the fallen man. "No," rasped Medwin again, "don't kill her." The old man's face was screwed up in pain, and blood soaked his shirt.

"She's killed you!" he yelled back, angry tears filling his eyes.

Medwin shook his head. "I'm not dead, yet, Laith. Get us both to the house. The girl first."

Laith stared at him incredulously through his teary vision, and shook his head.

Medwin sighed, a rattling, gasping sigh, and pointed to his left arm, then at the girl.

Dizzily, Laith bent over the fallen princess, lifted the sleeve of her left arm, and saw the mark there. She was a Vessel.

CHAPTER 41

Burr stood at the edge of the crowd of robed Bellarians, the two Pelasar men on either side of him. In front of him, less than thirty paces away, was a hangman's platform. Burr had never seen anything like this structure. It was not a simple and unfrequented wooden object, but a large, heavy, white stone, permanent structure.

Burr glanced behind him, furtively taking in the mass of spectators filling the square. He shook his head. What kind of people worship death so much that they would create this shining edifice on which to sacrifice mere thieves and outcasts, and then gather together in morbid delight to witness it? Surely a cold heart was a worse flaw than a quick hand.

An insect-like buzz erupted among the spectators as a dark, horse-drawn wagon rounded the corner and entered the square. A black-eyed, bloody-lipped John Merrick turned Pelasar was tied up in the back. The wagon halted a few feet from the platform, and two of the guards stationed there roughly pulled Merrick out and led him up the steps toward the awaiting noose. The guards placed their prisoner on the square stone in the middle of the platform and draped the rope around his neck, where it hung loosely. Burr watched as John Merrick scanned the crowd. For a moment, their eyes met. Merrick's face registered no recognition of any kind, but Burr knew that he had seen him.

The crowd had begun shouting angry epithets and insults. Burr recognized the common outcry of "Pelarus," which he had been told was a skewing of the term "Pelasar," or pit-dweller, to pit rat. Burr was taken back by their vitriolic outrage and the mad noise they created, especially when he reflected on the cold detached manner in which they had behaved on his first entrance into the city.

Suddenly, the noisy crowd was silent. The only sound was the rustle of the paper-thin leaves on the silver trees, and then, horse hooves. Royal riders on black horses had entered the square, and behind them was the large black and silver carriage. *Reyne morel has arrived,* thought Burr.

The royal carriage drew up, and the fat prince, dressed in deep purple, emerged. Surrounded by his armed guards, he ascended the platform, faced the waiting mass, and held up a long silver scepter. There was a rustling in the crowd, and Burr felt himself being yanked down by his Pelasar escorts. He fell to his knees, and his head was smashed down to the ground. Cautiously, he peeked up from his prostrate position to see that the throng of people were all similarly bowed down, and that Oswald blinked at them condescendingly, his plump face shiny under his dark curls and glittering crown.

Eventually he lowered the scepter, and the crowd rose to their feet once again. Oswald had begun to address the crowd in a loud and foreign tongue, but Burr was not paying attention. Instead he was carefully pulling out the glass jar he had been keeping under his robes. He held it cautiously in his hands and looked at the hundreds of dark little creatures moving within. Termites. At a soft and nearly indistinguishable volume, he began to hum. He had done this kind of thing so many times when he was young that it was almost unconscious. He just had not really realized the power behind it until he had met Medwin and learned about gifts.

The little insects were mulling around restlessly in their prison. Carefully, and with continued humming, Burr opened the lid of the jar and placed it on the ground. The termites rushed out and scattered across the ground. Separate, they were almost impossible to see, but Burr was aware of their position, and continued to direct them with his voice and mind.

He looked back up at the platform. The portly prince was approaching the captive. Burr felt a nervous flutter in his heart as Oswald moved around Merrick, slowly inspecting him. This plan's success depended on Merrick going unrecognized. He stopped at Merrick's side and, taking his right hand, inspected the royal brand. The Prince held up the hand, presented it to the crowd, and then lowered it to his mouth and spat into it meanly. The crowd again erupted in insults and murmurs.

Burr was aware that some of his termites had reached the top of the beam from which the hangman's rope was attached. They covered the rope and began, slowly, to eat through it.

Oswald had dropped Merrick's hand, and the crowd was again pacified. Oswald asked Merrick a question that Burr did not understand, but Merrick seemed to have been waiting for it.

"*Alwa*," he replied, carefully.

Oswald squinted at him for a moment before nodding. Then, turning to one of his guards, repeated the word as a command: "*Alwa*."

Presently, a certain guard mounted the platform and placed a clear glass of water in Oswald's hands. Oswald delivered it to Merrick. Tradition had been upheld. The last request had been asked and granted. Merrick opened his mouth and emptied the entire glass, then returned it to Oswald's outstretched palm.

The crowd's eyes were on the prince as he turned toward them, held up the glass, and then dropped it to the ground where it shattered dramatically on the stones of the square.

Burr, however, was watching Merrick carefully and could see that the man's cheeks bulged with un-swallowed liquid.

Oswald spoke a few more words to the crowd then turned and began to descend the platform. Burr's breath caught in his throat. Time was running out, and his termites had not yet finished with the rope. Oswald's men were clearing the platform. Soon only the two original guards remained.

Burr closed his eyes and increased the volume of his hum slightly, willing the creatures to hurry, to get through the rope faster. Some of the nearby Bellarians began to glance at him strangely, and he could feel the Pelasars tensing next to him. When he opened his eyes, John Merrick was staring directly at him. The rope was still intact. Burr shook his head slowly, and Merrick's eyes widened.

Then, abruptly, the guards swept the stone from under Merrick's feet and he dropped.

The crowd gasped. Burr hummed louder.

All of the sudden, the rope frayed and broke, and Merrick came crashing to the platform, gasping for air. The guards looked at each other, confused, and below Oswald barked out a command. The guards closed in on Merrick, and one bent to lift him to his feet. Merrick raised his head slowly and spit at the man.

However, it was not water that came from the prisoner's mouth but deadly sharp shards of ice. One grazed the man's cheek and the other lodged itself in his eye. The guard screamed, clapped his hand over his eye, and ran, falling from the platform into the awestruck crowd below.

In the meantime, Merrick had fired another ice shard at the second guard, finding his neck, and causing him to retreat in fear and pain.

Burr and his two companions lost no time moving to the dark horses. Within moments the majestic animals were rearing, neighing, and stomping wildly, causing the crowd to push back with fear and trampling some of the bystanders.

Leaving the horses to the pit-dwellers, Burr hurried up the platform and began untying Merrick, whose mouth was now empty of his self-made weapons.

"Cutting it a little close, there," he said to the boy.

Burr shrugged. "I wasn't a bit worried," he lied.

Merrick smiled, and the two dashed down the steps of the platform. At the side of his vision, Burr caught a quick glance of a large steed delivering a swift kick to Prince Oswald's knees, which buckled. Burr grimaced, then smiled, hurrying on as their Pelasar friends joined them.

No one seemed to mind their departure in the pandemonium the horses were creating. The four raced toward the nearby alley in which was hidden in the stone ground another entrance to the royal tunnels, and safety.

◆　　◆　　◆

Saffi Beval glared at the three Bellarian soldiers who blocked her path in the doorway. She was trying to decide on a particular action when, on the other side of the balcony, Gilda Reed extended her hand and propelled the vine she was still grasping at the guard in the middle. It wrapped quickly around his ankles, and the man tumbled to the floor.

The balcony erupted in movement. Fergus and Nabra followed Gilda's example and entwined the other two soldiers. Simon was instantaneously on the middle one, his knee in the man's chest as he wrestled away the sharp sword and bound the man's hands tightly with his own vine. Saffi moved toward the guard on the left to similarly bind him, but this man was thrashing about so unpredictably that his sword grazed Saffi's cheek before she could knock it from his hands. Gilda was near her soon, helping her to bind the hands.

When Fergus and Nabra had bound the third man, the group stood, catching their breath and looking at each other. Gilda gently placed a hand on Saffi's chin, examining her wound.

"It's not deep," she said. "It might leave a small scar, but you'll be fine."

Saffi felt reassured in spite of the stinging. She once again attained her calm and directed the group to follow her, cautiously, into the palace.

The room they entered was spacious and cool. The walls and ceiling were of smooth gray marble, and massive pillars lined the sides, each bearing unlit torches. The space was largely empty of furniture; but at the head of the room, at the top of a platform, was a gaudy golden throne overhung with shining fabric and stuffed with soft pearly cushions. Saffi nodded, relieved.

Her source in the palace had informed her that, without fail, Oswald kept his most valuable items in a locked chamber behind the throne room. She had chosen the right balcony, and now had only to get into the rear chamber to find the stones.

The others followed her as she moved quickly up the stairs and to the little door concealed behind the shining seat. She turned the knob to confirm that it was locked. Then, pulling out the chunk of iron she kept in her pocket, she knelt on the floor and bent over so that the keyhole was at eyelevel. She briefly touched the chain on which her stone was hanging and then pressed her bit of iron against the hole. She closed her eyes and focused on the metal, understanding its makeup and willing it to mold into the little hole in the door.

She could feel the metal warming and moving in her hand. She imagined it changing and filling the space. Soon, the movement stopped. She opened her eyes and stood. Carefully, she turned the piece of metal still in her fingertips and felt the locking mechanism release. She turned the knob and the door opened. The chamber was very small and windowless. Shelves lined the walls, and on them sat various jewels, trinkets, and an occasional bottle of wine. Saffi scoffed at the ridiculous pig prince and his precious treasures.

The group spread out into the room, searching the shelves and scouring the area for signs of the stones. In the rear of the room, on a low table was an ornate little box. It was deep blue and decorated with golden moons and stars and elaborate gold trimming.

Saffi approached the little box and tried to open it, but it too was locked.

"I think they're in here," she said quietly, repeating her words in Bellarian. The others gathered around the little box as Saffi knelt and once more extracted her piece of metal. This keyhole was very tiny, and Saffi had to focus deeply to move her metal into its desired shape. Eventually she stood, turning the self-made key and opening the box. The stones were inside.

There was a collective exhale of relief and delight. Simon and Gilda reached quickly for their own stones and put them on. Saffi collected the others, hiding them in an inside pocket of her jacket. *This wasn't so hard,* she thought, then instantly remembered Merrick and wondered if things had been as successful for the others.

She followed the group out of the room, looking down at her feet as she crossed the threshold. Suddenly, she was completely knocked off balance as she ran into Fergus's back. The others were all stopped still just outside the doorway.

Saffi stood quietly and pushed past Fergus and Nabra. In the center of the throne room was one man. Normally it would seem strange that one man would be a deterrent for five Stone Mages, but there was something different about this man. Saffi noticed right away the wild green of his eyes. She guessed without having to see the man's arm that he was a Vessel, probably a minion of Abaddon. The more arresting detail, however, was the fact that in both of his outstretched palms were angry spheres of flame, which he casually moved about.

"I thought I might find you here," he said in clear Lyrian. Then he pushed one of his flaming spheres forward. It extended to become a vicious pillar, licking at the ends of the shimmering fabric over the throne and catching it on fire. Saffi and her companions ran down the stairs quickly to avoid the flame as the material fell and writhed, a burning serpent on the ground.

Saffi's mind reeled. Swiftly, she pulled her bit of metal again from her pocket, shaping it into a sharp flat disk and flinging it at the Fire Wrake just before he shot out another spout of flame. The iron hit him squarely in the chest, and his hands flew to his torso with the pain of the blow. He stumbled backward.

"Run!" Saffi shouted, hoping to take advantage of his momentary confusion to escape. The group bolted for the balcony. Gilda's hand was on the door when Saffi felt the stinging heat on her back. She fell blindly to the floor. She could hear the others coughing in the smoke, and could smell her own singed hair. She reached a hand to her back and felt the shreds that remained of her thick jacket. If burned again, it would be her skin in shreds.

"*Vala!* Go! " she yelled. Simon helped her to her feet. Gilda and Nabra were out the doors and Fergus close behind when the second blast came. Saffi watched over her shoulder as it came straight for her, and she felt dizzy with dread. Before the flame made contact, however, Fergus jumped for her, pushing her out of the way and taking the force of the raging fire. Saffi screamed, jumping to her feet, and ran to her cousin, flame lapping the edge of his clothes and singeing his hair.

The Fire Wrake was moving closer, and Saffi knew this was the end. She bent over Fergus, extinguishing the flame and trying to lift his shoulders, while Simon rushed over and took his feet.

"Stop," hissed the Wrake. "Move toward that door, and you will surely die. You know the location of the other Lyrians. Stay where you are, and I will spare you."

Saffi was vaguely aware of what the man was saying but could not tear her eyes from her unconscious cousin and friend, his singed and bloody head resting in her lap. She would not let him die here, and she would not lead this man to her people. She looked at Simon, his back to the Wrake. He nodded, seeming to understand her expression. *Get him out,* he mouthed. *I'll take care of the rest.*

He nodded again, and Saffi quickly pulled her cousin for the door. She watched as the Wrake lifted his hands, preparing to throw his final fire at them. She moved faster, holding Fergus under his arms.

Suddenly, Simon tore across the room with unnatural speed. To Saffi it did not seem as if he took more steps in the brief second in which he closed the distance but that his steps held more significance. He dashed toward the Fire Wrake, whose arms were lifted and full of flame. The flame-filled hands descended on Simon as he drove his dagger into the Wrake's stomach.

The Wrake fell to the floor, dead, and Simon crumpled next to him. Saffi's heart thudded as she watched from the doorway.

CHAPTER 42

Dawn was creeping over the Fringe hills as Laith Haverford climbed them, dried tear streaks lining his face and the old man unconscious in his arms. Eventually, he entered the glass house, slowly making his way toward Medwin's bedroom, but then reconsidered and took him to the library, laying him gently on the sofa nearest the fire and rushing to the little pantry to find the healing herbs Medwin had showed him a few days ago.

Laith was sore and short of breath, his leg was throbbing, and everything seemed strange and disjointed. He ran his shaking hands across the line of bottles and boxes until he found what he was looking for. He pulled it from the shelf and brought it to the kitchen, setting it on the table while he filled a bowl with warm water and found some clean linen in a cupboard.

Somehow, he returned to the library, cut aside Medwin's outer cloak and jacket, and carefully lifted his shirt, so as not to pull away skin. He cleansed the wound with water and a salve made from the herbs and then gently wrapped the wound. He examined his own wound, but the cut was not deep, and the bleeding had stopped.

He laid a light blanket over the old man. Medwin's face was ashen, but he was breathing evenly. Laith stood over him for a moment, considering. Then he grudgingly left the room, exited the house, and headed back down the hills to retrieve the girl.

When he had left her, she was staring resignedly at the sea, blood issuing from her wound. Laith had felt no guilt in leaving her. Even if it was the Shifter inhabiting her body who had actually killed Medwin, she had allowed it access to her body and power by choosing the life of a Vessel. That revelation had offered insight regarding her, but not sympathy.

Now, as he approached her again, she looked pale all over, and her head was tossing deliriously. When he stood over her, she looked up at him vaguely and then turned away.

"Leave me," she moaned.

"I would like nothing better," Laith murmured, but knelt, scooping her into his arms. He was careful with her wounded leg, but still, she tensed in pain, and fell unconscious. She was light and limp in his arms, a bit like a fallen, rain-soaked leaf. Laith felt his anger melt into weary indifference as he carried her up the hill and into the house.

He brought her to the library as well, placing her on the other sofa in the room, removing her rain-soaked cloak and outer-dress. He mixed another herb poultice and applied it to her laceration.

He was covering her with a blanket when her eyes opened, and she looked up at him, murmuring a request for water. Laith went to the kitchen and returned with the liquid. She took it in her trembling hands and drank deeply, then coughed and lost the contents of her stomach on the floor.

Unthinkingly, Laith cleaned up the mess and refilled the glass. As he mopped her face with a warm, damp cloth she studied him.

Laith saw a wandering look in her eyes and was wondering if it was confusion or delirium when she spoke to him.

"Who are you?"

Laith did not answer immediately, but held the glass of water to her lips, allowing the liquid to slowly run into her mouth. He gave her a few more sips before setting the glass down.

She looked up at him with a momentary directness in her brown eyes. He blinked.

"Laith Haverford."

He watched her face as the name registered. Her face turned up in an ironic smile.

"My long-lost betrothed," she said, and laughed weakly before passing out of consciousness again.

Laith gently placed a pillow under her head, then crawled to the soft rug in front of the fireplace. Without even removing his cloak and sword, he sprawled on the floor and slept.

CHAPTER 43

Simon stood in a field of ripe white wheat, the Adler cottage at his back and the setting sun warming his face. He was waiting for someone but he could not quite remember who it was. He walked farther into the field. His feet were bare and the dirt in the furrows was warm and soft.

At the far edge of the field a figure appeared. A silhouette, backlit by the descending sun, was walking toward him, and suddenly, Simon knew whom he had been waiting for.

"Roger!" he called, and began to run through the field. The silhouette continued toward him, steadily, and soon Simon could see the familiar face, hear the golden laughter, and feel his brother's big arms encircling him in an embrace.

"You're home," Simon murmured into Roger's big shoulder. "You're alive." Simon held the embrace, and Roger returned it steadily and at length before gently releasing Simon and holding him at arm's length.

Simon took in all the details of the face he remembered so well: the strong chin, kind smile, and gentle eyes. The brothers turned and walked through the field together, talking, laughing, and sharing memories. Eventually, they reached the edge of the field and stood in silence, and

Simon could see that the sun had mostly disappeared over the horizon, a mere sliver remaining.

Roger turned so that his back was to the sun once more. "It is good to be home, Simon," he said. He began to step backward slowly, and Simon moved to follow him, but his older brother held out a hand to stop him.

"My battle is fought," he said, placing his hand on Simon's shoulder, steady and warm. "But yours is not finished." With his other hand, Roger pushed Simon, who stumbled backward into the field as the sun disappeared over the horizon, and everything was dark.

Simon was awake in a different darkness. His eyes closed, and intense and overwhelming pain entrenched him. He felt cold, but his skin felt on fire, and he was vaguely aware of gentle hands lifting his body. The very movement was excruciating, and he moaned with the pain.

The hands lowered him into balmy water, and he felt a mild relief on his arms, shoulders, and neck as he was immersed in the liquid. Only his face was above the surface, and someone was gently wringing a wet rag over his head, allowing more water to trickle down his forehead, across his eyes, around his mouth, and over his chin.

He was aware of nervous whispers about him. As cold and dark began to envelope him once more, he pictured the face of his Uncle Miles, laughing at him.

Simon was conscious several more times before he was really awake. There were more immersions in the cool water. Once he felt kind and careful hands wrapping his pain-filled skin in soft bandages. Other times he was given warm broth that slid down his scorched throat, but always he drifted back into his heavy sleep.

When Simon really woke, he opened his eyes to a familiar sight. A young, curl-framed and concerned face hovered over him, but this time it was a familiar one, and the look of her made his heart begin to beat more quickly.

Surprise overtook Ivy's features as she stared down into his open eyes, and she was cautiously still, as if one movement on her part might propel him back to his unconsciousness. He smiled at her and watched her face warm and eyes sparkle as she smiled back.

Almost as soon as the smile graced her features, however, it was gone, and tears began to fill the bright eyes. Stifling a sob, and turning in embarrassment, the princess fled the room.

Simon blinked after her, confused, and wishing she would return, as he took in his surroundings. He was in one of the sleeping chambers in the pit, but this one had an actual mattress and bed rather than a hammock, a little table scattered with ointments and bandages, and a low-burning candle. He slowly began to feel the pain, warm and throbbing, that spread over his head, neck, shoulders, and arms, but was aware that the deadening burn he had experienced at first was passed. He breathed in deeply and was relieved to find that he could do so without rattling and rasping.

The cloth was being pushed back from the entrance to his chamber, and a very pleased looking Gilda Reed entered.

"Awake at last!" she said, glowing. "You're feeling better, then?"

Simon smiled and nodded.

"We are all glad to hear it, and everyone wants to see you, but your physician insists that there must only be one at a time in here. We shouldn't be overexciting you, I suppose."

"My physician?" Simon croaked.

Gilda nodded. "Yes. It turns out Beathas is quite a gifted healer and earth worker. I have been learning a great deal from her. She has been supervising your recovery, but we have all had a turn in caring for you." She nodded toward the door. "The princess has spent all her free moments watching over you."

Free moments, thought Simon. He processed this. He had surely been sleeping for quite a while. He wondered what had gone on in his mental absence. He wondered if Merrick had returned safely . . . and Fergus.

He swallowed and framed the difficult words carefully, "What have I missed?"

Gilda's smile wavered as she sat on Ivy's vacated stool next to his bed. "I had thought to wait before burdening you with information, but I can see by the look on your face that you will not rest until you've heard."

Simon looked her in the eye and nodded once.

Gilda looked at the ceiling, as if searching for an answer there, then began. "Well, Simon, our Merrick and Burr were able to escape safely, and thanks to you we made it back to the pit with our stones and no Wrakes in tow. Saffi was a bit burned, you were badly burned, and Fergus died shortly after we returned." She paused, and Simon felt a stabbing sorrow in his chest.

"They've given him a hero's funeral," Gilda continued. "He has been greatly mourned. And while most push for the success of our venture, so that he would not have died in vain, there are some who want to use his death as a reason to abandon our plans. Ivy has been taken to the site of her mother's door and has spent almost all of the nighttime hours working to open it, but I'm not sure how much success she's having. I think your recovery will give her hope and also allow her some daytime sleep to renew her energy." Gilda smiled at this, but Simon looked away, feeling slightly ashamed.

"She feels responsible for me," he murmured.

Gilda was quiet for a moment, considering. "I don't think responsibility is necessarily what she feels, Simon. But I know that the best thing you can do is to recover your strength and give her your brave help once again. She needs that from you."

Simon looked back at the woman, returning her smile this time. "I live to give it," he said.

CHAPTER 44

Abaddon's broad figure was framed in the dark doorway, which led onto a balcony overlooking the barracks of the Southern army. From the darkness in the room at his back came a deep, raspy, and vaguely female voice.

"You are come to me on my deathbed, Abaddon."

Abaddon's voice was casual. "Are you dying?"

A sickly chuckle issued from the prostrate creature in the dark room. "You know as much, and you are here not to mourn my passing but to get my deathbed vision."

Abaddon's voice remained casual. "Your what?"

"Don't play dumb with me, boy!" was the abrupt reply. "You must believe the rumors that a Seer's last vision is her most powerful. But what do you need to see? Your army is ready."

Abaddon nodded his assent.

"Your Wrakes—"

Abaddon cut her off. "My Wrakes are prepared for war."

"You are missing a few, I have seen."

"Dead."

"Killed by you, you mean."

Abaddon turned to face the old seer. "I have recently disposed of two Shifters. The rest died of their own incompetence."

"Disposed?"

"I sent them to complete tasks. One was to have lead her Vessel in the disposal of the old man; but instead she returned to her body here with only the news of dead Wrakes, her Vessel about to be destroyed, and no guarantee that the mission was a success. She was not permitted to live to make more such mistakes."

"The other?"

"The other I sent into a Fire Wrake Vessel in Bellaria. The Lyrian Stone Mages walked into his open palm. But he failed, and his Vessel was destroyed. I killed him instantly."

The old woman's eyes narrowed at his accounts. "You do not have so many Wrakes, Shifters especially. Perhaps you are too hasty to invoke death rather than punishment."

Abaddon moved into the darkness of the room where he could see the woman before him more clearly. "I have no patience for punishment, and my victory is sure."

"Then why this obsession with a few Stone Mages? Why waste so much time and energy on them if they are not a real threat?"

Abaddon waved an impatient hand at her questions. "I am here for your sight, not for a personal interrogation."

The old woman pulled the dark stone from her side and studied its murky surface. Abaddon watched her, unmoving. Her breathing was becoming labored, but she smiled and coughed and looked him in the eye. "I will give you your sight then," she said and turned her gaze once more to the orb in her hand.

Eventually she lifted her head. "Very well," she rasped. "I see your war. For the first and last time I see a vision of the future."

"War?" Abaddon seemed surprised. "You do not say my domination. There will be a battle, then?"

The woman coughed again, her body curling in pain, but she nodded.

Abaddon's face was expressionless. He turned again toward the balcony, but the old woman's speech made him stop.

"You know that a future sight is nebulous."

"I do."

"Ask me what you want to know," the woman whispered, her eyes intense in her pain.

"Have you seen my victory?"

The response was a mere whisper. "I have," the Seer Wrake replied, then she turned her head and died.

CHAPTER 45

I've brought you some soup," Laith announced as he entered the library one evening. Medwin's eyebrows rose interestedly as he endeavored to sit up.

"Don't get too excited," the young man said, setting down the tray and helping his old friend to rise. "It is rather bad, I'm afraid."

Medwin smiled, and Laith was glad. The seer's wound was slowly healing, but the old man still looked haggard, his pale face tired and creased with wrinkles. Laith knew he would never fully recover.

"You've become quite the nursemaid," Medwin commented as Laith set the meal before him.

Now Laith smiled, inclining his head slightly. "It fills the hours," he said.

"How is your other patient faring?"

Laith shrugged. "Her wound is healing, I suppose, but she is weak and unresponsive. She sleeps a great deal and eats hardly anything." He ran a hand through his tousled hair. "I don't see what the point is, really. Why save her, Medwin?"

Medwin put down the hard bit of bread he had been picking at. "I understand your reservations, Laith, but she is no danger to us now. Those who sent her surely think she is dead." He paused for a moment. "I have seen some of her in my mirrors over the years as, I may remind you, have you . . . and not just because you were to have married her, I think. What I have seen makes me believe she is more lost than malicious. I don't know why she became a Vessel, but I think it would be important to find out before we condemn her to die."

Laith pondered this response for a few minutes before looking again at the old man. When he did, Medwin's face was turned up in a sour expression.

"What?" Laith asked.

"You are right," he replied. "The soup is rather bad."

Laith scowled at him good naturedly and left the room to bring more of his soup to the other patient. He had moved Princess Mara into another nearby chamber, where he expected he would find her as she usually was, sprawled on the bed in a fitful sleep. However, when he entered the room, she was sitting up in bed, staring calmly at his intrusion.

He cleared his throat. "I've brought you some food," he said.

She did not answer.

"Medwin says it is vile, but I'm sure you'd better eat some."

She nodded. "Thank you." Her voice was soft, but it was the first clear speech he had had from her, and he nearly dropped the tray in surprise.

He recovered, though, and delivered the meal safely to the table at her bedside, before turning to go.

"Where were you?" she asked with quiet directness.

He looked at her, confused.

"I mean, where did you disappear to all those years ago?"

Laith blinked. "I didn't disappear, really. I was in the shipyards, then at sea."

"Why did you go?" she asked, looking down at the hands folded neatly in her lap as if ashamed of her own boldness.

Laith stood before her stiffly. "I don't know anymore. I suppose I just wanted to escape, so I ran."

She nodded, as if accepting that answer. "I was glad you ran at the time. I was young, and I thought I would not have to be married at all if you never returned."

Laith smiled slightly, and then narrowed his eyes. "Why did you become a Vessel?"

She kept her head bowed, and was quiet for so long that Laith wondered if he hadn't better just leave. "I began, years ago, to become aware of some of my father's more corrupt practices and plans for Lyria. I was angry and disillusioned, but doubted my own power to do anything about it.

"Soon after this, a few dark and powerful people approached me. They said they served the Southern Lord, and that they planned to overthrow my corrupt father and build a better Lyria. They told me that they practiced an old magic, and that it was a power I held as well. They said they would share their knowledge with me if I would help them spy on my father. I agreed.

"They taught me to do extraordinary things with water. They schooled me in control and chaos, and I felt a certain exhilaration in the power I wielded. However, when they told me more of what it meant to become a Vessel, I became afraid, and told them I would not undergo that process, but would spy on my father as I was. They said if I refused, they would kill me, so I became a Vessel.

"I lived a tortured life. I was forced to only observe my own actions when I was being inhabited, vaguely aware of my own existence. I spent the rest of my uninhabited time fearing another takeover. I came to understand that my father was a mere pawn to the real evil of the man I served. I realized that my kingdom and loved ones—my sister—were in danger.

"After my father forfeited Lyria, and the South came in control of our lands, I went straight to the South's Lord, Abaddon, and told him I would no longer serve him and that he could kill me if he liked. He just laughed at me. He said he would not only kill me but my sister.

"I should have known he would kill anyone who might oppose him, regardless of my involvement, but I didn't. I have served him, albeit unwillingly, since."

As she spoke, Mara had gripped and twisted the bedclothes. By the time she finished she had grasped them so harshly her knuckles were white.

Laith watched quietly as she slowly looked up at him. He could read the pain in her face, and he swallowed heavily. Gradually, she relaxed her fingers, and her face became pale. She looked suddenly fragile, as if she might fall over any minute.

"Are you feeling weak?" he asked.

She nodded and he helped her to lie down.

"I have always been weak," she murmured as she turned her head away to face the wall.

"I know what you mean," whispered Laith. He stood and left the room.

CHAPTER 46

Ivy felt impatient, and she dressed quickly, exchanging her daily dress for the dark, loose-fitting clothing she always wore to the doorway. She looked forward with anxious tension to these trips, longing for the freedom of the leggings, the dark open night and warm desert wind above ground, but mostly for another chance to complete her task. She knew that she needed to succeed before it was too late, but the means of success continued to evade her.

She hurried from her chamber and agilely climbed the ladder to the top of the pit. Nabra was at work opening the tunnel entrance as usual, and Saffi was there, waiting for her. They had just exchanged kind greetings when Simon joined them.

His fair hair was a bit darker and close shorn. Beathas and others had taken special care of his damaged skin, but there was still some scarring on his face and exposed forearms. His movements were slower but surprisingly agile, and his usual youthful exuberance was replaced by a kind of steady solemnity. He seemed somehow older, and Ivy found herself somewhat reticent in his presence.

He greeted her formally, even bowing slightly to acknowledge her, and she stood mute. Saffi moved forward and took his arm warmly. She bore a small scar on her cheek, but Ivy thought it only served to make her look more strong and beautiful than before.

"Thank you for coming, Simon," she said. "We'll be glad of your protection and assistance."

Simon shrugged away the compliment with a kind smile, and the three moved to exit the pit, when a voice behind them made Ivy turn.

"Leaving without me?" John Merrick asked, his face dark as he walked toward them.

Saffi sighed. "I told you, Merrick, we won't need you tonight. I've asked Simon to take a turn."

"So you have," Merrick replied, acknowledging Simon indifferently, "but I intend to join in. The guard should be sufficient."

Saffi's face reddened with emotion. "Simon was *sufficient* in the palace, Merrick. I owe my life to him. He will be sufficient tonight."

A tense silence followed this speech. Simon looked down, embarrassed, and Merrick fumbled to explain his statement.

"I only meant—"

Ivy cut him off. "There is no reason you should not both come. I would appreciate the extra support, and it would be wise to have another set of hands should a problem arise."

The others accepted this without argument, but Saffi shot a hard glance at Merrick before storming past a bewildered Nabra and through the freshly opened tunnel entrance. Merrick hurried after her, offering up explanations that soon evolved into forceful arguments. The two disappeared into the tunnel, their raised voices becoming muffled by the surrounding earth.

Simon turned to Ivy. "I think they'll have forgotten us completely. I suppose we'll have to hurry unless we want to be unavoidably lost."

Ivy smiled at him, taking up the lantern Nabra offered before she relaxed into her sentinel post.

"Actually," Ivy said as she entered the tunnel, "I really know my own way by now, but Saffi insists that I still need her to be my guide. She and Merrick are more alike than she would ever wish to believe."

"Yes," Simon said, "the same way water is like oil."

By the time the tunnel had narrowed and Simon and Ivy were on hands and knees, the angry interchange ahead of them had become inaudible. Ivy wanted to ask Simon about the state of his injuries and how recovered he was feeling, but felt inhibited by shyness.

It was actually Simon who broke the silence first to ask, kindly, about her progress.

She sighed. "It's hard to say. I can feel the presence of the door, similar to the one at the Fringe. But it is faint. My efforts to strengthen the portal seem to be inhibited by the fact that I don't actually know where it leads."

"What do you mean?" Simon asked.

"We know she was going back to Lyria, of course. But I think she and my aunts would have had a specific location in mind. I have asked those in the pit who were around when she came if they can remember them speaking of a destination, but no one really remembered except Beathas. She told me my mother just said she was taking them home, to Lyria, someplace safe."

"Safe?"

"I assume she meant safe from the tyrants here in Bellaria. But she had to have also been thinking about Abaddon and his followers, perhaps even my father."

"Can you think of such a place?" Simon asked.

"When Beathas first told me that, I was sure my mother must have been trying for her library in the Lyrian palace. It was a favorite place of hers, and my father had little interest in it. I never saw him there. It was a large room and in an outer wing of the castle. It could have held the travelers she meant to bring and have given them time to form a strategy without drawing notice."

"It sounds likely."

"Yes. But, I have been focusing on that space in my attempts, and it does not seem to make a difference. I feel I am wrong about the library being her choice. I wonder if I did not know her as well as I might have believed."

Ivy had spoken the last sentence quietly, to herself, but she was sure Simon had heard. After a long silence he responded.

"I remember her," he said.

Ivy nodded, unsurprised. "She was memorable, well-loved. You saw her when she rode out in procession? Or did you actually visit the palace?"

"Perhaps I did both, but I remember her most in a different way. There was an orchard at the far end of our land, an apple orchard, and beyond it was a seldom-traveled road that wound through the kingdom. Sometimes after a long day, or to escape a little work, I would climb the trees and eat the apples, or juggle them, and write. Once or twice your mother rode by. I was so surprised the first time I saw her do that. She came barreling down the lane, riding the horse astride, skillfully, and very fast. She was without escort and seemed free and happy. She looked up at me in my perch and waved as she passed."

This small view of the queen from an outside observer was so clearly like the mother she remembered that Ivy's throat closed off and her eyes began to water. She was saved a response by the mere fact that they had reached the exit. She indicated the opening above to Simon and tried to wipe her eyes surreptitiously. Simon handed her a clean handkerchief, however, then waited silently while she made use of it before following her up and out of the tunnel.

A stone-faced Merrick and sheepish looking Saffi waited for them above. Ivy smiled weakly at Saffi before moving out into the night. The location was an undistinguishable patch of desert, lit by the large Bellarian moon. As she felt her way to the space where the almost-doorway hovered, she heard herself whisper to the night, "Where were you going, Mother?"

CHAPTER 47

The grass under Laith Haverford's feet was thick. Princess Mara's arm was tight on his, and she leaned into him for support as she limped along at his side and along the slopes at the Fringe. Medwin had insisted that the leg needed use, but Laith had opted for a more gradual strengthening of the wounded limb than the one Medwin had led him through those months ago.

When the girl's breathing became heavy, Laith led her to a low-lying rock for a rest, helping her onto it and then sitting next to her. They were fairly high up on the mountain, where they could see down to the wild and glistening sea. There was a gentle breeze, and light clouds shielded them from direct sunlight. Sprigs of foxglove dotted the grassy incline.

"It's actually quite lovely," Mara said when her breath returned.

Laith smiled slightly. "Surprising, huh? The end of the world is a nice place after all. Which is a good thing considering we might be here for a while."

Mara was quiet, and Laith could see out of the corner of his eye that she was staring out at the sea with a faraway look. He wondered what she was thinking.

"I'll never leave," she said with tiredness in her voice. Laith was about to reassure her that someone would surely come for them, when he realized her meaning. She was safe now, but only because those who knew she was a Vessel assumed she was dead. The minute she set foot in Lyria, she would again be in danger of habitation.

"There must be some way to undo—"

"Believe me," she interrupted, "there is no way but death. And I would rather die than return to the life of a Vessel once more." The wind blew her dark hair in front of her eyes, and she brushed it aside. "I may be a danger to you even now. Abaddon has a seer, and if she happens to discover me . . ." Her voice trailed off.

She looked at him with sudden directness. "Why did you not kill me?"

Laith met her gaze as directly. "I wanted to kill you," he said. "I would have, I think, if Medwin had not stopped me. . . . He was right, though."

"Yes, but at the time I'm sure I wished for death as much as you wished to administer it. These few days of freedom have been valuable to me. But, Haverford?"

He looked back at her. "Laith."

"I need you to promise me something."

"What is it?"

"Promise you will finish what you began that day if I am ever inhabited again. Promise you will kill me."

"I can't promise that."

"Please . . ." Her voice was soft, almost a whimper.

Laith looked out at sea and said nothing. Slowly he stood and held out his arm. "Let's get back to the house," he said.

They made their way back to the glass house in silence, their combined reflections in the shining surface growing slowly closer.

The house was quiet when they entered. Laith led the princess to the library, where Medwin sat, his face grave.

"Are you unwell?" Laith asked, concerned.

Medwin shook his head. "I have taken up my mirror just now."

"And?" Laith prompted as he helped Mara to a chair.

"Abaddon is preparing for an attack. He has left the South and has taken up residence in the abandoned Lyrian palace. His army is moving toward the pass, and our friends have not yet retuned."

"But the Lyrians," Laith breathed. "Certainly they will try to defend themselves."

"They will try—" Medwin began weakly, but Mara interrupted.

"There is no one to organize them. My father is dead, my sister and I presumed so, and the castle has been left in charge of a mere steward who is loyal to Abaddon. He will forbid the use of the army for some reason or another, and the people will be left on their own to organize a defense. They are largely outnumbered. They will fail."

Medwin nodded. "We must pray that the others return," he mumbled, "and soon."

Laith felt the usual heat redden his face with frustration and despair. He was about to storm out of the room, when he heard a sound. He started up from his chair and stood, poised and listening, wishing he would hear the wonderful, familiar sound once more.

He heard it again.

He darted out of the library and into the glass-walled corridor. He looked out at the sea with hopeful anticipation and saw what he had expected. He let out a whoop amidst the questioning voices of Mara and Medwin from the library.

The sound he heard once more was that of a ship's bell. The sight he saw, far out in the shoal, was the *Sapphire*.

Mara strained to keep up with Laith as he pulled her down the sloping descent from the house to the seaside, all his previous gentleness forgotten.

"Come on," he breathed, his hand tight on her arm.

Her leg wound screamed with the pain of the movement, and sweat ran down her face and pooled in her eyes so that she had to blink to see clearly. She felt a churning nausea in her gut, but it was not from the pain. Anxiety brewed inside her. She knew why Laith was pulling her down this mountain with hopeful abandon. He wanted her to use her magic.

When they reached the shore, Laith placed Mara ankle deep in the water. She could feel its pull and familiar rhythm as it wrapped around her limbs. She shivered.

"There," said Laith, pointing out across the rocky shoal. "Can you see them?"

Mara followed his gesture to where a longboat was inching away from the greater vessel, heading bravely towards them. She nodded slowly, trying to catch her breath.

Then the command came. "Help them," he said. "Help them through the rocks."

Now that she had stopped moving, all the blood seemed to rush to Mara's face and to course through the throbbing limb beneath her. She felt dizzy and weak. She swooned.

Laith extended his arms to right her. "Steady now," he said. "Pull yourself together. They'll need your help out there."

The nausea rose in Mara's stomach and she swallowed hard. "No," she whispered. "No. I won't."

Laith grabbed her by the arms and turned her to face him. "What?" he asked, his face a mixture of confusion and rage.

She looked away. "I won't use my power again."

Laith grasped her chin and turned her head abruptly so they

were eye to eye. "You will," he said. "These people are coming to rescue us at great personal risk. If you do not manage this water, it will likely overtake them. So I'm telling you again: you will help them."

Mara could not meet his angry gaze. She looked down.

Suddenly Laith pushed her from him, furious. "You told me you were weak," he roared, "but I didn't really believe it until now. You *are* weak, Princess. Don't you understand? These people can take us back to the continent. You could gain control at the palace and organize the army. Our kingdom is in your hands. But you shrink and you cower. So I repeat, you are weak."

Mara shook her head, trembling under his angry glare. "I will not be used again as a tool for power."

"Is that what you think?" Laith scoffed. "You make no distinction between servitude to the evil Abaddon and saving the good people of Lyria? After all these years of slaving under darkness, you have a chance to set things right. It was not your power that made you a force for ill, it was the way you used it. You *should* be powerful, and strong, Princess, but you should use it for good, and this is your last chance."

Goosebumps rose on Mara's arms as he spoke. When he finished he stormed into the waves, his back turned toward her. She looked out at the little vessel in the water and then closed her eyes, willing her breath to slow and her mind to clear. She shut out the feeling of the pain in her leg and allowed his words to sink in. She tried to sincerely see herself for a brief moment, to determine who she really was and who she really wanted to be.

"All right," she said, opening her eyes. Laith turned around. "Help me," she whispered.

In two brisk strides he was at her side, his arm around her, pulling her out further until the water swayed around her knees. She began to hum, low in her throat, as she worked to harmonize herself with the sea. She saw the little boat and understood the waves that tossed it, threatening to overturn it. Her song was a calming one, and in her mind and outstretched arms she lulled the sea, smoothed it, felt it wrap around the boat and carry it safely past a rock, and then another, over a swell and around a hidden crag. She allowed her mind to hope for the survival of the people in the boat. She wanted, and the water wanted, their safe passage. This time the magic did not heat and burn in her. It tingled and crackled. She forgot Laith's supporting arm around her, forgot the Fringe, forgot herself, and knew only the cool, deep, undulating water at the sides of the boat growing closer, winding over and around danger, until it was before her.

Laith released her and splashed out over the crags and into the surf, catching a rope that was thrown him and pulling the boat ashore. Mara allowed the magic to go, and felt calm and weary as the power faded and her awareness of her surroundings again increased. She saw that Medwin was near her, having hobbled down to greet his visitors, cane in hand.

She saw the three strangers climb out of the boat, the oldest among them embracing Laith in a happy "hullo!"

The two old friends laughed. "I can hardly believe my eyes, Abner Murray," said Laith with a jovial slap on the other man's back.

"You didn't think I'd just leave you out here to perish did yeh, Hastings?" said the older man. His kind eyes scanned his surroundings and lighted on Mara and Medwin. His eyes widened.

"Where are the others, my boy," he whispered to Laith, "and who in the name of Lyria are they?"

◆　◆　◆

Ivy sat up in her hammock, suddenly awake. She knew where her mother's doorway led.

In her excitement, Ivy hastily dressed and dashed from her chamber, off to test her hypothesis. She was ascending the ladder leading to the upper level when she realized it would be foolhardy to go alone in the middle of the night. She would be sure to hear a lecture from several sources if she left the protection of the pit alone. After a short consideration, she climbed back down the ladder and circled the corridor to the round chamber joining the men's sleeping quarters. She moved close to the cloth partition of one of them.

"Simon," she whispered, or at least that was what she had meant to whisper. Her throat was dry, and her utterance was more of an indistinguishable rasping than a name. Nevertheless, she could hear him stirring, and soon he pushed aside the curtain, blinking at her with amused interest.

"May I help you?" he whispered.

"I'm sorry to wake you, Simon, but—"

"You didn't wake me, I was—"

"I think I know where it leads!"

"Where what—"

"My mother's door!" Ivy was having difficulty sustaining a whisper in her excitement. Simon smiled slightly at her. "I must go try it, now," she continued. "But I need you to come, you know, for protection. So get dressed, and let's get going."

Simon shook his head. "It's too late now . . . or early. The sun will have already begun to rise."

Ivy's shoulders fell. "You're sure?"

"Yes, it will have to wait until tonight."

Ivy nodded, resigned. She turned to go. "I'm sorry to have bothered you."

"Wait," Simon whispered, and she turned. "How did you figure it out?"

Ivy's eyes sparkled, even in the dark chamber. "It came to me in a dream. Ever since my mother was abducted, I frequently have these dreams that I'm her, being taken by the warriors. They haul me across the plains and ferry me out to sea where they weight my ankles and throw me overboard. Then, I wake up."

"Sounds wretched," Simon commented.

"Yes. But this time in the dream I shook off my captors before we left the palace. I ran from them, and found myself in a corridor. A faceless but friendly figure at the passage end beckoned me to follow her, so I did.

"She took me through a doorway, and I was suddenly outside at this charming cottage near the Lyrian forest. Now I could see the woman. She was gray-haired, with wise eyes and a friendly smile. There was an older man as well, with broad shoulders and strong features, sitting in a chair in the shade of the trees. Two handsome, curly-haired young women were setting out a meal on a low table. They looked up and waved when they saw me."

Ivy paused.

"So you think this was a vision to show you where your mother was going?" Simon asked.

"It was not a vision, Simon," she replied, quietly. "It was a memory."

Simon raised his eyebrows. She continued. "Do you remember telling me of your memory of my mother the other day, of her riding past your orchard in happy speed?"

"Yes."

"That's where she was riding in such a hurry, to see her family, my grandparents and aunts. She took me there once or twice when I was young, telling me it was to be our secret. My father must not have approved, and she probably wasn't able to steal me away to visit as I got older. I had almost forgotten them altogether until Beathas told me my mother had come with her sisters all of those years ago."

"Ah," whispered Simon.

"Yes," Ivy whispered back. "I should have thought of it sooner. When she told the Pelasars she was taking them home, she could not have meant the tall castle walls and forced formality of court life, but rather the free companionable simplicity of her childhood home, a safe and unpredictable hideout where she could be sure of loyal help and protection. I must be right. I hope I'm right."

Simon reached out and gave her hand a reassuring squeeze. "I'm sure you are. We'll find out tonight."

"Tonight," echoed Ivy as he released her hand and disappeared once more behind the curtain.

◆　　◆　　◆

Laith loaded the final parcel onto the waiting longboat and stood for a moment watching the *Sapphire* where she swayed out beyond the shoal. He did a mental inventory of the items on the boat, ensuring he had not forgotten something important. Space was limited on the little vessel, so he had had to choose carefully.

That last parcel had contained a collection of some of the various healing herbs of the Fringe from Medwin's stores. They had done a great deal to heal Mara. He looked at her where she stood a few feet away, standing straight, watching the sea, and smiling slightly behind her dark hair. The new strength of her resolve seemed to carry to her wounded leg, and though she still walked with a slight limp, she seemed generally more whole.

She must have felt his gaze, and turned to look at him. Her eyes scanned the coast. "Where's Medwin?" she mouthed.

Laith shrugged. The old man had been hiding away all morning, hoping to avoid the inevitable good-byes, most likely. Laith beckoned for Mara to follow him, and with a promise to the sailors that they would return shortly, they climbed the hill one last time.

The early sun was still behind the glass house, framing it in a warm glow. Its face reflected the mossy hills and crags and the cloud-scattered sky behind the two figures. Neither spoke.

They found Medwin in the mirror room. He was hunched over his table, and Laith assumed he was staring into one of the many hand mirrors on it. The two stood quietly in the doorway, their reflections still and waiting.

"It seems I can't escape after all," Medwin mumbled without looking up.

"You're not big on good-byes, huh?" Laith teased.

When Medwin looked up, Laith saw in his eyes something resigned, and tired, and suddenly the old man seemed infinitely older than he had a few weeks ago. "No," he replied, and smiled ruefully. "It seems so easy to run away from difficult things, doesn't it?"

The three in the room stared at each other, understanding passed between them—and something else. Laith felt, for a moment, absolved.

Medwin crossed the room and stood in front of Mara. He took her pale smooth hand in his old red one.

"Thank you for a second chance," she said, quietly.

The old man leaned a little closer to her and spoke so quietly that Laith could not distinguish the words. Mara was very still, and he wished he could see her face better, as it was partially hidden behind her dark hair. When Medwin had finished speaking he wrapped the princess in a fatherly embrace. Quietly, she left the room.

Medwin turned toward Laith, studying him with eyes that were full of emotion but unreadable. The young man felt suddenly awkward. He cleared his throat nervously.

"Well, thanks for everything, I guess," he stammered. "I mean, I know that I have been less than pleasant at times."

"Rather," Medwin added, straight-faced.

Laith smiled nervously and fingered the chain around his neck. "And, thank you for this, I mean, I hope your wife . . ."

"Laith," Medwin interrupted, "let me tell you about my wife."

The younger man nodded, glad to relinquish control of the conversation.

"Her name was Liese. I knew her from my youth, as she belonged to one of the few Lyrian families, like mine, who kept the old secrets of the Stone Mages. We were connected by our gift of sight. She was the only person other than my mother who was like me, and we understood each other well. I loved her very much. We were married in Lyria and lived there happily for a few years. It was by our sight we were able to keep the Stone Mages safe, predicting possible danger of discovery by the Wrakes of the South.

"However, we were eventually discovered, perhaps seen in a vision by the enemy, or perhaps my hot head and loose tongue slipped in a too-public location. Either way, we had to flee for our lives. We were at one point overtaken, and Liese was badly injured. I was able to conjure up illusions and sword fight well enough that we eventually escaped. Our Stone Mage friends and family secured us passage on a boat and eventually hid us here. They would keep our location secret and avidly spread tales of danger concerning this place to keep others from us.

"Liese recovered from her injury, but the nature of the wounds left her unable to bear children. This was devastating for both of us, not only because we would never have the chance to parent but also because this amazing gift we possessed would end when we did.

"We weren't, however, totally alone or cut off. We built this house, complete with mirror room to connect us to the world outside and a library full of the ancient knowledge that was no longer safe to be kept on the continent. We had frequent visitors seeking magical knowledge or insightful mirror visions, always accompanied by a Water Mage for safe passage. Liese worked diligently to make our home a place where travelers felt welcome, and they came frequently enough that we were always able to obtain various items for the house or our personal needs. We learned about the native plant and animal life here and cultivated a garden. We were happy in spite of our underlying disappointment.

"As we grew older, however, it became increasingly apparent that Liese was declining in energy and health. The wounds inflicted on her young body had never completely left her. About twenty years ago, she died.

"I was bitter for a long time after her death, and felt very alone. More and more Stone Mages died out after Abaddon's rise on the continent. I did not seek visions in my mirrors, and wished for death.

"I found hope again, however, when I was visited by three Stone Mage sisters. I rejoiced that at least one family who knew the secrets was still living. They opened the doorway here, and even though I knew of their death and failure, I had taken up my mirrors again, and I believed that I would see another visitor some day, and that we might still triumph.

"I wasn't surprised at the arrival of the princess. I was not even surprised at the coming of brave others who had gifts, though unknown to them. But I was not prepared for you."

Laith looked at Medwin abruptly. "Me?"

"Understand, Laith, that as soon as we discovered my wife could not have children, I was convinced I would never meet another Lyrian with our gift. Imagine my astonishment, then, when you appeared. I had seen snatches of you in my mirrors when you were young but had written them off to your connection with the royal family. I was aware of your disappearance and guessed, soon after you arrived, your true identity. But I was amazed to get to know a young man with hair as red as mine had once been, with a temper as testy, a young man who, I came to suspect, had the gift of sight.

"I do not think it is mere coincidence, Laith, that led a man estranged from a family who maybe never loved or wanted him to a man who had wished so many years for a son, someone to pass on knowledge to, to teach, to be proud of, and to see himself in. I have found that in you. You are a runaway, a sailor, rightful duke, and a Stone Mage. But as far as I'm concerned, Laith Haverford, you are the son I never had. I want you to go live your brave life, but I'm loathe to see you leave."

Medwin's voice broke, and Laith felt sudden tears in his eyes. The old man embraced him and the two remained so for quite a time.

When they broke apart, Medwin smiled at the younger, taller man. "That stone you wear is yours forever, and this one at my neck will be yours when I'm gone. This place is your home whenever you wish for it."

"Thank you," Laith said quietly.

"Now go," said Medwin. He pushed the young man out of the mirror room and watched him walk down the hall and out of the glass house before turning back to the mirrors to watch him cross the sea.

CHAPTER 48

It was Gilda Reed's first time to visit the place of the doorway. She had not been needed as a guide or a protector on Ivy's journeys, but this morning the princess had squeezed her hand and told her that this was the night. Ivy's eyes had been full of hope and excitement. Gilda was not about to miss this, regardless of the orders to the contrary John Merrick had issued. Her response to his vehement "no's" and "absolutely not's" had been to smile and fall in behind the others as they entered the tunnels. He had sighed in exasperation and followed.

She was glad, however, that Burr had been successfully distracted. She had sent him off in search of Reuel, one of the animal mages who had accompanied him to the White City, to demonstrate his newfound ability to get groups of earthworms to dig holes in the walls of the pit. She would much rather meet his anger when he found they had gone off to do something important without him than see him harmed.

She was now simultaneously enjoying the relief of the warm, still desert air and dreadfully missing the cool, fragrant nights in her

Lyrian flower garden. She was glad to be helping in an important mission, and had learned a great deal from the earth mages in the pit, but sometimes her homesickness was overwhelming.

"I hope she opens it tonight," John Merrick mumbled, a few feet away, "time is running out."

Saffi scoffed. "Another insightful observation by the wise captain," she whispered. "Be patient with her, she's putting everything she's got into this."

Gilda peered through her spectacles at Ivy where she stood before them, eyes closed in deep concentration, arms scanning the open air.

"I hope you are not accusing me of criticism to my crown," Merrick said, and Gilda saw Simon wince. All his focus was on Ivy, but his fists tightened, and jaw clenched.

"No, no," Saffi replied, "I only accuse you of mere male thoughtlessness. Sometimes it is best for the slight of tongue not to speak at all."

"This from the woman I can't keep quiet in my own language, let alone hers."

Saffi nudged him sharply.

"That was much more eloquent," he replied.

Simon cleared his throat loudly, and there was silence again.

Gilda was watching Ivy's face. Her visage had transmuted from clear and calm to furrowed and perplexed. The poor princess had been pouring all of her concentration into that empty piece of air for over an hour now, and Gilda could see her shoulders slump in exhaustion, her frame bowing under the weight of her mission. Gilda began to feel a helpless concern that kept her staring, immobile, at the young woman.

The princess's movements were becoming increasingly frantic.

All at once she collapsed to the ground, gasping out a sudden teary frustration.

"It's impossible," she cried out to no one in particular. She ran a hand through her tangled curls. "I thought I could do this, but I can't. We'll just have to be stuck here. I have no more to give." She dropped her head and cried.

Slowly, Simon moved toward her, knelt at her side, and put an arm about her shoulder. Gilda followed, kneeling at her other side, and gently stroked her wild hair. Slowly, Merrick and Saffi followed. Saffi knelt before her, and Merrick stood a few feet back, watching her with shame and sympathy.

Eventually, Ivy's sobs slowed. She looked up, suddenly embarrassed, and wiped her red eyes. "I'm sorry," she murmured. "It's just, I'm sure I know where that doorway leads, but I can't seem to get a good grasp on that little cottage in the forest. It wasn't my home. Even when I feel a little clearer about *there*, I have no idea how to connect it with *here*. To me, that place is vague friendliness and *this* . . ." She paused, and sighed. "this is nothing but being trapped by the weight of the earth over my head, or being blasted with sand in my eyes. It is heavy and strange and the farthest thing from home I can imagine."

The little group was silent. A sudden thought struck Gilda Reed. "You have said," she began, softly, "that your mother and her sisters must have been aiming for home. You have decided that for them it was a little cottage in a forest where they spent their childhood. But is it possible that you are overly focused on the *where* at the expense of the *why*?

"My home," Gilda continued, "is where roses are growing, because my mother grew roses, and they remind me of her—her smell and her strong hands moving the soil and showing me how to tend it as well. Simon's home was a piece of land in Lyria, but more recently a crowded little home in the mountains."

Simon nodded, smiling. "The places my parents and my siblings have lived. The places I have memories of my brother."

"Exactly," said Gilda. "Don't you think, Princess, that your mother might have chosen that place because she shared a family bond there? Her connection here to that home had nothing to do with this wretched wilderness, but to the two sisters who were in it with her. People she loved, who loved her in return.

"But, Gilda," she whispered, "I'm not sure I even have a family anymore."

"You have memories, many devoted fellow Lyrians, and you have us."

Ivy looked at her four companions, all gathered around her. Saffi laid a hand on hers.

"It is *solely* our companionships that have helped us survive this hellhole all of these years. Imagine how loved you will be by all of us pit dwellers when you get us out of here," Saffi said, and Ivy smiled.

She stood up again and faced the would-be doorway. Gilda and the others began to retreat, but Ivy stopped them.

"Stay close," she said. She pulled her stone from her dress front and turned it over in her fingers before letting it fall once more. She lifted her hands to the air again, feeling the emptiness, but she kept her eyes open, staring wide-eyed into the empty desert, but looking as though she was seeing something completely different. Her face was blotchy and tear-stained but calm. The muscles in her arms became tense, and she reached out, directly in front of her and clenched her fists, as if holding onto the empty air. Then, she slowly moved one arm across her chest and behind her. Her eyes sparkled with intensity.

Out of the corner of her eye, Gilda saw a vague movement or

flash. She turned from Ivy to look at the empty air in front of her and saw that the very texture of the space shimmered around jagged edges, then blurred, then became liquid like the door had so long ago at the Fringe. She heard Ivy's surprised gasp next to her and felt goose bumps rise on her own arms and neck. The door was formed, and open.

CHAPTER 49

Princess Mara felt more alive than she had in years, maybe ever, as she rode horseback down the deserted road toward the mountain castle. She rode swiftly, her hair flying free under the cloak of night. Her thoughts had been dominated in the past few days by anxiety over the boat she was guiding as safely and quickly as possible over wild summer seas, and by fear of what she would meet once the ship made port.

Now, however, those concerns were a dull background to her current feelings of strength, freedom, and being, at last, in control of her own fate. Laith rode just behind her. She felt secure with him near, as if he would not only support her, but that he actually trusted her.

Some paces behind Laith, other men rode, and some, even farther back, walked after her. Abner Murray, Mr. Niles, and Russ, who owned the Arrow and who had given them use of these horses, and many other trusted Lyrians who would follow to the castle and obey her command there.

She could now see the outline of that stronghold, silhouetted in moonlight, and she gradually slowed her horse. Laith's horse moved adjacent to her own.

"I'll tell these men to wait on the low road, then?" he asked.

"Yes," Mara responded. "The less attention we draw to my coming the better. We can't risk the wrong people leaking information. I would like the general public to believe it is Ivy who has returned to give commands."

"What about those inside the castle?" Laith asked. "Murray says Lord Mockford was placed in charge after you left, and that he is most assuredly loyal to Abaddon."

"Anyone who is a threat to the safety of my kingdom, and who might expose me will have to be restricted to the palace, imprisoned." She exhaled slowly, and Laith nodded agreement before riding back to give commands to the other men. Only he and Murray would accompany Mara as far as the palace.

Laith thought it best for them not to encounter stable hands that they were unsure of and, therefore, the three travelers dismounted at the foot of the castle hill and proceeded to the gate on foot. When the guard moved forward to question them, Murray announced to the nervous-looking man that he had better open up for Duke Haverford and "the Princess" herself. Mara kept her head bowed under her hooded cloak but extended her hand, brandishing the royal ring, and the man quickly complied, his eyes wide with surprise, and, Mara thought, hope.

Once inside, she led the others to a small receiving chamber and sent one of the scrambling servants with strict instructions to bring her Talbot and no one else. She paced nervously as she waited, hoping she was right to trust her father's steward.

Murray and Laith were standing helplessly by, watching her, when the thin, haggard-looking man entered the room. Mara dismissed the servants who went reluctantly, glancing behind them. Talbot bowed before the princess, and when the doors were closed, she removed her hood.

Talbot looked up into her face, and immediately stammered, astonished. "But . . . Princess Mara . . . I'm sorry . . . I thought it was . . . and that you were . . ."

"Dead?" Laith finished for him. Talbot looked toward the two other men in the room, seeing them for the first time.

"Yes," he replied, a bit more calmly. "We had received word that you had been killed at sea, that you were serving. . . . When the servant told me the Princess had returned, I assumed it was Princess Ivy."

"That is what we would like everyone to assume, Talbot." Mara was feeling more relaxed. The look on the man's face when he referred to her supposed loyalty to Abaddon had given his own loyalties away. "Sometime, perhaps, you will know of my past, or what has brought me here, Talbot, but for now, be sure that I am Abaddon's sworn enemy and that I have returned to help my kingdom defeat him." Talbot nodded his head, looking slightly relieved.

"It is essential that my identity remain confused for the current time," Mara continued. "Can you promise to help me retake command of this castle while protecting my identity?"

The man nodded. "I promise, Your Majesty."

Mara smiled at him. "Good. Now tell me what's going on here."

◆　◆　◆

Saffi Beval stood sentinel at the newly re-opened entryway to the tunnels, her fellow Pelasars standing en masse before her. All were donning their most practical clothing for travel and were carrying packs and satchels filled with practical necessities and souvenirs of their lives to this point.

Next to Saffi, Beathas was raising a mound of earth for Eben to stand on to address the waiting group. Saffi saw her feelings echoed before her in the faces she knew so well. They were alternately afraid and excited.

As Eben commenced to address the people in their own tongue, Saffi moved closer to the Lyrians, who were also nearby, to whisper translations.

"Some of us," Eben began, "have spent a large portion of our lives in this pit, and some of you younger ones have never known another life. This pit has been the source of our power, and our refuge. It has been our home, but it has also been our prison. Some of our brothers and sisters whom we have loved dearly have given their lives to help us flee this prison. We remember them humbly and rejoice that today their dream will be realized.

"We are grateful for our Lyrian friends who have come to offer us a way out and a new home where we can begin again. We realize we will have to fight for that home, and all of you who are able have promised your hands and your gifts to help our friends in this fight."

Eben paused, and Beathas, who was standing nearby, indicated that she had words to add. She was helped up next to Eben. "After today," she said, her voice comfortable but determined, "you will no longer be just Bellarians, or even Pelasars. You will be Lyrians and, most importantly, Stone Mages. So, as we leave today to face new and unknown challenges and opportunities, I offer you this simple advice: do not look back."

Eben helped the old woman down from the post, shouldered his own pack, and entered the tunnels. The crowd began, slowly, to follow. As they passed by, Saffi could feel their tense exhilaration. When the Pelasars had all disappeared into the tunnels, the Lyrians followed them in.

Saffi, alone in the pit, lingered at the entrance momentarily. She inhaled the familiar aroma of smoke and earth. The cavernous space was so uncharacteristically dark and quiet. She thought of her father who lay buried deep beneath her, then moved into the tunnel.

Once inside, Saffi had to hurry to catch up to the others. John

Merrick had been the last one to enter, and he was holding the last lantern. Saffi knew the tunnels well but did not trust that knowledge in the darkness.

"So, you decided to join us," Merrick whispered without turning around. "I was beginning to think you were going to opt for stones and solitude rather than more Lyrians."

"I'm not opposed to Lyrians, in general," Saffi replied to his back.

"Just me, specifically, then?"

Saffi did not reply.

"It's just as well," he continued. "I'm not a fair representation of your everyday Lyrian. I'm far too extraordinary."

Saffi coughed. "Is that what you call it?"

"You have another word in mind?"

"No. There are no words to describe you."

Merrick laughed. "I'll take that as a compliment."

"Yes, I'm sure you will," Saffi replied.

"So," Merrick whispered in a changed tone, "do you suppose this journey will flow smoothly, or do you predict opposition?"

Saffi scowled at the darkness. "I wouldn't presume to predict, but I certainly have my worries. As you know, our history in this effort is not encouraging."

"But surely your pig prince is far too ignorant to apprehend for the second time?"

"Oswald alone poses little threat, but he represents those whose interest in us seems as constant as it is dangerous."

"You mean Abaddon."

"I don't mean that Abaddon would dirty his own hands here, only that he has a seer and a number of dangerous Wrakes at his fingertips."

"So we can only hope to escape their notice."

"Yes, that is my hope," said Saffi.

CHAPTER 50

Laith blinked at the mirror in his hands as his vision ended and the surface once again reflected his own face.

"What did you see?" Mara asked quietly. They were alone in a small antechamber to the throne room in the mountain castle. By Mara's command, Talbot had gathered a number of the loyal remaining Lyrian leaders for her to address and instruct, and they were waiting for them in the next room. The princess had asked Laith to consult a mirror before she addressed them, and now she was eagerly waiting to be told what he had seen.

"I'm not sure," he replied after a few moments. "I was targeting something useful to us, like Abaddon discussing battle plans, or at least the present location of the Southern army. Instead I've seen a burial of an old woman."

Mara drew in her breath, suddenly. "Describe the woman," she said quickly.

"Old," Laith said, straining.

"Was she holding anything?" Mara prompted.

Laith stepped closer to the princess. "You know her? Yes, I

noticed she was holding a large dark globe of sorts before they closed the coffin."

Mara's eyes were bright. "She was a seer, Abaddon's seer. Are you sure she was dead?"

"Very."

Mara put her hand on his arm, and squeezed. "We just might have a chance," she whispered, and then turned to enter the throne room.

Six men, including Talbot, were seated in chairs surrounding the throne, looking equal parts surprised and nervous as Mara ascended the throne. They stood when she entered and did not take their chairs again until Mara was seated on the throne. Laith took the empty chair at her right.

"You are here," Mara began, "as the last remaining courtiers loyal to Lyria. No doubt you are wary of me, and also reluctant to take a stand against what you see as an unbeatable foe." There were nods and murmurs of agreement from the men.

"Those feelings are natural, justified, even. But if we succumb to our fears, Lyria will cease to exist today."

The oldest man in the circle, Duke Ramsay, Laith thought, made a motion to speak.

"Please speak freely," Mara prompted. "This is no time for formalities."

"I hope Your Majesty will forgive me," the man said, with no forgiveness in his features, "but many would argue that Lyria has long ago ceased to exist. We no longer reside on our Lyrian soil, but hide in the mountains, and it has been ages since we had real direction from the crown. You yourself left us in Lord Mockford's corrupt grasp, and now he has been unceremoniously locked in the dungeon."

"That aside," said the square-chinned, hollow-eyed General

Rune. He had been shifting uneasily in his seat as though there was nothing quite so chaffing as a formal meeting among dignitaries. He was not old, perhaps thirty-five, and had been newly appointed as general based on his rumored prowess in battle and professed loyalty. He now spoke unfalteringly. "If you suggest that we fight the Southerners, we surely will cease to exist. Our remaining soldiers are not armed and ready, not solely because Mockford immobilized them. They know as well as we do that they don't stand a chance against Abaddon's armies. Wouldn't it be wiser to evacuate as many as possible by boat, soon?"

The men suddenly erupted in conversation, proffering criticisms and arguing points with each other.

Laith watched with growing anger as Mara attempted to speak, only to be drowned in the contentious noise. He could feel his face growing red as he stood and shouted, "Quiet on deck!"

The men looked up in dumbstruck wonder at Laith, and the room was quiet.

"Thank you, Duke Haverford," Mara said, clearing her throat and concealing a smile. "Gentlemen, your fears are real, and your criticisms have their foundation, but we have no time to bicker. You suggest that we can get on boats and sail away from our conflict, but you know as well as I do, that we haven't enough seaworthy vessels to save even half of the Lyrians here in the mountains. Even if we could get a good number safely away, where would they go? What kingdom would welcome poor Lyrians as anything better than slaves? Those who argue that point are only thinking of saving their own skin.

"I think that our best and only option is to fight. Our foe is great and powerful, but these mountains will act as our stronghold. I suggest we enlist all who are able to fight to arm themselves and head off our enemies at the pass. If we can hold them there, we will restrict the number of exposed fighting soldiers that have access to our armies, and we just might survive until help arrives."

"Help?" General Rune spoke, his eyes trained closely on the princess.

Mara swallowed. "Princess Ivy did not die at the Fringe. Duke Haverford and a small number of other Lyrians mounted a rescue party for her and found her safe. She and those others have embarked on a mission to find and bring back aid to Lyria. I do not know if they will succeed, but I believe they will."

The room was quiet. The small group of men around the circle seemed suddenly alive. "I believe in my sister," Mara continued, "and I think you do too."

◆　　◆　　◆

John Merrick exited the tunnels and offered a lifting hand to Saffi, who was just behind him. To his surprise, she accepted it.

Through the crowd that surrounded them, Merrick spotted the princess. She was threading her way through the people, who seemed to throng around her in support and encouragement, closely followed by Simon. Merrick smiled. Adler wouldn't let that girl out of his sight, and good for him. The princess could not ask for a more diligent bodyguard. He was now kindly asking the people to create a space for her as she faced her doorway.

Merrick glanced at Saffi and followed her gaze across the vast desert behind them to the distant lights of the White City. From here it seemed another sparkling star, but rather than being warmed by its light, Merrick felt chilled—especially when he thought of the cold, colorless people; the brutal blows and insults they had thrown; the gallows and dungeons; and that fat, lying prince. He looked down.

Saffi reached over and grabbed his arm with such abrupt urgency that he actually jumped. He turned a questioning look to her, but saw her panicked face and looked once more toward the White City.

The distance between them and the city was being closed with inhuman speed by a smudge of dark figures, horses, and even, Merrick thought, a long, dark carriage. He turned again to Saffi and their eyes met, communicating identical fear and determination. She nodded to him, and they moved.

Loudly and calmly, Saffi spoke out warning and direction in Bellarian to the surrounding people, while Merrick made his way to the princess and the Lyrians. The crowd was growing frantic, and Merrick had to push his way through them, glancing back over his shoulder in amazement at the caravan's speed. When the princess came into view she was standing still, her back to the unopened doorway in the sky. Simon was, of course, at her elbow, and Burr and Gilda were close by.

"We've got opposition incoming, and fast," he yelled to them. "Princess," he said, now standing directly in front of her. "You've got to open that doorway as fast as you can. We've got to get all these people out of here, women and children first. The men can stay to fight off the threat until they are through." Ivy nodded with impressive calm and turned her attention to the doorway.

Merrick shouted to Simon, "Adler—"

"Yes. I'll protect her." The young man's eyes held that characteristic determination Merrick had begun to recognize. He nodded at Simon and turned back to the group. Gilda and Burr had already made their way to the front of the group that was now watching the incoming enemy, transfixed. He found Saffi quickly.

"You've got to get the children behind us, they'll go through first, with their parents. Any others able to should be prepared to fight this off." Saffi shouted the commands, and the parents began gathering their children closer to the doorway, which, Merrick noted, was not yet opened.

He turned to study the incoming threat and wished dreadfully that they were at sea. He felt helpless. "We need a plan," he shouted at Saffi.

She nodded. "They've obviously got some Animal Wrake at their command making those horses move like that. They'll be on top of us in no time."

"We've got to use our gifts, but from what I can tell the only element here at our disposal is earth."

Saffi turned immediately to the crowd to call forward the Earth Mages. The caravan was coming so close that Merrick could make out the silver lining on the dark carriage. Ten or fifteen figures came to the front of the crowd, Nabra, Beathas, and Gilda Reed among them.

"Tell them to try and make a wall of this sand," he called to Saffi, and she again repeated his instructions.

Before any of the Earth Mages even raised a finger, however, the impending caravan halted. The door of the carriage opened, and a large figure emerged. John Merrick could see, even at this distance, the hideous deformation of his face and the limp in his walk. The kicking Oswald had received from the horse that day in the White City had left its marks, and the man was here to wreak his angry revenge.

The Pelasar mages were moving around Merrick, and he watched as the sand began to rise up before him, creating a translucent barrier between the opposing groups. He looked behind him frantically and noticed that the door was still closed. *Come on, Ivy,* he thought.

The wall of sand was growing thicker and taller, when suddenly it blurred and blew asunder with great speed. He looked at the enemy group and saw Prince Oswald and two Wrakes at the fore-front, on foot, waving their hands about them angrily. John Merrick realized with momentary clarity that he had been wrong when he had told Saffi the only available element was earth. These Wrakes were moving the wind.

The barrier blown asunder, Oswald's minions advanced. Saffi shouted another command, and again the wall of sand began to rise, this time thicker and higher than before. Once again, the wall was obliterated in three large gusts of wind. The enemy moved in. The wall was again raised. Merrick watched, transfixed, until a commotion behind him made him turn. The door was open.

Saffi, too, had noticed and began issuing commands for the children and their parents to start moving through. Wind was beginning to whip around Merrick as he watched the Pelasars scramble toward the doorway and disappear through the undulating surface. He could not see Ivy or Simon.

Sand blasted around Merrick and those surrounding him. It filled the air and stung his eyes. The shouts of the people around him became muffled, and he could no longer see the Earth Mages, or even Saffi a few feet from him. He tried to move toward her but found himself being pulled into the spiraling force of the wind. He felt it could easily lift him off his feet and carry him away.

Merrick knelt on the ground to feel the weight of it under him. He closed his eyes and covered his head with his arms. The wind chafed the exposed skin on his hands and arms. He felt a deep, aching stinging. He let out a low, bellowing scream, and the noise of it disappeared in the furious storm.

Suddenly there was a hand on his arm, pulling him, leading him through the thickness of sand and wind. He followed the person, pushing with all his strength against the blasting sand until he felt its pull intensify, then lessen, and he was running.

John Merrick opened his eyes to see that his rescuer was Gilda Reed. Her broad shoulders were determined, and her feet rooted to the earth that was hers to control as she led him toward the liquid opening of the doorway. The princess was standing before it, leaning toward it, her hands extended, and Simon Adler had his arm around her, as if rooting her to the ground.

Gilda released Merrick's hand, and he turned to watch her run back toward what Merrick could see now was a vicious tornado. Beathas was emerging from the sand, her feet sure like Gilda's had been despite her old age. Behind her, grasping her hand tightly, was Saffi Beval. Beathas relinquished Saffi to Gilda, and Merrick rushed forward to meet them, putting his arm around Saffi's shoulder and pulling her toward the open doorway.

Gilda was pushing both of them, shouting for them to get through the opening, when something made them stop, and turn.

Beathas was standing still, facing the tornado, head high and arms opened wide, as if she would embrace the ferocious storm that looked to devour her at any moment. The sand beat about her and tore at her gray cloak, but her feet were planted and she did not move. She raised her hands high above her head, and in one vast motion lowered them, as if pushing down on some unseen force before her. As she did so the swirling sand began to condense tightly at the storm's center. Then, slowly, it began to descend, pushing down with great pressure and force.

Suddenly, Merrick knew it would fall, that it would crush and destroy Prince Oswald and the mages, and Beathas, and them, and without thinking he grabbed Gilda's and Saffi's hands in his and pulled them to the doorway, glancing over his shoulder to see that Simon was pulling Ivy close behind. Together, they all went through.

◆　　◆　　◆

Mara sat in the dark throne room, her eyes closed. She tried to steady her breathing and still her shaking hands. She felt the air change as the door opened and quiet footsteps approached. She opened her eyes.

Laith made a small bow at the foot of the dais. "Your army awaits, Your Highness."

Mara almost scoffed at this address, especially when she thought of the contrast in his manner today to the first time they had met, him looking down at her with anger and loathing. She was about to tell him so, when she looked in his eyes and saw the sincerity in them.

"Are they all assembled, then?"

Laith nodded. "We have gathered all who would fight."

"The women and children—they are all moved safely within the castle walls?"

"Yes, it's close quarters, but they should be safe, and there are enough supplies and food stored to last for a while. They seem content, confident in our army to protect them."

"Would many come fight?"

Laith ascended the few steps to her throne and held out his hand. "Come and see."

She took his hand and they left the dark room. A few men were assembled in the corridor, including General Rune, who approached her, his dark eyes unreadable.

"We are ready for your command, Your Majesty."

"Thank you, General," Mara said, tying the cloak Laith had just placed on her shoulders. "Remember our aim. We keep them at the pass. Do not advance, and do all you can to keep them from breaking through our defenses."

General Rune nodded as the group moved toward the castle gate. Mara pulled the great hood of the cloak over her head.

"Also, General, remember that it is absolutely imperative my identity remains unknown. Let them assume I am my sister. Our enemies must not know I am in command here."

General Rune nodded, then, as almost an afterthought, he held out his rough hand and looked her in the eye. "Victorious," he said, in the longstanding tradition of the Lyrian army, and she placed her hand briefly in his.

"Victorious," she returned, feeling for a small moment as if the word just might come to fruition.

They had reached the gate. Mara felt her heart jolt as the portcullis was raised. She thought of what lay ahead, closing her eyes for a moment. When she opened them, she crossed the bridge, lines of soldiers saluting her hidden self as she passed through them. Her breathing was strained, but when she reached the edge of the bridge and looked down the hill at the army below, it stopped altogether.

The mountain valley between Mara and the pass was filled with Lyrians. Some on horseback with proper armor and weapons, others on foot, much more humbly outfitted. They ranged in age from youths barely out of boyhood to men well past their prime. All of them, heads held high, turned their thousands of eyes to her.

Her knees were weak, and she found herself unable to speak. Laith was soon by her, bringing her horse, and she was glad she would be able to mount and hide the shaking in her legs. He helped her up to the saddle, and she turned the dark mare toward the waiting people. They stared at her, waiting.

Mara took a deep breath and, in a bold gesture, raised her arm high, her fist clenched. Below her, there was a stirring cry among the people, and they raised their sword-wielding arms in response.

◆　◆　◆

Ivy felt a somewhat familiar, heavy grounding in her back and arms. She opened her eyes to see a blur of green and blue, and then realized that her eyes were wet. She blinked away the watery film, and a leafy canopy against an afternoon sky came into focus.

She sat up abruptly, registering the success of the journey she had just attempted, then, amidst the dizzy swaying that soon overcame her, she remembered why there were tears in her eyes and why there was an aching somewhere in her chest that refused to be quieted. A series of images reeled in her mind: the windy desert, the vicious sand, the incoming opposition, confusion, madness, and then that glance over her shoulder, that brief view of a little old woman bringing the earth crashing down upon the enemy and herself with them. *Beathas.*

The tears returned. Ivy blinked and looked about her. Nearby, on the soft ground and under the trees, people were sitting up and looking around. There were quiet whisperings and sorrowful glances as the Pelasars learned of the fate of their old leader and friend. Arms encircled nearby shoulders, and mouths sighed out sad cries.

Simon, next to her, sat with his head in his hands. She found Saffi's face across the clearing streaming with unembarrassed tears, seemingly unaware of the arm Merrick had placed on her slender shoulders.

However, it was the lined face, the drawn sad mouth, and the meaning-filled eyes of Eben that held her gaze. He was watching her, and his face communicated something to Ivy that made her sit up straight and wipe the tears from her face. She saw in his look the hint of command and responsibility that marked him as a leader. She understood that in spite of his great sorrow in the loss of a long-time friend, he was thinking of his people, of the present mission at hand, and he was asking her to do the same.

Ivy surveyed the glen where they were gathered. She turned around to see the little cottage of her memory not far off, overgrown and crumbling. She stood and moved toward it, running her hands over its rough stones and peeking in the dark window. Eben had followed her and was now at her side.

"What now?" he asked, in rough Lyrian.

Ivy met his gaze honestly. "I had not thought past this point," she admitted, shrugging to communicate her meaning. "I don't know whether or not Abaddon has brought war to my people in the mountains, or if there is anyone there who would oppose him, but I have to get there and find out."

As the princess spoke, others joined Eben and Ivy at the cottage. A dazed Gilda Reed came, with Burr trailing close behind, unusually quiet. Saffi and Merrick came, and Simon. They made a circle around her, swallowing tears and wiping their faces.

Eben spoke in Bellarian, and Saffi translated. "Some of our people will need to stay here and protect the children and their mothers, but the rest of us are resolved to go with you, and help you fight our common enemy."

Ivy nodded. "This place will be safe for them." She pointed through some trees at her right, "there is a stream just through there, and there is plenty of fruit on these trees, and in that neglected garden at the side of the house to keep them fed. Not everyone will fit inside the little cottage, but the trees provide protection, and it will be warm enough in this summer air."

"Should we prepare to head toward the pass then?" Gilda asked.

Merrick frowned. "The Southern Army could be there already, and we are not enough to get through them alone."

"How else will we get to the Lyrians?" Simon asked.

"We could sail around," Merrick replied.

"In what ship?" Burr barked. "Every stinking boat on this side of the mountains could be full of Southerners."

"I don't suppose we could go over the mountains?" Eben offered.

Simon shook his head. "These mountains are more like cliffs. Really, they are impassable."

"We have Earth Mages," Saffi offered. "Perhaps we could tunnel through, or create a stairway."

Ivy looked up, some memory tugging at her mind.

"We could," said Merrick, "but these cliffs are thick, and it would take more time than we have."

"It doesn't seem that we have any other option," Saffi retorted.

"Actually, we might," Ivy said, almost to herself; but the others turned to look at her, questioning.

Ivy was not looking at them, however.

She was somewhere else, or some time else, running through these very trees, chasing something, a bunny or a small deer maybe. She had been running for a while, and soon found that she was following the creature along the cliff face, her small hands brushing its surface, when suddenly her hand met air, and she turned to see a dark opening in the cliff face, big enough for even an adult to pass through. The fawn forgotten, she had stepped into the shady entrance, imagining a secret cave full of treasure and mystery. She had taken only a few steps when she had felt a hand on her shoulder.

She had turned abruptly, catching her breath, to see her grandfather, his kind eyes unusually stern.

"Do not go in here," he had warned, and led her gently but firmly from the cave.

"What's in that cave, Grandfather?" she had asked. He had turned and looked down at her with eyes that could not lie to a child.

"It is not a cave, darling," he had said. "It is a long passage, leading all the way through to the mountain valley, but it is dark, and there are holes and bends. It is not a safe place for a child to play."

Ivy looked up from her reverie, her eyes suddenly clear. Without a word to her waiting companions, she ran through some nearby trees and disappeared from sight.

CHAPTER 51

Severin squinted his red eyes and dismounted his horse. The Southern encampment was sprawled out on the plain before him. The sun was setting, and while he couldn't make out the distinct figures of the warriors amidst the tents, he could feel in the earth beneath his armored feet their energy and anticipation. They were hungry for the killing.

He spat in the dirt, disgusted with these base creatures at his command; and yet, he was scarcely less anxious to begin fighting. The sound of approaching horses interrupted his thoughts, and he turned to see his leading five Wrakes dismount and walk toward him.

"Another day gone, Severin, and still my sword and hands are clean," Caddock hissed as he approached.

"Patience," Severin replied.

"Patience?" spat Rona. "We have just been to the pass, Severin. Every day those Lyrians are building up more courage and man-power, and we sit and wait."

"It is not a matter of patient waiting but foolish hesitation," sneered Dougal.

"They're right," Tynan's gravelly voice entered the mix. "We are weary with waiting, let's finish them, now."

Severin stared at his angry peers, unmoved. "We will wait for Lord Abaddon's command. No matter how long it takes."

"And if the command never comes?" Nysa spoke low and advanced on Severin as she spoke. She watched his countenance waver briefly and stopped only when her face was mere inches from his. "When was the last time you heard from Abaddon at all, Severin?"

He swallowed.

"Not for a long time, I'd wager," Tynan answered for him. "He sits up in that gaudy Lyrian palace hanging on the every word of that ancient seer woman while we prepare for war. I say it is time we make our own commands from here on out."

There was silence in the circle for some long moments. The sun had now descended below the horizon, and Severin felt unusually chilled as he watched their shadowed faces. He turned away.

"Well?" Caddock demanded. "Will you act, or are you too afraid of Abaddon?"

Severin turned to face him, a ready response on his tongue; but Caddock's face did not wear the taunting, accusatory expression he had expected. Even in the growing darkness, Severin could read the panic that had taken sudden hold of the Wrake's features. The others had seen it also and had begun to move warily away from him.

Severin watched as Caddock's face grew red and his eyes wide; and soon Severin became aware of the long-fingered, black-gloved, and disembodied hand clutching Caddock's throat and apparently restricting his air.

Severin and the other Wrakes took more steps backward as the hand grew to include arm, shoulder, neck, and broad chest. Finally, the cool, strong-featured face of Abaddon appeared. He seemed to be unaffected by the strain of strangling the man in front of him, and it was with the calmest voice that he spoke.

"The wise will always fear me, Caddock."

Caddock's face was becoming blue, and his eyes were rolling back in his head.

"You will remember that after this, I think," Abaddon said.

He turned his attention to the cowering group before him. "All of you should remember that," he said. "Imagine my surprise in coming to my most faithful servants only to hear them plotting against me in a most pathetic fashion."

The other Wrakes, Severin excluded, cowered; but Abaddon did not move toward them or release his grip on Caddock, who had begun to flail about madly.

"The seer is dead," Abaddon said, "but she has assured me that she has seen our victory. What does it signify when we begin fighting? We will win. We must simply carry it out." He looked at the five shrinking Wrakes with the utmost loathing and patronization. Then he turned to Severin.

"As for you, your patience will be rewarded."

Severin bowed deeply.

"Command the army to prepare themselves," Abaddon continued. "We bring our final war to the Lyrians in the morning."

Then, suddenly, Abaddon disappeared from sight. Caddock fell to the ground in a heap, gasping for air.

CHAPTER 52

Saffi lifted the torch she was holding and squinted into the darkness of the cave before her. "You're sure about this?" she questioned the princess, who was standing beside her.

"Yes," was Ivy's confident reply, "this will take us straight through the cliffs."

"But you've never actually traveled it?"

"I have not." Ivy's tone was unconcerned as she moved into the darkness. The others, Saffi included, followed reluctantly. Saffi could not help but notice the princess's calm. Indeed, Ivy's clear-minded leadership had been impressive since their return to Lyria, and Saffi had never been so aware of her resemblance to her mother.

At the same time, Saffi felt cold and unsure of this pathway they were taking and wondered why she, who had spent most of her life underground, was so unsettled by the dark cave. Saffi moved slowly, and soon others began passing on either side of her.

Presently, John Merrick was at her side. "Keep up," he whispered, and took her arm, linking it through his. She was forced to quicken her pace to match his long stride.

"You all right?" he asked.

"Fine." Her brusque reply quieted him, and they walked in silence for a while before she spoke again.

"I suppose I'm a little unsettled by being in a space that I'm not familiar with every inch of."

"Yes, I can imagine that would be unsettling for one like you, not to mention you were just wrenched from your only home, have lost a dear friend, and are now marching straight into a battle with unbeatable odds against a largely unknown foe."

He chuckled dryly.

"Considering what you have gone through in the last twenty-four hours, your reaction is totally normal, even if it is not normal for you."

"I'm not invulnerable," Saffi murmured.

"Yes, I know," Merrick answered quietly. "Stubborn and sure and strong, maybe, but not invulnerable."

They were quiet for a time before Merrick spoke again. "I am feeling a bit anxious myself at the thought of facing the Southern Army again."

"Are they so formidable?"

Merrick sighed. "They are of a tradition where the men are born and raised to imbibe warfare. They have always been fierce and bloodthirsty; but they were tribal in the early days, divided and disorganized, so less of a threat. Then Abaddon came, seemingly out of nowhere, and gave them unity and focus for all their violence. They fight with reckless cruelty and seem to need no reason to kill or maim. I'll never forget the masses of them marching toward our small army across the Lyrian plain, spitting and swinging their maces. They were like a sea stretching out as far as we could see. I can imagine they have only grown in force and number since our last meeting."

Saffi shivered in the darkness. She soon began to realize, how-ever, that at perceptible intervals, the space was becoming lighter. It was not the brash light of day or even moonlight approaching, but something of a glow.

Saffi began to grow warm. The glow was coming from the walls of the tunnel itself. As they moved further along the path, others began to take notice, and whispers echoed through the tunnel.

Eventually the walking slowed, and the travelers stopped, star-ing around themselves in amazement, their wondering murmurs becoming audible exclamations. The tunnel had opened up into a larger cavern. It was not of magnificent size or shape, but its walls were lined with exquisite glowing gems and stones of many colors and shapes. Bejeweled stalactites hung from the arched ceiling, and somehow the very air of the room seemed to hum with the energy from the rocks.

Saffi's eyes, however, were not on the ceiling or the walls but on a mess of obscure dark objects on the cavern floor.

She had stooped to carefully pick one up, when she heard Ivy, who was standing nearby, say to herself, "What is this place?"

Saffi stood, lifting her torch in one hand and the pick she had found on the ground in the other. "It's a mine," she announced, and everyone turned to look at her. She was smiling broadly. "This is your Lyrian Stone Mage mine." Saffi dropped the pick and pulled her own stone out from her tunic and held it up. It was warm and glowed with resonance to the stones in the room around her.

The others began to extract their stones, and each of them glowed as hers did.

"Our own mine became nearly depleted many years ago," Saffi explained. "It was only a weak echo of what this one is, untouched after all these years. Merely being so near this mine will strengthen our stones and us. There is no better place we could have come before a battle than this path, Princess Ivy," she said. "You have led us well."

·   ·   ·

The summer morning hung unusually cold and heavy around the Lyrian Army as they took their positions at the pass. Princess Mara looked down at them from horseback atop the hill, feeling anxious and slightly impatient.

General Rune and his commanders were ordering the little army sprawled before her, and they were readying themselves, alive with anticipation.

A deep, pulsing rumble began to resonate through the ground. Mara could feel it move through the stiff form of the horse beneath her, and it made the tips of her fingers tingle. Her Lyrian Army below grew still at the sound, waiting and watching. The advancing Southern Army had reached the pass and had begun to move through the tall cliff face to meet the Lyrians, their marching shaking the earth and sounding in the hearts of their waiting foe.

Slowly, they began to fill the narrow pass like a dark, viscous river. The passage through the cliffs was only wide enough for about twenty men to pass through abreast, but it was long. Abaddon's army was quickly closing the gap between the armies, and Mara knew at once that it was time to go out to meet them.

Sitting tall on her horse, she pulled out the sword that was sheathed at her side and raised it above her head, signaling General Rune below. He raised his in response, and then cried out the orders to march. Without hesitation, swords drawn, the Lyrians began to march forward into the pass.

The Southern Army seemed to her a single entity, an enclosing wall, but she suddenly found that the Lyrian Army before her was hundreds of arms, legs, heads, and hearts—thousands of individual people courageously putting forward their singular will. Among them were people she recognized, people she knew. Duke Ramsay sat astride a horse not far from her position, his wrinkled visage alive with brave determination. She could see General Rune riding back and forth among his men, shouting orders and encouragement as they moved slowly forward. Closer to the pass she recognized Laith's shipmates, Murray, Niles, and others. They were on foot, not far now from the opening of the pass.

She cast about looking for Laith himself. He had insisted that he be on foot, among the first to enter the pass. She had been equally insistent that he hold back and stay on horseback. She had convinced him that he was too indispensable as a seer to be reckless.

But now she could not locate him, and a feeling of dread began to possess her. A loud war cry arose from the men below, and she looked to the pass to find that the gap between armies had disappeared. The Southerners were upon them. The clash of swords seemed deafening even above the shouts and cries of war.

She continued to scan the crowd for Laith. Her horse began to stomp and shuffle, and she held hard to the reins holding him steady, feeling frantic. She forced herself to look back to the pass.

She could see that some at the front line were falling under. She was impressed by the size of the Southern warriors and by the brutal vitality with which they fought, swinging maces and thrusting their large swords. But she also saw the desperate bravery and determination with which her men were fighting and that, at least for the moment, the line was holding; the Southerners had not advanced. She wondered how long they could maintain this position.

Mara was overwhelmed by the noise of the fighting; she had never imagined it would be this loud. Her ears were ringing and she continued to scan the fighters before her, looking for a snatch of bright red hair under a helmet, hoping to catch a glimpse of his sturdy shoulders or his gray mare.

The Lyrians continued to move forward into the pass, each ready for their turn at the front line. She could no longer see Abner Murray and his men. The sun had just risen, and her view of the confrontation became obscured by the sunlight filtering through the dust and dirt that seemed to fill the air around the pass. This "not seeing" increased her anxiety, and she shifted nervously on her horse. She could see movement before her, the dusty silhouettes of horsed and unhorsed men, of swords and shields. She tried to picture them in her mind, but found that the only image she could see was that endless sea of Southerners, filling the pass and stretching out far across the plain that had once been her home.

Mara was afraid. She could see in her mind the way this battle would go. Those brave men, young and old, would keep fighting in the pass, while their families prayed for them within the castle walls behind her. Eventually they would tire, and fall. More would fill their places, and more would fall, until they were all fallen, trampled in the dusty, bloody ground. Then Abaddon's endless army would pour through the pass like deadly ooze, overtaking the captains and leaders, overtaking her, and climbing into the fortress where the rest of Lyria would be annihilated.

She was glued to the saddle, unmoving, sick and dizzy. The sun was blinding her, and she closed her eyes. She felt herself sway slightly as her horse moved beneath her, and she let go of the reins.

Suddenly, there was a hand on her arm, grabbing her, stabilizing her. Startled, she opened her eyes.

"Look!" she heard Laith shout next to her.

The sun had crested the eastern mountains and risen in the sky. The light had changed, and she could again see the many Lyrians spread before her, ready to enter the pass. She could see their own eyes and heads, turned toward the west where the morning sun shone on a group of people, maybe a hundred or so, emerging from the folds of the cliff face in the distance.

She blinked and squinted at the vision in the west, leaning forward on her horse. The group was coming toward them, toward her. They were crossing the mountain valley with determination. One figure, toward the front, was waving a long arm back and forth, as in greeting.

Mara focused on that figure with its erect carriage, pale face, and wild, windblown hair. Recognition struck, and tears sprung to Mara's eyes. She held up her hand and waved in return. Then she spurred her horse forward into a gallop down the hill and across the distance between them.

The wild-haired girl dropped her arm and ran also, and somewhere in the middle the two met and stopped, and the battle seemed far away to Mara as she climbed down from her horse and looked into the other princess's eyes, unbelieving and suddenly hesitant.

Princess Ivy's face was dirty and tired, but her eyes were strong, and Mara smiled at her. Ivy reached out her long arms and held Mara by the shoulders for a moment, then pulled her older, smaller sister into an embrace.

"Welcome home, sister," Mara whispered at her ear. "It's been a long time."

⋄　⋄　⋄

Laith had approached slowly on his horse, watching the sisters, and giving them time to greet each other. But, as he neared the group, the happy reunion was interrupted by an outburst from the group of travelers.

"What the blazes are *you* doing here?" Laith knew who had spoken even before he spotted young Burr, who had pushed his way forward to gawk up at Laith. The boy received an immediate box on the ears from Gilda Reed, who smiled up at Laith apologetically.

Laith dismounted and moved slowly toward Burr, narrowing his eyes and baring his fists. The boy, still smarting from Gilda's chastisement, backed up cautiously. Then Laith laughed and dropped his fists. "I'm glad to see you too, you little rodent."

The group relaxed, and John Merrick moved forward, clapping him on the back. "It *is* good to see you here, Hastings, and mended too. How'd you pull it off?"

Laith smiled, shaking hands with Simon and Gilda. "I had help, and Murray came back for me. It's a long story," he said, now scanning the crowd of foreign-looking strangers behind his friends, "one to tell another time."

The sounds of battle behind Laith seemed loud once more, and the group looked sober.

"I see you've brought help," Mara said.

"Yes," Ivy nodded. "We also have a long story to tell another time. Needless to say, I have brought friends who have abandoned what home they had to come help us. We are not a great fleet of reinforcements, Mara, but each one of these good people are Stone Mages." Ivy watched Mara as she said this, as if trying to ascertain if the words meant anything to her. The amazed relief that dawned on the delicate features of the elder princess's face indicated that she did.

Princess Ivy pulled a distinguished looking older man and a dark-haired young woman forward. "This is Eben," she said, indicating the older man. "He is the leader of this group, and here is Saffi Beval, another leader and good friend. She knew my mother and speaks Lyrian well."

Mara bowed her head in greeting, again looking amazed, as Ivy introduced her in return, Saffi translating.

Mara greeted the others as Saffi translated, and then she directed them to higher ground so they could form a plan.

Mara moved closer to Laith, taking his arm as he led his horse back up the hill. "Laith," she said close in his ear, "while I debrief them, could you look in your mirror for us? I would like a little direction before we decide just what to do." She looked toward the pass where the battle was raging. "And we've got to move quickly," she said.

They soon reached the hilltop, and Mara sent for General Rune, gathering the others around her. They were soon deep in conversation, and Laith moved apart, pulling out the small mirror he now kept on his person. He closed his eyes for a moment, endeavoring to find some calm and to push aside the sounds of war all around him.

He opened his eyes and looked down into the mirror, directing his thoughts toward a clearer view of the ensuing battle. He was surprised when the image that appeared was not of the army at the pass. Instead, he saw the Lyrian harbor. He had not been there since he was very small, but he immediately recognized its landscape, and the design of the boats. He had helped to build many of those vessels, before the harbor, shipyard, and most of the Lyrian fleet had been left behind to the Southern invaders. Only a few sailors had managed to save a few vessels—the *Sapphire* had been one—by sailing them around the horn to the small mountain port in time.

Laith stashed the mirror inside his tunic and rushed to join Mara and the others, cutting her off mid-sentence.

"They're coming by sea," he blurted. "They're coming from the Lyrian Harbor to ours, to surround and overtake us."

The group was instantly silent, and Laith was aware of many questioning eyes on him; but he merely watched Mara, her face a study of shock and calculation.

"Can we stop them?" she breathed.

Laith nodded. "We'll have to try."

The circle of people was quiet for a moment, all watching each other in a moment of inaction.

John Merrick suddenly cleared his throat, breaking the silence, and all eyes found his face. His mouth turned up slightly in a subtle smile. "I have an idea."

CHAPTER 53

John Merrick knew he was sailing against a formidable enemy, with much at stake. He was exhausted and hungry, and the summer sun, now high above, burned the back of his neck. However, he felt strangely at ease, happy even, to be standing at the helm of his *Sapphire* once more.

He looked behind him in the harbor to mark the progress of the two other ships. He had put Abner Murray at command of the *Hammer,* another old naval vessel turned fishing boat, and Niles in charge of *Moon Tide,* a newer and moderately armed merchant ship.

His crew was motley, most of them he knew only a little if at all, but Gilda Reed and Burr were on board, staying below as commanded. He didn't like having them at all, but knew they were crucial for the second phase of his plan, as were a number of other Pelasars hiding below on all three ships.

The older princess was also on board. She had approached him earlier with some nonsense about killing her if her eyes changed color and she started behaving in a way that would endanger the crew. He had merely stared at her in bewilderment. But when she wouldn't leave him alone about it, he had agreed to the task before turning his full attention to the water ahead.

They were now nearing the horn at the edge of the harbor. Merrick shouted orders to his crew, and the *Sapphire* began to slowly make the turn.

Merrick inhaled. He was well aware that the ships they were sailing against would be more numerous and better armed. He knew the Wrakes on board these ships would have more experience and skill in using their elemental gifts.

He also knew that no one aboard those ships was expecting them. They were merely acting as ferries for ground troops, and he hoped that the Lyrians/Pelasars could use surprise, and all the Water Mages available to them, to win this confrontation.

"Ready!" he shouted, and knew by the relative silence on board that the cannons were manned and the Water Mages were prepared. The land receded, and in moments the Lyrian harbor and four large ships were visible.

Merrick cursed, disappointed, but not surprised, to find that they were outnumbered. "Hold steady," he barked. The *Sapphire* made its final turn and straightened out. Merrick saw that the other ships were still close behind, about to round the horn as well. The wind filled his ship's sails, and he exhaled, glad they would have the advantage of wind to put them upon their enemies speedily.

The enemy ships were already turning about and bringing out the guns, and Merrick knew it was time to act.

"Take the wheel, Mr. Jones, you're in control," he said, relinquishing control to his newly appointed first mate. Jones looked suddenly young under his fair hair, but his eyes were steady.

"As soon as the water rises," Merrick commanded, "turn us about." He could see that the *Hammer* and *Moon Tide* had come around and were sailing the straight course, now on either side of his ship. He looked both directions, glancing at the mages flanking the front of both decks. He saw Princess Mara and the two other mages on the *Sapphire* watching him with ready eyes. Then he raised his hands and shouted at the top of his lungs.

"Raise the water!"

On his command the mages also raised their arms, some humming, others staring at the water with tense concentration. Merrick sought to find his focus as he studied the water before him. He saw that it had already begun to swell, moving his vessel forward, and the sight gave him courage. He added his power to that of the other mages, and felt the water move and swell under them.

The *Sapphire* began to turn sideways, as directed, and Merrick was vaguely aware of the orders flying about the deck as the ship moved into attack position. He looked up and saw that they were now fast closing in on the enemy vessels. They were close enough to see the individual figures moving about deck, and he strained his eyes, scanning the bodies and faces, trying to ascertain how many Wrakes they had along.

He knew there was at least one Wrake, because the water around the large Southern-controlled ships was moving out and away toward theirs, trying to push them back and gain more time to prepare for conflict. He watched the figures on deck closely and finally decided that there were only two Wrakes, two figures not engaged in the usual business of sailing. They were on the decks of the two ships nearest them. *Good,* Merrick thought, *once we take them down, the other ships should fall easily.*

Merrick was preparing to command his men to fire, when he saw that the ripples of water moving out from the Southern ships were increasing in size. They were no longer mere undulations in the water but full-blown waves, growing rapidly larger as they approached.

"Meet them," he called to his fellow Water Mages. "Make some waves!" He concentrated on the water, watching as his power, combined with the others', formed swells in the water that grew to waves, matching those of the enemy.

Waves met waves, crashing and spraying, then canceling each other out. More waves moved up toward them, and Merrick and the other Water Mages made answering waves. Merrick began to grow weary and impatient, worried that this water war would give the enemy ships time to turn about and face them equally or with an advantage.

The warring swells grew until Merrick could no longer see the Southern ships over the water and spray.

Then, without warning, the enemy waves stopped. Merrick lowered his arms in surprise, and their answering swells also died down. The sea became flat as he stared across the water at the ships, turned and ready for battle. Then Merrick looked to the South's decks and felt a spasm of shock that pulsed in his throat and ran through into his gut where it sat, turning into fear in the pit of his stomach. He saw now not the two solitary Wrakes on the front two vessels, but instead four decks lined with dark-cloaked Wrakes, men and women, hands raised and ready for attack.

◆　　◆　　◆

Simon pushed through the throngs of Lyrian fighters on foot. He had been offered a horse, but knew that horsed warriors wouldn't be seeing any action for a good while yet. He had to get to the front lines. General Rune had been rotating men in and out of the pass so that those fighting on the front lines did not just die of weariness. Simon approved of this and was hoping he could force his way through these fighters and finally get a taste of the battle.

Soon, however, he became so surrounded by men that he lost

his bearings and wasn't sure if he was actually getting closer to the mountain or farther away. He stood on his toes and strained his neck to see above the heads of his peers, glad that he had the Adler height, and saw a small rise of men not far off. He pushed his way toward the rise and found a large, freestanding stone. There were several men atop it, and he had to squeeze to fit on its surface, elbowing his way in between the small gathering of young and old soldiers.

From this vantage, he could again see the pass, its entrance now only about twenty yards off. He fixed the image in his mind, and was about to climb off the rock, when he felt a hand on his shoulder, pulling him back.

He turned to confront the offender, annoyed, but the irritation immediately gave way to surprise and joy.

"Dad!" he yelled, as Marcus Adler pulled him into a strong embrace. Soldiers jostled about them, and Simon pulled back to look into the lined face of his father.

"What are you doing out here?" He'd had to yell the question to be heard over the noise.

His father's eyes twinkled. "What do you think, son? I'm here to defend my kingdom."

"Your leg, Dad," Simon said, his brows furrowed. "You shouldn't be out here, you're not fit for battle anymore."

His father scowled. "Simon Adler," he bellowed, "I've been waiting all my life to see my fellow countrymen get out and defend themselves. One of my sons gave his life for this cause . . ."

"Yes," Simon cut him off. "I'm not about to lose another family member in war."

Marcus did not respond immediately to this outburst, but studied Simon's face for a moment before he spoke, pulling him close, so that every word would be heard. "I've been standing here for a while, son. I saw you ride in, Princess Ivy at your side, and help following close behind. I can see in your face that whatever you went through to get them here has molded you. You are not the same young son I sent off months ago. I'm every bit as proud as you as I am of Roger. I couldn't ask for braver sons. I need you to give me the chance to be worthy of them."

Simon looked into his father's eyes and slowly nodded. "I'll fight here by your side, Dad."

Marcus looked off into the distance, his expression changing. "No, Simon," he said. "I think your battle is a different one." Marcus nodded off at something in the distance, and Simon followed his dad's gaze, his arguments melting on his tongue.

In the distance, a horsed rider was speeding across the low hills, toward the mine. He knew in an instant who it was.

"Go," his father commanded, but Simon had already jumped from the rock, pushing himself through the crowd. He could see in his mind's eye the speed with which Ivy rode, and he knew that he was moving much too slowly to catch her. He opened his eyes wide and reached out onto the strings of time—and pulled. The increasingly familiar sensation returned, and everyone around him was suddenly dragging, moving slowly while he raced through them. Presently, he was through the crowd, barreling across the hills on foot after the princess, and then, before her.

He planted his feet in the direct path of her steed. She screamed and pulled back on the reins, her horse rearing wildly. She looked down at him, angrily.

"Get out of my way, Simon," she shouted.

Simon ignored this order. "Not until you tell me where you're going," he replied, just catching his breath, and feeling the weariness of using his gift throughout his body.

She looked about to refuse but seemed to realize its futility. She relaxed in the saddle. "Listen, Simon. Hastings, or Haverford, has been breaking his head trying to catch some vision of our friends at sea, but sees nothing. Even if they do succeed, and this plan works, it means nothing if Abaddon sits safely in our Lyrian palace ready to clean up our leftovers. I have to do something other than sit back there and worry. I may be the only one who has any chance to defeat Abaddon."

"Why? Why you?" Simon asked.

"I share his gift," she shrugged. "I know that I'm a mere novice, but for some reason Abaddon was worried enough about me to send me off to my death. That fact alone gives me hope that there is some chance I might defeat him."

Simon stood there, watching her, then nodded. "I see."

"You can't stop me, Simon. Move."

Simon looked up at her. She was magnificent on that tall white horse, her wild hair framing her determined face. "I don't plan on stopping you, Princess," he said, "I'm going to help you."

Her twisted brow cleared. "Thank you," she said, and held her hand out to him.

In a few long strides he was at her side, taking her hand and swinging into the saddle behind her. Then, together, they rode toward the mine, and through it to Lyria.

CHAPTER 54

Mara observed herself, detached, to gauge her own response to the horrendous sight before her and was surprised to discover that she was not afraid. She had become so quickly certain that there would be no escape for her and her comrades that she felt resigned, calm even.

Everything and everyone seemed to move slowly except those four ships bearing down on them. The sailors were moving around her as though swimming through a thick liquid, and she understood that the *Sapphire* was ready to let loose its fire on the enemy ships. She knew, also, that all the cannons in Lyria could not stop the army of Wrakes they faced.

A deep, dark fog was rising around the enemy, and it crept toward her, moving subtly but steadily. She turned involuntarily toward the captain some feet from her. He glanced at her, and their eyes met. This man was in no way like her; but in this strange moment she saw her own feelings in his eyes: acceptance, a touch of sadness, and a large measure of determination. He nodded at her, and she returned the gesture, then they turned again to face the enemy, standing tall and unafraid.

The fog had reached them. Mara felt the cold moisture wash over her, blinding and hiding her. She removed the hood of her cloak and felt the cold on her face and the dull breeze move through her hair. She was isolated in this misty blindness, but she remembered the captain and the other fighters on the other ships, some who had traveled great distances to come to her kingdom's aid. She did not feel alone.

Somewhere in the mist, a man called, "Fire!" The ship rumbled under her, and she saw flashes in the fog and heard the sound of the great lead balls as they sunk into the sea and eventually crashed into the wood and metal of the great ships in the near distance.

Mara could not see more than a few feet in front of her face, but she sensed, almost as clear as real sight, what was coming for them. Great water. She planted her feet firmly on the deck, closed her eyes, and raised her arms, feeling the great wet mass moving toward them with much speed. She felt its wetness and saw in her mind's eye the way it rolled and rushed, the way its particles worked together and moved to destroy her, and she pushed back. She moved the particles. She listened to their rhythms and changed them. She felt the mass hesitate and subside momentarily, then move forward once more, and then it was upon her.

It crashed over her, arresting her breath, pulling her hair, and knocking her to the deck where it swirled around her and away. She could hear the coughing and sputtering of its other victims around her as it slid with sudden docility over the deck.

Another wave was coming. She pulled herself to her knees and found it again through the blind mist. She held it, tried to move it, to change its course, and felt it sway. She knew that someone— perhaps several someones—was helping her, but this wave and the powers guiding it were stronger than she and her companions. The wave again assaulted them, offering a brutal beating. The

Sapphire swayed and tipped. Mara flew across the deck and slammed into something hard and unmoving on the other side. The mass of water abated and sloshed around her where she lay, aching deep in her chest, drenched and weary.

More water was coming, and she forced herself to her knees, and then her feet. She moved forward to meet this wave angrily. She spoke to it ruthlessly and pushed and tried to move it, but this time it did not waver in the slightest. It was larger and faster than the previous two. The chaos around her was suddenly amplified. She could hear muffled screams, most in a language she did not understand, shouts of "Pelasars" and "*terata.*"

Soon the wave was again before her. Mara could see it in her mind, with absolute clarity, and she raised her chin. She opened her eyes wide and saw the huge tower of liquid and spray as it hovered over her and then fell, largely and heavily, enveloping her.

The cold pressure swirled around her and did not subside. She opened her eyes to see nothing but bubbles. Eventually the water cleared, and she looked down to see that the ship lay beneath her. It was completely submersed in water and tilting slowly away. She looked up and saw that the surface was far above. She began to feel pain in her chest, followed by panic.

She moved her arms and legs frantically but felt that the water was working against her. She grasped for the peace of mind to use her gift but could not find any calm as her pain intensified and her sense of alarm increased. She continued to struggle madly upward, but the surface still seemed distant.

Mara's eyes began to sting, and she closed them. She kicked with her legs and paddled with one arm, the other extended above her, hoping to soon feel the water make way for the air above. She began to feel faint, and ill, and her strength waned, and there was no air on her fingertips.

Her arms fell hopelessly at her side. Her legs curled beneath her, and she drifted, panic gone, her mind clear, and tired. In her mind, she saw her frail, dark-haired mother withering on her deathbed. She saw her trembling father, poisoned by her own hand, writhing in pain as death overtook his features. She saw Abaddon's cruel, laughing eyes when he told her she had no choice but to serve him.

But then, suddenly, Mara saw Medwin's kind eyes and remembered his whisper in her ear that day she had left the Fringe. *You're stronger than you know,* he'd said. She saw Laith kneeling at the foot of her throne and looking up at her with trust and respect. She saw Ivy riding across the rocky field, sisterly love shining out through her eyes.

The pain became intense, and she saw white, and then she thought she felt something heavy beneath her, pushing her limp frame upward. She found this strange but could not move or open her eyes. She was suddenly lying flat on the hard surface beneath her and rushing upward. The water moved away from her face and hair and limbs and she gasped for the air and felt it fill her lungs. She coughed and sputtered and breathed, rolling about on the deck and relishing each breath. Eventually, she laughed and planted her wilted hands on the surface beneath her and sat up and opened her eyes.

The fog was gone, and the brightness was all she could see. Eventually her eyes adjusted, and she saw that she was on the deck of the *Sapphire*. Captain Merrick was getting to his feet not far from her, and others were getting their bearings on the deck.

She felt strange, dizzy almost, and there was an odd noise, like the sound of rocks grinding. She realized, slowly, that the ship was still moving up, into the sky. Then she saw at the forefront of the ship, crowded around the railings, the woman Gilda Reed and many of the foreign Stone Mages, all using their gifts.

Mara stood, ignoring the weakness in her knees and the aching in her chest, and moved toward the ship's rail. She looked down.

The *Sapphire* was perched atop a rising mountain that was slowly and steadily emerging from the sea beneath them. These Earth Mages were lifting the ship from the ocean, two ships, actually. Mara could see *Moon Tide* perched to their left atop the same newly made rise. She inhaled deeply, amazed at the sight, and then scanned the sea below.

There were three of the enemy vessels still visible, one was actually split in the middle and sinking—some of the cannons had found success. Its deck was abandoned. The other two were whole, the Wrakes moving agitatedly about their decks. There was no sign of the *Hammer.*

The *Sapphire* had stopped its upward climb. Mara moved over to where the Stone Mages stood, looking weary but slightly pleased.

"Well done," Captain Merrick was saying, and the foreigners nodded, seeming to understand his meaning.

Mara saw that the young boy was among them, and it was he who spoke next. "We'd better do something else before those filthy scum think of a way to get us up here."

Captain Merrick nodded at the boy. He scanned the other ship, and Mara followed his gaze, noting the number of Stone Mages standing on that other deck, watching and waiting for the next command. Then he looked at her.

"Let's flood them," he said.

•   ◆   •

When Laith Haverford finally pulled the vision he had been searching for onto the surface of his mirror, the sight was not what he had expected.

The *Sapphire* was perched atop a strange rise of land, with another ship, *Moon Tide,* in the close distance. The inhabitants of the ship that had once been his home were huddled on one side of the deck, deep in argument. He strained to hear their voices.

"Raising the water now will only raise the enemy up to our level," Mara was shouting at Captain Merrick.

"As I said, Princess, I'm not talking about raising the water. I'm talking about a flood, instantaneous, like a tidal wave," Merrick shouted back.

Gilda Reed was looking at him quizzically. "You think you have the skill to bring a tidal wave to this bay in the next few minutes?"

"I don't know," Merrick replied, "but I'm not the only Water Mage aboard these ships, Ms. Reed."

"I've never done anything like that," Mara cut in, "and I've been a Water Mage for years. I can push and move the water in front of me all you'd like, but call it in from afar off, on that kind of scale? When our energy is already at a low? I'm not sure it's possible, Captain."

"Do you have an alternative to suggest?"

Through his mirror, Laith watched Mara glance toward the land—toward the Lyrian plain and its crumbling buildings, fields, farms, and homes. "There must be another way," he heard her murmur. "If your plan works, we'll be destroying much of the kingdom we are hoping to reclaim."

"Yes," Merrick said impatiently. "And we'll be destroying a good number of the army on that land that we now have little chance of defeating alone, with sapped energy, as you point out."

Suddenly, Burr appeared in Laith's mirror, bursting into the scene with characteristic mayhem. "There might be another way out of this here mess, people," he announced. "But nothing we'll come up with in time." He pointed to the rail. "The Southern ships are practically on top of us. I say we soak 'em, and we do it now."

Laith saw everyone, including the foreign mages, rush to the rail and look down. Two Southern ships, fully armed and decks teeming with mages, were closing in on the rise of land.

He saw the indecision vanish from Mara's face and heard her calmly speak: "Okay, we'll try it."

Laith strained to see what was going on in his mirror. The decks of both ships seemed to be in chaos; and here he was, miles away, useless to their cause. He could hear Merrick shouting orders and watched his friends—old and new—carrying them out in compliance. Burr had remained at the *Sapphire*'s rail and seemed to be reporting on the progress of the adversary.

"They're at the bottom of our hill now!" he heard Burr shout. The boy pointed to water below him, and Laith could see Burr's own magic in play as a number of gray shark fins circled the Wrakes' ships, causing fear and havoc below.

Mara and some of the other Stone Mages, the Water Mages, Laith assumed, had gathered at the opposite side of the ship's deck. They looked out, away from the harbor and over the open sea, and waited for the command to begin the strange task.

Laith could see Princess Mara's face. There were dark circles under her eyes, and her features were slack. He had not seen her looking so weary since that day he had almost killed her on the shore below Medwin's house. He wondered what she had been through already, and if this plan would sap the remaining energy she had.

However, he could also see something in her features that had not been present the day she lay wounded at the Fringe. He saw courage and determination.

"They're leaving the ships," Burr yelled at the rail. "My sharks got some of those filthy Wrakes, but the rest have started climbing our mountain!"

Laith watched Merrick rush over to join the other Water Mages. They all seemed to watch the captain, waiting for his command. He fingered the blue stone at his neck briefly before extending an arm.

In the distance, outside the bay, Laith saw an undulation, a rise in the surface of the water.

"There," Merrick shouted, and "Now!"

The Stone Mages came to life, some concentrating on the sea with stiff focus, others moving, swaying, or humming. As they did so, the water in the distance formed a wave, long and low.

"They're getting closer!" Burr shouted. Laith flexed his muscles in tension, grasping the mirror tightly.

Out in the distance, the wave was growing, rolling forward and reaching upward. He could see Merrick's back bend with the weight of it, and Mara began to shake.

"Closer!" Burr shouted. Laith's knuckles were white.

The water was at the edge of the Lyrian bay, and it had become a wall vast and tall as it moved toward the harbor. Laith swallowed the lump in his throat.

The wave was so close now it began to roar, drowning the sounds of the Stone Mages, the scream on Mara's lips, and the roar of the land battle going on around Laith. It was right before his friends now.

"Hold fast!" shouted Captain Merrick, and the wave hit.

Suddenly, Laith was looking down on the harbor, and he saw the wave as it crushed and covered the unprepared enemy. He saw the mass of climbing Wrakes as they were swept away and covered in its depths. He saw *Moon Tide* and then the *Sapphire* tip and sway as the great water reached their sides, carrying them along its crest. He saw the Stone Mages and Mara fall to the deck and slide about in unconscious chaos.

Finally, he watched as the wave, full and furious, carrying two small ships, moved inward, over the land and buildings and roads and trees and toward the Southern Army.

Then he was looking at his own pale face, his eyes wide, and he jolted into action.

CHAPTER 55

Change it up," yelled General Rune, who watched as the men in the front lines fell back, their waiting reinforcements rushing in ahead of them. The tired men came toward him, their faces covered in dust and blood, their arms supporting their wounded comrades or dragging dead ones.

He felt bile rise in his throat, but swallowed it down, ashamed of his own queasiness. He had seen some battles in his lifetime. But never before had he seen men fight harder or with more brave abandon. Never before had the battle's stakes been so high.

He hoped the signal they were waiting on would come soon. He had already changed out the men at the front line more times than he could count, and no one was really "fresh" anymore. Each time he called a change, there were more who came out of the pass injured or dead.

He looked back up the hill, scanning the horizon for the princess, and saw the redheaded duke, Haverford, waving frantically at him. He left his second in charge and rode carefully through the weary soldiers up to where Haverford stood. By the time Rune reached him, the young duke was issuing urgent commands to a regal-looking young foreign woman. He looked up when Rune drew near.

"The signal will be coming soon, but even if it does not, we must proceed with the plan regardless. Look to me, General and Ms. Beval. One way or another we'll need the Stone Mages ready at the pass and the soldiers prepared to withdraw in an instant, understood?"

The woman nodded and mounted her horse, rather clumsily in General Rune's opinion, and rode down toward the pass to command the "Stone Mages." General Rune nodded his assent and rode off also. He again wended his way through the Lyrian soldiers and positioned himself near the mountain-side of the pass. He glanced back up at Duke Haverford, but the young man was merely watching the sky.

General Rune could see that the new group of front liners was already wavering. The fierce Southern fighters had advanced their line, taking down his men with single blows. He was about to switch his men out once more, when something changed.

It was barely perceptible at first, and it seemed to sweep through the Southern fighters slowly before it began affecting his men. Soon the battle slowed, and he realized what it was: quiet. There was a stillness in the soldiers that began to alter the general mood of the battle.

From atop his horse, it took General Rune longer than his men to understand the noise that came next, but he soon recognized the seeping sloshing that began to fill the pass and surround the ankles of the fighters, both friend and foe. It was water.

Before anyone had time to question the strange sensation, a cry went out from among the men.

"Up there," someone shouted, and General Rune looked skyward.

Standing out against the moody afternoon sky was the figure of a large white bird floating peacefully over the soldiers and the mountain pass. It was the signal they had previously agreed upon.

All at once he heard the shouts of Haverford and the foreign woman. He looked down at his men, dazed and confused.

"Retreat!" he yelled, but was disheartened to see that few obeyed immediately. Some turned and fled upward, out of the pass, but others merely looked about, disoriented.

Rune was barely less disoriented. "Retreat!" he called again.

On either side of the gap at the top of the pass, the "Stone Mages" seemed to be working frantically, and it took Rune a moment to realize that they were actually moving the sides of the pass, closing in the gap that provided access to both the Lyrian valley and their mountain refuge. He had been told the plan, but until now had not believed it actually possible.

More of the men were now issuing from the narrowing pass, leaving their pursuers momentarily confused. Rune knew that confusion would be short-lived. He urged the horse into the pass and began to physically hurry the Lyrian soldiers from it.

"Move!" he called. The Southern warriors were no longer watching their fleeing foe, but instead were glancing nervously back over their shoulders. General Rune was aware of the increasing depth of the water coming from the valley side of the pass as his horse splashed about. He wondered, vaguely, how the water was pouring in, but his curiosity was overshadowed by his urgent need to get his men out before they were trapped.

The gap was becoming narrower. Rune had positioned himself in the pass between the rest of his fleeing men and the Southerners. It was going to be a close call to get all these men, let alone himself and his horse, through the narrowing space up ahead.

"Faster!" he called to the men, and watched them scramble and push each other forward with more haste.

There was a tumult behind him. General Rune turned and saw the Southerners moving about in a panic, fear and dread clouding their faces. The pass had become crowded behind him, and Rune realized that the waiting enemy out on the Lyrian plain had begun to flee *into the pass,* looking for an escape from the rising waters. Of course, this was happening at the same time the enemy already within the pass was growing conscious of the mountain walls closing in up ahead.

Rune turned back to account for his men. Most had almost reached the narrowing gap; there were a mere handful of men left in front of him. He rode toward them and then held his breath as he watched them rush through. He urged his steed forward with urgency. He could hear the Southerners behind him, and then smell them. He felt a large hand on his shoulder. He shrugged it off. His mare leapt through the opening, screaming wildly as the closing stone pushed in on its sides. And then they were through.

He turned around, and before the gap closed completely, he saw a mass of angry heads, and frightened eyes, and brutal fists. He saw the water rising to the Southerners' thick knees and watched as it seeped through the remaining space in the gap to pool around his horse's feet.

After the gap was closed and transformed into solid stone, Rune shook his head. His last glimpse had puzzled him. He could not be positive, but he was pretty sure that the last snatch of color he had seen in the distance, above the heads of the angry warriors, was the topsail of a ship.

◆　　◆　　◆

From the crow's nest, high up above the deck of the *Sapphire,* Burr could see about him more clearly than he had ever seen. This particular bird's eye view of Lyria was not one he had ever imagined seeing. Burr had been only a small boy when the Lyrians had moved into the mountains after fighting that last battle. His memories of the kingdom were few. But still, it was a strange sensation to look about him and see the effects of their great wave.

The vast wall of water that had carried them inland had swept clear across the plain, only retreating as it met the rise that led to the forests and the Lyrian palace. Everything else had been flooded.

Now, however, the water had receded some, leaving the *Sapphire* and *Moon Tide* grounded not far from the pass, surrounded by the puddled remains of their old kingdom and the strewn and still bodies of most of the Southern Army and, sadly, some of their own.

What remained of the Southern Army existed in two parts: those who had fled toward the palace, retreating inside its walls before the rising water could overtake them, and those who had crowded up into the safety of the pass, where they had been closed off from the mountain side after he had sent his graceful fulmar bird.

Those in the pass were now being held there, against their will, as Gilda Reed and the other Earth Mages worked their magic to speedily close in this side of the pass. Burr knew this had been the plan: to obliterate as much of the Southern Army as possible, then close the pass, trapping the rest. He also knew that those awful warriors would kill the Lyrians if allowed the freedom to move about on the plain. But even knowing this, Burr could not watch their frantic desperation as they were walled in.

Instead he looked skyward for the return of his fulmar. Reuel had called this particular bird, and Burr had sent him. They were supposed to send a brown bird next, as a signal that their side of the pass was closed.

Reuel called up at him from the deck below.

"Pey morne!" he cried, the nickname Reuel gave him, which Burr had ascertained to mean, roughly, "little wizard." Perched on the

older mage's arm was a large hawk of some kind. Burr extended his arm and screeched for the hawk, which came floating up toward him, his great wings beating easily, and landed on his outstretched arm.

He stroked the bird and looked into its copper-colored eyes, endeavoring to distract himself from the frantic shouts and groans issuing from the pass. The fulmar had returned and perched near him on the rail of the little crow's nest, eyeing the new visitor with a cocked head.

"Now!" someone cried out. "The pass is closed, send the signal!"

Burr held the hawk close to his head and felt its restlessness, its hunger, its longing for the hunt, and its curiosity. He cooed softly in its ear, communicating with and directing the creature, and felt its understanding. He raised his arm, and the bird launched off, opening its wide wings and soaring over the mountains that were now closed in a solid line.

Then, after essentially releasing the fulmar to fly under its own command once again, he climbed down from the crow's nest. When his feet touched down on the deck, Burr immediately felt cramped and confused. Bodies of the wounded and dead lay about the ship. Some were sailors, jarred and killed by the movements of the ship during its carriage by the wave. Others were those he recognized better, those who had fallen with the strain of what they had created. Among them was Captain Merrick. Burr could not see the princess at all.

Burr swayed where he stood and soon felt Reuel's hand on his shoulder, steadying him. Gilda Reed and the other mages were climbing back on deck. She found his eyes instantly and beckoned him to her. Then pulling open the large pouch that she had worn on her waist since they left Bellaria, she extracted different pouches and bottles, healing herbs and liquids. After distributing them among the Earth Mages who did not possess their own, she handed some to Burr and Reuel.

"I ain't no healer," Burr rasped, but she held up her hand to silence him.

"Just follow me, and watch, Burr," she said. "I need another pair of hands. Can you do that?"

Burr nodded, swallowing the lump in his throat, and followed Gilda to where she soon knelt at the side of the crumpled, water-logged figure of Captain Merrick.

◆　　◆　　◆

"What do you see?" Saffi asked the redhead, Laith, as he pored over his little hand mirror.

He did not respond, but she read deep concern, even pain on his face. Saffi clenched her fists and began to pace back and forth in front of him.

Around Saffi and Laith a noisy pandemonium was in progress. As soon as they had closed the pass, and then seen the hawk, cheers of joy and victory had erupted from the Lyrian army. Not long after, a host of their anxious families had poured forth from the palace. Some fathers were now embracing wives and children. Other women knelt, wailing over fallen sons and husbands, oblivious to the happy reunions of their peers.

Even the Pelasars on this side of the pass had been pulled into the celebrations and lamentations, but Saffi merely paced, and Laith pored over his mirror.

"Well?" Saffi asked again, impatient irritation plain in her voice. He merely shook his head at the mirror before him, but seemed as if he would soon speak. Saffi held her breath.

Without warning, Laith stood, abruptly pocketing his mirror, and without even a sideways glance in her direction, moved toward the nearest free mount.

Saffi rushed after him, rapid in her anger and frustration. "You tell me what you saw," she shouted at his back.

He turned to her abruptly, his face red and his eyes ablaze. "I can't see everyone. Some of our friends are probably missing or dead, others lay unconscious. Some are alive and helping to heal and rejuvenate the fallen. The princess . . ." Laith's voice trailed off and, forgetting Saffi again, he turned and mounted the horse.

She ran to his side and grasped his ankle. "What of Captain Merrick?" she shouted at him.

Laith paused at this, as though waking from a trance, and looked down at her. His brow furrowed as he studied her face for a moment, as if he were reading the desperation there.

Presently, his countenance cleared and he looked at her with seeming understanding. "Captain Merrick is among the unconscious. I don't think he is dead, but some of the Water Mages were brought down by the effort of what they created. I do not know how long he will live."

Saffi felt an ache in the region of her chest, and she closed her eyes. When she finally opened them, Laith was still near her on his horse, but he had brought another mount over and offered her the reins.

"Princess Mara is missing. I intend to go find her at once. It is foolish, and there is not likely much I can do. I would advise you not to come with me, but it is clear that advice is not likely to be followed."

Saffi was overwhelmed with gratitude, and she nodded at Laith as she very clumsily mounted the beast before her.

"You haven't ridden much, have you?" asked Laith, without really expecting an answer. He spent a few minutes explaining the reins and the way she should sit and lean to guide the creature and stay the most comfortable in the saddle.

When he had finished, Saffi extended her hand. "Saffi Beval."

He nodded. "Laith Haverford," he said, returning her handshake.

Then, as if unable to restrain himself any longer, he prodded the horse and galloped away in the direction of the mine. Without hesitation, Saffi followed.

CHAPTER 56

Simon knelt next to Princess Ivy in the undergrowth beneath the trees outside the old Lyrian palace. He was in a state of immobility, counting figures in his head.

He guessed there had to be at least fifty soldiers guarding that gate—not ordinary soldiers, but fifty brutally angry and disappointed massive Southern warriors, ready to replace their taste of defeat with slaughter.

From where Simon and Ivy sat, they had a pretty clear view of not only the palace but also the sodden plain below. They had surmised what had taken place with the water, and could see only too well the disappointment and frustration of those survivors at the gate in front of them.

He shook his head. "We'll just have to wait for reinforcements, Princess," he whispered.

"We have no guarantee there will be reinforcements, Simon," she replied.

"Everyone knows Abaddon is hiding out here. Once they dress

their wounds on this side of the pass and the other, they'll realize coming here is the next step."

"That may be true, but by the time they come, it will probably be too late."

"Too late for what?" Simon considered that his question may have sounded impertinent to her, but he felt a great degree of caution on her behalf. "What harm is there in leaving Abaddon locked up in there for a while?"

Ivy was quiet. She seemed to be considering his questions, or perhaps just how to best answer them. "I can't really explain it, Simon, but I have the feeling that Abaddon is never really locked anywhere. I cannot imagine what powers a man with his kind of ambition and focus has developed over the years. I don't think he would have stood back and allowed his army to be obliterated if he wasn't up here feeling sure of his victory."

Simon could hear her sincerity, and accepted her answer. "How will we get in?"

Ivy turned toward him. "Do you remember how I used to move things from room to room in Medwin's house?"

"Yes."

"Well, I think I might be able to move myself in there. I know the rooms in that palace perfectly, and I think I might be able to place myself inside of one."

"You'll have to take me with you, then."

Ivy smiled, sadly. "Even if I could move us both in, Simon, it would only deplete my strength more. I'll need my remaining energy to face Abaddon."

"I can't let you go in there alone."

Ivy was looking directly into his eyes. She reached out and gently took his hand in hers. "You'll have to, Simon."

Simon looked away but held her hand more tightly. He was

thinking, and she was waiting for his answer, his approval. He looked back toward the castle gate and the warriors. His eyes narrowed.

"All right, Princess, you will go alone, but when you do it will be with all of your strength. I'll create a diversion, draw their attention away from the gate, and when I do, you will slip in."

Ivy smiled at him, and he quickly explained the details of his plan. When they stood to go, however, Simon still held onto her hand.

"I'll get to you as soon as I can," he whispered. "Hopefully we'll have help sooner than we think."

"Thank you, Simon," she whispered back, "for everything." He released her hand and she moved away.

Simon stayed where he was for some minutes, watching until he could see Ivy was in position, and then studying more carefully the men at the gate. He was assessing his audience, as Uncle Miles had taught him, and realized that this audience was unlike any he had ever performed for. He hoped he had made the right choice.

Simon stood, drew his sword, and moved steadily and with confidence from the cover of the trees and straight toward the men at the gate.

It did not take long for the Southerners to spot him, and Simon soon heard their anticipatory grumbles as they prepared to come out and obliterate him.

However, before they could actually move, Simon acted. With great flourish, he tossed his sword in the air. It flew up at least twice his length, spinning above him. He heard the collective intake of breath from the warriors and tried not to smile.

The sword came down, and Simon caught it easily by the hilt, and then swung it up again, this time higher. The Southerners moved unconsciously forward in expectation as Simon caught it once more and tossed it up a third time.

Simon concentrated on the spins of the blade and its arc as it fell down again toward him. This time its hilt landed perfectly on his outstretched palm, and he balanced it, upright. A surprised murmur echoed through his audience, and at that perfect moment he saw a flash of color out of the corner of his eye as Ivy slipped behind them and through the gate.

Simon smiled; he couldn't help it. Unfortunately, something about that smile broke the trance under which he had held his audience, and they began to move in on him.

Simon took the sword in two hands, swinging it in front of and across his body, as he moved with skill through a routine he knew by heart. He could feel the advancing warriors hesitate for a moment, but they now seemed spurred on by the challenge he presented. They came toward him hungrily, swinging their maces and broadswords in answer to his own graceful movements.

Simon desperately wanted to take steps backward but forced himself to hold his ground. He passed the sword from one hand to the other swinging it through his arms, over his head, and around his body. When the warriors were a mere matter of yards distant, Simon threw the sword in the air with all his strength. The Southerners couldn't help but look up to where it flew high above their heads.

In that instant, Simon ran for it. He bolted into the trees, stretching time here and there to increase the distance between him and his would be pursuers. It wasn't long, however, before he could hear their angry shouts and knew that they were close on his heels.

◆　　◆　　◆

Ivy blinked in the dim light of her former home. It was cool and quiet in the palace, and she saw at once that in the interim years, it had fallen into a state of disrepair. She shivered.

The large, open entry hall appeared to be empty. Ivy had never heard the palace so still and silent. She was facing the wide steps of the grand stairway but she did not ascend them yet. Instead she turned to an adjacent room, searching for movement or life.

Ivy had explored the entire first floor, kitchen and servants' quarters included, before she realized she was stalling and felt ashamed, especially when she thought of Simon facing those fifty warriors outside. Somehow, she knew that Abaddon, if he were here at all, would be in some upper chamber and that she needed to find him.

She climbed the large stairway step by step, but when she got to the second floor landing she did not stop. She moved on to the third floor, and when the stairs ended, she automatically moved through the hallways until she came to the long spiral staircase at the back of the palace and climbed some more, ignoring the doorways and side-branching corridors on her way.

The stairway ended at a single closed door at the top. Ivy pictured the room behind the door. It was the tower room, tall and rounded with a pointed ceiling and opening out onto a large balcony that overlooked all of Lyria.

There was a strange noise behind the door, and Ivy was suddenly aware that her heartbeat had escalated. It was beating so rapidly and loudly that she had a hard time distinguishing between it and the mysterious sound coming from the closed chamber. It seemed to be a rushing roar. Ivy swallowed and reached for the doorknob. Her hand was shaking as she turned it and entered the room.

Ivy had never actually met Abaddon, but as he stood at the far end of the room, his back to her, and his face to the open balcony doorway in which he stood, she realized that he looked exactly like she'd imagined him. The sun should not yet have set, but no evening light peeked through the cracks of the doorway in which he stood. She was puzzling about this when he spoke.

"It's taken you long enough," he said without turning. His voice was deep and calm, and Ivy could barely hear it over the roar as she scanned the room, looking for the source of the sound.

The chamber contained a strange smattering of old benches and chairs. At one side of the room was a recently slept-in bed and at another a table littered with papers and books. There was a round fireplace in the middle of the room, and a fire was lit, but it was not, Ivy realized, the source of the roar. The sound seemed to come from Abaddon himself.

She looked at his back, and watched, transfixed, as he turned slowly toward her, his large frame obscured in darkness. As he moved a step closer to the firelight, she saw his eyes first, and in them equal parts intelligence and coldness. He smiled at her.

"I wondered if it might be you who would first walk through that door."

Ivy merely swallowed, not trusting her voice and unsure of how to proceed now that she was here.

His smile broadened, a seeming laugh at her insecurity. "Please come in and make yourself comfortable," he said, indicating a chair not far from where he stood.

Ivy remained where she was, her feet grounded. The roar and rush seemed to be growing louder.

"Suit yourself," he said. He also remained standing, and Ivy began to get the impression that the noise was coming not from him, but from behind him on the balcony. She tried to see over his broad shoulders.

"Oh, don't worry," he sneered. "It is only a matter of time before your curiosity will be satisfied, but first tell me: Where are your little Stone Mage friends? Have they left you to face my formidable self all on your own?"

Ivy found her voice. "Perhaps you do not know that my 'friends' have practically obliterated your army. While you were hiding up here, your men have lost this war." The words sounded raspy and less confident than she had hoped.

He laughed aloud. "Congratulations to the honorable Stone Mages, then . . . from me." He laughed again, and she scowled at him, feeling the anger rise up from her stomach into her throat. "Really, Princess, for someone with your gift you really are naïve and unimaginative. You are also incorrect about one thing: I never hide."

"What would you call what you are doing here, then?"

"Again, so curious. The way I have developed our gift, little Princess, allows me to move about very stealthily. Why, just today, in fact, I have stood among your pit rats, hooded, and watched you ride across the hills to meet your sister, my Vessel. Oh, this shocks you that Princess Mara works for me? Well, keep listening. Later today I was aboard one of your Lyrian ships, the *Hammer.* I stayed just long enough to see that it was going under along with a ship full of your noble countrymen. I even bumped shoulders with your friend, the fool, in the midst of your fighters over in the mountains and watched him race after you as you galloped away on horseback. I should also tell you that my men down at the gate have eaten him alive by now, his excellent sword tricks notwithstanding."

Ivy glared at him, her heart thudding. "I don't believe you. I thought Shifters could only travel through Vessels."

Abaddon smiled. "I am no mere Shifter." He shrugged, his smile growing above his chiseled jaw. "None of that really matters for you now, anyway, as you are about to die."

Slowly Abaddon moved away from the doorway. Behind him, obscuring the balcony's view, was a vast, swirling blackness. Ivy squinted and slowly moved closer. It was as though there was a great hole in the fabric of the sky, spiraling into nothingness.

"What is it?" she breathed.

"This," Abaddon announced, "is my greatest creation, or, I

should say, discovery. You see, Princess, not all doorways have to go somewhere. You Stone Mages feel so superior in your ability to connect two places; but I have finally found the value in opening a doorway in space that leads to absolutely nothing. When you enter this opening, you will be lost in that nothingness, not only dying, but ceasing to exist. There will be no trace of you for anyone to find, you will simply be gone."

The roar of the hole was deafening, and Ivy felt doom settle in her stomach. At the same time, she felt the pull of the opening; her whole body seemed to lean toward it.

"Why?" Ivy's mouth felt dry.

"Why open it?" Abaddon seemed pleased by the question. "To answer that, I'm afraid I must delve a bit into my past. You see, as a young man, I gradually became aware that I possessed great power, perhaps the greatest gift in all of Bellaria. But others failed to recognize my gift and refused to give me the power and influence I deserved. Because they would not give me the status that was rightfully mine, I took it, as you well know, and became the ruler of Bellaria.

"However, that dominion did not satisfy me for long. The people were weak and easy to lead, and my powers and abilities called for greater challenges, so I moved on to the next kingdom, looking now to control and govern every place I could. Lyria, however, has taken a bit more time. There was more of a will among your people. But don't look so pleased; it was only a matter of time. I could have marched my armies into the mountains to conquer long before now, but I have, instead, taken the time to be thorough. I have slowly infiltrated the Lyrian court, and today, with this crowning achievement, I will be victorious."

"How can you call today a victory?" Ivy interjected. "You may kill us with this . . . hole . . . or cow us into submission, but you have lost an entire army, and if you kill us all, there will be no one left to govern."

Abaddon smiled. "Don't mistake me, Princess, my initial desire was to rule; but governorship is too easily won, people too easily led. If I am the only one left on this continent it will not make my victory less potent. My need for power has gone beyond mere people. I seek to rule everything. Land, nature, and yes, space. I will have ultimate power to command and destroy. That is my victory."

"You will not obtain that goal," Ivy said. She was fighting hard to breathe, and the swirling darkness was pulling at her fiercely. "No man was made to control everything."

"That's right," Abaddon said, cynically. "You Stone Mages still hold onto the belief that you can work with nature, move with the elements, and that harmony is the key to great power. You cling to those little stones about your necks without realizing that they are really nooses, keeping you tied to others, and the earth, and strangling out your potential."

"You are wrong, Abaddon," she said, stepping forward. "We are not seeking for power at all. We wear the stones and believe in the harmony of the elements insomuch as it will help us fight for balance, and unity, and eventually peace. Power is your game, not ours."

Abaddon sneered, and Ivy was surprised to see that her words had affected him. His cold, snide features showed anger. She moved closer to the hole. She felt its pull, and she knew that she had to close it, but knew also that she couldn't.

"I will show you," he said, his voice low and unsteady, "what comes of your ideas of peace and balance. You will die here and disappear into darkness. Sometimes in real life, little Princess, doorways lead to dead ends. People are essentially weak; and power, might, and evil triumph. Today is one of those days."

Suddenly, Abaddon reached behind him toward the spiraling nothingness and pulled. A strand of darkness eked out of the hole and wriggled into his hand. The pull of it became so strong that Ivy fell to her hands and knees, grasping at the crooked floorboard to hold her in place.

Abaddon was moving toward her. Slowly, he wrapped that strand of darkness about her waist, and she could not move, could not push it off. It held her, squeezing the breath from her lungs.

Abaddon moved back now, and she saw only a short glimpse of the angry triumph on his face before the dark rope that held her reeled her in. The roar encompassed her, drowning out the sound of her own shrieking. The dark hole was before her, and around her, and she surrendered and then knew nothing as she was hurled into darkness.

◆　◆　◆

Simon was out of breath, but still moved with amazing speed up the spiraling staircase of the palace. He pushed onward and upward, ignoring his failing energy and sense of weariness. He had had to use his gift more than he would have hoped in order to evade the guards below and now hoped he would have enough strength to help the princess. He had ceased calling out her name and now merely focused all of his energy on pushing himself up the stairs toward the strange rushing noise.

Soon he began to hear voices above, snatches of speech from a deep voice drifting down to him over a strange roar that grew louder every moment. He knew the speaker was Abaddon, describing the triumph of evil, and Simon felt ill. He pushed himself harder, stretching time, but still, the stairs seemed eternal.

As Simon reached the doorway at the top, he suddenly realized that the voices had ceased. He put his hand on the doorknob, and as he turned, he heard a sound that stopped his heart.

Ivy was screaming. It was a desperate, fearful, pained shriek. He burst through the door just in time to see her wrapped in darkness, being pulled toward a black tunnel. He ran toward her, but he was too late. She was thrust into the swirling hole, and was gone.

Simon screamed and fell to his knees, staring at the hole with emptiness, shock filling his insides.

Then, slowly, in his emptiness, Simon began to hear the low laughter at his side. He turned and noticed for the first time the tall, dark, and menacing man standing only feet away from him.

The emptiness inside Simon was pushed aside, and anger began to take over. He blinked away the water that had accumulated in his eyes and turned on the man in rage.

"Where is she?" Simon shouted, advancing on Abaddon, who merely smiled.

"Gone," he said. "Dead. Lost in nothingness, never to return."

Simon's heart broke, and his eyes stung. How could she be gone so completely? Where were her straight figure, wild hair, and determined mouth? He couldn't even take her limp form in his arms and wish to revive her. She was gone.

Simon screamed again and faced Abaddon, but before he could grasp the evil man's neck with all of his angry strength, Abaddon reached toward the hole and pulled a seeming strand of black into his hand. Simon realized he would be next, but the thought was not, for some reason, frightening. He felt very little will to fight or live.

Abaddon's dark strand began to wrap around his chest, pulling him, forcing him toward the black space. He screamed as he neared it. Hollowness began to possess his chest, his heartbeats strained. Soon, he was through the hole, black coldness engulfing him. His screams became hollow with despair, blindness, and devastating regret.

If only he had been faster. If only he had arrived earlier. How is it that a man who could bend time could arrive so everlastingly too late? Simon's breathing tightened, and anguish made way for realization. *He could bend time.* Simon wondered, and then hoped. He closed his eyes, and tried to shut out the tightening on his chest, to ignore the intense pull. He felt around him in the emptiness and reached out to find the fabric of time. He shut out the roaring that was growing louder around him, and pulled on time, pulled as hard as he could for as long as he could, holding on to the direction of the past.

His arms and chest and head began to ache, then burn, but he did not let go, he pulled on time, succumbing to the pain, and ignoring the darkness on the backs of his eyelids. He began to gasp for breath and felt as though any minute he would fall to pieces.

Then he collapsed.

Simon opened his eyes to find himself sprawled on dirty ground. He blinked and discovered that someone's hand was in his. He looked up.

Bending over his prostrate frame was a sight Simon thought he would never see again. Her forehead was wrinkled in confused worry.

"What happened, Sim—" Ivy began, but was cut off as Simon sat up and threw his arms around her, smelling her hair and feeling the real breath move in and out of her.

"You're alive," he whispered, and then realized that she was tense in his arms and let her go. She smiled at him confusedly, and he returned the smile, a surreal relief filling him.

"Alive?" she whispered, and shook her head, looking a little dazed. "Simon, we've got to move. I'll get into position now." She stood, pulling him up with her. They were in a familiar spot in the trees outside the Lyrian palace, Ivy ready to go and Simon not relinquishing her hand.

"Thank you, Simon," she said, "for everything."

Simon felt his grip tighten. "You cannot go."

She shook her head, "We've been over this, Simon. I have to face him." She tried to pull her hand free.

"No!" Simon said. "Look at me, Ivy," he said, and saw her surprise at his informal use of her name. "You have to trust me. If you go in there, you will die."

She blinked. "You don't know that, Sim—"

"I do!"

She seemed to waver and stopped pulling against his grip.

"Simon," she said, her voice quiet and slightly condescending, "you are no seer."

"Ivy," he said, softening his grip and covering her hand now with both of his, "I don't have to see the future. I've been there."

Ivy's eyes widened, and she suddenly seemed to see him, his tired stance, his legs so weak he had fallen to the ground, and especially the sincerity in his eyes.

"Simon, what did you—"

"I will tell you everything, someday, Ivy," Simon interrupted, "but now I need you to trust me."

Princess Ivy looked at him steadily for a while before sighing and nodding. "Okay," she said quietly. "We'll think of a plan; you can come with me."

"I can barely stand. Look at me. I won't be any help to you. If you are so determined to go up there, then we'll just have to wait for the others."

"They might never come," Ivy said, but she sounded as though she were giving in.

"They'll come." Simon hoped he sounded sure of himself. She seemed to accept that this was part of his experience in the future. Slowly, she helped him back to the ground where they sat against a tree.

Simon relaxed into the forest floor, happy in Ivy's company. He scanned the horizon in the direction of the plain and hoped the Stone Mages wouldn't let him down.

CHAPTER 57

Laith's head buzzed from his hard ride in the saddle. He glanced behind him to see if Saffi Beval was still keeping up and found that she was close behind. He had to admit, she'd ridden well enough.

The flooded ground was soft, and getting softer as they rode. Mud caked his horse's flanks, and his own boots were coated to the knee in the filth.

The setting sun cast a low, straight light at the grounded ships now in his line of vision. He could see people moving, and he had to force himself to breathe as they drew closer.

As they closed in, Laith could see a group of ten or fifteen people congregated at the base of the nearest ship, the *Sapphire*.

He squinted, trying to find that small figure and dark head among the gathered survivors. He began to panic as they got closer and he did not see her. He could see young Burr in conversation with a tall, foreign Stone Mage. He saw Niles and inhaled sharply when he saw his former shipmate talking with a wilted but characteristically resolute Captain John Merrick.

"There's Merrick," he shouted back to Saffi, and heard her

intake of breath as she spotted him as well. She was off her horse
in an instant and was striding, rather angrily, Laith thought, toward
the captain.

Merrick looked up and smiled largely when he saw her.

"Were you *trying* to get yourself killed!" she shouted, and
Merrick laughed.

Laith also dismounted. In a matter of seconds he had looked at
every face in that group. Mara was not among them.

Laith dropped to his knees on the muddy ground, despair engulfing him. His breathing was coming in fast, his head pounding.
He was vaguely aware that someone was walking toward him and
looked up to see Gilda Reed, her broad shoulders slightly hunched.

"Where is she?" he asked, trying to keep his voice calm but not
looking up.

Gilda Reed slowly knelt near him in the mud. "We cannot find
her. She fought very bravely—it never would have worked without
her, but after the rush was over and the water receded, she was just
gone. She was most likely taken by the wave, Hastings."

Laith lifted his head and cried out, a sharp, angry growl that
turned to a mournful cry, which died in his throat. He stood
abruptly, kicking at the muddy ground and turning his back on the
pitying faces nearby. His head was full of angry fire, and his fists
clenched.

Soon, though, in the silence, the fire receded. His body went
slack where he stood until he could see only her face. Mara's face
with those dark eyes, bravely determined as they had been up in the
palace and in the mirror before she had helped make the monster
wave.

He turned around, mildly aware that his face was wet.

"Haverford, Ms. Reed," he said, and she looked at him, confused. "I am Duke Haverford. She was my betrothed once. Last I

knew her, though, she was a fighter. I'm ready to join her. I'll kill Abaddon myself."

He moved for his horse, the others staring after him dumbly.

Their reverie was interrupted by young Burr, who bellowed, "What are we standing around here for? Let's get to the castle and finish off that ruddy tyrant."

The little group was unanimous in its agreement.

◆   ◆   ◆

The sun had set. Ivy blinked in the darkness, battling to keep her eyelids open. Simon had fallen quickly asleep and was slumped quietly next to her. Ivy decided that the moon must be full, or nearly so, because she could still make out the strands of his sandy hair and the little burn scars on his face, intermingled with freckles.

A distant noise interrupted her observation, and she sat up abruptly. She leaned forward, blinking through the trees at the dark horizon. She crept slowly ahead on her hands and knees and lowered the obstructing branch of the bush before her.

In the near distance, a tight group of people was moving toward her. There were two horses, and maybe ten more on foot. Immediately, she recognized the small, slender boyish figure at the front: Burr.

Simon was right; her friends had come to help them. She roused Simon, after a few less-than-gentle shakes. In a matter of moments they were both peering over the bushes, simultaneously watching the advancing Stone Mages and the restless palace guard.

"As soon as the Southerners see them," Simon whispered, "we'll join them, but there's no use in alerting the brutes early."

Ivy nodded, hoping that the other Stone Mages had come up with a plan. Elemental gifts notwithstanding, fifteen against fifty was not good odds.

A cry went up from the direction of the palace, and Ivy knew that their friends had been spotted.

"Now!" whispered Simon, and they broke free of the bushes, running out to join their friends who were advancing quickly now.

Simon and Ivy were soon among the ranks of the other Stone Mages. She felt the joy of seeing her friends, and then concern when she noticed Mara was missing. Their reunion was clipped short by their advancing enemy. Dozens of massive Southerners were bearing down on them. Captain Merrick drew his sword, and the others followed suit.

Ivy had only a few moments to prepare herself before she was facing a drooling, mace-bearing Southern giant. She swallowed, bringing her sword up in front of her face to block the falling ball of the mace, remembering gratefully her swordplay lessons on all those long afternoons at home.

He swung again, this time he went low and she jumped, countering with a jab to his stomach. He moved aside, and her thrust found his right arm instead.

He bared dirty, angry teeth at her and lifted his mace above his large head with both hands, swinging it swiftly down at her. Ivy knew that she could not move fast enough. She closed her eyes, focusing, and listening to the space around her.

She felt the moving sensation, and when she opened her eyes, she realized she had done it. She had disappeared from that space under him and had landed herself directly behind the warrior. He was bent forward, almost in two, doubled over by the force of his blow without contact.

Without thinking twice, Ivy thrust her sword into his side, and he fell forward with a thud. She shuddered, turning around to face her next adversary, but found none immediately near her.

Simon was darting about several confused Southerners, bending time. Ivy could see that he had already killed two men, but she could also see that his previous use of power had left him with little, and that he would not last long. She rushed toward him, hoping to give him aid, when someone caught the sleeve of her dress.

She turned, and Gilda Reed's urgent eyes met hers.

"Help me draw them toward the trees," she said, and then was gone, her hands shoving earth from the ground in front of her toward a nearby opponent.

Ivy rushed into the middle of the fray where Simon was fighting. She could also see Merrick doing serious damage with his sword, and Saffi Beval bending her sword around and through her attackers.

A few Southerners saw her advance and moved toward her. She took a deep breath and then moved herself a second time, landing squarely in the underbrush at the foot of the nearby trees. She could see her confused pursuers a distance away.

She planted her feet. "See if you can catch me, you ugly oafs!" she screamed. The insult sounded ridiculous, but it was apparently effective. The two warriors who had been chasing her and a dozen others looked in her direction and then slowly began moving toward her.

Ivy had done this much, but now began to feel nervous as the big men advanced on her. She cast her eyes about for Gilda Reed but couldn't see her. The princess drew her sword and swallowed, preparing to move again when she heard a yelled command and felt the ground shudder beneath her.

She turned around to see her backdrop of trees tilting toward her. They were falling, fast.

Ivy was standing, paralyzed, when she clearly heard Burr yell, "Move, idiot."

Ivy tugged on space, and moved a distance, gaining her bearings just in time to see at least five massive trees fall on a group of mus-cled brutes.

Ivy barely had time to smile at Gilda Reed's plan when she felt a presence behind her and turned quickly, drawing her sword just in time to run it through the stomach of the warrior waiting there. His eyes got wide, and he toppled forward, like the trees.

This time, she could not get away in time, and he fell on top of her, his weight crushing her to the ground, her face muffled in fetid armpit. She turned her head and gasped, screamed, but no one seemed to hear. She tried pushing the brute off of her, but it was in vain. Her breath was strained, and she tried to move again, to find space and free herself, but she could not gather the strength.

Her vision began to blur, and she closed her eyes. She felt dizzy. She knew it was only a matter of time before she went unconscious. It was just as this thought crossed her mind that the weight eased and then lifted, and she was looking up at a group of tattered but pleased-looking Stone Mages.

Simon Adler was at the forefront, and he bent down to help her up. Slowly, she stood, leaning on him while her breath returned and her vision cleared.

When she could finally see around her clearly, Ivy observed that every Southern warrior was fallen or slain, and that every single one of her comrades was surrounding her in elated companionship, alive and victorious.

CHAPTER 58

The scene played and replayed in Mara's mind, and she studied it. She had called the water to come, as had the others, but her magic had been reared in chaos and there was chaos still in it. It was wild, and she had never been trained to control it. She had willed it toward the land where it had flooded the plain—and the warriors and Wrakes—and she had gone along with it, losing her grounding on the *Sapphire* and following the wave to the end of its course where it had eventually receded, leaving her in the mud far inland, alone. She had coughed its remnants up from her body and lost the rest of her stomach on the ground and in her hair.

She knew she would probably die. The magic had been too much for her, and she could not move. There was pain everywhere, and her heart ached, so she just laid and waited. It was a comfort to know that she had come here by her own choice, not a pawn in her own body, and that she might have done some good.

She found herself thinking of the old first mate, Abner Murray, who was now at peace, she thought, his body at the ocean's bottom, having died bravely himself. She wondered if any of the others had met their ends, but somehow felt that they would live on and finish this.

She allowed her mind to find Ivy and smiled at the picture of her sister riding across the mountain valley toward her. She wished that there had been more time.

Finally, she thought of Laith. Then she cried. She had known him so briefly, but it seemed she had known him so long, and the loss of him seemed too much. She sobbed then, turning her face to the muddy ground to hide the terrible sadness of it.

When the tears expired, she felt empty, and then her mind became strangely clear. Laith would have told her to quit being weak. He would have told her not to lie down and let death take over. So, she lifted her head up. Then she moved her arms and pushed herself to sitting. She moved to her knees and rested there, her strength waning and the pain of movement threatening to overtake her.

Yet she pushed her body upward. Soon she was standing, then, slowly inching out of the mire. She found her bearings and looked toward her childhood home. Then she walked, one step at a time.

By the time the sun was setting, Princess Mara was running, her chest aching, her throat dry, and her eyes blurred and she pushed on, resolute, toward the palace.

◆　◆　◆

The euphoria of success began to wear off as the Stone Mages entered the shadowy palace, shoulder-to-shoulder, and arm in arm.

Ivy naturally assumed the lead, and no one spoke as they followed her up the grand staircase to the second and then the third floor. Simon was at her side, close and wary.

Saffi was walking closely to and slightly ahead of Merrick, who found himself studying the graceful curve of her neck where it sat on her resolute shoulders. Saffi looked behind and around her at her fellow Pelasars, walking upward and forward courageously as they left behind their low past.

Burr looked up at Reuel. The man had stayed near him during the battle below and was even letting Burr wear his stone. Gilda Reed, too, had saved his life down there more than once. He liked that she looked after him, and he knew she was standing close behind him even now. But he had fought as well. No one was telling him to turn back or get lost. He smiled.

Laith came last, surety in his silent step.

When they reached the landing on the third floor, Simon told them all to stop, and they did, each of them gathering around to look at him.

"We're going to climb up one more long set of stairs," he said, "and when we get to the top, we will face Abaddon." He watched their faces for a moment before continuing.

"He has opened up a hole in space, a spiraling doorway into nothing, and he will pull us all into it unless we can close it and kill him."

He looked at Ivy. "Princess Ivy is the only one who can close it. I think our best plan will be to enter that room and confront him and, if not kill him, keep his attention for as long as possible, so that after we have entered, Ivy can move herself, undetected, into the room and work on closing that doorway before he even realizes she's there."

They all stared at him blankly. "I have thought through this," Simon said, "and this is the only solution I can come up with."

Ivy spoke softly next to him, "If I fail—"

"You won't fail," Simon said.

"We'll obliterate that lowlife," said Burr.

Ivy turned and led them up the long staircase.

They paused for a moment at the top, listening to the rush

inside the room. Ivy took Simon's hand briefly before she moved aside and he burst open the door. The Stone Mages rushed into the room.

When Abaddon turned from his post at the doorway, he seemed surprised to find the motley group before him. He blinked before smiling calmly and moving toward them.

"The noble Stone Mages have come to stop me from my evil deeds," he sneered. "You're just in time to witness my greatest exhibition of wicked power yet."

He began to extend one arm toward the dark mass behind him, but Simon spoke quickly. "We already know about your hole, Abaddon," he said.

Abaddon dropped his arm and looked unsettled for a small fraction of time before his face became a picture of pleased scorn once again. "Yes, well," he said, casually. "You aren't the only one who knows a seer. Unfortunately mine is dead, but I should tell you that before she died she saw this moment, and she saw me victorious."

Simon grimaced for a moment, because he had seen Abaddon win as well. He was not about to let it happen again.

"We'll see about that," he yelled at the man. Simon unsheathed his sword and rushed forward, the others moving with him. Abaddon lifted his arm again, but in his haste did not have the time or focus to draw a strand from his abyss of darkness, and therefore, moved himself.

The Stone Mages were practically on top of him when he disappeared. Reappearing altogether on the other side of the room, he smiled at them, as though he had just played a little joke.

They rushed for him again; but this time Abaddon was prepared. He was gone at once. He reappeared in the center of the room, near the fire, the flames lighting his face, and reached for the hole, drawing out two of the dark strands.

On the far side of the room, the group could feel the pull of the strands. It was then that Ivy appeared behind Abaddon. Simon tried to control his face and hoped the others had done the same. Abaddon was moving in on them and appeared not to have noticed the addition to the room.

Ivy took in her companions' predicament at once and, without another thought, moved toward the doorway, raising her hands to its dark mass and endeavoring to find a way to close it.

Simon took a deep breath, wishing they had something other than Water and Earth Mages in the room, when he saw that the prongs in the fire began to melt and slither off the stone like serpents. They moved across the floor, and Simon gratefully remembered Saffi's metal molding abilities. The molten serpents wound their way around Abaddon's advancing ankles and hardened.

Abaddon looked down in surprise, dropping his dark strands, just as John Merrick hurled a sword at him. The dark mage disappeared again, leaving his metal shackles behind. Merrick's sword fell to the floor with a clang as Abaddon reappeared on the other side of the round fireplace, his back still to the princess.

He reached a hand out again to grasp a binding string, but felt a terrible pain in his hand. He screeched as he looked to see a large spider resting in his palm, its pincers ready to strike again. Burr laughed and advanced on the momentarily distracted Abaddon. But the angry man recovered himself just in time to move once more. This time, he appeared near the door they had come in.

The Stone Mages were now between Ivy and Abaddon. The Mages were still for a moment in the knowledge that if they advanced, they would reveal Ivy behind them. Likewise, Abaddon was aware that he would have to move again to get access to the power of his doorway, but his strength was waning. He knew if he moved through space again he might not have the energy he needed to finish them off.

Looking to distract them as he moved closer to the balcony, Abaddon gave them his most charming smile. "Funny isn't it," he said, "all these mighty Stone Mages can't quite take care of one dark mage like me."

He began inching slowly along the wall of the round room. The others seemed to shadow his movement, staying between him and the doorway, but they did not advance. He laughed inwardly at their stupidity.

"Why don't you just take those weights off from around your necks and face me with your unbridled power." He inched close to the balcony, and they mirrored him, but then, suddenly, he darted toward the doorway, reaching out to grasp two strands of darkness as soon as the doorway was in view.

It was only when he held them in his hands that he saw Ivy. He knew right away that she was trying to close his doorway. He knew that she was failing, but the very sight of her made him so angry that he raised his hands and hurled both of the dark filaments at her.

The Stone Mages, however, had used his moment of hesitation to once more interject themselves as a barrier. They moved between attacker and prey just in time for the ropes to miss Ivy and instead grasp Reuel and Laith.

Abaddon's anger increased at being thwarted in his chosen target. Without a second thought, he tugged on Reuel's string, and the man had disappeared into the hole in an instant. Abaddon was about to throw the other man through, when a shout caught his attention.

It was not the shout itself, but the voice that uttered it. A hooded figure had burst into the room and removed her cloak. Abaddon saw that it was Mara, his little Vessel.

"Take me instead!" she cried. She was pleading, and Abaddon liked her desperation. He held the redhead from the hole for a moment to laugh at her. "You silly little fool," he said. "Did you think I did not know you were alive? I knew the moment you set foot in Lyria. How touching for you to offer yourself like some sacrificial substitution for this nobody, when I could be in control of your insignificant frame any time I wanted."

He laughed again, and then raised his arm as if to dump Laith into the abyss. But suddenly he choked, and his eyes grew wide, and his face pale, and he looked down.

Wrapped around his midsection was a thick strand of his own dark nothingness, and holding the other end was the other princess, Ivy.

He was so surprised that he let go of the bit he was holding, and Laith fell to the ground, gasping.

Ivy was pulling on his thread. He reached down, desperately trying to pull it off him but was ineffective in his panic and exhaustion. The roar of the nothingness filled the room, and in a matter of moments he was close enough to the girl at the abyss to see the whites of her eyes, and those of the young blond man who stood close at her shoulder.

The young man looked at him with a knowing that made him freeze at the mouth of his own death.

Simon looked straight into Abaddon. "There are times when heroes meet dead ends, and evil prevails," he shouted over the growling rush of the nothingness, "but in the end, Good always triumphs."

Then Abaddon was thrust into the hole and surrounded by blackness—and nothingness. He was gone.

In the room he had left behind, a wild-haired woman pushed and pushed until the nothingness folded in on itself and screamed and swirled and disappeared. All that remained on the balcony was Lyria below, and moonlight above.

Princess Ivy slumped to the floor to finally rest.

CHAPTER 59

Far away, in a room full of shadows and reflected light, an old man smiled. He was sitting on the floor before his largest mirror, and his back and legs were stiff and sore.

Tears filled his eyes, and he laughed on that floor, and cried some more with the emotion that prevails at the end of a long ordeal, when there have been losses but peace is once again restored. His old body shook with sobs, and then he laughed once more, drying his eyes and feeling ridiculous.

Medwin had really only watched this ordeal as a distant observer. He had not been present for the rushed emigration through the doorway from Bellaria to Lyria. He had not fought at the pass, battled a host of Wrakes on the water, or defeated the evil man whose name had made him shudder for years.

But then, he knew those people in the mirror. They were fellows in a cause, friends, pupils, and surrogate children, and he loved them. In a very real sense he had been with them every step of the way.

He sat up on his dusty floor and breathed more deeply than he had in years, maybe ever. When he finally stood on his weak legs, he felt calm but tired. There was a pain in his old wound, but it seemed quiet as he moved into the glass hallway.

Medwin stood, looking out of those windows for a long time, hours maybe. Eventually the sun began to rise, and he could feel its light reflected from the bay where it touched his hands and face and eyes. He began to move along the corridor, running his hands along the glass.

Soon he was down the stairs and out once again on the grassy summer slopes of the Fringe. Without turning back, he began to climb.

His breathing grew labored, and his cheeks flushed with the exertion of the climb, but he was determined to reach his destination. There, he would rest.

Medwin moved past the dormant surface of the glacier and felt the cool breeze waft from its quiet valley. He moved into thick spruces beyond it and then up again, and out of the trees, and soon he was at the pond, the quiet still pond backed by the stone of the cliff and dressed in summer wildflowers. He knew the pond was deep and calm, and he knelt in the soft grass at its edge. He had avoided this place for many years, as it was *her* resting place. But today there was only peace here. He whispered her name.

He looked down at his reflection and knew that his time had come. His face was white and pale, and his breath rattled in his chest. He studied the surface, wondering if moments from his life would flash before him.

Instead he saw faces. First his mother and father, then a beloved and long-gone sister. Then more faces came in succession—friends, old and new. He saw two princesses. He saw a sea captain and a brave young fool. He saw a strong, bespectacled woman and a precocious young boy. He saw his son, with the red hair and the fierce eyes and the mirror about his neck.

In the end there were two faces. One was his own, before grayness and beard, full of life, but with wisdom remaining in his eyes. The last face was Liese's. She looked the way she had when they were young and love was new. But in her eyes were warmth and intelligence and deep, enduring love. Then, she beckoned.

Medwin leaned forward slightly and extended his arms just as he breathed his last breath. His body broke the surface. The picture blurred, and soon the pond was once again still, calm, and quiet.

CHAPTER 60

Princess Mara sat at her old pianoforte in the Lyrian palace but did not touch the newly dusted keys. Some of the palace men had actually carried it from the mountain castle and through the mine to her, as a gift. She had longed to play it, but there was so much quiet serenity in the palace, the sun streaming in through the windows lining the high ceiling, that she had not the heart to break the peace.

Soon, however, she began to hear a song in her head, one she had not played for many years, and she moved her fingers across the keys without pressing on them, trying to recall the notes.

Then Mara closed her eyes and began to play, surprised at the sweet sound that began to issue from the instrument and from her memory. She cleared her mind, allowing the music to flow through her, and she swayed slightly as she played, wondering where the song would take her. Almost as soon as she had begun, she finished. Her mouth turned up slightly, and she opened her eyes.

Laith was standing in the doorway. She started, surprised to see him, but he merely stared at her unabashed and slightly red-cheeked. She met his gaze and found she could not look away.

"I'm sorry," he said eventually. "I didn't mean to spy. It just sounded so perfect that I didn't want to interrupt."

Mara felt she should stand to welcome him but found herself rooted to the seat. She indicated one of the chairs near to the piano, inviting him to sit.

He nodded and came toward her but remained standing, resting his hand hesitantly on the pianoforte.

"You have news for me, then?" she prompted.

He nodded. "I have questioned General Rune, as you asked. He says, according to reports, that there were several surviving Southerners scattered about Lyria. They have retreated once more to their Southern forest. Several men say that there were some Wrakes among them. They are much too weak to do anything . . ."

"For now," Mara finished his sentence, and felt the color drain from her face. She closed her eyes. "Thank you, Laith," she whispered.

When she opened her eyes, he had moved nearer. He was standing by her bench.

"I hope you won't deprive Lyria of its rightful queen," he said.

Mara smiled at this. "You and I both know that I am not the queen this kingdom needs." She heard protest in his throat but cut him off. "I have no desire to be queen, Laith. I never have. I want to see Ivy rule Lyria. I had only hoped I could help, be near . . ."

"You can," Laith said, suddenly moving to sit next to her on the bench. "We can protect you."

"There will always be a risk," she said quietly. "I cannot allow myself to jeopardize my sister's safety or the kingdom's well-being by remaining close to her. I won't be weak any longer. I have to leave, to hide. It is the only way."

They were quiet for a time, and Mara was surprised to find that in such a moment she had time to be aware of how close Laith was sitting next to her on the bench, facing away from the piano. He was so near she could hear him breathing.

"Where will you go?" he asked after a while, his voice deep and a bit shaky.

She shook her head, looking straight ahead, away from him. "I'll find somewhere. Perhaps I'll sail away, try to start a new life on another continent somewhere."

"You don't sound sure," he said.

"I'm not."

They were quiet again, and Mara was sure he had moved closer to her. His arm was touching hers. Almost unthinking, she moved to his side and placed her head on his shoulder. He rested his head lightly on hers and his arm went around her. They remained that way for quite some time, eyes closed, listening to each other breathe.

When he spoke it was barely above a whisper. "I know a place you could go."

Mara exhaled. "You do?"

His voice was steadier and more audible. "I do. It's a little out of the way, practically the end of the world, but it's mine, or at least it will be some day."

Mara could feel her heartbeat in her head. "What is this place?"

"We call it the Fringe."

"I see," she said, keeping her voice steady. "And will the rent be steep?"

He laughed, his voice deep, and then was quiet again for a while before he spoke. "I was thinking maybe I could share it with you."

Mara lifted her head and sat up straight, looking directly into his eyes with sudden seriousness. "You have no reason to give up your life here, Laith."

He returned her gaze with equal gravity. "I have many reasons.

Among them is the fact that Seers are almost as hunted as Vessels at times; but the only reason that really matters is you."

Mara studied him and was aware that her heart had started to beat faster.

Laith reached up and gently brushed a strand of dark hair from her face. "We are betrothed, after all," he said. "If nothing else, we should at least honor our parents' promise."

Mara smiled and covered his hand with hers as he bent to kiss her. "At least," she agreed.

•　　•　　•

In the past, Lyrian memorial services had been held at night, candles lighting the hollows of the hillside cemetery; but on this particular occasion, as Simon stood amongst his family and fellow Lyrians with gravestones at his feet, there was soft morning light all around.

Quiet prevailed under the cemetery trees, the quiet of waiting. All eyes were on the doors of the little church at the top of the hill. In a few moments, a handful of people would emerge, among them the newly crowned queen of Lyria.

She would come out in all her glory and address her subjects; but Simon knew she would not be giving a typical coronation speech. Instead, her first act as queen would be to honor the dead.

Everyone was looking at that door, anticipating—everyone but Simon, who looked at the ground. He had come to hear his queen. He knew there could not be a better ruler for his kingdom. He wanted to hear her voice and feel the comfort of her words as he thought of those who had died, so he had come. Underneath all this, however, was the ache of knowing that although he would be near her, that he would see her and hear her, she was farther away from him than ever.

The bells of the church rang, loud and clear over Lyria, and there was a movement among the people. Simon felt his father's broad hand on his shoulder. He took a breath and heard the door of the church open as the new queen emerged.

A cheer went out from among the people, and Simon looked up, silent. She was magnificent in red and gold, a train flowing behind her, and the great crown at home on her head. Almost immediately she raised her arms to silence the people.

When she spoke or, more accurately, shouted her words to the vast multitude, they were hushed, listening.

"I'm honored," she stated, "to stand in front of my valiant fellow Lyrians as your queen. Among you are those who were loyal to my mother and the other queens and kings before her, as well as those who are new pioneers, valued friends and fighters.

"Today, I especially want to honor the men and women who lie at my feet, literally and in spirit, those who gave their lives so we could stand here today, the sun on our faces and the morning air in our lungs, free from fear and able to make a new start."

She paused for a moment before speaking a final few words. "If you wish to honor me today, to honor this crown, do so by honoring those who made it possible for me to be standing here wearing it."

There was a reverent hush in the crowd. Simon closed his eyes and felt the sun shine on his face. He breathed in the clear air. On the backs of his eyelids he saw Roger in a hundred glimpses, memories of their childhood together, of his quiet bravery. He smiled at the face of his brother and felt Roger smile back.

He felt his father take his arm and lead him forward, and Simon followed the procession of the living Lyrians as they moved toward the rough stone monument that stood near their new queen, a memorial to those who had fought for Lyria.

When Simon was before the queen, he looked up, he couldn't

help it. He met her eyes as they met his, then he turned, placing a deep purple flower before the monument, and moved on.

• ◆ •

Gilda Reed, newly appointed chairwoman of the Council of Witchcraft, hustled through the long, crowded building under construction, carrying a large basket and trying unsuccessfully not to look too smug.

"Ms. Reed," called a young man nearby, rushing toward her, building plans in hand. "I have a question about the entry to the storerooms through the kitchens," he said, and she stopped to survey the plans he thrust in front of her.

"No, no," she mumbled, shaking her head. "I couldn't tell you about the numbers, Bernard, but the storerooms must be accessible through here." She pulled a piece of charcoal from his hand and sketched the change. "Understand?"

The young man nodded and rushed off. Gilda smiled. This place, the Earth Hall, would be a training center, designed and presided over by her. She had been appointed by the queen herself and was looking forward greatly to teaching those in the kingdom with real earth talent how to use it.

She walked through the classroom, where a hodgepodge of long tables had been assembled. She looked in on the kitchen to see how the cabinet structure was progressing and eyed the area that would soon be the storeroom, shelves lined with the healing herbs and mixtures they would create here. She then passed into the green house area. It was open now, but would eventually be enclosed to let in light, like in Medwin's glass house, so plants could be grown here year-round.

This was one of a number of buildings that were to be constructed at this location so that magic could be reintroduced and taught in the kingdom. There would be libraries and classrooms, and Lyria would once again be a place of learning.

"Gilda," called a harried female voice, and she turned to see Meg coming toward her. She smiled.

Meg smiled shyly at her. "Everyone has arrived," she announced. "We are all ready for you in the council room." Gilda nodded and followed her old friend into the final room of the building, the council room. It was small, and still only roughly finished, but functional. Gilda took her seat at the head of the table, setting down the basket she had been carrying.

Other members of the council included Nabra and two other Pelasars, as well as Meg and two of the lower ranking former council members, who seemed suddenly much less sure of themselves than she had ever seen them.

Gilda Reed smiled and began to pull several items from her basket. "We may as well have something to eat while we talk, don't you think?" she asked without really expecting an answer. She pulled forth a teapot, passed around matching cups, and then produced some warm raspberry tarts. The council looked pleased.

"Alright, Meg," she said, when everyone was lost in berry deliciousness, "what is the first matter of business?"

Meg cleared her throat. "Unfortunately, we are addressing a complaint of one of our members."

Gilda had expected this. "Show him in."

Hobart Andrews, former head of the Council of Witchcraft, pushed through the door, thrusting forward his pointed nose in angry confrontation. "I demand to know why I am denied my rightful seat on this council," he said, and slammed his fist down on the table in front of Gilda.

Gilda considered him carefully through her spectacles while taking a bite of raspberry tart. "Unfortunately, Mr. Andrews, it seems you have insufficient witching ability. Your enthusiastic arm flailing has yet to show an ounce of control over the earth element."

"Why that's ridiculous," he spat. "You have no right to banish me. I am a man of great power and ability."

"Oh, Mr. Andrews," Gilda crooned softly, "we have no intention of banishing you. You are most welcome to come and participate in our classes; you could at least learn the mixing of herbs. Who knows? Perhaps your gift will surface eventually. In the meantime, I hope you will feel free to continue wearing the green stone, as I'm sure it holds at least sentimental value for you if nothing else."

Mr. Andrews gritted his teeth at her in silent rage.

She smiled at him once more and proffered the tray before her. "Raspberry tart?"

◆　　◆　　◆

John Merrick stood on the Lyrian docks, gazing up at and admiring his old ship in its newly repaired state. He whistled low in his throat and began climbing the plank up to the deck.

"My girl," he said, "you've never looked better."

"Why thank you," said a voice behind him, and he turned. Looking up at him from the dock below was Saffi Beval, and it was true, she too had never looked better. She was wearing trousers and a jacket of practical material in the most stunning blue. She wore her dark hair down, plaited with small silver ribbons. For a moment he was speechless.

"You seem a bit surprised to see me here," she said.

He cleared his throat, taking a few casual steps down the gangplank. "Not at all," he said, smirking. "I knew you would feel compelled to come see me off."

She scoffed.

He ignored it. "Pretend all you'd like, I'll probably be gone a long while, and you're bound to miss me."

Saffi raised an eyebrow at him, her eyes sparkling with humor. "No doubt."

"I, on the other hand, will hardly have time to think of you," he continued, advancing down the gangplank a few more steps until he stood directly before her on the dock. "The queen, you see, has made me an official in her navy and is sending me on a diplomatic mission to the other continents."

"Really?" she said, in mock adoration. "Couldn't that be a dangerous mission?"

"Likely," he replied casually. "We have never before had any friendly intercourse with the neighboring countries and governments; they might be just as likely to fight us as welcome us."

"Indeed," Saffi said, looking up at him with a vague smile.

For a moment the smile disarmed him. "What *are* you doing here?" he asked quietly.

She glanced down and, following her gaze, Merrick noticed for the first time the two small trunks at her feet. He scrunched up his forehead. "What are those?"

Saffi stepped closer to him, and he caught his breath. She was so near he could smell her. Then, however, she moved around him and began walking up the plank.

He turned abruptly to confront her. "Where do you think you're going?" he demanded.

She turned around casually to face him, her head now a few feet above his. "Did you hear, John Merrick, that I received an appointment from the queen as well?"

"I had heard something like that. Didn't she make you and Eben advisors or something?"

"Something like that, yes. One of my duties will be to specialize in diplomatic relations."

Merrick shrugged. "Sounds fascinating."

Her cool reserve erupted into a grand smile, but she stifled it quickly, and was again impassive. "My first task will be to accompany you on this particular diplomatic mission." She lifted her chin and turned once more, walking up the plank.

He bolted after her. "Oh no you don't," he shouted. "A naval vessel is not a place for a *lady*, and like I said, this could be dangerous. Do you really think I'll let you parade onto my boat, just like that?"

She laughed. "I'd like to see you stop me," she challenged. But when he advanced, she put her hand out, pushing on his chest to keep him from her. "Besides," she said, "did you really think that the queen would leave diplomacy to warring sailors? Of course they would fire cannons rather than sign treaties if the conversation were left to you."

"It's too dangerous," he said, but his reserve was melting. She dropped her hand from his chest.

"Come on, Merrick," she said, looking him in the eye, "you know I am more a rogue thief than a lady. Besides, you and all your many strengths will be there to sail me safely and stand as my protection. I will be there to do the talking."

She winked at him, and he shook his head, smiling.

Saffi Beval extended her slender hand toward him, beckoning slightly. "Come on, Captain," she whispered, nodding toward the waiting ship. "It's time we set sail."

John Merrick hardly hesitated before following her closely up the plank and onto the deck of the *Sapphire*.

•   •   •

Queen Ivy walked the pathways of the palace gardens, deep in thought. She was aware that these gardens were not the same manicured, flourishing gardens of her youth. However, the palace gardeners had already begun planting and pruning, cleaning out and cleaning up the area so that the hedges, trees, lawns, and flower beds were more in a state of repair than disrepair.

She hoped, sighing, that the kingdom was in the same state. She acknowledged that much had been done since they had reclaimed Lyria, but there was still so much more to do. She was glad to be out in the cool evening air where she could still remember that she was Ivy and not just the queen. She needed reprieve from the meetings, speeches, documents, and decisions.

It was not that she wished *not* to be queen. In fact, she was certain that this was the right path for her. There was just so much to learn and do and become. She could not help but feel that the new good was bittersweet in its partnership with some kind of loss. She was only twenty, after all. Not, by far, Lyria's youngest queen, but she was missing certain freedoms, and especially the camaraderie of equals and the daily association with peers that she had taken for granted over the past year.

Ivy was drawn from her thoughts by a slight noise behind her. She turned to see Simon Adler coming up the path toward her from the direction of the palace. She felt slightly nervous to see him and wasn't sure why. She had been waiting for a visit from him for weeks since she had written him a letter telling him she would like to see him at his leisure. Now that he had finally come, she was not sure what she meant to say to him.

"Hello, Simon," she said when he was close enough to hear.

He stopped a small distance from her and bowed his head, "Your Highness." He did not altogether look up to meet her eyes. "I apologize for not coming sooner." His statement was final, without explanation, and Ivy felt disappointed and a little annoyed.

"I hope I haven't inconvenienced you," she said.

"Not at all."

Silence.

"You wanted to see me?" he prompted. Ivy wondered at his cold tone. He seemed to be studying every inch of the garden but still did not look at her. She cleared her throat and pointed down the pathway.

"Will you walk with me?"

He joined her, and they walked quietly, him slightly behind her. "I guess I just wanted to thank you," she said, feeling the words were awkward and inadequate. "I wanted to thank you for everything you have done for me, and for Lyria."

"My service for Lyria is hardly greater than yours. I am sure there is no debt of gratitude owed, Your Majesty."

The way he said the last two words touched a nerve, and Ivy turned, grabbing his arms and forcing him to turn and look her in the eye. "What's the matter with you, Simon?" she almost shouted.

He pretended confusion, "I did not mean to offend, Your Highness—"

"Stop calling me that!" she interrupted.

Simon's face broke, and he looked her in the eye. "I, a mere fool, have received a summons from my queen which I have answered." He looked at the ground. "If you just meant to thank me you could have done that in the letter."

She shook her head and turned away. "You're right, Simon, it looks like *I'm* the fool here. After all we have been through together, I hoped that I could meet with a friend, no, perhaps the best friend I've had, and have a conversation. I wanted to see you and tell you that I miss you, and yes, thank you for doing that little thing—saving my life. I'm sorry to have imposed on you." She started walking down the path again. "You may go."

But he didn't. She was only a few steps away when she felt Simon's hand on her shoulder. It was a gentle touch, apologetic, so she turned, and Simon put his arms around her and held her close. She relaxed in his arms and felt a great measure of comfort fill her.

"I'm sorry," he whispered. "I've missed you terribly. I just assumed that you wouldn't need me anymore."

Queen Ivy pulled back to look at Simon Adler, her hands in his. "You were wrong," she said, studying his face. "I need you, but not as my royal subject, Simon, as my friend and equal. Please, will you be that for me?"

Simon looked at her with solemn eyes. "Always," he said. Ivy looked at him, taking in the familiar sandy hair and freckled face, and saw the young man, a stranger, who had mounted an impossible mission to save her all of those months ago. She also saw the weight of experience in his eyes that had not been there before. She saw the way his stone of power hung importantly about his neck. She saw the burn scars that made small faint lines on his face, and she suddenly, somewhat distractedly, wished she could trace them with the tips of her fingers. Instead she kissed him softly on the cheek and he closed his eyes for a moment. Then he stepped away from her and, flashing a smile, swept a grand bow and offered his hand, which she took with equal grandness, and together, they continued down the garden path.

◆ ◆ ◆

Burr sat on the rock wall outside a cottage covered in flowers, turning a small stone over and over in his dirty palm.

He did not look up as Gilda Reed emerged from the cottage and sat by him without a word. The two of them sat in silence for a few moments before she spoke.

"I've never seen you so quiet, or so still," she said. "Do you regret deciding to come and live with me?"

"Nah," said Burr. "Although I guess I did end up living with the old witch after all, eh?" He ducked before she could box his ears. "Your cooking is worth it," he amended, and she seemed mollified at that.

"Then what is on your mind, young man?" she asked.

Burr held up the amber stone on a heavy chain in explanation.

"Ah," she said. "I didn't know you had that. Was it from Reuel?"

"Yes," the boy said, unusually solemn. "He let me wear it the night we faced Abaddon, the night he died."

Gilda put a sturdy hand on the boy's small shoulder. "I think he would want you to keep it, Burr, and use it."

"I'm not so sure I *want* to wear it," he said, a slight edge in his voice. He looked at Gilda and saw the confusion on her face.

His explanation came out in a rush. "It seems to me the thing is pointless anyway. I've learned how to use my gift without wearing one before and I've been just fine. The stone might just weigh me down and make me weak. I don't need any weight on my neck, binding me to anyone or anything." Burr's words came out faster and increased in volume. "I don't want to die!" he shouted.

Gilda did not touch or coddle him, just sat by him and listened and thought, and he felt himself begin to relax again, despite the tension that had built in his chest.

"That decision is certainly yours to make, Burr," she said. "I think you are right that you could still use your elemental gift without wearing a stone." She paused, and he let this sink in. She wasn't treating him like a child, or telling him what to do.

He looked up at her, interested.

"The sad but real truth is that everyone dies eventually. It can be terribly painful for those of us left behind, but that does not mean we should live our lives avoiding it. It is inevitable. What we can do is decide how we will live the lives we have left.

"If you wear that stone, Burr, you might realize a greater harmony with the animals you move and communicate with; but as you say, the difference may be small. However, when you make the choice to put that chain around your neck, you are telling the world that you will be using the gift you have been given to unify rather than to destroy. You are telling your friends, and especially your enemies, that you will do what is right. It will mean that you are not a lone mage, but that you belong to a family of fighters. No longer will you be a thief, an orphan, or some insignificant boy. You will be a Stone Mage."

She looked down at him. "And that, my Burr, is a great thing to be."

Then, as quietly as she had come, Gilda Reed stood and walked back toward the cottage that was now theirs to share and disappeared behind the door. He wondered later if she had watched from the window as he took the stone and chain he had been turning back and forth in his hands and lifted it deliberately over his head.

DISCUSSION QUESTIONS

1. Many of the characters have active dreams in the novel. Ivy dreams of being abducted by Southern warriors; Simon relives memories with his brother. Others dream of the missing princess or the use of their gifts. How do these sleeping experiences shape the characters' waking decisions and actions?

2. There are several references in the novel to the hope the Lyrians place in Ivy. In what ways is it beneficial for them to have a single unifying figure in which to place their trust? In what ways could it be complicated or even dangerous?

3. In Chapter 11, Abner Murray tells Simon that Captain Merrick is fearless, but not reckless. What is the difference between these characteristics? Based on what we see of Merrick in the book, do you think this description is accurate? What other characters might also fit this description?

4. In Chapter 22, Medwin tells Ivy, "The only you who really matters is who you are right now." What do you think he means by this? Do you agree with him?

5. Roger Adler once told his brother Simon that actions are not

necessarily heroic because people are there to applaud, but because they are the right thing to do. Where in the book do Simon and the others demonstrate this kind of heroism—performing courageous or selfless deeds without recognition or praise?

6. During the time he spends with Medwin, Laith Haverford learns to use his gift to see images more clearly in the mirrors. How does this reflect the personal changes he is making during this time? What other things might he also be learning to see more clearly?

7. In Chapter 35, Medwin convinces Laith to use his skills at deception for a good cause. Laith later encourages Mara to do the same with her abilities. How can these characters become stronger, better people without changing what their gifts and powers are? What might this say about the difference between what people do, and why they do it?

8. When Burr observes the Bellarians' attitude toward public hangings, he decides that "a cold heart was a worse flaw than a quick hand." What does he mean by this? Do you agree?

9. When Ivy is trying to open the doorway back to Lyria, her friends remind her of the importance of having people she loves and trusts near her. Why is this advice so important in general? How might it be especially important advice for Ivy?

10. The title of the book is *Journey to the Fringe.* Medwin explains in the story that a fringe is not an end but an edge. To what "edges"—both literal and figurative—do you think the characters in the story are journeying?